M

Midnight Red

For Ken Burke &
Becky Riordan,
my friends & colleagues
& fellow raconteurs,
Best, [illegible]

Steven Rudd

Dec '05

ISBN : 1-4196-1240-9

To order additional copies, please contact us.
BookSurge, LLC
www.booksurge.com
1-866-308-6235
orders@booksurge.com

Midnight Red

In memory of Perry Rudd, who cherished words and loved a mystery.
And for Lurline Weeks Rudd, the greatest profiler of them all.

CHAPTER ONE

Kris Van Zant's prime concern at the moment was not the psycho who was still at large in Atlanta after ripping the throats out of two victims, bleeding them white, and leaving their gnawed-over corpses behind like a predator in the wild showing off its trophies.

Much more pressing to her just now was the state of her uncle Hank's health. As one shrink to another from opposite ends of a forensic career, they'd been conferring by long distance at the close of the day. They'd just been going over the details of the killer bloodsucker case. As usual, the local authorities had consulted Hank as a profiler.

Then the senior psychiatrist blurted out something about chest pain.

"No, it's nothing," he said quickly. "I'm sure there's no reason for you to concern yourself, Kristin.

Typically Uncle Hank tried to laugh it off, but to Kris it sounded forced.

"I'm afraid it's merely another instance of dietary indiscretion on my part," he added. "Now to return to the 'Buckhead Vampire,' as our media people insist on referring to this matter, I think you make quite a telling point—"

"No, hey," Kris cut in on him. "Whoa up there, big uncle."

She caught herself making a time-out sign over her desk. While they talked, Kris had been cleaning out her office. She was just winding up her fellowship in forensic psychiatry at Saint Elizabeths Hospital in Washington, DC.

"Describe that symptom you mentioned a few seconds

ago," she urged him. "And this time just you listen to what you're saying to me. All right?"

"Kristin..."

Hank let out a long sigh.

It was the same forbearing exhalation Kris had been getting from him ever since she was a little girl. When he came back on the line, his voice was as deep and measured as ever. But still she caught the trace of pain in it.

"As I just noted, my dear," he said, "your point about the, ah, presentation of the victims is very incisive."

"Thanks."

Before he could go on, she spoke up again and pressed him hard.

"But I want you to tell me what it was that cut your wind off just now and made you grunt like that," she said. "You hear me, Uncle Hank? Out with it. Speak to me. Now."

"It's nothing," he muttered again, sounding rueful to her. "Merely a touch of gas. I confess I had a chilidog for lunch, purchased from that vendor who's always to be found at midday lurking in front of the medical school."

He gave another half-stifled belch.

"Now," he said, "to return to the crime-scene details that seem to have fired the public's imagination. I refer to your point as to the appearance of the victims at the time of their discovery. With the doors all locked and the windows secured, that is.

"And no indication of forcible entry," he said after a pause. "And the signs of struggle far too slight for the extravagant degree of violence on display, not to mention the nearly total absence of blood..."

As her uncle's voice trailed off, Kris's impatience rose with her concern for him.

"It's way too Hollywood for a working vampire," she filled in. "As if I could tell *you* anything in that department.

"But still," she added, "most of the psychopathic blood fetishists I've read about or dealt with myself were way less fastidious than that. Too, this sucker comes off as downright exhibitionistic. I mean he might as well be pitching his own movie ideas, right out in plain view...

"Uncle Hank?" she demanded when she got no reply. "Hello. Please, are you okay there?"

He groaned, and this time Kris caught him as he tried to cover it.

"Ah, I'm perfectly fine, thank you, Kristin," he said. "I—you're right, my dear. I must learn to be more discriminating in what I eat."

"But you never get indigestion," she pointed out. "That's why you're way too fat as it is."

"As always, my dear Kristin," he said dryly, "you remain a bulwark to my self-esteem."

She got to her feet, set to spring into action on his behalf.

"Get real, Uncle Hank," she pleaded, "You're pushing sixty. You've refused to take care of yourself ever since we lost Aunt June. You work all hours at your desk and keep on smoking that smelly old pipe to boot.

"And the last time you even thought about taking the stairs instead of waiting for the elevator was back during the Carter Administration," she wound up. "Okay?"

"Your point, girl?"

Hank's strict paternal tone held for a moment before his voice broke with another heavy groan.

"I—beg your pardon, Kristin," he said. "It's merely... *uumf*."

"Okay," she snapped. "That tears it."

With a forefinger poised over the phone and a plan in mind, Kris had already flipped up the numbers and extensions she needed on her Rolodex.

"You sit tight, Uncle Hank," she told him. "I'm going to ring the cardiology department down there direct. I'll have 'em send a wheelchair—no, unh-uh, let's make that a gurney. They'll come straight over for you and get you plugged into CCU protocol stat. I'm on my way, too, so I'll see you soon. Stand by."

Not for the first time, he sounded outgunned as he let go another moan.

"Kristin," he said. "Oh, for God's sake, girl."

"You know I'm right, Uncle Hank."

That phrase had been cropping up between them ever since her childhood, Kris reflected, much like the valediction she gave him just before she punched the button.

"So resistance is futile," she said. "I love you."

❧

People who knew Kris well told her that even in those rare moments when she was standing still, it was easy to see how fast she could move.

She'd jumped a last-minute connection out of Reagan National in DC and talked her way onto the Delta feeder flight to Hartsfield Atlanta. Then she'd taken a cab straight in from the airport to Emory University Hospital. Now as she hopped out at the curb, she was a study not just in speed but of focus and follow-through as well.

In the words of a colleague, Patriot missiles had nothing on Kris Van Zant.

Kris didn't look like a force of nature, though, at least at first glance. A slight young woman, she had fair skin and a piquant oval face and wore her glossy dark hair cut short. In a white cotton button-down blouse, chino skirt and penny loafers, she was more likely to get taken for a freshman headed home from college than a doc with a tall stack of honors to her name.

People made that mistake all the time. Kris was just a few months shy of her thirtieth birthday. Still, bartenders would ask to see some ID before they served her.

"Yes, CCU?" she said into the cell phone she held pressed to her ear. "This is Dr. Van Zant. Kris Van Zant."

She juggled her purse and flight bag in her other hand as she cut past the info desk up front and began to thread white-tiled corridors.

"You say my uncle is out of the cath suite now and back in the unit," she said on the line. "And Dr. Friedrich and his crew're in there with him? Good, good..."

Even though she'd grown up next door to the medical

campus here and knew all the shortcuts from ward to ward, Kris double-checked the floor plan by the elevators. She didn't break stride as she pushed through the stairwell door. Light on her feet as always, she jogged up two flights to the Cardiac Care Unit.

Kris carried herself straight as a lance, which made her seem taller than the five-foot-three she stood in flats. But in spite of her posture and the great tensile strength of her spine and limbs, a natural grace made her come off more like a dancer than the killer gymnast she'd been in school. It also took the edge off the stance she'd gained from a bent for martial arts.

But for those not inclined to take Kris seriously, just one look in her eyes served to change their minds.

Sharp and bluer than blue, her eyes cut right through to indigo violet. They seemed to take in the whole world and give back no light at all. To match gazes with Kris Van Zant was to step into a shade so deep it could hide any motive and hold any secret. It was plain to see why she'd never feared the dark.

She nudged the door back from the landing and skirted the waiting area outside, and then she headed for the wide sliding doors under the sign marked CCU.

Sounding surprised to meet her, someone called her name in the hallway. Instantly she recognized the tall man with the deep seams in his face, obsidian eyes and bare brown scalp. In the same glance, she took in the Atlanta Police Department badge clipped to the front pocket of his suit coat.

But she didn't stop. She just nodded and waved to him with her free hand. Not even slowing down, she dodged through the doors of the heart unit before they'd hissed halfway back. Kris knew where she was going now. She almost always did.

"Uncle Hank!" she yelled. "Uncle Hank, thank God you're okay!"

Charging across the open-plan floor, she startled the unit nurses in scrubs who were hovering by the door to his cubicle. Over apologies, she dropped her bags by the nurses' station and trotted over to the bedside. As careful and as ready to scold as a mother hen, she swooped down on her uncle with her arms spread wide.

For his part, Hank seemed chastened to her.

He lay flat on his back in a hospital gown with his half-moon glasses riding down the bridge of his long, pinched nose. Hank's milky blue eyes were mild and now looked wry under a thatch of shaggy hair the color of iron filings. As Kris leaned over him, he reached up long-armed to cradle her shoulders and mumbled something reassuring in her ear.

Grizzled and curt at his side, the chair of the cardiology department introduced her to the other doctors in attendance before he returned to Hank.

"It was a close call," he said. "But lucky for you, Hank, that's all it was."

"At angiography, doctor," an associate professor of medicine told Kris, "there was one solitary, distal stenosis of the circumflex branch of the left coronary artery present. So, we were able to open it right up and stent it. Since the rest of the coronary circulation appeared widely patent, very minimal myocardial damage was incurred."

Looking ready to get on to the next case, Dr. Friedrich winked at Kris.

"Bottom line," he grunted, "is it was damn smart of you to get us to go direct to catheterization instead of screwing around and waiting it out like a lot of folks'd do and risk winding up with a full-blown heart attack. Well, Hank, young lady, good evening now."

Outside, the ward staff parted ranks for the chief and his colleagues as they rejoined a small army of medical students and residents in short white coats and trooped away on late-hour teaching rounds.

"Very well, Kristin," Hank said once they were alone. "It's not the first time I've been forced to admit it, and I'm sure it won't be the last, but you were right, my dear. Now..."

He warmly clasped her hand in his on the bedrail. Then as he looked up, his eyes darted past her. Catching a flash of alarm in them edging into stark terror, Kris spun around to see.

Just past the curtains, the tall bald man with the policeman's badge was making placating gestures to fend off the CCU nurses who blocked his way.

"'Scuse me, 'scuse me here," he said at large. "I know I'm not even supposed to be back here, y'all, but if I could just have me a word or two with the good Dr. Van Z...?"

"It's all right, ma'am," Hank called to the nursing supervisor. "Please, I'm sure my dear old friend Detective Lieutenant Judson will be very brief, if you'd just allow him to join us. Thank you."

Reluctantly the stern-looking woman backed down, and the detective sidled in to face Kris across the bed.

"Doc, hoss, whoa," he boomed, pumping Hank's other hand. "What that other doc was saying in here a little while ago was pretty much Greek to me. But it sounds like you just dodged you a bullet, my man."

"I couldn't have translated it better myself, Matthew," said Hank. "Ah, I believe you recall my brilliant and quite relentless niece Kristin."

"Miss Kris!"

Kris judged there was more hope than nostalgia in Det. Lt. Judson's smile as he overlapped her fingers with his and gave her hand a fond, avuncular shake.

"Seems to me like it was just yesterday you's sitting on my knee," he declared. "And bugging me to tell you one more story before I had to get on back to work."

Kris smiled at him and didn't hold back.

Her teeth were white and even by the deep, soft dimple in her left cheek. Bright and sweet, that expression was much at odds with the darkness in her eyes. When Kris smiled like that, most people would blink. Sometimes they'd even take a step or two back from her while they looked around for a fire exit.

"Seems that way to me, too," she said. "It surely does, Uncle Matt."

Aunt June and Uncle Hank had had no children of their own. Good Southern liberals alike, they'd always seemed pleased by the way their niece would welcome this black man into their home when she was growing up there. Matt was one of rising stars in the Department then, and he often came to call on Hank's expertise.

For her part, Kris didn't give a rip damn what color Matt's skin was as long as he'd fill her in on his exploits with the Homicide Squad when nobody else was listening. The detective knew the story of what had happened to the rest of her family, too, in all its detail. That had made for an understanding between them from the start.

"You've had yourself some kind of stellar academic career in a hurry," Matt said now. "Haven't you, Kris?

"If memory serves," he added, "you went and earned you a master's degree in psychology from the university here, with top honors and everything. And that was by the time you was twenty years old."

Hank drew a long, proud breath from below and between them.

"I'm sure my niece's native humility would prevent her from giving you the rest of her résumé, Matthew," he said. "But immediately following that precocious graduate work, she enrolled at Harvard Medical School. After graduating magna cum laude, she embarked on the general psychiatry residency at McLean Hospital and Massachusetts General in Boston.

"Then," he went on, "she turned down an offer to be chief resident in order to work at Saint Elizabeths Hospital in Washington under Stephen Laszlo the—"

"Hold on," the detective broke in. "Beg pardon, doc." He kept his gaze fixed hard on Kris.

"We talking about *the* Stephen Laszlo here?" he asked. "Man who literally wrote the book on serial killers and sexual predators and won't even give the time of day to anybody that lacks an IQ like a bowling score, like him. That Dr. Laszlo?"

Kris gave Hank's hand a squeeze as she decided to grab the initiative.

"I've been Laszlo's fellow for the past year," she said. "But this isn't just a social call for you, is it, Matt? You came here to consult on a case, didn't you?"

The detective looked all around before he ducked closer and held up three fingers between them.

"Oh, dear God..." Hank whispered, shutting his eyes. "Is it like the other ones?"

"Worse," the other man rasped. "If possible. My gut tells me, too, the only way we going to come close to busting this one is by profiling from the scene while it's still fresh."

As Kris watched, the lines by Matt's mouth and eyes seemed to dig down to the bone.

"That's why I had to come see you, doc," he said. "We need us an all-star psych pro—preferably homegrown—to come in right now, right on the ground."

"Take me," Kris begged. "Please, Matt. Uncle Hank, I can be your eyes."

The smile he gave her seemed to cost him dear.

"Yours were sharper than mine ever were," he said. "So's your brain, for that matter."

Matt looked to Kris to be bridling to go now.

"Doc?" the detective coaxed Hank. "Is she really...?"

"Kristin is already better that way than I ever was," Hank told him. "She's as good in the field, in fact, as any violent-criminal profiler I've ever heard of."

He didn't quite manage to meet Kris's eyes. At length he let go of her hand. Then just over his breath, he gave her his blessing.

"She's as good at it now," Hank sighed, "as anyone would ever want to be."

CHAPTER TWO

At the admitting ramp in front of the hospital Matt hailed a big, towheaded man who stood by a dun Ford Taurus with municipal plates. Kris took the car for unmarked if you didn't look at it too closely. A foot shorter than Matt, she easily outpaced him on the sidewalk.

"Over here, Yuri," the detective called out at her back. "Dr. Van Zant's coming with us."

The other man, whom she placed his mid-thirties or so, gave an easy salute and then did a double take at Kris.

As tall as Matt and a good deal wider, he was solid-limbed and blocky through the chest and shoulders. He had on a khaki suit, navy tie and high-buffed shoes. Next to the older man's rumpled seersucker, that gave him a military cast. But something in his jock's slouch and quick-eyed, heads-up bearing told Kris he'd be much more at home on a team than in an army.

This Yuri, she judged, would be as good at calling plays as he likely was at running them.

"I beg your pardon, lieutenant," he said. "I understood you to say that Dr. Van Zant was to accompany us, but in this I was mistaken perhaps?"

His accent was Slavic and so broad that Kris wondered for a moment if he was kidding.

"No mistake, partner."

Swinging open the front door on the passenger's side, Matt offered introductions on the run.

"Detective Yuri Chernenko, meet Dr. Kris Van Zant," he said. "She's the next generation, you know. Dr. Hank's niece and one righteous psycho-killer hunter in her own right."

Yuri returned her fast, firm clasp with a hand that felt like solid callus and bone and then opened the passenger door on the driver's side and held it for her.

"Is my pleasure, doctor," he said. "It has been my privilege to work with your uncle on several cases, and in each of these matters his insight was quite invaluable."

Kris said thanks on Uncle Hank's behalf and got nimbly in the back.

As Yuri turned and buckled in in front of her, she noted how his face ran to broad flat planes in the cheeks and jaw and brow. She could tell his nose had been broken more than once and set not quite straight the last time. Still, there was an aspect about him she found dashing and even handsome in a durable sort of way. Irresistibly he put her in mind of a cavalry officer out of Tolstoy.

Half-expecting to see Cyrillic lettering on the badge-holder on his jacket, instead she recognized an Atlanta PD sergeant's shield with a Criminal Investigations Division tab.

"Now how we standing as to security on the scene?" asked Matt. "Boys in blue still got the lid on tight up there?"

Starting up and cutting deftly into traffic, Yuri shook his head over the wheel.

"I regret not," he said. "Already Fourth Estate is out in force."

As Kris listened to Matt swearing under his breath, she caught Yuri's eyes seeking hers in the rearview mirror. They were the light, warm green of coastal seawater. In the midst of all that heavily guarded bone structure, his gaze was as active and curious as a boy's.

"Excuse me, doctor," said the young investigator. "Is no disrespect I mean, but may one inquire as to your experience in this regard?"

"Don't sweat it, man," Matt said before Kris could answer. "The doc here's a stone pro. Fact of the matter is, she's Dr. Laszlo's own protégée."

Yuri's eyebrows, bristling thick and so blond they were nearly white, went up sharply.

"This is correct?" he said over his shoulder. "It was my privilege to hear Dr. Laszlo lecture when I attended FBI National Academy couple of years ago."

"The Bureau seems to think a lot of his abilities," Kris said. "Even if it isn't mutual."

"My own assessment, humble to be sure," said Yuri, "is Dr. Laszlo is genius, one who is disdainful of those whose gifts are less than his own and who suffers fools not at all. In this you would agree, doctor?"

"Pretty much," Kris said. "At least, that's been my impression over the past year."

With a laugh Yuri hoisted his brows again in what Kris guessed was self-parody.

"Whole year you spent with him?" he said. "It seemed to you much longer than this perhaps?"

"Not at all, detective," Kris chuckled with him. "I learned a lot."

Yuri turned sober, his eyes grave and level as they shifted from the road to meet hers in the mirror.

"Forgive me, Dr. Van Zant," he said. "Is not that I wish to make light of your training. I wish merely to make clear that what you are about to witness is not at all suitable for the inexperienced."

Kris glanced at Matt, who looked as if he'd been biting his tongue all the while he'd followed their exchange.

"Please don't be concerned on my account," she told Yuri. "Let's just say I've already gone over some pretty bloody crime scenes in my day. That is, in a professional capacity."

Shooting the long curve of Clifton Road in the dark, Yuri speeded up and drew a deep breath.

"I am afraid that is not quite my point, doctor," he said. "Rather, is that I believe this to be *least* bloody homicide you will ever see."

The house was on Blackland Road off Roswell, in the ritziest district of upscale Buckhead. Strung up out front, the yellow police-line tape struck Kris as a major lapse of taste. The press contingent bearing down on the scene only bolstered that impression for her.

"Bloodsuckers," Matt muttered, shaking his head. "Y'all know what I mean."

As they passed a line of vans with TV-station call letters on their panels, the senior detective kept his eyes to the front. The crowd outside the fence bristled with light bars, shoulder cams and boom mikes. Passing them by, Yuri pulled up at a checkpoint by the looming black-iron gate.

"Chernenko and Judson, Homicide," he told a uniformed policeman. "And this is Dr. Van Zant who will be acting as official consultant to task force."

The patrolman held a flashlight up to their badges and jotted on a clipboard before he waved them through.

"This would be good night to boost car off street in Buckhead," Yuri said, whistling. "It would appear most of Zone 2 Precinct is right here, yes?"

Kris smiled back at him and began to reply.

Then she sat up even straighter than usual as she looked ahead and caught her breath. The four-pointed red stars and red-green-and-blue stripes of APD patrol units filled the courtyard. But it wasn't the fleet that grabbed her attention.

Rather, the house itself made her stare as it reared up from a stand of live oaks trailing beards of Spanish moss. With ease it commanded a lawn that seemed to sweep to the horizon before it rolled away under floodlights. A massive colonnade in gray-veined marble fronted the Greek Revival pile, and fluted white columns at the top of the steps spread and soared like redwoods against the dark misty sky.

"Wherever he is now, David O. Selznick must be green with envy," Kris said. "So who lives here anyway?"

"Macdonald Fisher," Matt said. "Mr. Fisher, that is, he *used* to live here."

As he turned to Kris, he kept an eye cocked toward the policemen who stood sentinel on all sides of the main building.

"As in Fisher & Wales, the developers," he added. "You heard of 'em, Kris?"

"Sure, I haven't been away that long," she said. "As the saying goes, F&W's had the biggest impact on the Atlanta skyline since Gen'l Sherman passed through here."

Yuri pulled to the canvas-topped porte cochere on the side and jerked a thumb at the pearl-gray Ford Crown Victoria parked beside it.

"Heads up, lieutenant," he said in an undertone. "Looks like boss lady herself is on deck."

"Right," said Matt. "Okay, Yuri, Kris..."

He put a finger to his lips before they got out together.

"I'm going to go try and hack me a swath through a whole bunch of red tape in a hurry and make life simpler for all concerned," he told them. "So y'all come back me up with the high brass, hear?"

They fell in step and headed for the cluster of suits, gold braid and taut frowns under the awning. Looking to Kris as if they were co-conspirators now, Yuri grinned and gave her a wink behind Matt's back as he went ahead to address a stately woman dressed in pinstripes. She had café au lait skin and a prim, thoughtful face under a gray bun.

"Chief Radcliffe," Matt said. "I'd like to introduce to you if I may, ma'am, Dr. Kristin Van Zant, who I'd like to strongly recommend to be the latest addition to our serial-homicide task force."

The chief of police offered Kris a warm if tentative handshake and gave her an appraising look over rimless glasses.

"Oh?" she said. "I'm very well acquainted with Dr. Henry Van Zant, of course, but...?"

"I'm afraid my uncle's indisposed just now, Chief Radcliffe," Kris said quickly. "But since our training has been very similar and he's been my mentor throughout my career, Uncle Hank asked me to come in his place tonight so I could relay everything to him. Then we can both put together a psych profile for your department."

"You seem very young to me, Dr. Van Zant," the chief said. "And as to your 'training' you mentioned...?"

Matt took Kris's shoulders under his arm in a proud, proprietary gesture that she sensed he meant everyone around them to see as he spoke up for her.

"Dr. Kris comes to us straight from Washington, DC," he said. "Most recently, chief, matter of fact, she's been working side-by-side with none other than Dr. Stephen Laszlo himself, and—"

"Washington?" Chief Radcliffe cut in. "Laszlo?"

"Yes, ma'am," Kris said. "But I've just accepted a position back here at home, at Emory."

On instinct she decided to stretch the point by a couple of months, since her faculty appointment and status as an attending wouldn't take effect until September.

"I'm assistant professor of psychiatry," she stated. "At the medical school."

"Oh?" the chief said. "Very good. So you're one of our own."

She'd spoken just loud enough for Kris to hear, and then in spite of the palpable tension around them she smiled openly and gave her hand an enthusiastic pump as she raised her voice.

"Well, welcome aboard, doctor," she declared. "On behalf of the rest of the force, I must say I look forward with great anticipation to your contribution to all our efforts to solve these horrible, horrible crimes."

Rumbles of assent from the surrounding brass followed Kris as Yuri and Matt flanked her on either side. Overshadowed by the two men, she took a set of fieldstone-flagged steps up to the entrance in the mansion's east wing. At the threshold of the crime scene, the ranking detective dropped his head to speak in her ear.

"A little later, doc," he pledged, "I'll clue you in on the political side of the case."

Then under the anxious gaze of the patrolman who was guarding the way in, Matt put his arm across her shoulders again and sounded relieved and grateful to her as he bent even closer.

"In the meantime," he whispered, "I got to hand it to you one more time, Kris. Even when it comes to batting back interdepartmental BS like that, kid, you're a natural."

❧

From the detectives Kris gathered that Macdonald Fisher's corpse had turned up in the library on the ground floor.

"In the *li*brary now, uh-huh. Just like something out of Agatha Christie," Matt said with a scowl. "But after that, doc, I got to tell you in advance that any similarity to your ordinary decent, civilized homicide drops off sharp-like."

Conducting her past a two-story-high double staircase with crimson runners, he exchanged grim looks with the policemen stationed at every doorway they passed.

"We have instructed even evidence techs to give body wide berth for time being," Yuri told her. "Not even Medical Examiner's people have touched it so far. Is for you, doctor, they are waiting."

Straining not to let her eagerness show, Kris nodded as she stepped up to the towering oak doors at the end of the hall.

"Thank you," she said. "Thank you, so very much."

Matt had a word with the two patrolmen who stood at parade rest by the doors. They both were big men, roughhewn and hard-faced. Kris judged that neither of them was close to being a rookie. Still she could tell that whatever lay inside had spooked the sheer mortal daylights out of them.

Matt put his hand on her arm then. It felt like a father's touch. But she couldn't be sure whether he was trying to steady her or himself.

"Okay now, doc," he rasped. "Let's go."

She bobbed her head again.

The doors parted for them. Lamp glow from inside struck highlights off Kris's hair like sun on a raven's wing. With Matt and Yuri at her side, she didn't pause going in. Hissing discreetly, the doors slid shut at their heels and sealed themselves with a click.

As Kris took a look around inside, old money plus taste and privilege were the first associations that came to her mind.

Heavy silk drapes hung drawn to the casement of the bay window, and brass floor lamps lit the space. Bookshelves full of hardback spines and well-tended calfskin bindings covered most of three walls. From over the mantelpiece a gracious, sporty-looking couple in formal clothes from the turn of the last century gazed down in gilt-framed oils.

"I know I don't have to tell you, doc," Matt said hoarsely. "But long as we're in here, we strictly supposed to look but don't touch."

Kris gave him a nod and crossed the broad, spotless Bokhara rug to where the body lay full length on its back.

She noted how the arms turned out at the sides with the shoulders lined up square in front of the hearth. While not a pathologist herself, Kris had gowned up and gloved in on more than her share of coroner's autopsies. Already she'd taken part in a career's worth of forensic clinicopathological conferences. As always, the urge to touch and probe and trace the signature of wounds ran strong in her.

So, she took care to clasp her hands in front of her while she lightly knelt down and leaned over the head of the mutilated corpse.

Long-shanked and lean, Macdonald Fisher looked to Kris as if he'd been a tall and striking man in life. His face and form were still intact for the most part, but now they were as white and waxy-skinned as a museum effigy. He had on a light-blue, open-necked cotton shirt with the sleeves lapped up past the elbows, crisp white ducks, tasseled loafers with silk socks, and a narrow leather belt with a gold clasp half snapped off it.

Pale-hazel, the dead man's eyes were wide open and fixed on the distance. To Kris they still seemed to brim over with horror. Below a sharp-angled widow's peak of fair hair shot through with gray, his features were bold and aquiline.

Whoever had eaten through his throat, Kris noted, hadn't even slowed down before hitting cartilage and bone and sucking every vessel dry.

She considered that most people who could keep their eyes on a wound like that would take it for the work of a wild animal such as a wolf or coyote or maybe a rabid dog. Kris knew human bite marks when she saw them, though, and there was no way she could blame this carnage on any other species. Like an art appraiser tracking an Old Master's brushstrokes, she tilted her head from side to side as she inched her way around.

Now and then she nodded judiciously at the way the attacker had chewed straight through the strap muscles of the throat and torn them back to expose the thyroid gland and trachea. In frank appreciation she narrowed her eyes at the gnawed, ripped-open jugular veins and carotid arteries. The only other wounds she could see were on the hollows at the crooks of the arms.

Teeth had severed the basilic veins and brachial arteries there, apparently not just with a feel for anatomy but with gusto as well.

Kris's face at that point might have been a chess prodigy's who had sat down to a game with a grandmaster and had just glimpsed an opening to checkmate. Then as she got to her feet, her smile could have been that of a little girl on Christmas morning who had just got the pony she'd been praying for. Turning around, she saw both detectives staring hard and looking unnerved.

It took her a beat to realize they weren't gaping at the body but at her.

It's mine, she'd been thinking. Yes, yes, mine. This has got to be a true creature of the night, filled with raw blood desire and lethal unnamed needs, and no faking it either. For sure, it's what most folks would call a monster.

It's inhuman, she exulted. It's the real thing. It's at large. And now it's all, all...*mine*!

Kris gave an easy shrug as she rejoined Matt and Yuri by the door.

"So what can I tell you?" she said aloud. "This sucker was way thirsty."

CHAPTER THREE

Still looking around with a tracker's eye and a hunter's instincts, Kris had got halfway across the foyer when she cocked her head to the side. From close by, she heard someone sobbing and wailing. She turned back to Matt and Yuri to ask who it was.

"Roan Fisher," the younger detective told her quietly. "Victim's daughter, his only child. She was one who found body."

"Says her daddy wasn't expecting her and nobody picked up the phone when she called here," Matt filled in. "So she went and took her a cab in from Hartsfield, straight off an international connection that got way delayed tonight. Times she gives checks out with the taxi's log and our Airport people, too.

"You'n just about imagine what it was like for her," he added in an undertone. "What with nobody else here in the house, and all."

Following the deep-lunged crying, Kris hauled up at the threshold of the dining room.

"Nobody?" she asked. "Literally? With a place like this you'd think they'd need a custodial team the size of the Smithsonian's."

At her side, Yuri inclined his head toward the library they'd just left.

"Entire household staff and everybody on grounds had whole night off," he said. "On orders from deceased."

"Just like that?" Kris pressed him. "The late Mr. Fisher just up and declared, 'I want to be alone, crew, so clear out. You're on your own tonight.'"

Yuri shrugged, shifting long ridges of muscle under his jacket, but his eyes never left Kris's.

"Custom of long standing here, so we are told," he said. "Is his place, after all. Who is to argue with boss man, doctor, yes?"

"Good point, detective," she said. "Now I'd like to talk to Ms. Fisher, if I may."

Matt raised a hand to the two blue-suited policemen on guard by the banquet hall. Then he cracked the door and spoke for a few moments with someone inside. As he stepped out and held it open wide, Yuri stood back for Kris to go in ahead of them.

It was a lofty formal space. Lining the black-oak panels were framed prints of hunting scenes that Kris took to be originals. A crystal pendant chandelier like an inverted pyramid overhung the center of a mahogany table. As Kris sighted down the mirror sheen of its top, she estimated that forty guests could sit down around it at once and none of them would have to worry about their elbows.

Now the table was empty except for a young woman who sat in a chair at the head. Doubled over, she hugged her sides as her chest heaved. Her breath came out in harsh, panicked catches and moans.

Flanking her were a man and woman in plainclothes with APD shields and ID showing. After Kris introduced herself, they took a few steps back but still seemed wary. Neither looked away as she pulled up a chair and sat down facing Roan Fisher.

"Hi. I'm Dr. Kristin Van Zant," she said. "I'm a psychiatrist."

Taking the other's hand in both of hers, she held on to it with care and warmth while she leaned in close. Wide golden eyes stared at Kris from under moppy, sun-streaked bangs. She reflected that the dead man's eyes must have looked much like them in life.

"I—I—thanks," Roan mumbled. "But I already have, like, a therapist?"

Big surprise, thought Kris. From behind a blandly supportive expression she took the other woman's bearing.

Coltish and wiry in a cropped white tee with shredded Levi's and scuffed-up trail shoes, she looked to Kris like an adolescent on hold.

Roan must be within a year or so of her age, she judged, but the heiress was still punked out in rebel metal and ink. The silver-plated snot ring in one nasal wing looked purely excruciating to Kris. So did the ratchet-toothed piercing in her navel. A sunburst tattoo on one biceps complimented the stylized yellow crescent moon below her ribcage.

At least that bindi looks daubed on, she mused as she considered the red dot between Roan's eyebrows, so likely it'll wash off.

"I'm working with the police," she said aloud "They're going to find who did this. And I'm going to find out why."

The younger woman sputtered and thrashed her head. Kris gave her fingers a big-sisterly squeeze with a confidence she didn't have to force. Roan locked gazes with her then and seemed to find some grounds for comfort, maybe even hope, in those sunless depths.

"But—but—I...*no*," she gasped. "This is too much. I mean, like, I just got back to the States. I just flew in..."

"From India?"

Kris had already spotted the dog-eared *Bhagavad-Gita* sticking out of the backpack propped on the table leg beside them, and with a closer look she made out the *Lonely Planet* maps tucked in beside it.

"You've been spending some time in Nepal, too," she prompted. "Right, Roan?"

"From—flew in direct from Mumbai, yeah," she said, even wider-eyed than before. "How'd you know that, doc?"

"Wild hunch. Call me Kris," she urged her. "Everybody does. Now, Roan, I take it your dad wasn't looking for you to show up tonight?"

"He never is, Kris," she said. "But it's like, he's always willing to take me in when I do."

Roan's unlined, tanned face put Kris in mind of a child's

from a primitive tribe before she seemed to catch herself using the present tense and scowled again.

"I—I mean, he would," she said. "Like, like Mom never would. She's in Milan or Florence now—maybe Provence, Cannes, Monaco, wherever. And just now Daddy's, like, between marriages, you know?"

"Sure," Kris said. "And I'll bet this house has always been, like, his castle."

Roan's smile revealed a small fortune in orthodontia, and then with Kris's encouragement she seemed to grow fond and forgetful of the moment.

"You know it," she said. "This place's like—like nothing ever gets to him here, man."

"But the furnishings," Kris said. "You know, like that wallpaper up front in the hall? Something tells me your dad didn't pick that out himself."

"You mean that tacky flocked paper out there," Roan giggled. "Like Early Victorian Whorehouse? Whoa, dude, isn't that too Mancusi & Rennie for words?"

"Oh, the decorators?" Kris laughed with her. "Local, huh?"

"Flavor of the week," said Roan. "What can I tell you?"

"The color scheme," Kris coaxed her on instinct. "I mean, c'mon, Roan, that's got to be the most downright oppressive shade of..."

Roan mugged and clung to her hand as if, Kris imagined, they were staying up late together swapping secrets at the Chi O house.

"Midnight red, that's what they call it, Kris," she said. "What can I tell you?"

"Uh-huh."

Kris sensed it was time for a changeup, even if it was bound to bring this session to a crash.

"Your dad's such a resourceful man, isn't he, Roan?" she said. "He's always been so much in control and so on the lookout. I guess it'd be really, really hard to think of him ever getting taken off guard, huh?"

"No way, Kris, uh-*unh*."

Roan tossed her loose fair hair, which brushed Kris's forehead as she ducked closer.

"Daddy's like the original big-time paranoid," she said. "He's the kind that's built to last, you know? I mean, look how he's got this place all sealed off and wired up."

Long-armed, she gestured around them.

"Like tonight," she said, "I had to climb over the fence with the closed-circuit cameras on me and everything before I even hit the door. And like *I've* got the keys and codes. Okay?"

Kris saw her suck her gut in tight.

"Okay, *look*," Roan burst out. "I mean, it's like total fuckin' Fort Knox around here! So hey, there's no way anybody could ever get close enough to..."

Then doubt seemed to catch up with her fast. All at once her pupils blacked out the brown of her eyes and her lips went dead white. Kris could tell it was something Roan had just remembered or added up for herself. She also sensed that there was too much terror in the way and it was still too fresh for anyone to get past it now.

"Roan, you listen to me," she said like a doctor. "I'm going to make sure you get something that'll let you go right off to sleep, right now. You won't even have to dream, okay?"

Half standing, she braced the younger woman's shoulders.

Then over Roan's head she caught the eyes of the attendant plainclothesmen. They looked back at Kris stone-faced for a few seconds as if to let the newcomer know who was in charge here. Then they nodded to her at the same time.

"And after you've had a good long sleep, I want you to talk to me again, okay?" Kris whispered to Roan. "Listen to me. Don't think about it now. Don't you give it a second thought then.

"Just call me right up," she urged her. "We'll talk. Just us two, start to finish. Okay?"

"But—yeah, sure, Kris," she said. "I want to. I really do, but...?"

Kris gave her arms a quick, deft shake.

"I will," Roan said again, blinking. "But whoever, whatever got in here tonight and...?"

Kris held out one of her cards to her. She'd already crossed out the extension for her fellow's office at Saint Elizabeths Hospital. In its place she'd inked in the number of her personal cell phone.

"Whatever got to Daddy," Roan said just over her breath. "I know it couldn't have been...it wasn't really human, was it, Kris?"

"Maybe not," she said. "But we're going to catch it just the same."

Kris pressed her professional card into the other's palm and firmly closed her fingers on it.

"I promise, Roan," she said. "Because, you see, that's what I do."

❧

Kris lingered in the grand foyer with Matt and Yuri. Together they watched the latest arrivals go past. On their lab coats the serpents of a Caduceus staff twined around the Scales of Justice in the round, yellow-blue-and-red logo of the Fulton County Medical Examiner's Office.

"I assume the ME'll post the body in the morning," Kris said. "So if it's at all possible, I'd really like to scrub in on that autopsy."

"I believe this can be arranged," Yuri spoke up. "Yes, lieutenant?"

He raised his snowdrift eyebrows and shot his colleague an imploring look, and after Matt nodded, he asked after Kris's plans.

"I will come for you in morning, doctor," he promised. "I will conduct you to Medical Examiner's myself. Is necessary, you see, to exercise some degree of discretion in this matter."

"Yeah," Matt said. "As it is, we got the press and TV swarming all over this thing like flies on a dead pig in—"

He cut himself off and glanced around them before he went on more softly, directly to Kris.

"I know I don't have to worry about you keeping a secret now," he said. "Still and all, Kris, I surely wouldn't want anybody else to get wind of what you just said to young Ms. Fisher in there."

"Is matter of public perception, I believe," said Yuri. "As you can imagine in setting like this, doctor, great many rumors and theories are in circulation."

He gave Kris a wry look.

"Many of these suppositions are of quite frankly superstitious nature," he added. "To imply that official credence is given to supernatural origin for these murders would only add fuel to fire, yes?"

"I said the murderer might not be human," Kris replied. "But when it comes to inhuman behavior—even with acts like these killings—you hardly need to invoke the supernatural. Do you, detective?"

Yuri looked thoughtful. Then he met Kris's eyes and gave her a smile head-on. Something in his expression suggested to her, disturbingly enough, that they might just be kindred souls.

"I quite agree, doctor," he said cheerfully. "Excellent point you make."

"One more thing," said Matt. "I know it's a hell of a lot to ask of you, Kris, since you've already gone some distance out of your way for ol' Hank's sake, and everything."

He'd pressed his palm to his crown and was giving his scalp a vigorous massage, which Kris recalled as a familiar sign of stress with him.

"What?" she said. "C'mon, Uncle Matt. Please now. Out with it. Tell me."

"Hank's been going over the files on the first two victims," he said. "He's got 'em all locked up in his office at the hospital. And he was all set to give a preliminary briefing tomorrow to the Vam—er uh, to the serial-homicide task force, that is."

"Vampire Squad is whimsical little nickname we use, yes?" Yuri put in. "Strictly hush-hush, you know, doctor."

"Of course, detective," Kris said with her eyes on Matt.

"Actually, Hank and I've been discussing these cases for quite a while now. Matter of fact, that's what we were talking about when he—well, when it got to be obvious that I needed to be back here.

"So trust me, Matt," she pressed her case. "It wouldn't take much time at all for me to get up to speed on this myself."

"It's a hell of a lot to ask of you, Kris," he said again. "But we need the psych input bad just now. That much even *I* can see, doc.

"And for reasons I'll have to fill you in on later," he sighed, "we under a lot of pressure from downtown right now to keep this local and not bring our friends the Feds in on it."

"Don't you worry, I'll take up the slack for Uncle Hank," Kris said. "Starting with that briefing tomorrow, I'll be ready. For everything."

"Kris, I...don't know."

She could see the desperation and gratitude in Matt's eyes warring with what he knew to be her personal stake in this.

"If you would," he said at last. "If you would."

"It's okay, Uncle Matt."

Kris caught herself smiling at full intensity. As usual, that seemed to unsettle Matt. By his side, though, Yuri grinned back at her with his whole face.

"You know," she chided, "I'd be really, really hurt if you didn't ask me to."

CHAPTER FOUR

Kris had the patrolman who drove her back to University Hospital drop her off by the emergency bay. A white-haired security guard who had been a fixture in the ER for as long as she could remember smiled and waved her in even before she could hold up her state medical-license card. Familiarly then, she cut through the bustle and throng to the central corridor and took the stairs up to CCU.

The unit nurses told her her uncle's vital signs were good and stable. His ECG hadn't budged since his admission by way of the cath suite. So, it took little coaxing from Kris before they let her look in at his bedside one last time tonight.

She found him just as she'd come upon him a thousand times before, in his study late at night. Uncle Hank's half-lensed spectacles perched near the tip of his nose as he softly snored. Propped open on his midsection was the latest edition of the *American Journal of Psychiatry*. As usual, he'd filled most of the legal pad beside it with the chewed-on Bic pen by his hand.

Kris watched him in silence for a few moments. For good measure she counted the pulse at his wrist with one eye on the monitor overhead. Finally, just as she'd done a thousand times in the past, she slipped off his glasses and laid them aside without waking him.

Then she bussed Uncle Hank's forehead and left by the way she'd come in, with as little sound and as hard to track as a shadow at twilight.

Before Kris left the ward, the unit clerk retrieved her bags for her. It wasn't hard to talk Security into turning her uncle's keys over to her for safekeeping. That was all she needed for now. She let herself into Hank's office upstairs in the psych wing, unlocked his filing cabinets, and raided them for pertinent documents.

Sitting down in the outsize swivel chair, Kris adjusted the desk lamp to her height. Methodically she arranged his case notes on the blotter. Beside them she laid out reprints from forensic and clinical journals, press clippings, the official path reports from the ME's office, and the police records of the Buckhead Vampire's first two homicides. All the while, she took notes.

It took her less than an hour to commit the facts to memory. As to theory, she decided to confer with Uncle Hank in the morning and see if he still agreed with her. Now it was getting late.

She checked her watch, compared it with the brass clock on the desk, and conceded that midnight was as good a time as any to call it a day. In the same order she'd taken them out in, Kris returned the papers to their files and locked the cabinets back up. Mindful of shadows, she took the stairs down to the hospital-security checkpoint up front and crossed the street to the parking deck where Hank kept his Volvo.

Alone then and as at home in the night as ever, Kris drove back to the house where she'd grown up.

Kris had never been afraid of the dark, but she'd never taken it lightly either. At sundown she grew even warier than usual. If possible, her senses got even keener then. She had her reasons for vigilance.

She pulled up to the sprawling old white-clapboard house on Baker Place just off the university campus and parked at the head of the drive. After she let herself in by the front door, she stood in the hall in the dark for a few seconds. As soon as she put the lights on, she caught the fine sheen off Aunt June's piano in the front room.

The sheet music was still in place on the concert Yamaha grand. Two years after his wife's death from cancer, Hank still kept it that way even though he was an indifferent pianist at best. He was just barely a better player than Kris, in fact, even after all of June's longsuffering efforts to teach her.

But then as Kris had come to recognize not long after she moved in here, Hank was the one who could see where his niece's real talents lay.

She paused at the foot of the stairway and peered up into the dark. At age seven, on her first day in residence here, Kris had gone up to the bedroom off the landing. After trying the window in its sash and looking out over the roof of the trellised porch below, she'd decided it was much like her room in the house she'd lived in before.

"This one, please," she'd said. "If it's okay with you guys, I'd like to sleep up here."

"But—but, dear," said Aunt June. "Wouldn't you rather take the bedroom downstairs, closer to us?"

She was a pretty, upbeat woman but seemed vague to Kris except when she was seated at the ivory keyboard.

"I mean, a big old creaky house like this," she went on. "When it's dark at night—that is, don't you think you might get...well, uhm, lonesome up here?"

"No, ma'am," Kris said. "If it's all the same to you, please, this is where I'd like to be at night."

"It's all right, dear," said Hank. "After all, our Kristin knows her mind."

Kris's first home was a weathered Colonial pile that had stood for over a century on the Warrior River flats, near Tuscaloosa. Van Zants had lived there for generations as country docs and gentry, more or less. Like his twin brother Hank, Kris's father Will was a Harvard-trained psychiatrist and an idealist.

Will came back home to be chief of staff at Bryce, the state mental hospital. He was set on remaking it from the infamous Southern Gothic asylum it had come to be into a proper twentieth-century mental-health facility. Meanwhile, his wife

Christina taught psychology next door at the University of Alabama.

"So now, Miss Kris, you want to be on your own in this little room all the way up here at the top of the stairs," Christina chided her. "Wouldn't it be better to stay on the ground floor with Petey and the rest of us, with a nice big room of your own?"

Kris kept her eyes away from the windowsill as she reflected that her brother Pete, who was two years younger she was, was also louder and might be even higher-spirited but still tended to shy away from the dark.

"No, ma'am, thanks," said Kris. "I like it up here, Mom. Honest I do."

"Well, if that's the way you feel," her father allowed. "I guess there's no reason for you not to make it your room now."

Will waited until they were alone to ask his daughter a question.

"Honey," he said. "You're not still trying to get away from monsters, are you?"

"Oh, no, *sir*!" said Kris. "I swear. Cross my heart and hope to die, it's not that."

Behind her back, she kept her fingers crossed on both hands. She guessed Dad had glimpsed her trying out the trellis at the top of the front porch. Plus, everyone around here seemed to know what a prodigious climber she was. A natural acrobat, Kris hardly ever lost her grip or got taken off balance.

"I mean, I just like it up here," she insisted. "Especially at night."

"Krissy," Dad sighed. "There aren't any monsters that come out at night. Or anytime else, for that matter. I promise."

"But what about the Werewolf, Daddy?" she asked. "Isn't *that* a monster?"

It was late in the 1970s, and the local news was full of the Tuscaloosa Werewolf. An elusive intruder who struck only when the moon was full, the Werewolf had broken into a number of homes nearby and left his victims hacked to pieces. Seven-year-old Kris had made it her business to find out the meaning of such long and intriguing words as decapitation, mutilation and dismemberment.

"Honey," her father said. "What the TV and newspapers keep calling a 'werewolf' is merely somebody who's just like everybody else but who for one reason or another goes out from time to time and does bad things."

"But why?" Kris asked. "Why does it—why does he do stuff like that, anyway?"

"He's a bit mixed-up in the head, that's all," Dad told her. "He's not well, so he just needs somebody to help him get better. And you know we'd never let anybody hurt you, not in a million years. Don't you, princess?"

Kris nodded politely and kept her opinions to herself. She loved her parents and even her brother Pete. But they were only human, after all. That meant she was going to have to look out for herself.

That was her state of mind as she lay down to sleep in the upstairs bedroom in her folks' house. It was the night of the last full moon in spring. The season had turned off much crisper and cooler than was usual in the river bottoms.

On the edge of sleep, she made out the rattle and grind of a pickup truck. Its engine shut off as tires crunched on the gravel driveway right under her window. Rory, the redbone hound who patrolled outside, always barked when strangers came close. Tonight Rory didn't so much as growl, though, not even when a door banged shut and heavy footsteps crossed the drive to the front porch.

Kris hopped out of bed to look out the window, and then she saw why. In the moonlight she recognized the man who got out of the truck as Mr. McCandless. A longtime orderly at Bryce Hospital where her father took care of mixed-up people, he was a familiar figure around the household. From time to time he'd hire on to do odd jobs and see to all the repairs the ancient homestead needed.

Big and gaunt, he was an easygoing man with scruffy hair and downcast eyes the color of tobacco juice. Tonight as usual he had a smile on his pale, loose-jawed face and wore a patched-up windbreaker over his customary scrubs and gumboots. While Kris watched, he bent down to pat Rory's head. Then as the dog trotted off, he took the steps up to the porch and knocked on the door.

She heard her father call out and McCandless answering. The bolt shot back, and the front door opened. Some more talking carried from downstairs. Then came silence. To Kris it held on for way too long.

She didn't even have to think as she slid the window up without a sound and pushed the screen back from the frame. On a hundred other nights when she'd thought she heard something, she'd done the same. Kris put on jeans and a woolly pullover against the chill and laced her sneakers up tight to her ankles. Then she kept still in the dark and listened hard.

At length she heard a deep, sharp gasp from below. Or maybe it was a half-choked scream. It might have come from her mother or Petey. Kris couldn't be sure.

Still she wasn't afraid. At the same time, she was too smart not to know when to cut and run and try to save herself. But then she thought maybe she could still help her folks get out. Maybe they were okay down there, just trapped.

Okay, sure, she reasoned, even if they hadn't believed her about the night monsters, they still had a right to get rescued.

So with her ears pricked up so high they were humming like crickets in summer and her eyes peeled to see in stray moonbeams and shadow, Kris pushed open the door to her room and eased her way down the hardwood boards in the hall to edge up on the top of the landing.

As she got closer, she saw the light was shining in the front hall below but everything else was dark. From experience she knew she could get almost all the way down the stairs before the third riser from the bottom squeaked. So she held back a step and looked down.

McCandless stood with his back to her in the middle of the hallway, between the front door and the ground-floor bedrooms. At his feet lay a wrack of long bones and ribs and square-cut slabs like sides of beef and pork shoulders. Kris had seen something like it in a butcher's freezer, but these had a lot more blood on them.

Her folks' old handyman was holding up a knapped-edged sling blade in his right hand. In his left he had something else Kris couldn't quite see. Leaning closer, she forgot and put her foot down on the tread below. Before she could draw back, it let out a creak and made her start.

McCandless spun around at the noise. As he pivoted at the waist, she saw he was palming her brother's head like a football. It was chopped off clean at the chin.

Kris didn't scream. Instead she scrambled back and began to climb. With a grunt McCandless shambled after, and then he dug in up the stairs.

He was quick, but she was much lighter and even faster on the incline. She heard the soles of his boots slap down on the boards in the hall, but she'd already made it back to her room. With a kick she slammed the door shut at her heels.

She jumped for the sill and slid over it on her knees, and then she landed on the shingles outside on the balls of her feet.

At double time, Kris bucked a dozen sidesteps to get to the top of the trellis. She'd shinnied halfway down it when McCandless clambered out the window right over her head. Sounding frenzied, he took a dive for the edge of the porch roof. Then he heaved himself over and made grab for her with one rangy arm.

The trellis's gracious old woodwork shivered and cracked like matchsticks under his weight. He flailed his arms and kicked his legs out as he took a header for the gravel just clear of the veranda rails. Trailing ivy on his way down, he missed Kris by inches.

The bellow and squeals he let out with his fall told her he'd come down square on his own blade, but she didn't look back.

Knees up and elbows pumping, Kris lit out for the stand of water oaks by the drive. Then she cut past them through the tall grass of the meadow. She didn't let up until she came out at the back of the old stone farmhouse on the Turnbulls' holding, hard by her own folks' land.

"It's the Werewolf!" she cried out as loud as she could. "It's the Werewolf, for real!"

She hammered on the door with the flat of both hands until lights came on and Old Man Turnbull gaped out at her through the glass.

"It got my mom and dad and Pete," she kept yelling. "And now it's out in the front yard. And please, Mr. Turnbull, please, you've got to stop it before it gets away. Let's get going, right now. *Please*!"

All of a sudden the night filled up with high-beam carbide lamps fit to outshine the moon. Ramsay Turnbull and his three big sons went clumping through the brush as Kris led the way back to her house. All the men ported twelve-gauge pump guns with their dogs yapping and baying in front of them.

Sirens went off just as Kris and her party made it to the Van Zant property line. Right beside her, a squad of county sheriff's patrol cars came barreling down the road running all their lights. As they cut into the drive, their tires shrieked and sent gravel flying at the end of the blacktop.

They found Lyle McCandless in a sweat to get the door of his pickup open. He had one arm clamped to his side but still couldn't stanch the flow of blood from the gash in his ribcage. Facing a pack of sharp-toothed rawboned dogs up for the hunt, he stared down the barrels of as many shotguns and pistols.

To Kris he looked shaken-up bad and stymied. Strangely, though, he didn't strike her as scared at that point. Even when two sheriff's deputies bigger than he was hauled his arms behind his back and snapped handcuffs on him, he still didn't seem alarmed.

Now as Kris got ready for bed in her uncle's house, she couldn't help but dwell on that scene. She decided once again that the Tuscaloosa Werewolf had shown fear just one time that night. And that had come when he finally looked down.

Then he met her eyes.

CHAPTER FIVE

Kris woke up fresh and ready to go just before the alarm she'd set for 5 AM went off on the bedside table.

Not bothering with lights, she clicked it off and hopped out of bed. After a quick loo stop, as her New Zealander roommate in med school used to put it, she pulled on the warm-up togs she'd laid out last night. Then she laced her Nikes tight and knotted them snug to her ankles for her morning four-miler.

Before she hit the street, Kris belted on a jogger's pack and slipped her wallet and three other items in it. The first was her cell phone from its charger cradle, and the next was Uncle Hank's key ring. The last she'd taken from the gun safe in the den last night.

The blued-steel SIG Sauer P225 double-action semiautomic was a match for the piece she'd had to leave behind for her airline flight. She favored it because the compact grip just fit her palm and balanced out to point like a coon dog. It packed eight full-house 9mm hollowpoint rounds in its clip, too, plus one up the breech.

Fondly, the little SIG reminded Kris of the .22 plinkers she'd won a string of Girl Scout merit badges with. At age twelve, she'd aced the NRA pistolcaft course the first time she took it. Since, she'd wangled civilian handgun licenses and concealed-carry permits in three state jurisdictions and the District of Columbia so far. These days she went strapped most of the time.

Alert and well armed then, Kris padded downstairs and left by the kitchen door.

By the fading glow of streetlights, she stuck by the sidewalk and hedgerows. Taking her old gym-team training route, she headed up Baker Place for the long flat stretch of Dekalb Heights Road so she could double back around Sherrinford Circle. At the corner she overtook an old neighbor.

A distinguished emeritus of the physics department at Emory U., Prof. Teitelbaum shuffled down the walk in his slippers and bathrobe. Picking up his *Constitution*, he seemed pleased to see Kris again. As she passed him by at full tilt, the gray-bearded scientist exchanged greetings with her on the crisp morning air.

Kris admitted that her dawn run was as much for her mind's sake as for exercise. Usually the play of her muscles and the pumping of her blood cleared away any dogging, unhelpful dreams and memories. This morning, though, she found it hard not to think of the correspondence she'd carried on for over ten years before it ended a decade ago.

Her pen pal was Lyle McCandless, aka the Tuscaloosa Werewolf.

Kris had written her first letter to him when she was eight years old. In her best schoolgirl copperplate, she'd addressed the envelope in care of the Alabama Department of Corrections. As she'd made it her business to find out, that was how folks on Death Row got their mail.

Since they hadn't really got a chance to talk at his murder trial, young Kris wrote to the condemned man, maybe he had something on his mind he'd like to say to her now that he had the time.

The first reply was full of longwinded remorse and semiliterate pleas for forgiveness. He just hadn't been able to help himself, Lyle told her. Furthermore, as he begged to make clear, since his sentencing he'd gone and let Jesus Christ into his heart and accepted Him as his personal Lord and Savior.

Immediately Kris wrote back to congratulate Lyle on the saving of his soul, and then she urged him to keep on writing to her.

Tell me what it was like for you, she coaxed him. Tell me how you went about doing what you did. Let me know what you thought about and what you felt while you were doing it. Please, Mr. McCandless, she wrote. Tell me your story.

Most people found it hard not to open up to Kris even when she was a child, and Lyle the Werewolf proved to be no exception.

At first he'd only go on to her about growing up dirt poor in the hardscrabble backcountry. He told her about going hunting all the time to help feed his family and how he'd field dress the deer he shot, and so on. None of this was news to Kris.

Then after a couple of years of writing back and forth, Lyle began to confide in her the indescribable but uniquely tantalizing thrill he got when people became his prey. From the start he'd known it was wrong. The fact was, he never doubted just how wrong it was. But the lure of the hunt was so great and the tang of satisfaction so sweet and deep and keen in the blood...

It was like poaching, prompted ten-year-old Kris. Wasn't it, Mr. McCandless?

Exactly, he wrote her back. That's what it felt like, Miss Kris, exactly. It was surely a relief, too, to be able to let go and get it all out to somebody like her. To a fellow soul, that is, who seemed to be able to appreciate just what he was all about.

Dang if it wasn't a pure old comfort and a true blessing to be able to speak his mind to her, said Lyle, who swore he'd never trusted anybody else that way.

All the while Kris was writing to her family's slayer, Uncle Hank honored her privacy. Then when she was fifteen and had over two hundred letters from the Werewolf precisely sorted out and cross-filed with her own notes, she let him go over them with her. In his scholarly way, Hank suggested sharing what she'd learned. That led to the first of their many joint publications in a peer-reviewed psychiatric journal.

A little later, a trade publisher got wind of Kris's correspondence. When he approached her about a book deal, she thoughtfully said no. She was already taking graduate-level psych courses at the U., and her professors were convinced she'd initiated a dialogue with one of the purest cases of a human predator on record. Kris was sure she didn't want to risk screwing it up now.

In the meantime, the case of *Alabama v. McCandless* reached the US Supreme Court. The appellate lawyers handling the Werewolf's defense had challenged the testimony of the medical experts for the prosecution. That was what the trial judge had relied on to deny their client a plea of not guilty by reason of insanity. As soon as she heard from the defense team, Kris was happy to send them Xerox copies of all her letters.

In reply she got nothing but silence.

Soon the state attorney general's office in Montgomery made the same request. Under threat of subpoena, Kris complied. This time the result was plain to her.

On the first day of May, quoth the State with the backing of nine Supreme Court Justices, Lyle McCandless would be put to death in the electric chair in Holman Prison and may God have mercy on his soul.

"*What?*" said Kris. "C'mon, that's just stupid!"

Now a teenage grad student in abnormal psych, she broke her silence with a vengeance when a reporter from the *Birmingham News* called her up with the final verdict and asked her for a quote.

"The best thing for everybody," she elaborated, "would be to study and work with Lyle McCandless—not *kill* him, for crying out loud."

After her outburst made the news, a dozen editorial writers opined that the interests of society and of justice itself would best be served by carrying out the capital sentence on a vicious killer like McCandless who clearly knew the difference between right and wrong.

"I can't say I've given much thought to theories of justice and punishment," Kris told the *Atlanta Journal* writer who got to her first for a comment. "But I have studied human personality in some detail. And I believe it would be a waste of a once-in-a-lifetime opportunity to execute this complex, fascinating man."

What young Miss Van Zant cannot bring herself to face up

to, declared a Southern Baptist clergyman of national repute, is that some folks are just plain evil and deserve to die for their crimes.

"Of *course* what Lyle McCandless did was evil," said Kris. "He slaughtered my family right in front of my eyes—in cold blood, for pity's sake. If *that's* not evil, then what is?"

Then she tried to strike a scientist's detached pose for the Associated Press staffer who had called her up to relay the parson's remarks.

"But isn't evil what we ought to be analyzing if we're ever going to figure out how to keep from destroying ourselves on this planet?" she went on to the AP man. "I mean, what if we were to discover a kind of bug—a parasite, say. And what if it turned out to carry a highly evolved strain of disease that was lethal to humans?

"Now I ask you," she concluded. "Wouldn't it be a lot smarter to keep it alive in the lab to study it for a cure than to just step on it and squash it?"

In pious tones, an international human-rights group then demanded whether Ms. Van Zant was comparing Mr. McCandless to an insect.

Can this victimized and no doubt psychically scarred young woman, they asked, really be suggesting that such a disturbed individual is subhuman?

"Look," Kris told the *New York Times* in a follow-up call. "That was *not* my point.

"What I meant," she said with care, "is that the best thing for everybody, Lyle McCandless included, is to keep him away from society. Six lock-ins deep behind stone walls and razor wire and guards all around with sniper rifles—hey, sure, okay, whatever it takes. But in the name of humanity, don't throw away the chance to—to...

"But why do I keep talking to you media vultures anyhow?" she snapped at the phone. "Just go *away* now."

Desperate then, Kris sat down and drafted an impassioned plea. In concise detail and with lucid reasoning she petitioned the state to commute the sentence of her family's murderer to life imprisonment without possibility of parole. She sent it by certified mail, to be delivered in person to the Governor of Alabama.

By return post, the governor invited her to take his place in the observation gallery at Holman Prison for the execution of Lyle McCandless.

On the first of May Kris drove herself down to Atmore, Alabama. It was near the Florida line but too far from the coast to be anything but flat and hot and scrubby. She requested a final meeting with the prisoner on site. But as the Holman officials explained to her, Lyle was too busy praying in his cell to talk.

Kris took her ringside seat in the death house to watch but never stopped taking notes, as a Reuters correspondent put it, "in her quite indecipherable shorthand."

Then in a Wirephoto snapped right after the electrocution, she appeared alone. Kris was shoving her way past a group of nuns and priests as they held up candles in a midnight vigil outside the prison. Various onlookers described the look on her face as disgusted, exasperated, or perhaps deeply anguished.

But what she really felt that night was screwed over.

Once she got back home, Kris applied to med school. A renowned criminal psychologist who had been courting her for his PhD program at Johns Hopkins called her up to protest. As her would-be mentor pointed out, she was phenomenally gifted in the field. In the academic study of dysfunctional human behavior, he maintained, she was like a one-in-a-million math whiz or an equally talented musical prodigy.

Surely, the Hopkins prof entreated her, in her case getting an MD would be slumming.

Kris heard him out politely, much as she'd listened to her college gym coach when she'd predicted that if only Kris would spend a few more hours a day on the parallel bars she'd be a sure bet for the US Olympic team.

But in the end she went her own way, for her own purposes. The experts had just shown her whose word counted when it came time to decide what to do with people who had broken the rules in a big way. Now she saw her mistake. She'd been like a little girl who had trusted the grownups to protect her.

At that point Kris swore that she'd never again let those shortsighted, narrow-minded, self-important bastards get between her and the truth.

Now as she clocked the end of her run at twenty-four minutes flat, she didn't slow down but kept on going straight through her uncle's front yard. She still had a cool-down drill of tae kwan do kicks and lunges ahead of her before a quick shower and breakfast. Then she'd confer with Hank at the hospital, attend the autopsy of Macdonald Fisher's body, and brief the Atlanta PD serial-homicide task force.

After that, she could get down to work. Kris knew where she was going now. She almost always did.

❧

"So that," she said at the bedside in CCU, "is how I put the profile together so far. Now what d'*you* say, Uncle Hank?"

"I'd say that on the essentials of these cases, we are in complete agreement."

The senior psychiatrist folded his hands like a Buddha over the mound his belly made under the sheet.

"In fact, Kristin," he went on, "I'm sure I couldn't have boiled it down nearly as succinctly and brought it to the point as you just did."

"Whoa!" she laughed. "I'm flattered."

Then she caught the troubled look in Hank's eyes as they blinked shy of hers behind his low-riding glasses.

"But...? C'mon, big uncle," she said. "Please. Tell me what's bugging you."

"I confess, my dear," he said. "I'm very glad that you are out there doing the field work on this matter, and not I. Very glad indeed."

As he shut his eyes, Kris couldn't mistake the wave of pain that crossed his face.

"Hank!"

She grabbed his arm to take his pulse. He gave her a smile

at that and shook his head. When she persisted, he took her hand and patted it on the bedrail.

"C'mon," she said. "Are you sure you're okay?"

"I'm fine, Kristin," he said. "Just fine, as long as I don't have to look directly at..."

He swallowed, and from the taut lines by his mouth she sensed that his discomfort wasn't physical but ran deep to the bone all the same.

"You see," he said, "this 'Vampire' matter has been trying for me precisely because at this stage in one's career, one would like to think that one could face up to any manifestation of behavior that is, after all, a part of the human condition.

"But still," he muttered. "Still..."

"You don't have to get close," she said. "I'll be your eyes on this one. Remember?"

"And for that I'm more grateful than I can say."

He gazed at her in a way that was as fond of her as it was uncomprehending. It was more paternal than anything else, she judged. Then just as he'd do when she was a child and he was offering her advice, he reached out a big rangy arm and put his hand lightly on top of her head.

"Kristin," he said. "You know I love you."

"I know. I do, too," she said. "Love you, I mean. But...?"

He drew her closer and brushed his lips to her forehead.

"Please, my dear," he sighed. "Be careful."

"Don't worry, Uncle Hank."

She pecked his cheek and straightened up, set to go.

"I'll watch my step," she said. "I always do."

"That isn't quite what I had in mind."

He looked wry as he regarded her over the tops of half-lenses.

"It's your methods I was referring to," he said. "Please try to remember as you go about this matter, my dear, that the rest of us are inclined to fear and recoil from that which moves by night and would seek to maim and kill us."

"Oh."

Kris barely missed a beat as she half-turned at the door.

"I'll be careful what I say in public this time," she pledged. "How's that, Uncle Hank?"

"That's my girl."

She waved back at him. Outside, she intercepted the cardiology fellow hovering by the nurses' station on early rounds. After he'd satisfied Kris as to her uncle's progress, she took the sliding front doors out of the unit.

"Dr. Van Zant," called a CCU nurse at her back. "There's somebody out there in the waiting room looking for you. I can't pronounce his name. I think he's, like, Russian or something?"

"Yuri!"

Kris just held back from colliding with what she at first took to be a slouching brick wall draped in neat, pressed khaki.

"I mean," she said as she got back her footing, "hi, detective."

"To you also good morning, doctor."

His hand as it clasped hers might have been a brick, too, if a warm one.

"Since we are to be working together," he said, "I would be very pleased if you would call me merely Yuri, yes?"

"Yes."

She was still a little off balance as he stepped aside and held the stairwell door for her.

"And please," she said. "Call me Kris. Everybody does."

"Very well, Kris."

He was casual and jaunty, but the hunter's glint in his eyes was much like what she'd seen in the mirror this morning.

"I beg your pardon for asking personal question like this," he said. "But are you by any chance, Kris, what is know as perky morning person?"

"Well...yeah."

She shrugged, about to take the stairs down.

"Sorry," she said. "I guess we all have our crosses to bear, huh?"

"I myself believe this is not such bad thing."

Keeping in step with her between the metal railings, Yuri whistled tunelessly to himself on the way.

"Car is waiting downstairs," he told her. "I will drive us straight over to ME's. They promised me not to start postmortem examination of Vampire's last victim before we arrive."

"All right," said Kris, impressed. "Good deal, Yuri."

"Good deal."

Echoing the phrase with a smile, he seemed appreciative as he stepped down on the ground-floor landing and opened the door for her.

"Is almost like date, Kris," he said. "Yes?"

CHAPTER SIX

As they cut south down Pryor Street in an unmarked car, Kris recalled the grand opening of the new Fulton County Medical Examiner's Center.

Hank had filled her in on the event just over a year ago. Sprawling a couple of blocks west of Turner Field, the center hulked dead ahead now. From somewhere Kris dredged up the fact that the FCMEC took up more than thirty thousand square feet of downtown real estate.

Yuri kept going past the gracious, glass-roofed public entrance at the front of the administration building. Instead he headed for the staff parking deck in back by two massive, anonymous structures. Kris knew those housed the autopsy suites.

The sunny facade was a good touch, she thought. She appreciated how it took the edge off the facility's morbid enterprise and held out some comfort for the bereaved. Too, when needed, it ought to help keep the press in bounds.

"Out in force," Yuri said from the wheel. "Big story, yes?"

Seeming to read her thoughts, he turned and hooked a thumb back. Kris followed and saw all the TV trucks out front. Bristling with microwave-relay gear and swarming with sound-and-video crew, they'd lined up all the way across the visitors' lot.

Kris nodded but kept her eyes on the skyline to the north.

Already bright, the rising sun struck tracks of red and gold down the sides of all the office towers and convention hotels. From this angle, the buildings loomed together. Peachtree Street was a steel-and-glass-box canyon to Kris's eye.

Yuri spoke up again as he pulled to the booth by the gate and held out his badge to the parking attendant.

"After all," he said, "is not every day billionaire developer turns up in property worth millions of dollars with last drop of blood sucked from his body, yes?"

"True," said Kris. "In these parts, it's usually the other way around."

❧

Mindful of house rules, Kris changed into scrubs in the staff locker room and gowned up. Then she fitted an OR cap and mask over her hair, snapped on latex gloves, and donned a pair of clear-plastic safety glasses. But still the chief medical examiner singled her out as soon as she entered his autopsy room.

"Little Krissy Van Zant!" he boomed. "Well, I'll be a sorry ol' son of a..."

Of long standing in office and no mean reputation in his field, Rob Mackenzie looked up from the exam table. He stood on a stool opposite a tall, stooped young figure Kris took to be one of the docs doing a fellowship here in forensic pathology. Wiry and set close to the ground himself, the ME let out a chuckle.

"I couldn't miss those laser-beam peepers of yours anywhere," he said to Kris. "So it really is you, child, pinch-hitting for the great big profiling shrink. And how the hell's ol' Hank faring today?"

Kris put her native drawl back on for the occasion.

"In the pink, Uncle Rob," she sang out. "Turned out it was just a li'l ol' bitty MI he had yesterday."

"Damn lucky's what he is."

The pathologist drew his grizzled brows together and set his jaw behind his mask.

"That ol' boy's got way too fat for his own good," he added. "I expect you let him know it, too. Didn't you, Krissy?"

"Yessir," she chimed back. "You bet that's just what I told him, Uncle Rob."

"Attagirl."

With effort Kris held back and waited her turn to get near the body. She saw Matt come in with a long gown and paper shoe-covers over his street clothes. He nodded and joined her by Yuri and a handful of staff personnel at the white-tiled wall in back.

"Okay now, let's have at it," said the ME once everyone was in place. "As to the external exam..."

One of the techs nudged another footstool toward the far side of the table, and Kris thanked her and stepped up on it.

In front of her, Macdonald Fisher's corpse lay supine and naked on the stainless-steel tabletop. A wooden wedge at the back of the neck propped up the head, and that made the hole in the throat gape wider. Otherwise, the wounds looked much the same to Kris as they had last night.

Now, though, the signs of an older injury drew her attention. The tracks of surgical incisions stood out dusky-blue against stark white flesh. In long, puckered lines they ran from hip to knee on the outside of both thighs.

Rob met her eyes and turned to the path fellow, who'd just begun to dictate into the overhead microphone.

"Hang on a sec, Jimmy," he said. "Before we go on to address the obvious traumatic lesions of the neck and arms up there, let's us give just a tad more notice to these chronic, well-healed scars down here."

"Looks like big ol' railroad-track suture lines," said Kris. "Is this some kind of major orthopedic work up and down the legs here, Uncle Rob?"

"I haven't got the patient's old medical records for review yet," he told her. "But my guess is, it'd be bilateral open reduction of multiple fractures of the femurs."

Wide-eyed and deferential, Kris inclined her head to him.

"And from the look of it 'em," he added, "I'd put the timing of surgery as sometime in mid-adolescence. Say, not long before long-bone growth was completed."

"Long time back, yessir," Kris said. "But there's nothing to indicate a more recent hospitalization, is there, Uncle Rob?

"That is," she pressed him softy, "unless something turns up in the patient's recent medical history to explain these—oh, I dunno. Would you call 'em restraint marks, on the extremities here?"

"Ah...yeah."

The ME looked over his shoulder at the detectives. Then as he leaned over the table facing Kris, he glanced up at the mike. Presently he went on in a monotone.

"What Dr. Van Zant just referred to is these subtle, circumferential premortem discolorations," he narrated. "Mild bruising, in a nutshell. They are most apparent on the dorsal aspects of both wrists and extend to the distal forearms. They also appear around the ankles just proximal to the dorsa of both feet."

"Looks like something you'd see at post on some of *my* old patients," Kris put in. "I mean, with institutionalized folks who had to be strapped down in bed to keep them from hurting themselves. You know...?

"What's the pathological term for it, Uncle Rob?" she asked lightly. "Something like 'humane restraint' contusions?"

"Close enough, Kris," Rob grunted. "Glad to see you keep up with the literature outside of your specialty. More'n I can say for some of your colleagues. Good ol' Hank excepted, of course."

"Thanks."

Kris looked up and beamed at him over the top of her mask.

"And say," she asked blandly, "didn't you describe much the same incidental findings in your autopsies of the first two cases like this?"

"You read 'em."

It wasn't a question.

"Just like in the other Vam—serial cases," he caught himself before he proceeded with the dictation. "These markings are in striking contrast to the manner in which the body was found, which was positioned unrestrained and with no sign of ligature material close by. Now, to get on to the primary assault lesions…"

He paused and looked hard at Kris over the body.

"Unless, doctor," he said to her, "you have any further questions or comments you'd like to make at this point?"

Keeping her gloved hands folded primly in front of her shoulders, Kris shook her head.

"Oh, no, sir," she said. "This is a learning experience for me, all right."

With another grunt, Rob gestured over the ripped throat.

"Okay," he said, "looks like we got us some good, clear soft-tissue impressions here. I'll leave it to our forensic odontologists to say for sure after we've got casts made whether these bite marks match up with the other two.

"Which is to say," he elaborated, "they are indicative of a probably young, male, big-jawed individual in a state of good dental health without obvious prostheses or missing teeth or malocclusion. And now…"

Seeming distracted, the ME raised his head and fixed Kris with a black-eyed glare.

"Dammit, gal!" he burst out. "You're doing it again."

Kris gave him an innocently questioning look.

"You've got that way about you that says, 'I'm the smartest kid in this here classroom and I'm just adyin' to put my hand up,'" said Rob. "So give us all a break, child. Speak your mind now. Out with it, hear?"

"'Scuse me, Uncle Rob," Kris said. "But I was just wondering if you'd be willing to predict that the internal exam'll turn up the same cause of death here as in the other two victims."

With a show of sorely tried patience, Rob shut his eyes for a few beats.

"Oh, well, judging from the lily-white cadaver with severed carotids and jugulars I see before me," he said, "I'd be willing to go out on a limb here, Krissy, and say in advance that we're like as not to find us a bunch of hypoxic-ischemic tissue changes and generally shocked-out organs.

"Which is to conclude, in fine," he barked, "that this here poor, luckless son of a bitch got himself bled to death!"

"Yessir," Kris said. "Thank you, so much."

Then before he could open his mouth again, she spoke much faster.

"But what did you make of the dry trachea and esophagus and the absence of ingested or aspirated blood in the stomach and lungs?" she asked in one breath. "In the previous two posts, that is, along with the histologically 'clean' findings of the wound margins on micro exam."

The pathologist straightened up and turned to shoot accusing looks at the two detectives who flanked him.

"Trust me, Dr. Mackenzie," Matt said. "I did *not* discuss any of the hold-back findings from your office with either of the Drs. Van Zant when we went and consulted them as psych profilers in these cases."

"Nor did I," said Yuri. "And I beg your pardon, doctor. But I believe it would be mistake to imagine that younger Dr. Van Zant could not read between lines and figure out on her own what you have already discovered for us."

Once again confronting Kris, Rob blew his breath out through his mask.

"Okay, okay, I'll say it out loud for you then," he told her. "Whoever or whatever—

"Oh, hell," he spat out. "Let's just call it the Buckhead Vampire like everybody else in town's doing, all right? Well, it looks like your goddam Vampire'd just about drained those bodies of blood even *before* it chomped down on the vessels in the arms and damn near bit the victims' heads off. Must've been like suckin' on a dry hole...

"Okay," he said again. "Happy now, Krissy?"

"Just about delirious," she said. "Thank you, Uncle Rob, thank you. But there is just this one other thing...?"

The senior physician urged her on with both hands

"Yessir," she said. "I just wondered, since these wounds look deeper and wider and yet more precisely inflicted than what you detailed in your posts of the other two, would you say the assailant is getting—well, more adept in his technique?"

"You talking about a learning curve here, Krissy?"

She bobbed her head in encouragement, and Rob shut his eyes before he spoke again.

"Yes, " he said at last. "And before you go on and ask me straight out, Kris, I'll tell you it looks like he's getting hungrier, too."

"Thank you, doctor," she said with feeling. "*That's* all I wanted to know."

"Thank *you*, doctor."

The ME bent forward over the colorless chest and stuck his hand out to an assistant.

"Let's go," he snapped. "Knife!"

Kris kept quiet for the length of the procedure and watched closely. But just as she'd suspected, even in a leading-edge forensic lab like this one there was little more to learn. She couldn't help thinking of a comment in a similar context from Stephen Laszlo, her erstwhile mentor and sometime lover.

You can always tell more from a body, said the great Laszlo, when the soul is still in it.

The Atlanta Police Department headquarters was in City Hall East out on Ponce de Leon Avenue. It looked like a rundown commercial building from the outside, and its offices were nowhere near as new and grand as the ME's. All the same, Kris sensed that the place was just as focused on nailing the city's best known and most dreaded killer.

Standing in front of a whiteboard at the head of a squadroom that looked more like a lecture hall to her, she cleared her throat.

"I'd like to thank Det. Lt. Judson for that kind introduction," Kris said. "And on behalf of my uncle Hank, thank you for all your good wishes while he's on the mend in University Hospital."

Two-dozen police detectives sat facing her in plastic chairs with writing arms attached. They gave her some sounds of assent and a few muted benedictions in return. But mainly they met her eyes with a set of hard, attentive stares.

On the way over, Matt had explained that he'd had a free hand in picking the members of the task force. Calling in his markers in the Criminal Investigations Division, he'd creamed off all the talent that Homicide/Assault, Burglary, and Sex Crimes could spare. It occurred to Kris that the investigators she was about to brief were likely to hold as few illusions about human nature as she did.

So as she faced her audience with a felt-tipped marker in hand, Kris strained to hold back a grin of anticipation.

"We have three victims so far," she said. "The first to get drained, back in April, was Wade Hazlitt. He was only thirty-seven years old and already the chief exec of one of the largest HMOs in the Southeast.

"I'll bet," she mused, "there wasn't a dry eye in the state medical association then."

Jotting names and dates on the board, she heard appreciative-sounding sniggers at her back.

"Then over Memorial Day weekend," she went on, "the Vampire swooped down on Ms. Halley Cantrell. She was a forty-six and a trial lawyer. I'm told that up until the time of her demise, she held the state record for cash damages from a jury verdict in a personal injury action."

"*In*surance companies was real broke up over that one, too, doc," called a voice from the back. "You know it."

"I'll bet, detective."

She finished writing on the board and faced back around.

"Then last night it was Mr. Macdonald Fisher's turn," she said. "He was the fifty-three-year-old CEO of Fisher & Wales, the real-estate developers."

Kris glanced out the window, which faced west and caught the glitter of the soaring cityscape.

"Now there was a man who needed no introduction in this town," she added. "So, what did these three have in common before they got their veins and arteries nipped into and turned up with all their blood missing?"

From the back came the same country-and-western baritone that had spoken up before.

"They's all high-class whitebread folks that lived up in Buckhead, doc," he called out. "And all of 'em rich as hell, too."

"Plus," she prompted, "they were all currently unattached and living alone.

"*And* they'd made sure no one else was around on the nights when they got murdered," Kris pressed her point. "No servants, no caretakers, no live-in significant others. Nobody. Just a quiet evening all by themselves in their palatial homes, with the very best security systems that money could buy."

"Excuse me," said a young woman in the front row. "Dr. Van Zant?"

She had cut-glass features the shade of mocha and eyes like agates.

"I'm sure you know it already," she said. "But no matter what they hear from the Department, the media's been treating these homicides from the start as if they're some kind of classic locked-door mystery."

"Thanks, detective," said Kris. "That's my point exactly."

Like the fresh-minted assistant professor she was, Kris faced the room and spread her arms wide.

"And in real life," she demanded, "who always turns out to be the perpetrator in a locked-door scenario?"

"That's easy, doc," said her interlocutor in the back row. "Sumbitch that's got a key."

"Damn straight, bubba."

Kris had taken to pacing up and down, and she hit her stride as she primed the others.

"That's what's going to pull these cases together and put a face on the Vampire," she said. "I believe each of these victims in fact *welcomed* his or her killer."

"Hey, hold on, doc."

A heavyset, buzzcut detective by the one she'd called bubba held up his hand.

"Aw, c'mon now," he said. "'D'I understand you to say you

think this here bloodsucking business was, some way or other... consensual?"

"Don't know if they lean that way up in Buckhead," said the detective beside him. "But where I come from, doc, that's kind of kinky."

"Psychiatrically speaking," said Kris, "it's kinky as hell. But trust me, serious blood fetishism exists. And I hear there's an old saying in the S&M scene. It takes two, at least, to tango."

Some of the younger investigators nodded and spoke together behind their hands as she let them all think about it.

"But of course," she went on, "I'm not talking about those gothed-out, multiply pierced deathrock punks and vampire wannabes you're liable to run into out on the street.

"No," she sighed. "Obviously, this is more than just some thrill-seeking kids tugging on nipple rings and taking bites out of each other's necks and so on in that vein...

"Yes," she said, looking around. "Question there, Det. Sgt. Chernenko?"

From his chair by the door, Yuri spoke as formally as she had.

"To return to physical evidence if I may, Dr. Van Zant," he said, "I would like to make one point clear. Medically speaking, is possible to drain body of blood merely by biting and drinking from vessels in this manner?"

"Good point, detective," she said. "The answer's no, of course not."

Kris caught herself picking up her pace.

"Not even if you managed to sink your teeth straight into the carotid artery," she went on. "Of someone who's still kicking, I mean. Believe me, in that case it'd be like trying to take a sip from a fire hose.

"Not to mention the fact that the average person has five or six liters of total blood volume onboard," she added. "Make that ten or twelve pints, more or less. So in all, we're talking about more than a whole Anne Rice fan club could handle at one sitting."

"Okay, doc, I'll bite," said Bubba. "So where'd all these folks' blood go, anyway? And how?"

"It's not that big a deal to bleed out a living body, detective," Kris said. "Not as long as the victim doesn't put up too much of a fight."

Pacing faster, Kris shrugged.

"Think of when you've donated blood to the Red Cross," she said. "Remember how the nurse sticks you with a needle and plugs an IV tube in an arm vein. Then she keeps that limb below the level of the heart so blood pressure and plain ol' gravity'll do the job, no suction required.

"Pretty soon that way," she proceeded, "you could drain off a dozen units. And that wouldn't be too cumbersome to carry off in phlebotomy bags."

In front of Kris, the detective with the stony eyes shook her head.

"But what about the meticulous placement of the bodies, doctor?" she asked. "There weren't even any bloodstains around 'em and no tie-downs we could find. Obviously they'd been moved a ways from where they'd been murdered. Don't you agree?"

"Sure," said Kris. "And that's the part I don't like."

Still in motion, she frowned.

"It's fussy, it's cute, and it's way too Hollywood," she fretted. "Maybe it's even reaching for some kind of arcane symbolism or trying to send a message. Maybe...

"I don't know," she admitted. "And that's not like our Vampire."

"It's not?"

The investigator up front bit her lip hard, her eyes on Kris.

"You already seem to have a picture of the actor in mind, doctor," she said. "Care to share it with the rest of the class?"

"Hm? Oh, sure."

Remembering herself, Kris stood still and began to lecture.

"As to the standard-probability profile," she began, "we're

most likely dealing with a white male, stronger and larger than average. He'd be in his mid-twenties to late thirties, a loner but holding down a steady job. Maybe he works in a medical setting and has some background or training in healthcare. And as the saying goes, he's presentable enough to gain entry to the very best households.

"But from what I've seen of his work so far," she went on, "his most distinctive psychological trait is also the one that clashes most with the layout of the crime scenes. What I'm getting at is his sheer single-mindedness and the seriousness of his intent. I mean, everything points to his being able to get his victims right where he wants them to be.

"But then," she posed, "what does he do? Does he take their money or property? Does he go for sex? Personal revenge? Does he act out some other kind of sadistic gratification?"

Kris raised her arms high, as if leading a cheer.

"Hell, no, team," she called out. "What's our boy want? Huh? All together now! It's got to be—"

"*Blood*," said a dozen voices. "Blood..."

Kris picked up the quaver in some of them, not least Matt's as he looked on from the corner with his arms folded tight.

"And it's not just that he wants it either," she said. "Uh-uhn, no. This sucker *needs* it. He's getting thirstier, too. It's plain to see how his habit's snowballing on him. He—yes, Det. Chernenko?"

"I beg your pardon, Dr. Van Zant," he said. "Not to belabor what is obvious, but to me it seems as if you are giving profile of addict and not just killer, yes?"

"Bull's eye!"

Kris couldn't hold back a smile of triumph.

"And that's got to be our biggest advantage in tracking the Vampire," she said. "Maybe he looks enough like everybody else to keep his head down and blend into the crowd, sure. But sooner or later—and my money's on sooner—he's going to trip himself up like any substance abuser's bound to when he's starting to hurt bad for a fix.

"He'll be at his most vulnerable when he's about to come

down off his last hit and he's a threat to withdraw," she added. "Because that's when he knows he's got to go out and score or he's going to lose it big-time. See?"

She decided it was time to wrap it up.

"That's the profile I'm convinced we're faced with," she said. "Junkie dynamics, in a word. In the end when the need hits him hard, he's just going to have to make a grab for blood and he won't have time to think about it either.

"A predator's reaction, pure and primitive," she concluded. "Like shark reflexes."

Seconds went by, and nobody said a word. Then Kris saw some nods followed by acutely thoughtful looks. All across the room, these seasoned manhunters seemed to buy into what she'd just told them.

Kris felt relief as she picked up her briefcase and got set to go. She could tell she'd struck a chord with them and now it was resonating. Too, even if she doubted that anyone here would admit it, they all looked to be in mortal fear now.

For Kris's needs that was a lot better than a round of applause.

CHAPTER SEVEN

Back at the psych department at University Hospital, Kris blithely commandeered Uncle Hank's office.

She'd found out that several of the senior tenured staff were off on sabbatical for the summer. That included the chair, Dr. Luttwick. So, Kris had little to distract her from her plan to get a jump on the Buckhead Vampire.

"No one was really expecting you to show up until September, Dr. Van Zant," said Terri Frank, the departmental secretary standing in for Hank's vacationing assistant. "But if there's anything I can do for you, doctor...?"

Kris looked up from clipping her new medical-center ID to the lapel of a crisp white ward coat, which she'd just cadged from the linen service.

"I'd been planning to take a little time off after my fellowship," she told the young woman. "But then I saw a chance to—well, just say I changed my mind. And since you mentioned it, Terri?"

"Actually, Dr. Van Zant," she said, "most folks around here just call me by my initials."

Slim and chestnut-haired, she was as wide-eyed and proprietary as a Persian cat as she hovered by the door with a notepad at ready.

"It goes back to when I used to work down in Transcription," she explained. "As in 'T.F.' You know, like at the bottom of letters and consult notes and such?"

"Check. And call me Kris," she said. "Everybody does."

Hauling an armful of files out of the cabinet, Kris sat down at the desk. In a white coat with a stack of police reports laid out in front of her, she was feeling more at home here by the minute. She drew a deep breath and looked up.

"Okay, TF, stand by," she said. "Pretty soon we ought to be getting a bunch of faxes under confidential cover. It'll be some patients' records I requested from the Medical Examiner's office. They ought to include copies of old hospital and clinical summaries on Wade Hazlitt, Halley Cantrell and Macdonald Fisher."

Terri arched her eyebrows at the victims' names as she jotted herself a note.

"If you don't see 'em within the next hour," Kris proceeded, "I need you to call up the ME's for me. Ask for Dr. Mackenzie's personal assistant. And if they give you any pushback over there, I want you to use both my name and my uncle's *and* refer to Det. Lt. Judson from APD Homicide when you repeat the request. Got that, T.?"

"Yes, ma'am! I mean, Dr.—uh, Kris." Terri said fast. "I'll sure keep a lookout for 'em. Anything else I can do for you?"

Kris held up a folder for her to see.

"My uncle's been keeping a file of press clippings," she said. "And it looks really, really thorough and well-tabulated. By any chance, T., did you put it together for him yourself?"

Terri looked shy but beamed at her.

"I sure did," she said. "I'm sort of a media watcher. I'm, like, working on a communications degree, from Georgia State? If you like, Kris, I could keep on updating the file for you."

"Please," said Kris. "But I'd like you to add a little something to it."

She got to her feet, drawing closer to Terri as she dropped her voice.

"It'd be a good thing, too, if you could pull this off without letting anybody know who's doing the asking," she said. "See, I'd like to find out which of the local radio and TV call-in shows have been getting the most phone traffic on the Buckhead Vampire just lately."

Not even blinking, Terri bobbed her head and made some more notes on her pad while she backed out the door.

"I can do that," she said. "I'll get right on it, Kris."

"Good deal, T.," said Kris. "Oh, and one other thing—"

She'd turned back to the desk. When she looked around, she found that Terri had already disappeared into the anteroom. One of the buttons on the console was labeled *TF*, so she picked up the phone and punched it.

"I'm expecting to hear from a Ms. Fisher," she said on the line. "I gave her my cell-phone number. But she struck me as having the sort of inquiring mind that might just go looking for me where I'm working. If she calls here, T., you can put her right through to—"

"'Scuse me, Kris," Terri broke in. "But if you mean Roan Fisher, I've got her right here."

"Oh?" said Kris. "Which line, TF?"

"I mean she just turned up out here," Terri said. "She's, like, right in front of me, Kris."

Springing up, Kris was already headed for the doorway.

"Now *that's* what I call efficiency," she called to Terri. "Send her right in."

Kris strained to square the appearance of the composed young woman who sat by her at the desk with the prodigal child she'd met last night.

"Man, it still just doesn't seem real to me," Roan said, downcast. "It's like this nightmare that won't quit. You know what I mean, doctor?"

"It's Kris," she said. "Yes, I do know. It's natural, Roan, after a shock like you had."

The other met her eye, but the contact lasted for only a second.

"And as we say in my line," Kris went on, "sometimes even nightmares have a logic of their own."

Today Roan wore a demure short-sleeve gray silk blouse with black cotton slacks and closed-toed leather pumps. She'd taken her nose ring out and powdered over the piercing. Kris mused that with none of her tattoos showing and her hair brushed back, she wouldn't look out of place in a corporate boardroom or at a meeting of the trustees of a charitable foundation.

She also reflected that those were posts the heiress had likely had just come into.

"I know this is supposed to be like a 'smoke-free facility,'" Roan was saying. "But d'you mind if I...?"

Tentatively she held up a silver-plated Tiffany lighter. At a glance Kris also recognized the bright yellow cone she was clutching in her other hand. The packet of Ranvir Beedies took her back to the imported-tobacco counters she'd seen in the kiosks on Harvard Square.

"I mean, like whoa," Roan muttered, sounding lost. "Who'd've even thought there really *were*...?"

Kris found Hank's old leaded-glass ashtray in the lower left-hand drawer of his desk and set it out between them. Looking grateful, Roan rolled her smoke tight and lit up. Soon the air was pungent with Indian broadleaf and cloves.

"Vampires? Jesus, dude," she said, exhaling. "I mean, talk about some deeply twisted medieval shit from the Dark Ages. Who knew?"

"Oh, they're around," Kris said. "Just not like in folklore or the pop-cult icons. Even if their fashion sense might tend that way sometimes, none of the ones I've dealt with looked much like Bela Lugosi."

"The ones you've dealt with," Roan repeated. "Uh-huh."

As she looked over the diplomas on the wall, Kris refrained from pointing out to her that they were Hank's and not her own more recent ones.

"Kris, c'mon," Roan said. "I can tell you're a pro, for sure. But what's the story on these bloodsuckers? I mean, like, the real deal?"

"D'you have any academic psych background?" Kris asked. "Some college credits, say?"

"It was my major at Mount Holyoke," Roan said. "But I got kicked out from up there after the first year. Then over at Hampshire College, or was it Hollins—or no, wait, down at Rollins...?"

"Whatever," Kris said for her. "My point is, vampirism is a well-recognized psychopathological entity."

She'd got up to pace. In front of her, Roan sat up straighter in her chair. Still, she didn't quite look at Kris.

"You think it was a psycho that got to Daddy?" she said. "Like maybe a schizo or something that was all wacked out in a major way?"

"Could be..."

In motion, Kris decided that for openers it would be best to take a professorial tack with Roan.

"If you'd like to read some reports in the professional literature," she said, "Benezech has a really intriguing paper on vampirism and paranoid schizophrenia from back in '81 in the *Journal of Clinical Psychiatry*. Jaffe and DiCataldo did a nice wrap-up on psychopathy and vampire tendencies that's a little more up to date. That was in the *Bulletin of the American Academy of Law and Psychiatry*. From '94, I think.

"The bottom line's the same," she added. "As fetishes and compulsions go, Roan, the craving to drink blood is a really powerful one."

"You're talking about some kind of weird-ass sharp-edge S&M trip," Roan said just over breath. "As in, like, hardcore fetish pervs that go in for cutting and drinking blood and that kind of fun stuff. Right, Kris?"

Pacing up and down the middle of Hank's worn Kashmiri rug, Kris gave her a nod.

"There's a general rule in my line," she said. "The stronger the urge you're dealing with, the more room it opens up for kinks. And when it comes to the human sex drive, even the survival instinct can run second to it.

"Sometimes," she went on more softly, "it's not even a close second."

She came to a stop square in front of Roan, who started and looked up at her but then dropped her eyes again.

"Your father," Kris said. "He was badly injured in his youth, wasn't he? He broke both his legs, I take it."

"Sure, yeah," Roan said. "I think he was, like, fifteen or sixteen when he was in this plane crash."

Kris kept quiet and stood still to wait while the other gazed at the carpet.

"Their Gulfstream went down," Roan told her. "Or maybe it was a Learjet or a Cessna prop job. Anyway, whatever kind of airplane they had back then. That's when Daddy's folks got killed on him. All I know is he got banged up real bad, but in the end he came through it okay."

"I see," said Kris. "But I'll bet it took a really long time in the hospital for him to get back on his feet. Plus, I'm guessing, an even longer time in heavy-duty PT. Physical therapy, that is, for rehab and reconditioning."

She'd gone back to pacing, and when she spoke again she took care to make it sound as if she was just musing out loud.

"You know, Roan," she said, "it's hard to imagine what it's like for folks who get to be really, really successful in their own right. Not just rich but powerful, too. In effect, not having to answer to anybody.

"Sometimes," she went on, "they find that they want to get back to a time when they didn't have to bear up under all that power and responsibility. Sometimes even, they might want a taste of what it was like when somebody else held the power over them. When they were pretty much helpless, I mean, literally at the mercy of someone else."

Kris paused at the door with her back to Roan.

"Sometimes," she said one more time, "they want very badly to get back into a situation like that, even if it's just for a little while. You know?"

"Kris...?"

Roan's whisper sounded to her like the opening to a prayer.

"Kris," she said even more lowly. "Can you, like, keep a secret?"

Kris pulled open the door and looked out both ways. Then she shut it without a sound. Returning to the desk, she perched on the side facing Roan.

"Keeping secrets is what I do for a living," she said. "Remember, I swore an oath that way."

"Oh, yeah," said Roan. "Right."

She stubbed out her cigarette in the ashtray and leaned closer to Kris.

"There was this one time when I came back to the big house, here in town," she said. "It was, like, maybe a year ago? I'd just flown in from Jakarta, see, after I got into this kind of major-drama blowup with Hans-Pieter. He was this photo-shoot guy I'd been trekking with, down in Bali?"

"Your father was always willing to take you in," Kris prompted, quoting her own words from last night. "But he was never expecting you when you turned up."

"Like exactly," said Roan. "That time, I don't think he ever even saw me. Nobody else did either, for sure. 'Cause I just turned right back around and snuck out."

"Because, before you took off," Kris coaxed her, "you saw..."

Turning childlike again, Roan mugged and grimaced.

"Daddy was in, like, his bedroom, upstairs?" she said. "He was, you know, tied down? Spread-eagle, like, to the bed?"

"Tied?" Kris asked. "Or strapped? Restrained, I mean. Like in a hospital bed?"

With her eyes closed tight, Roan scowled and bobbed her head.

"That's it," she said. "And it was like—I mean, you could tell how everything looked staged. Like for bondage and whatever, you know what I'm saying? Dude, it was like Discipline City in there.

"He had on this hospital gown, too," she said after a beat. "And there was this needle thingy and tubing, kind of, in his arm?"

In a strain to keep her voice down, Kris nearly bit through the tip of her tongue.

"Who else was there, Roan?" she asked. "Who was with your father then?"

"I saw—she had on a mask...?"

"Leather?" Kris asked. "Hooded?"

Kris's heartbeat began to drum in her ears, the way it tended to whenever she found out just how right she'd been all along.

"C'mon, she demanded. "Somebody had on a mask. Was it latex? Chain mail? Spandex? Like Halloween? *What?*"

"She was dressed up like a nurse," Roan said. "Like, you know, what d'you call'em? A scrub nurse, like in surgery?"

Looking hapless and bewildered with Kris bearing down on her, Roan gestured at her own face and chest.

"Scrubs, that's what she was wearing," she said. "With a cap and mask on. And—and rubber gloves, too."

"And besides your father, only one other person was in there?" Kris asked. "It was just her?"

Roan nodded.

"Okay," Kris said. "You couldn't see her face then, but what did she look like otherwise? Size, build? How tall, say? C'mon, Roan. Try to recall. Height?"

"Well, uhm, you know," Roan mumbled. "She was taller than you are, I guess."

"Who isn't?" Kris said. "As tall as you, then? What, five nine?"

"Yeah, about," Roan said. "Chick was built, too. Dude, like out to here."

Roan cupped her hands and held them up.

"Maybe a 'plant job but primo tits anyway," she said. "You know?"

"Uh-huh."

On impulse Kris took both her hands and gave them a squeeze.

"Keep going, Roan," she urged. "There must be something else you picked up on then. Some little thing you can remember for me. Something. Anything? Tell me."

"Oh, well," Roan muttered. "He said her name."

"Her *name?*"

"Hot *damn*," cried Roan. "You're strong!"

At the other's gasp of pain, Kris let go of her hands and braced her shoulders with care.

"I beg your pardon," she said. "I'm sorry, Roan. I didn't mean to hurt you. But please, tell me her name."

Crinkling her nose as she rubbed her knuckles, Roan looked to Kris like a little girl whose elder had mortally embarrassed her.

"It was just something Daddy, like, moaned at her," she said. "He called her Nurse Nell."

"Nurse...Nell?"

"Dr. Kris!"

Terri's voice from the speakerphone made them both jump.

"I'm sorry, doctor," said Terri. "But Dr. Stephen Laszlo's on the line for you. From Washington. DC?"

"Remind him I don't work there anymore," Kris snapped. "All right, T.?"

"But he says it's personal," Terri persisted. "In fact, doctor, he said it was very personal."

"Then tell him I'm out, tell him I'm in conference," Kris said through her teeth. "Tell 'im I'm up on the roof with a deer rifle and a big box of ammo. Just take a message. Please, TF."

Roan stared at her as the interoffice line clicked.

"Stephen Laszlo?" she said. "Isn't he that big-time psycho-killer analyst guy? The one they call the 'shock doc,' the 'brink shrink'? Wasn't his picture on the cover of *Time* a while back. Or was it *Newsweek*?"

"Both," sighed Kris. "Plus *Psychology Today*."

It was plain to her that the spell was broken and that for now, at least, she wouldn't get anything else out of Roan that she could use.

"Laszlo hates publicity, too," she said. "If memory serves, 'vulgar, mindless curiosity of the benighted masses' was the phrase that sprang to his lips."

"And *you're* the one he wants to talk to," Roan said. "Hey, wow."

"Dr. Kris," Terri's voice came back. "I've got *another* call from Washington, doctor. DC? This time it's a Ms. Jezreel

Thornton for you. She says she's an attorney. With the US Department of Justice?"

"Whoa, man. Wow," Roan repeated. "I'd better give you, like, some room to work here."

She unfolded her legs and made for the door.

"Hang on, T.," Kris yelled. "And Roan, please, wait."

Scrambling from the desktop, Kris caught up with her at a trot.

"Please," she said. "Promise me you'll get right back in touch if you remember anything else about what we were just talking about, or anything even remotely like it.

"Or for that matter," she went on in the same breath, "if you want to talk to me about anything, anything at all—whatever, regardless. Just call me right up and we'll talk it out. Okay, Roan?"

"I promise, Kris," she said. "I—it's just..."

As Kris gingerly hung on to her fingers, she returned the pressure. She took a look all around the airy, sunny corner office that Hank's seniority merited. Then she shivered, hard.

"Dude," she blurted. "It's like I just can't get my mind around it.

"I mean, here you are," she said in Kris's face. "You're like this happy, friendly, perky little expert in all this dark-side-of-nowhere bizarre-ass monster mash shit like bloodsuckers for keeps and head games in bed that're way out on the edge and God only knows what other kind of life-threatening kinks and twists like that."

Eyes wide and nostrils flaring, she snorted and took a step back.

"I mean," she said at last, "how can you, like...cope?"

"Oh, well," said Kris. "You know how it is."

Seeing Roan to the door, she laughed lightly and gave her a smile she meant to be reassuring.

"After all," she said, "it is an age of specialization."

CHAPTER EIGHT

Warily Kris picked up the line Terri had put on hold and took her second call from Washington.

"Hey, Jez," she said on the phone. "It's me."

"Got your message, Kris," the voice of Jezreel Thornton chimed in her ear. "Glad to hear you uncle's doing okay."

A lawyer on the rise at Justice, she shared the lease with Kris on a Capitol Hill condo.

"Question is, Buffy old girl, how're *you* getting on?" she asked. "'Cause from what I see in the news, this must be some kind of high-class vampire you're stalking down there in your ancestral region."

"Don't believe everything you see on CNN, counselor."

"Hey now," Jez chortled. "C'mon, Kris."

Kris pictured her friend's skinny brown features under frizzy, untamed hair. Somehow when Jez laughed, her freckles seemed to spread out wider than her face. Even then, her eyes behind steel-rimmed glasses would stay as sharp and on point as a blue jay's.

"You know," she went on, "the *New York Times* ran a piece this morning that comes close to implying that the elemental forces of evil're running loose on the streets of the Big Peach."

"If that's what the *Times* thinks, then who am I to quibble?" said Kris. "Hey, I just work here."

"So it's true, just as I suspected."

In character all of a sudden, Jez turned sober and lawyerly.

"You really are on the case, aren't you, Kris?" she said. "It's official with you. Fact of the matter is, you landed right in the middle of it and that's just where you've wanted to be from the start. Right?"

"Right," Kris confessed. "And so it's probably just a matter of time before somebody recognizes my name from ten years ago and goes on to connect the dots from the Lyle McCandless flap to where I am now."

"Right, right," Jez said. "It's inevitable, I guess."

Kris caught more than a trace of Carolina Low Country drawl breaking through her businesslike mid-Atlantic accent. With Jez, that had always been a sign of unease. So was the giggle that followed.

"Hard to keep a background like that undercover," she said. "What with you being a woman with such a colorful past, and all."

The two of them were confidants of long standing. In Jez's phrase, they'd been fellow members of the Southern-girl Mafia up at Harvard. Then while Kris had stayed in Boston for residency after med school, Jez had taken off for DC right after law school to clerk at the US Supreme Court. Over the years, they'd kept in touch.

Jez remained one of the few people Kris knew she could talk to about what had happened to her mother and father and brother, and what she'd done afterwards, and still count on some understanding in return.

"Sorry I had to take off like that right in the middle of moving out," Kris said now. "As soon as I can, Jez, I'll come get the rest of my stuff. And I'll clean my room up one more time, I promise"

"As it stands, you can already eat off the floor in there," Jez clucked. "Next to my mama, you're the most advanced case of neat freak I've ever encountered."

Kris could hear her draw her breath in deep before she went on.

"Something else you need to know," Jez said. "Looks like a certain unrelentingly smitten colleague of yours is all torn up. It's even worse than before, I mean, now that it's plain to see how you just up and skipped town on 'im."

Kris strained to keep her back teeth from grinding.

"It's okay, Jez," she said. "I'll deal with Stephen myself."

"Uh-huh?"

Kris heard the Charleston inflection take over as her friend's giggles came back, even louder than before.

"Well now," Jez said, "you want to go and take you a guess as to what the good Dr. Laszlo just sent over to our place?"

"His severed ear?"

"You *wish*."

Jez's voice had just gone up by half an octave.

"This time," she squealed, "it was *three* dozen roses."

"No kiddin'?"

Kris shot a longing glance at all the notes she'd spread out across the blotter in front of her.

"Well, I promise I'll let you know as soon as I can when I'll be coming back up there," she said. "In the meantime, Jez, just—oh, hey, I don't know. Would you put 'em in water for me?"

"You got it, girlfriend."

Except for the glow of streetlamps and the flicker of passing headlights, the sky had gone matte black outside the office window. Kris didn't care. Still pouring over the reams of notes and records at the desk, she was busy with her plans.

She'd looked in on Hank in CCU a little earlier. Pleased with his progress, she'd slipped off campus for a bite to eat. Now a neat stack of takeout cartons from her favorite local Cantonese eatery lay in the trashcan in the corner. Steam still rose over the extra-large Styrofoam cup of Guangzhou Ginseng tea by her hand.

From the FM band of the radio at her back came a seductive, compelling voice in the alto register. Kris had tuned in the late-night call-in show while she worked. She'd been listening and taking notes with equal intensity. And now she'd just hit on the best way to hook up with the Buckhead Vampire.

"All *right*, folks, you've got Kerry Jean here on *Hot 'Lanta*

Nights," the woman's languid voice carried from the speaker. "On the line with me now is Tom from Marietta. Hi, Tom, what's on your mind?"

"Hey there, Kerry Jean," said Tom. "How you doin'?"

As she sipped her herb tea, Kris sat back and cocked her head to savor the caller's earnest tone and north-of-Metro-suburban vowels.

"If I may," Tom went on, "I'd like to talk about the Buckhead Vampire."

"Oooh, original topic, that one," the host responded. "So what's your take on our very own night stalker, Tom?"

"To tell you the truth, Kerry Jean," he said, "I believe it's some kind of a satanic deal, is what it is."

He sounded sorely put-upon to Kris.

"Now I'm not pointing no fingers here," Tom insisted. "But I think that some these rich folks up in Buckhead, they went and they made 'em a pact with the devil some while back in they career. And now it's come time to pay the piper, pure and simple."

"So it's the Prince of Darkness calling in his IOUs? Interesting theory, Tom," Kerry Jean said. "But why's ol' Beelzebub so hot for blood in particular? You'd think an immortal soul'd square the deal in itself, now wouldn't you?"

"Now as to *that* matter, Kerry Jean—"

Before she could take in the rest of Tom from Marietta's viewpoint, Kris's cell phone rang. She swung her chair around and grabbed it out of its charger on the credenza. Ever since this morning, she'd been expecting a follow-up call from Roan Fisher. But the voice in her ear now was a man's, familiar and urgent.

"We just collared us a bloodsucker, doc," said Matt Judson. "Got 'im in the box down here at City Jail. Yuri's doing the honors sweating him right now."

"How about the victim, Matt?"

"She's okay," he said. "Thank the Lord."

To Kris the detective didn't sound any less anxious.

"Along about sundown," he told her, "this character went

and jumped a thirteen-year-old girl at Five Points right outside Underground Atlanta. Then he tried to bite her on the neck."

"Draw any blood?"

"Uh-unh, girl kicked back and crotch-bombed him before he could move in close," he said. "Bless 'er heart."

As Matt paused, Kris recalled that he and his wife had three young daughters of their own.

"But we did take a box cutter and some syringes and needles off him," he went on. "Plus he's got a hinky background I think you're gone want to hear about firsthand, Kris."

Already on her feet, she slipped a fresh notepad into her purse and switched her medical-ID laminate from the front of her coat to the belt of her skirt. At the same time, she crossed the room to the corner window and took a look out. Then Kris broke into a big smile.

On sight, she recognized the four-pointed red star on the side of the patrol car headed up Clifton Road. She knew the university kept its own security force and the campus itself was in DeKalb County, well beyond the jurisdiction of Atlanta PD. As she watched, the Metro cruiser put its blue flashers on and cut around an EMS van to pull into the admitting bay below.

Kris didn't have to wonder why.

"We'd truly appreciate your special input right now, Kris," Matt said in a rush. "Yuri tells me he's got a real strong hunch we could squeeze a lot more out of this li'l ol' dirtbag down here if you'd just come on over now and sit in during questioning."

Scampering down the corridor for the stairwell door, Kris hit her stride with the phone pressed tight to her ear.

"I'll be right there, Uncle Matt," she said on the run. "My ride just got here."

CHAPTER NINE

The desk sergeant at City Detention Center downtown gave Kris a visitor's badge to go with her doctor's ID, and a young patrolman saw her upstairs to Interrogation.

Matt greeted her there. He led her to the door of a long, narrow room with dim lighting. From waist level up, a half-silvered mirror took the place of the front wall.

Inside were a dozen other police in plainclothes. They all seemed to Kris to be holding their breath as they stood watching through the glass. On the other side, two figures faced each across a solid-looking table whose top was intricately nicked and scarred over with cigarette burns.

As Kris began to listen in with Matt, the hard-eyed woman investigator she'd met at the briefing at headquarters stepped up beside them.

"Det. Kelly Sims," the senior detective reminded Kris. "She's got some background info on this citizen we just pulled in."

"Normally I work out of Zone 5 Precinct at CNN Center, doctor," she said. "On Sex Crimes."

Like Matt, Kelly spoke in an undertone and kept her eyes on the questioning in progress in front of them.

"I've come across this individual before," she went on. "He's Beverly Dale Battle, age thirty-four. We picked him up on suspicion of trafficking in child pornography at his place of business in Underground Atlanta. Didn't pan out, though. No charges."

"No, of course not," Kris muttered. "Kiddie porn?"

Shaking her head, she took a fix on the suspect. He was

bony and long-limbed in a black T-shirt and jeans. Framed by a black goatee and lank dark hair drawn back in a ponytail, his face was white and sweaty with a hatchet edge at the nose and chin.

"He'd want 'em bigger than that, natch," said Kris. "Does he have any assaults on his record before this?"

"No violent priors," Matt said. "But as to that 'place of business' of his that Det. Sims just mentioned...whoa now."

"It's a sort of goth boutique, doctor," said Kelly. "You know, the kind of thing you tend to see these days on the fringes of malls and such. He calls the shop Crimson Kisses.

"It's real popular with the kids in all the vinyl and eyeliner and black nail polish," she added. "You know the ones I'm talking about? Your Hot Topic rats, the ones that always look like they could use some sunshine."

"And its line is vampirana and related paraphernalia," Kris said. "Right, detective?"

Kelly raised her eyebrows.

"I'd say this guy deals in 'dark' videos and games and 'zines," Kris went on. "Plus black candles and white face paint and other such fashion accessories. As for ambience, there's got to be a strong batwing-and-fang motif. Right?"

The young detective nodded.

"Okay," sighed Kris. "Innocent enough, so far. But how long's this guy been in business at that location?"

"Ten years or better," Kelly told her. "Far as I know, he's been down there ever since they got Underground restored and reopened the arcade levels."

Kris said thanks and leaned closer to the one-way pane. She could just about feel all the others' expectations boring into the back of her head. But for now she said nothing while she listened to the PA speaker on the wall.

"I'm telling you, man," said the suspect, "I thought that chick was way older'n she turned out to be."

Wheedling, he sounded frankly aggrieved to Kris. He kept his thin shoulders braced tight and bunched up high as he sat forward. A manacle on a short length of chain held one hand to the top of the wooden table in front of him.

"C'mon, I swear," he pleaded. "Really and truly now, I thought she was somebody I knew."

"So naturally," said Yuri, "you attempted to bite her on neck."

He slouched across the table from him. Hulking in shirtsleeves, he casually rocked back and forth in his chair. Kris noted how he kept the thumb of one hand hooked in the big empty holster of the shoulder rig under his arm.

"With romantic approach such as this," he prompted the other, "one would imagine that you have met with great success with women in your time, yes?"

"Hey, c'mon now, officer. Why don't you cut me a li'l slack here," the suspect groaned. "And what kind of accent's that supposed to be, man? Where you come from anyway?"

"Transylvania."

Yuri's smile impressed Kris with its unmistakable, finely controlled menace.

"This is to make you more at home with us," he added deadpan. "Yes?"

"Aw...*man*"

"No," Kris said. "This guy's not the one we're looking for. No way."

Kelly nibbled her lower lip as she watched over Kris's shoulder.

"You sure, doctor?" she said. "Just like that? To me he looks, well, kind of hungry."

Too keen to explain anymore, Kris broke away from Matt and the others and darted outside to get to the room next door.

"My point exactly," she called back. "He's not hungry enough."

"No, unh-uh," the suspect blurted out. "She's not the one."

Big-eyed, Beverly Dale Battle stared at Kris as she shoved her way in and lightly took the chair next to Yuri's.

"I'm telling you, man, she really looked older," he protested. "You'd've thought she was nineteen, twenty minimum. I swear."

Yuri didn't even turn his head.

"Dr. Kristin Van Zant," he said. "Please allow me to introduce to you, doctor, Count Dra—"

"Oh, hey, I'm sorry, doc," the other man broke in. "I didn't see y' ID there. Folks call me Bev, hear? Just plain Bev'll do."

Bat, Kris mused, would probably cut too close to the bone.

"Call me Kris," she said aloud. "Everybody does."

She folded her arms in front of her and let her elbows rest on the table.

"So, Bev," she said. "I take it you thought that was an old girlfriend you went swooping down on at Five Points just now. You took her for a personal donor of yours, didn't you?"

"I swear to God, doc—"

"You don't have to," she cut him off. "I believe you, Bev, because I know your kind. The blood kind. I'm a psychiatrist, and I've been around that track more than a time or two before."

She locked eyes with him head-on and let him have her full-bore smile.

"What's more," she said, "I'm a really, really good listener. Understand?"

After a few seconds, Bev swallowed hard and blinked. Sweat beaded his cheeks and brow and stood out like thorns in his beard. Tucking his chin down, he dipped his head to Kris.

"I understand the need," she went on. "I've heard from the folks who know. And trust me, Bev, there are folks who need it a lot worse than you do. They told me what it's like when you have to have it hot and wet and red in your mouth.

"And right away, too," she added brightly. "So I can well imagine how it is for you when there's just none to be had. Not a throat in sight. Not a drop to drink. Poor, poor, thirsty you."

With no effort at all, she stared him down again.

"That's the way it is on the local blood scene right now. Isn't it, Bev?" she said. "What with all the usual donors too uptight to bleed. I bet they're spooked just plain bite-shy by the big, bad ol' Buckhead Vampire.

"Just lately," she coaxed him, "you must feel like you're stuck way out in the middle of the Sahara Desert. Right?"

"I had to—"

Bev coughed and bit it off. He glanced up at Kris and then looked down again. Slumping low in his chair, he sighed.

"Yeah, right," he said. "You know."

"So you took to street to go look for snack," said Yuri. "And just for luck, with you you took blade and hypodermic syringes and—"

"Man, that 'blade' was for opening boxes," Bev broke in. "Like, videocassette and DVD shrink wrap. Okay?"

With his free hand, Bev made an artisan's gesture in the air.

"And as for that needle kit, man," he said, "I'm diabetic. You can ask my doc. Honest."

"Yeah?" Kris said. "So where d'you inject your insulin, Bev?"

He pulled up his tee. Over his abdominal muscles, a row of tiny bruises stood out against the white of his skin. Kris let go a whistle.

"All *right*," she said. "Well, dear me, Det. Chernenko. I'd say we're awfully close to dealing with an innocent man here."

"Just so, Dr. Van Zant."

Yuri matched her rueful, dismissive tone note for note.

"For sure is merely case of mistaken identity that brings him to us," he said. "But assault is assault, doctor, yes? And on innocent female juvenile, no less."

"As you say, detective."

Keeping her eyes on the prisoner, Kris slowly shook her head at Yuri.

"And everybody's out for blood in this 'Buckhead Vampire'

matter," she began. "Oh. Sorry, Bev. I wasn't trying to make a pun.

"Still, it looks as if everybody from the magistrate you're about to face on arraignment right on down to the guys who've just been pulled in off the street in the felony-detention cell with you, well," she said in one breath, "I'd say they're all going to be in a righteous eye-for-an-eye-and-a-tooth-for-a-tooth frame of mind.

"No excuses," she added. "That would be the prevailing mood, I'd say."

Decorously she looked away from Bev.

"I surely wouldn't want to be an admitted blood drinker," she said just over her breath. "Not when those bad boys get a load of you."

"But it's all a mistake, man! I'm telling you—you can't—" Bev stammered. "I—I want..."

Just as Kris had hoped for, he'd taken on the aspect of a mouse in a corner.

"A lawyer perhaps?" said Yuri. "But no. Yes?"

When Bev shook his head, the investigator laughed as if they were sharing a joke.

"No, no, no, Bev," Yuri said. "Of course not, my friend. Is plain to see you are sick man. So it is doctor you need instead. How fortunate indeed for you that good and gifted Dr. Van Zant herself is available to you here."

Damn, he's good at this, Kris thought as she took the handoff from Yuri that was just as smooth if they were out dancing together.

"What Det. Chernenko means, Bev," she said out loud, "is that what I say about you's bound to swing some weight with the judge. Okay?"

Bev bobbed his head.

"Okay," she said. "For instance, I could report to the court that you have this well-recognized psychiatric syndrome that includes impulses to do certain things.

"And while these things are admittedly suspicious and even scary at first glance," she proceeded, "they are clearly beyond your control. So, the best way to dispose of your case would be to plug you discreetly into some effective program of counseling and therapy.

"And if you please, your honor," she said as if they were already in front of a judge, "jail time would be in nobody's best interests here, least of all the public's."

The gratitude kindling in Bev's eyes was almost pitiful for Kris to see.

"Doc, I—" he sputtered. "Man, I just don't know how to thank you for, for..."

As soon as his voice trailed off, Kris spoke up just as she had before.

"*Or*," she said, "I could opine that you're just as dangerous and crazy as a sack full of rabid bats. Oh, sorry again, Bev. I beg your pardon for the allusion. No offense."

She spread her hands gracefully before she went back to her expert's stance.

"And so for everybody's sake, your honor," she said, "I deem that this man would be best off locked up for the rest of his days in the bottom of the deepest, darkest mental hole the great State of Georgia can provide."

"Wha—?" Bev burst out, recoiling. "Say *what*, doc?"

Businesslike, Kris ticked off a third finger on the hand she'd held up in front of his face.

"*Or*," she said, "I could report that I find nothing at all the matter with this boy, your honor, except that he gets off on sinking his teeth into those innocent little girls he stalks and accosts on the street and then slurping their blood like a wild beast. And that brings us to..."

Dimpling in a soft frown, Kris sat back.

"Oh my, Bev," she said. "I guess that would put us right back to where we started out, with you thrown together with all those narrow-minded badasses down in the violent tank."

The whites showed all around the prisoner's eyes as they darted between Kris's face and Yuri's.

"What do y'all *want* from me? I don't get it," he moaned. "I mean, I've already told you everything I know."

"Not everything, Bev," said Yuri. "Because, you see, we have not yet asked you everything."

"We want to know who *you* know, Bev," Kris said. "Name us some names on the local serious, sharp-edge blood-play scene. Okay?"

Looking helpless and uncomprehending, he shrugged.

"Tell us about the doms and masters and psychodrama pros who draw blood for hire," she pressed him. "And then tell us who pays for it or at least who likes to keep 'em company. I mean the clients and subs and slaves and cut-fet bottoms and donors. In short, the ones who bleed for thrills. Okay now, Bev?

"It's not like you're among squares anymore," she added. "*Tell* us. Out with it. Now."

Blinking hard, Bev pulled a face that assured Kris he was about to tell a lie.

"Jesus, y'all, I don't even know what you're talking about," he said. "I—look, me, I just run this li'l ol' shop for kids that like to go out and play like they're vampires now and then. 'Creatures of the night' play-acting's all it is. Honest."

"Save it for the tourists, sweetheart."

Kris leaned closer and showed him her teeth but not in a smile.

"Your habit's too real and you've been around here way too long not to know what *we* want to know," she said. "So spill it."

Bit by bit, she raised her voice to him.

"Who's pleased to bleed, and who's in the biz to oblige 'em?" she asked. "I want names, places, dates, styles. And unless you want your lily-white vampire ass to land in the tank downstairs in about two seconds flat with all that rough trade and the hard-eyed boys and the plain ol' honky-stompers...

"By God," she said after a beat, "you'll *talk* to us, bloodsucker!"

"I—please—she—"

Drawing back as far as he could from Kris, Bev shifted in his chair to face the impassive Yuri.

"I swear, man," he gasped, "the only thing I ever heard about on the scene that's even a little bit close to what she's talking about is this high-class dom. Word was, she had a serious way with tapping a vein. Used to call herself Sister Night. Okay?"

"This lady would be professional dominatrix, yes?" said Yuri. "I see. And if one were so inclined, where would one go to obtain services of Sister Night?"

"Hey, man, I don't even know if she's still in the business. I—"

Bev's eyes met Kris's, and then he cringed back from her even harder.

"I know she used to rent some dungeon space from this place around here," he said to Yuri. "Maybe you know it, too, officer. It's this mainstream S&M club they call Lucifer's Realm. All right?"

Kris glanced over her shoulder. Yuri nodded and slipped her a wink. At that, she jumped up and hit the exit as fast as she'd come in.

"But—but, hey, doc," Bev called after her. "How 'bout our deal...?"

"You are very lucky man, Mr. Battle."

Just before Kris kicked the door shut with her heel. Yuri's voice carried solemnly to the hallway.

"Dr. Van Zant likes you," he told the prisoner. "I can tell."

❧

Matt got Yuri and Kris into a closed conference room to themselves, just down the hall from Interrogation

"Awright, y'all," he demanded, "now what in the name of sweet sufferin' baby Jesus was *that* all about?"

In a few words, Kris filled the ranking detective in on what she'd learned about the late Macdonald Fisher's dealings with one Nurse Nell.

"Lord o' mercy."

Matt blew out his cheeks and did a slow exhale.

"So that's the territory we getting into now," he said. "Some of our leading citizens're turning up twelve pints low 'cause of they unusual taste in leisure-time activities. That it?"

Kris gave him a smile and nodded eagerly.

"I know this place called Lucifer's Realm that Battle was speaking of, lieutenant," said Yuri. "Is not too far from here."

"That weirdo whips-and-chains establishment, or whatever it is?" Matt asked. "Go there often, son?"

"I myself am old-fashioned kind of guy, lieutenant," Yuri chuckled. "I know proprietors, though. They have been very helpful, in fact, in previous inquiries."

"Really?" Kris said. "Are they informants of yours, Yuri?"

"Merely sources," he told her. "Let us say, Kris, they are quite public-spirited people who know how to keep secrets, yes?"

"Okay. Let's go pump 'em, partner," Matt said. "Problem is, yours truly is due to show up at the mayor's office about now."

He looked pained as he checked his watch.

"At this ungodly hour, too," he added. "Looks like I'm gone be expected to help brief Hizzoner up to speed on this ongoing threat to municipal safety, and all."

"So I'll go with Yuri," Kris offered. "We'll question 'em together, just like we did with our li'l pal Bev back there."

Looking paternal, Matt held up a hand to her.

"Miss Kris," he said. "I hate to have to be the one to go and state the obvious like this. But as you've likely noticed, this is a *po*lice matter. And not to put too fine a point on it, doc, you're a civilian."

"But she is official consultant to Vampire Squad task force," Yuri said. "Thanks to you, lieutenant."

"Besides, Uncle Matt," Kris said before he could open his mouth again, "you just saw what a cross-examination team we made back there. Now didn't you?"

"To split us apart now," Yuri said, "would be, as we used to put it back in Moscow, to send Butch Cassidy to rob train without Sundance Kid, yes?"

"Y'all—hold on. Just..."

For several moments, Matt gave his scalp a rubdown with both hands. At last when he waved them off, his tone reminded

Kris of Hank's. She also judged that his parting words had as little as her uncle's to do with their personal safety.

"Awright," he called at their backs. "But you kids be careful now, hear?"

CHAPTER TEN

Filling a corner lot a few blocks off Piedmont Park, Lucifer's Realm turned out to be a nondescript two-story building with cinderblock walls and a flat tin roof.

Kris and Yuri left the car at the curb by a streetlight and crossed to the front door. Under a white canvas awning, the entrance was unmarked except for the number. The place could be a warehouse or some kind of wholesale outlet, Kris mused, if it weren't for the flag on the roof.

She didn't need a second glance to recognize the banner in the floodlights. A white horizontal band ran down its middle between alternating black and blue stripes. In the upper right-hand corner was a red heart.

"Leather Pride," she said aloud. "So I take it they don't mind showing their colors around here."

"Not at all," said Yuri. "Jim and Martha Nilsson, who run this establishment, they are quite serious in their beliefs."

He smiled as he stepped back to hold the brassbound door for her.

"They are almost like missionaries," he added. "Something suggests to me, Kris, you will find them quite interesting."

The anteroom inside had an impersonal, efficient air about it. The oak paneling and chrome-framed airline posters put Kris in mind of an upscale travel agency or an orthodontist's waiting room. A counter with an ebony top spanned the back wall, and facing them behind it was a young woman in a white tunic.

Blonde and fresh-faced, she looked up and greeted them with a bright professional smile.

"Good evening," said Yuri. "My name is Chernenko, and this is Dr. Van Zant."

Kris noted how he palmed his badge for the receptionist to see even though no one else was around.

"I am told," he said softly, "owners are expecting us."

"Yes, sir."

Without blinking, she pushed a button on the console in front of her. Silently a door slid back beside the counter. Like a dental assistant, she turned her palm out to them.

"This way, if you please," she said. "Basil will see you to them."

The young man who stood in the doorway bore an air of deep reserve and had on a lambskin jerkin, white ducks and a pair of Converse All Stars. He gave Kris and Yuri a shallow bow before he led the way down a long corridor with bare white tiles. At the end, he knocked on a metal door and held it open for them.

With another half bow, he disappeared.

"Welcome once more, young Det. Chernenko!"

The booming greeting came from a big man with gray hair and a square build. At the threshold, he shook hands with Yuri and put a hand out to Kris. Then he saw them into a roomy, cluttered office.

"Dr. Van Zant, I presume?" he said. "I'm Jim Nilsson. This is my wife Martha."

"Please, call me Kris," she said. "Everybody does."

She put the Nilssons in their late fifties or so. Jim wore a faded golf shirt with khakis and loafers, and Martha had on denim overalls and Birkenstock clogs. Large and hale, they shared a homespun manner and had matching accents. To Kris they sounded like the upper Midwest, either western Minnesota or maybe South Dakota.

"Once again," Yuri told them, "I find myself in need of your help."

With Kris, he turned down an offer of coffee or tea. Together they took chairs facing the Nilssons. Stacks of paper and computer gear filled the desks beside them.

"We are looking for someone who may have rented space here from you at some time," said Yuri. "We are told she calls herself Sister Night."

"Uh-oh."

Silver highlights showed up in Martha's cropped auburn hair as she shook her head and eyed her husband over bifocals.

"Didn't I tell you, Jim?" she said. "I knew that one was bound to be trouble."

"I guess we both could see that one coming, Mama."

Jim set his chin and gave his wife a brawny frown before he turned to Yuri.

"What'd she do now?" he asked. "She hurt somebody?"

"Excuse me," Kris spoke up. "But given the nature of her work, why would you even have to ask that?"

"Why—? Oh, I get what you mean, Kris," Jim said. "I meant a real, significant injury of some kind. Which I assure you, doctor, is *not* what we're about here."

"In fact," said Martha, "it's precisely the opposite."

She looked as strict as a schoolmarm, but then she paused and let Kris have a wry smile.

"Begging your pardon, dear," she said. "But you can just imagine all the misconceptions we run into that way."

"Sure. I get that in my line, too," Kris said. "But naturally you'd expect the masochists who patronize someone like Sister Night to—well, to expect to get hurt."

With effort she looked away from the bank of closed-circuit TV monitors she'd spied in the corner alcove.

"They'd want their money back if they didn't suffer," she prompted her hosts. "Right?"

"S&M play, so called," said Martha, "is not primarily concerned with pain."

Waxing severe, she seemed to catch herself again.

"Beg pardon, Kris," she said. "But we prefer the term 'erotic power exchange.' We feel that conveys the nature of this form of human interaction much more accurately."

"Safe, sane, and consensual."

Jim smacked his fist into his palm as he pronounced each word.

"That's our motto around here," he said. "And by golly, it always will be."

"Soapbox, Papa," Martha clucked at him. "Now, now."

Meanwhile, Kris took in the images on the monitors.

The men and women onscreen were mostly young and mostly white, and most of them were in couples. Behind them, the sets ran to stone walls with iron bars and wooden pillories. Hooks and chains hung from pulleys suspended on staples in the ceiling.

Accessorized with leather belts and collars and vests, the dress of the participants ranged from none to boots and jockstraps to high heels and garter belts. Flogging and pinching and the probing of body cavities seemed to Kris to be the order of the day. Dripping candle wax and an enema here and there lent some variety to the proceedings.

It all looked to her like the last days of Sodom and Gomorrah, as enacted by midlevel account execs with way too much time on their hands.

"Sister Night wouldn't abide by your rules," she said aloud. "Would she?"

Jim flushed and shook his head at her.

"Sister Night," he muttered. "Why, she and the kind of folks she tended to attract are nothing but a threat to our whole way of life."

Martha looked judicious.

"Sister Night, as she called herself," she said. "Well, let's just say she chose to transgress boundaries in a way we cannot endorse in any way, shape, or form."

"If one may ask," said Yuri, "what was nature of this transgression?"

"Well, f'r instance, she damn near smothered this one fellow to death!" Jim burst out. "Sorry. But it was just totally uncalled for, that episode."

Automatically Kris called to mind the entry under 302.83

Sexual Masochism in the *Diagnostic and Statistical Manual of Mental Disorders, Fourth Edition.*

"You mean as in erotic asphyxiation?" she asked aloud. "Asphyxiophilia? Or 'hypoxyphilia,' if you're a taxonomy nerd like me and prefer the term from good ol' *DSM-IV*."

She caught Yuri cocking an eyebrow at her.

"That is," she said, "the kick some folks seem to get from having the oxygen supply to their brains temporarily shut off. Like that?"

"I mean no disrespect to you, Kris, as a mental health professional," Martha said. "But some preferences and practices are just plain sick and dangerous. And that's all there is to it."

She kept her voice down, but her steely classroom tone had come back.

"And such as that from the likes of 'Sister Night' or anybody else," she added, "will *not* be tolerated on these premises."

"Hear, hear, Mama," said Jim. "And now you mention it, that's the problem with kids today. There's no willingness to set limits and just back off when it's called for."

He waved his arms sturdily.

"Just you try to warn 'em about the risky tricks and fetishes you're liable to run into on the scene," he went on. "Or so much as breathe a word to 'em about traditional taboos or even just plain common sense. No, sir. No, ma'am.

"Why, they'll laugh in your face!" he declared. "'Cause they've already seen it done in a gosh-darn Gap ad or a video on MTV, or something of that nature."

"Now, now, dear," said Martha. "Soapbox."

"Of these dangerous attractions and diversions Sister Night had to offer," Kris asked, "did any of 'em involve bloodletting of any kind?"

Jim shrugged negligently.

"There may've been some piercing and pinning going on," he said. "But it goes without saying, we have strict house rules about sterilization and safety precautions when it comes to any kind of sharp-edge situation."

Nodding, Kris searched the Nilssons' faces but found nothing useful.

"Thank you very much for sharing these impressions of Sister Night with us," Yuri said at her side. "Now, please, how can we find her?"

"Beats me son," Jim said. "Good riddance, I say."

"Wait a minute, Papa."

Martha adjusted her glasses. With a grunt, she rolled her chair over to one of the computer terminals. Then she started tapping keys.

"I believe one of her old associates still rents from us here from time to time," she said. "Let's see. Oh, yes. Here we are. Dimanche Noir."

"Right, yeah," said Jim. "You mean that feisty li'l mulatto dom with the long legs and all the attitude."

He began to chuckle. Then he bit it off as his wife glanced up and gave him a sharp look. At the same time, the printer by her desk clicked on and whirred.

"Sister was pretty much a loner," Jim said. "Far as we could tell, anyway."

He coughed into his fist and ducked his head as his wife held out a sheet of billing info to Yuri.

"But those two gals were close," he added. "Mighty close. No question about it."

"I am very grateful," Yuri said. "Once more you have been so helpful."

Kris said thanks, too, and stuck by Yuri on the way out.

Basil met them again at the door. Without a sound, he showed them down another hall to a side exit. As they passed an arcade, Kris saw Yuri shake his head at the display behind the glass.

Against black velvet, mannequins in masks and hoods stood bound in leather harnesses and chains in a welter of poses.

"One does not wish to be prude or spoilsport," Yuri said. "But to me this seems to defeat purpose altogether of man and woman being with each other, yes?"

"No doubt," Kris said. "In practice, Yuri, fetishes like this tend to preclude having sex in any way you'd recognize."

"That as well, yes."

As he held the outer door for her, Yuri struck Kris as wistful.

"But I confess to you," he said, "what I had in mind in fact was making love."

❧

The address they got from the Nilssons was in a weathered brownstone in Midtown. It was just off Peachtree, not far from the Fox Theatre. At the front desk in the lobby, Yuri flashed his badge to the young security man.

"Det. Chernenko," he said. "And Dr. Van Zant."

As the guard reached to key the intercom, Yuri bent toward the mike and raised his voice.

"To see Ms. Noir," he said. "Atlanta Homicide."

From the speaker came a gruff basso rumble. The guard waved them on and made a note in the book in front of him. Kris caught the wink Yuri slipped her as they got on the elevator and took it to a loft at the top.

The doors rattled back, but a young man blocked their way. He was pale with a shaved scalp and thick muscles and wore a black mesh tank over sweatpants. Sleeves of tattoos covered both arms, and to Kris most of them looked like razor-and-ink work.

"Yeah?" he said. "Wha's problem, buddy?"

Yuri didn't make any threat that Kris could see, but still the other man backed down and stepped to the side.

"Is time for boss lady to come talk to authorities face to face," Yuri said. "About Buckhead Vampire killings."

The buffed-up young con scowled at him. Then he wheeled and swaggered across the bare room. The hitch in his stride told Kris how spooked he was.

Seconds later, a door banged back in the brick wall in front of them.

Before it slammed shut, a willowy figure about six feet

tall strode out. Her heels snapped time all the way across the hardwood floor. The young woman's hair was shiny black and hung down well past her waist. Flashing amber, her eyes turned up at the corners in a lean face with beige skin tones.

She was pulling on a long terry robe, and under it Kris glimpsed a leather bodice with rivet studs and thigh-high black vinyl boots.

"What is your *prob*lem, for Christ's sake?" the newcomer spat out. "I'm Dimanche Noir."

Sure you are, Kris thought as she took in her flat Metro-core drawl, and I'm the Grand Duchess of Luxembourg.

"I'm Dr. Van Zant," she said aloud. "This is Det. Chernenko."

Smiling wide, she'd put on her party manners.

"And if you're smart, Didi," she went on, "the next time you open your mouth it's going to be to tell us everything you know about Sister Night."

Kris didn't wait for an answer. Before the other woman could stop her, she crossed the room at her back. Then she yanked opened the door she'd come out of.

Banks of candles lit the studio inside, and a rigging of chains and straps hung from the roof beams. Alone in the middle of the floor stood a man lashed to a wooden whipping post like a St. Andrew's cross. Paunchy and chalk-skinned, he was naked except for a black leather hood.

Kris whistled silently as his erection, which she found all the more impressive given the dumbbell dangling at the end of a leash knotted around the base of his penis.

"Fair marks for ambience," she sighed. "But no points at all for originality, I'm afraid."

Shaking her head and rolling her eyes, Kris shut the door without a sound.

"Compared to Sister's act," she added, "I swear, this little gig of yours comes off like plain vanilla."

"You don't know what you're—"

Dimanche caught her breath and drew herself up, looking balefully from Kris to Yuri and back.

"Whoever you two think you are," she snarled, "you can't just come barging in here and threaten me."

"We wouldn't waste time that way," said Yuri. "Instead, Dr. Van Zant and I are trying our best to keep lid on tight until we get answers...mistress."

Kris savored the chilling, scornful twist Yuri put on his last word.

"What Det. Chernenko is trying to get through your head, Didi," she said, "is that if we weren't treading so lightly in this investigation, you'd be hitting the news like a twenty-car pileup."

She let a beat go by.

"Right here," she added. "Right now. In full color."

"For all of clientele to see, yes?"

Looming up with his arms folded, Yuri closed ranks with Kris.

"And what would paying customers think," he went on, "to see mistress in middle of biggest manhunt to hit town in twenty years?"

"Oh, me," said Kris. "I guess Didi here 'd be out on the street in a hurry, huh? I can see her now. Pounding the sidewalk, leaning in cars, hustling blowjobs to Shriners on convention..."

Kris judged Yuri's chuckle could chill the blood of a KGB veteran.

"Perhaps even going so far as to wait tables in all-night diner," he said. "Yes, mistress?"

"You're bluffing," said Dimanche. "You can't—you don't know...?"

"We know Sister Night's been really, really popular with thrill-seeking bleeders and smother freaks," Kris said. "So one would assume she's been dealing in near-snuff trips."

Dead on, Kris smiled in her face.

"Hence the cute name," she added. "Just a quick glimpse into the abyss, and then she'll snatch you right back to the land of the living."

Without warning, she broke into a carny barker's come-on.

"*Yes*, sir, *yes*, sir. Step right up, folks!" she yelled. "*Right* this way. Check out the raggedy edge of your own mortality and live to think it over!

"Real E-ticket ride, right, Didi?" she said more softly. "Too rich for your blood, sure. But that's just what ol' Sister's retailing. Right?"

"She, she..."

Dimanche sank her teeth in her lip, and then she threw her head back with a show of sinewy brown throat in a spiked collar.

"Okay," she said with a frown. "You know."

"But we do not yet know her real name, yes?"

Now Yuri sounded to Kris like an insurance agent who'd just sold a policy and was good and ready to see some ink on the contract.

"Or where to find her," he went on. "So you will tell us."

"She's Lu Ellen Reese," Dimanche said fast. "She's straight out of hard-cracker white trash up North Georgia way. Girl comes from way back in the country around Lake Lanier."

She shut her eyes tight then but kept on talking.

"I guess she finally went back there," she said. "On her own terms, too, like she always used to talk about. See, I haven't seen her or even talked to her in close to a year now."

"She retired from the scene?" Kris asked. "Is that what you're telling us?"

A head shorter than Dimanche, she moved up and crowded in tight to cow her down.

"Aw, c'mon, Didi," she said in her face. "We both know a li'l ol' country girl with a goldmine of a talent like that's not going to pack up and leave ATL after the city's been so good to 'er. She's not back chopping cotton in the noonday sun, now is she?"

"You *don't* know, you little—!"

Slowly Dimanche opened her eyes, and then she swallowed hard under Kris's gaze.

"Lu'd never give it up," she said. "No more'n she'd ever give anything away. But—it wasn't just a talent for near-snuffing folks she had. See, she could..."

"Oh."

The light grew in Kris's eyes just as it died in the other woman's.

"Now I get it," she said. "Silly me. Sister's a talent spotter, too!

"Of course, that makes sense!" she crowed. "She not only knows how to tease up a death trip *and* how to find somebody who wants one made to order..."

She paused and gave Yuri a nod.

"But she also knows how to scope out some other pro with the same gifts," she concluded. "Someone who can deliver the goods in her place."

Cocking her head toward the door behind them, Kris smiled at the dominatrix.

"But that's not how she got hooked up with you. Was it, Didi?" she said. "Oh, no. You're just a hardworking chick who knows how to hurt folks so they'll pay for it up front, and then you keep 'em coming back for more. Right?"

"I swear to God, I never wanted any part of that risky, twisted-ass near-death shit," Dimanche pleaded. "Not even when she offered me a piece of her action. Not even when she started to get her business all lined up so as to—so..."

"So she didn't have to get her hands dirty anymore," Kris finished for her "And that's how she's living it up right now back in the country, isn't it? She's got her whole operation here in town set up on autopilot.

"And more than likely," she added, "it's running so smooth for her, all she's got to do is kick back and take her cut while supply keeps on meeting demand.

"All *right,* Sister. Whoa," Kris laughed. "Nice job. Too cool."

"I'm telling you," Dimanche blurted, "you don't know the half of—"

As she shook her head hard, hair extensions rustled all down her back.

"That girl always had a mind for making things work just the way she wanted 'em to," she began again. "She'd have circles running inside of circles. She'd always keep the right hand from knowing what the left hand was doing.

"I'm telling you," she muttered, "if she'd ever got the chance to, Lu could've run the whole fuckin' CIA on her own."

"And you are her friend," said Yuri. "Everybody needs friend, yes?"

His smile spread like a little boy's with a big fish on the line.

"Friend to talk to, to trust," he went on. "Friend to tell all one's secrets to, yes?"

"After all," said Kris, "you're a smart girl yourself. So you can tell we're not the kind of folks you want to go away empty-handed. Right?"

"Smart girl like you," said Yuri at her side. "You see of course that Dr. Van Zant and myself are people you want to go away happy, yes?"

Dimanche balled her fists up tight and raised them over her head. Just barely, she choked off a scream. Spinning around on one heel, she marched for the door in back. Then she banged it shut so hard behind her it made the ceiling tiles thrum.

"I don't know the vibe you're getting off her, Yuri," Kris whispered. "But to me it's starting to feel like Christmas in July."

"Here!"

Dimanche came back with a shout. She thrust out a small, thick notebook to them. Bound in red leather, it had a tiny black padlock on the side.

"Sister—Lu gave it to me," she said. "That's the last time I saw her. She said if anything ever happened to her to give it to the cops. Or the papers, or TV, whatever.

"Me, I never even looked in it," she added. "And I damn sure don't want to now. Here!"

Yuri bowed at the waist as he took it from her.

"Department is very grateful for your cooperation in this matter, Ms. Noir," he said. "You would like receipt for this property, perhaps?"

She flashed sharp white teeth at them.

Then she stripped off her robe and whirled away to stalk back the way she'd come. After the door slammed at her back, Kris heard a whip crack inside. Behind it rose a shriek of pain.

"For once," Kris said on their way out, "I'll bet ol' Dimanche is about to give her client way more than his money's worth in there."

CHAPTER ELEVEN

Back at police headquarters, Matt slumped at his desk and pulled a long face as Yuri finished briefing him on what he'd turned up with Kris.

"Lordy, lordy," he groaned. "Dang, y'all. When did folks start to get all weirded out and twisted around like that anyway?"

"I don't know, lieutenant," said Yuri said. "Perhaps shortly after leaving Garden of Eden, yes?"

"Shoot, I reckon," Matt sighed. "Okay, partner. What else have you got there?"

"Current residence of Lu Ellen Reese," Yuri told him. "Aka Sister Night."

He gave Kris another wink behind his hand as he hung up the phone. Then he tore a pink memo slip off the pad he'd been jotting on. Looking up, he slid it across the blotter to Matt.

"According to DMV and state property title databases," he said, "this has been address of record for Ms. Reese since June of last year. Is near little town north of here, I am told, called Cumming.

"I swear," he said deadpan, "this I am not making up."

"I know, man," said Matt. "That's out in Forsyth County, not far from the lake."

He tipped his chair back against the wall and nodded familiarly.

"I know the sheriff up there pretty well," he added. "DA, too, plus a couple of judges. I could—say, Kris? You okay there?"

"I'm not sure," she said. "That is, no..."

Slowly she raised her head from Sister Night's private

notebook. She'd just scanned the last page. Now she gulped for air as her heart began to run away with her.

"'Scuse me, Uncle Matt," she choked out. "But what you just said—does that mean you could get us a search warrant for her place? I mean, like, right *now*?"

All at once both men were on their feet, peering over her shoulder from either side.

"See?" she said. "As best I can make out, most of this reads like some kind of master business plan. Or a marketing guide, if you will."

Kris took some deep breaths. Marking her place with a finger, she flipped back through the pages. She'd been in a strain to make sense out of the tight, cryptic scrawl ever since Yuri picked the lock for her.

"It seems to match up a bunch of doms she pimps for with their clients," Kris began. "In the case in point, that means some customers of a dominatrix who appears to specialize in a bleeding fetish.

"I mean a pro on the scene," she went on. "This would be somebody who acts as an enabler for these folks' addiction to hemorrhaging for kicks. You with me so far?"

Matt and Yuri gave her some encouraging pats on the back as Kris cleared her throat and fought to catch her breath again.

"Thanks," she said. "Too bad for us, though, Sister's handwriting is nearly as bad as mine is. Also, she seems to have used some kind of idiosyncratic shorthand with a lot of tricky abbreviations. See what I mean?"

"Uh-huh," said Matt. "Kind of like you do, too, Kris."

"Sure," she said. "But what I'm trying to get at here is..."

"Sister Night gave this to her most trusted friend for safekeeping," Yuri prompted her. "In case something happened to her, she said."

"Yeah..."

Coughing, Kris tasted dust and copper at the back of her throat. She shook her head over the entry that had jumped out at her. At length she got her voice back.

"That kind of arrangement would make sense, too," she

said. "As a kind of backup insurance policy or a fail-safe system, I mean.

"See," she went on, "Sister'd only want this grand scheme of hers to come to light if she'd been put out of commission *and* she knew that something had happened that'd serve to make all this comprehensible to somebody who could follow her tracks. You see where I'm going, here...?"

As her voice faded again, Matt leaned over and ran a finger across the rough block letters of the page's heading.

"Looks like 'BAR/NN,'" he said, squinting. "Guess that last could be your 'Nurse Nell,' Kris. But what about the first part?"

"I don't know," she admitted. "Not yet anyway."

She held the book up so they could see what she was pointing to. The ink was smeared, and the short list was barely legible as it ran down the rest of the page. As her heartbeat kicked up one more time and set in to hammer at her eardrums, Kris had to bear down hard to keep her voice steady.

"Take a look at this sequence down below," she said through her teeth. "See? I'm pretty sure it says 'macd.f.' and 'w.h.' and 'h.c.' and...?"

"Macdonald Fisher, Wade Hazlett and Halley Cantrell," said Matt. "Son of a bitch."

For some reason, Kris felt easier in her mind as he came down hard on each syllable of the victims' names.

"Also 'mdub.' and 'j.t,'" Yuri said. "Or perhaps it is 'j.z.'"

Kris heard him suck his breath in hard as he straightened up at her back.

"Point is, lieutenant, there are five sets of initials here," he went on. "So Vampire is only halfway down list so far, yes?"

"Damn straight," said Kris. "That means we've got to get to Sister Night before this goes any farther."

She sprang up from the chair and whipped around to face them.

"We've got to find out from her just who these people were hiring to bleed 'em before they turned up drained to death," she said fast. "*And* how they all got tangled up with my—with this serial bloodsucker, that is."

She was up on her toes waving her arms before she caught herself and pulled back a bit.

"We need to find out right away," she insisted. "Okay, Uncle Matt. *Right* now, okay? Okay. Let's get going right *now*."

"Just a minute," said Matt. "Just—hold on now, Kris."

He held up a hand to her with the palm turned out, but she couldn't read anything in his face.

"Way it is, Kris," he said, "things move a little slower up there than we're used to in our jurisdiction. See?"

She began to protest but decided to hold it for now and nodded.

"Okay," said Matt. "Now I'll go ahead and make some phone calls to those contacts of mine I just mentioned. But I expect we best let it go till morning. Meantime, you better let me have that."

Feeling blinkered and hemmed in on all sides, Kris handed the notebook over to him.

"But, c'mon, Matt," she said. "What if—?"

"In the morning, Miss Kris," he cut her off. "And not before. Hear?"

Impassive, he turned to Yuri.

"You, too, partner," he said. "I'm gone have to make that an order."

"I understand, lieutenant."

From Yuri's tone Kris could tell that he did, too, even if he wasn't free just now to share what he knew with her.

"So we will all hit trail together then," Yuri said with no inflection at all. "In morning bright and early, yes?"

The sun was up and well on the rise by the time the three of them set out in an unmarked car. Headed north, they took US Highway 19 into the Blue Ridge foothills. Soon they pushed into the piney woods and hollows of Forsyth County.

"Kris," said Matt. "I know I prob'ly don't have to ask you this. But still...?"

He spoke low from the back seat. As she turned to face him, he looked up at her over the tops of his reading glasses. In his hand was the supplemental report she'd just printed out in Hank's office at the hospital.

"By any chance," he went on, "have you let anybody else get a look at this set of victims' profiles you went and put together without being asked to?"

"Unh-uh," she said. "You don't have to ask me that, Matt."

As he kept his eyes fixed on her, she reached down and dug in her purse.

"I discussed it with Hank, of course," she told him. "But otherwise, it's strictly confidential. I didn't even save it to the hard drive. Here's the floppy right here. See?"

Matt held out his hand, and she gave him the diskette.

"Is much like method I heard Dr. Laszlo lecture about, lieutenant," Yuri said from behind the wheel. "And in my humble opinion, Kris has perfected it. To profile killer, one must study his victims as well."

"Goes double in this case," said Kris. "At least."

"Dang."

Matt's grunt sounded to her as if it came straight from the gut. She watched as he put the papers back in his briefcase and locked it. Leaning forward, he pointed to the off-ramp coming up.

"Take you a right down here, partner," he told Yuri. "Then head back left up the county road for a couple miles. That's where Sheriff Varner said he'd be waiting with his boys to link up with us."

The roadbed took a steep incline and went to gravel once they turned off the two-lane blacktop. By the sides of the winding drive, the woods ran to old-growth hardwood as well as pines. A blue-green haze blurred the horizon in front of them, and brown crags broke up the tree line in the distance.

Yuri rounded a long curve at the top of the rise, and then he hit the brake.

Dead ahead, Kris saw two patrol cars with county shields and seven-pointed stars on their doors. They'd pulled up in tandem to a chain-link gate between two tall redbrick posts. Waiting beside them were three deputies with sweat rings on their khaki shirts.

"Jimbo!"

Climbing out, Matt hailed a rawboned young man with a pink face and a black crew cut. He had on navy pants and a white uniform shirt. Kris counted five stars and three stripes on each epaulet.

"Man," called Matt, "it does my ol' heart good to see the high sher'ff out in the field mustering the troops like this. And on a Sa'day morning, too."

As Kris watched them, the sheriff slapped Matt's shoulder as if they were frat boys and pumped his hand with both of his.

"Well, Matthew," he said. "It'd do me a world of good if I could offer y'a cold one and a fishin' pole, 'stead of a li'l ol' piece of paper from Judge Osgood."

Gingerly he held up a document that looked official to Kris.

"Got the search warrant all signed and sealed," he added. "Looks like we gone be needin' 'er, too."

"*Why?*" Kris asked. "Won't Lu Ellen Reese cooperate with you? Why not? What's the problem? What'd she say to you anyway?"

Intent and impatient, she went up on her toes between the two men.

"This is Dr. Van Zant, sheriff," said Matt. "She's a consultant to our task force. You know, the one I was telling you about."

Looking startled, the baby-faced lawman took a few moments to recover before he lowered his eyes and put out a hand to Kris.

"Call me Kris," she said. "Everybody does. Begging your pardon, sheriff, but just what did you hear from Sister—from Ms. Reese, that is."

"Nothing," he told her. "Not a word, doc."

He darted a look uphill over his shoulder.

"And I'm afraid, ma'am," he added, "that's the problem."

She turned to look, and then she stared.

The house on the summit might have been a fairy fort. Rising from a bare slate plateau where the mountain laurel and rhododendron gave out, it looked to Kris as if it had started out as a massive gingerbread Victorian. Now it ran riot in white shingles, pink dormers and a host of turrets and gables lined in blue and black.

A crow cawed from deep in the bush, and Kris felt a chill go down her spine in spite of the hot sun.

"She went back to where she came from," she said just over her breath, thinking of Dimanche Noir's words. "'On her own terms.'"

"Miz Lu paid cash for this ol' place when she moved in," the sheriff said. "That's been just about a year ago now."

He made a sign for his deputies to open the gate.

"That caused some talk, like you'd expect," he went on. "But in these parts, if you mind y'own business and pay your way folks'll leave you be."

"It looks old," Kris said. "Who built the place?"

"Some city folks. Used to be a huntin' lodge," the sheriff told her. "Rumor has it, doc, they was Coca-Cola money involved."

"No doubt," she said. "And just how long's it been since anybody around here's seen Lu Ellen Reese out and about, sheriff, outside her hideaway?"

"Well, that's hard to say for sure, doc."

Trudging up the gravel to one of the squad cars, he shrugged.

"Way she set it up when she moved in, all Lu's utility bills and such get paid automatically out of her bank account in town," he said. "And I got to tell you now, she keeps a tidy sum on deposit at the First National."

"Please, sheriff," Yuri said by Kris. "Can you tell us how long since Ms. Reese has been seen in public?"

As the sheriff paused and glanced around with one arm resting on the top of the squad, Kris thought he looked sheepish.

"Well, I tell you the truth, detective," he said. "Fact is, most folks in these parts, they always tended to give this place a wide berth. That's because, well..."

"They think it's haunted," said Kris. "Don't they?"

The sheriff started again and looked down at her.

"Say, doc," he asked, "you ever been up here before?"

"Not since I was a Girl Scout on weekend hikes," she sighed. "But if I were a kid from around here, *I'd* damn sure walk wide of it."

❧

Nothing happened when they knocked on the door under the lodge's broad front roof. No one came to the side or back way either. Every entrance was locked.

As they all stood waiting on the oak-plank porch, Yuri pulled a set of lock picks out of his jacket pocket.

"Please allow me," he said. "This should just take minute, here...ah."

The door swung in under his hand, and the hinges let out a creak like a rifle shot. Kris had been expecting it, but still she jumped back and bit down hard. The foyer inside was sunny and empty, and its walls were bare.

The next room was a wreck. Broken glass, upended drawers and overturned chairs and tables choked the floor. Scraps of paper and pasteboard lay strewn in all directions. Sounding reverent, the sheriff whistled.

"Damn," he said. "Looks like somebody broke in and—"

He bit if off as he seemed to Kris to think it over.

"I mean to say, somebody sure went and tore this place up good once they got in here," he went on. "One way or th'other."

"Heard that, Jimbo."

Matt patted his arm. Then he met Kris's eye and cocked his head to the side. She saw his nostrils flare as he returned to the sheriff.

"Say, by any chance," he asked, "would there be a basement or a root cellar or something of that nature?"

"I b'lieve there's a door right under the steps," the sheriff said, pointing. "Ought to be right over here. Yep, there she is."

He doubled back the way they'd come and stopped by the staircase off the front hall.

"Uh-huh, that's it," he said. "Goes down to the cellar."

Kris dug a handkerchief out of her pocket and pressed it over her mouth and nose, and then she trotted to catch up with Yuri and Matt at the head of the party.

So far, the scent that came up through the floorboards was faint. Sickly sweet, it was waxy and gassy at the same time. Kris knew that nothing else smelled quite like that. It was a cross between old roses and beef gone high.

Reaching for the doorknob, Yuri turned politely to the sheriff and his deputies.

"May I?" he said. "Thank you."

They all hung back at his heels, and he pulled on a pair of latex gloves before he went ahead.

He tried the switch on the landing, but it looked as if the bulb downstairs had blown. Craning at his shoulder, Kris took out her penlight and clicked it on. Yuri said thanks as she handed it to him.

"Danny, yo!" the sheriff called back. "Gone need us a flashlight up here."

Going just ahead of Matt, Kris flanked Yuri down the stairs. At the bottom, she broke away from them. She'd got halfway across the cement floor when the high beam came on at her back. But the big light didn't help much in the cavernous space.

All Kris could make out along the walls were shelves full of pickling jars and potting shards. In the far corner stood something like a long box on its side. As she got closer, she saw it was a brassbound steamer trunk with thick carpet on the panels.

At her side now, Yuri leveled a finger ahead of them.

"Uh-huh," Matt grunted. "I'd say that's it."

Yuri held up the penlight and snapped open the latches on the trunk. On tiptoe at his shoulder, Kris held her breath and pressed her handkerchief tighter to her face. With one hand, Yuri eased the lid open.

Bending forward to see, the senior detective motioned for the sheriff to come join them.

"Uh-*huh* now," Matt said. "Say, Jimbo, any these clothes here look familiar to you?"

The sheriff edged up to take a look, and then he let out a gasp and drew back fast.

"Uh—yeah, yeah," he said after a little while. "That cross there, yeah. I'd say I seen that on Lu Ellen a time or two... yeah."

By the glow of the penlight, Kris took in the dead woman's clothing. She'd dressed for the cold in jeans, trail shoes and a cableknit sweater. The crucifix around her neck was black enamel with a gold inlay. It hung just clear of the three clean entrance wounds in her chest.

One of the deputies pushed up by Kris to see, and then he drew back and doubled all the way over as he started to retch.

Ignoring him, Kris considered the other bullet hole. It stood out black between what was left of the eyes. Caved in around it, the remainder of the face was the shade of parchment and might have been a mummy's.

But even at that, Kris marveled, she hadn't died all at once.

Impressed, she stared at the skeletal arms that reached out high overhead. The yellow claws at their ends spread wide like a point guard's hands in a freeze-frame shot. But each of the fingers had broken back at the top joint. All the tips were worn down to the bone with the nails torn off.

She might still have been scrabbling and fighting with everything she had to get out of the box.

"I would say six months dead perhaps, doctor," Yuri said in her ear. "Kris? Yes?"

She shook her head at herself as she realized he'd had to ask her twice.

"Sure, six month minimum," Kris said. "So what can I say? Rest in peace, Sister Night."

CHAPTER TWELVE

As she stood up to address the Vampire Squad the next morning, Kris was still trying to keep her teeth from grinding

"Before we go on to Plan B," she said between them, "I'd like to share with you some points from my profiles of the victims and tell you how I think they connect to Sister Night."

On his feet at the back of the closed squadroom, Matt caught her eye and dipped his head in encouragement.

"Besides being in the prime of their lives and at the top of their professions, they had something else in common," she went on. "Each of them in their early days had come very, very close to dying. From loss of blood."

Kris began to pace up and down by the lectern.

"Our megadeveloper Macdonald Fisher survived a plane crash in his mid-teens," she said. "But he suffered massive hemorrhage from multiple fractures, and he barely made it out of emergency surgery alive."

As usual, Kris didn't have to refer to her notes.

"Then there's Wade Hazlitt, healthcare entrepreneur and, at least on paper, a boy billionaire," she said. "When he was seventeen back in Nashville, he cracked up his daddy's Porsche and took a header right through the windshield.

"Not wearing his seat belt, natch," she went on. "According to the old records the ME got from Vanderbilt Trauma Center, young Wade had to be completely transfused to make it out of the OR and into ICU.

"As in," she said for emphasis, "total blood volume replacement. Before he got the IV, he'd shed every single drop of blood in his body."

"Holy…"

One of the detectives in back let go a whistle that sounded purely awed to Kris.

"That ol' Hazlitt boy still raced cars and showed up in a bunch of rallies around here, too," he told her. "If memory serves, doc, he come in first at the last three Road Atlanta runs."

"No surprise there, Bubba."

Kris gave him a nod without breaking stride.

"Then there's Halley Cantrell, Esquire," she said. "The plaintiff's friend, she of the multimillion dollar personal injury awards. At age sixteen, she broke up with her boyfriend. Then she sat down in a warm bath and used a Swiss Army knife to slit open the veins in her wrists."

Kris shrugged.

"I think you see the pattern shaping up here," she said. "Yes, Det. Dorfman?"

"Doc, hey, c'mon."

Seated by Bubba, he was a round but solid-looking man who Kris guessed gave his barber free rein with the clippers.

"You mean to say that from what happened to these folks, they picked up a hankering for near about bleeding to death?" he said. "Well, I got to tell you, doc, from my own personal experience I b'lieve that's a stretch."

Kris ignored the ripple of groans from the others.

"Please, detective," she coaxed him. "Do feel free to share."

"Looky here," he began in earnest. "A long time back when I was still in uniform, back when patrolling Downtown wasn't like the pussyfoot cakewalk it is today…"

"Uh-huh," a young woman's voice carried from the side of the room. "And dinosaurs still roamed Grant Park."

"Lot of glaciers over there, too," said another youthful detective. "They hadn't receded from Peachtree Center yet."

"Yeah, yeah, you kids've heard it all before," said Det. Dorfman. "But I nigh on went down the tube back then, and no joke about it. See, I was in hot pursuit after a armed robbery went down at the Varsity.

"I caught me five .38 steel-jacketed slugs at the intersection of North Avenue and Spring Street," he went on. "And I wound up leaving m'spleen and five, maybe six feet of gut in the Grady ER. Not to mention six or eight pints of blood, all told."

As he stood up, his belt strained at a belly that struck Kris as not lacking for girth in spite of a shortage of intestine.

"Not a day goes by but I can't help remembering how it was, doc," he said. "I mean getting so close to slipping down the drain I could just about see out to the end of that long, dark tunnel and hear that celestial music strike up to play from on high...

"Now you can talk about the big ride at Six Flags all you want to, but, but—" he began to stammer after a pause. "I mean to say...aw, hot *damn*, y'all. Whooee, now!"

Puffing out his breath as he sank back in his seat, he seemed to Kris to be rattled by the sheer seductiveness of his own narrative.

"A normal, healthy response to a brush with mortality," she assured him. "Thank you, detective.

"That's my point," she went on. "It's best that most of us never get that close to death before our time. Because while few of us could afford a round-trip ticket, even if we knew one was available, we might just cultivate a taste for...yes, Det. Sims?"

From the front row, the investigator with the model's face and rockbound gaze folded her hands under her chin and looked Kris dead in the eye.

"Okay, Dr. Van Zant," she said. "So maybe the decedents did have some kind of bizarre fetish for near-death by bleeding. And maybe they did act on it with the help of this Sister Night or her associates.

"It's not that hard to conceptualize," she allowed. "Not after you've had to tag some kids who wound up asphyxiated from jerking off with a belt around their neck."

Kris nodded and urged her on without speaking.

"But then," the detective pressed her, "just how'd these rich, high-class terminal thrill-seekers get tangled up with the Vampire to boot?"

"That's a really, really good question."

Deciding to keep her theories under wraps for a little while longer, Kris gave her a graceful shrug.

"I can't answer it, though," she said, looking up. "Yes, sir. Bubba?"

"Yes, ma'am," said the detective in back. "Got to ask you, doc."

He sounded a lot like Hank Williams, Jr., to Kris as he went on gravely.

"Even if it didn't go down on our turf," he said, "who d'you think it was that went and smoked Sister Night anyway?"

"Somebody she knew well," she replied. "Someone she trusted enough to open the door for and welcome to her hideaway."

Kris went back in motion up front.

"Somebody who bore her no grudge. Not personally," she added. "But somebody, still, who had reason to kill her and was cool enough to finish the job with three shots to the heart plus one in the head, with premature burial thrown in for good measure."

Wrapping it up, she glanced around the room.

"*And* someone who knew what to look for afterwards," she said. "Right, Det. Sgt. Chernenko?"

"Dr. Van Zant's impressions in fact match my own."

As Yuri spoke quietly from the corner, Kris noted how all the others followed his words.

"Not like professional wax job, as you would say, but same effect," he added. "Killer likely was not robber either but was very good at searching house. For you see, we turned up no trace there of Sister's business dealings."

Listening to him, Kris caught sight of a young policewoman who'd slipped in the side way. At the back, she passed a folded piece of paper to Matt. He looked at it and nodded to her before she left, but he kept his head down so Kris couldn't see his face.

"So is it fair to say then, doctor," asked Det. Sims, "that this leaves us with a circumstantial link at best between Sister Night and the victims? But none at all to that 'blood junkie' killer you profiled for us last time around?"

"True," Kris said blandly. "That's where we stand."

"And you don't have anything else to add to that?

"Just this, detective," said Kris. "Along with an addict's needs and reflexes, our Vampire probably has senses that're just as keen and on edge. So right now, he might well be watching out for us just as hard as we are for him. That's why I propose to..."

Putting his hand up for her attention, Matt crooked a finger at her from the back of the room.

"Thank you again," Kris said at large. "Please excuse me."

Smoothly breaking off the session, she cut down the aisle between desks.

"Looks like," she said just over her breath, "I'm going to have to get back to you on Plan B."

❧

Kris sat facing Matt across his desk. Before he spoke, he cut his eyes past her. Half made of glass, the wall at her back looked directly onto the Homicide squadroom.

"I told 'em downtown about this wild hair you got to go and try to make contact with the Vampire on the radio," he began. "One on one, like you said."

Kris bobbed her head.

"Well, the mayor himself, the chief herself and all the brass that matter, they heard me out," Matt went on. "And in the end, Kris, they said..."

She caught herself holding her breath.

"'You go, girl.'"

Kris barely kept back a war whoop.

"Just like that?" she asked. "Just the way I asked for, Matt?"

"Uh-huh," he said. "Our public affairs folks got in touch with Sun 99."

Referring to the leading local call-in station, he gestured at the Hallicrafters set on top of the bookcase by his desk.

"And Ms. Kerry Jean Cavanaugh, the one that hosts that show you so interested in?" he said. "Well, she jumped at the chance to book you on *Hot 'Lanta Nights*."

"You mean—?"

"That's the upshot, Miss Kris," he said. "Once the sun goes down tomorrow, you on the air."

Kris made a grateful noise that set up a hum in the glass behind her.

"I'm going to get results for you. I promise," she said. "Fast and big-time and right to the point."

"That's what I told 'em," he said. "So it's just what they expecting from you."

He winked and smiled at her like an uncle, but it only made the lines cut deeper in his face.

"Politics?" she asked. "There's a lot going on behind the scenes, isn't there, Matt?"

"Politics," he agreed. "Plus history. It's..."

He looked down at the blotter in front of him. For a few moments, he ran a hand over the old paving stone he used for a paperweight. Kris knew it was a memento from the first murder case he'd ever solved.

"Even before you went and opened up this 'consensual bleeding' angle on us," he said, "we'd been getting some warning signals. From Halley Cantrell's dad, f'r instance. You know who I mean, old Congressman Cantrell?"

"Isn't he the ranking Democrat on the House Ways and Means Committee?"

"Sure is," sighed Matt. "And he wields about as much clout back here in his home district as he does up in Washington.

"From the start," he said even more softly, "this congressional aide kept calling up the Department and giving us to understand just how much 'discretion' counted with 'em, see."

"Because," Kris suggested, "her folks already knew she had some dangerous kinks?"

Matt put a finger to his lips and wrinkled his brow.

"Politics," Kris said again. "I get it. And as to history?"

"Goes back over twenty years," Matt said. "Long time,

Kris, sure. But even with all the personnel turnover and office shufflin' and *re*organizations we've had around here since then, that last big serial case still casts a long shadow."

"You're talking about the Atlanta child murders," she said. "Aren't you, Matt?"

He sat forward over the desktop with his arms folded and his shoulders hunched.

"I'd just made it to Homicide then," he said. "And to this day, Kris, I can't tell you for sure which chafed my soul the worse.

"Not being able to crack that case while those bodies kept turning up," he went on. "Or having to listen to what folks had to say about how we's doing our duty."

Kris saw the pain in his eyes, and then she caught the rage that came with it.

"Word was," he said, "either we weren't up to the job or maybe we just flat didn't give a damn as to what happened to a bunch of 'li'l ol' throwaway colored chil'en.'

"As you prob'ly read about, Kris, at last we called in the Feds," he went on. "Yep, we went and took it up with the FBI profilers up at Quantico, which back then was like going and consulting a witch doctor. And not even local hoodoo, at that."

"Not exactly a bright shining moment," she softly prompted him. "For the 'city too busy to hate.'"

"We ain't Birmingham."

Mattt shook his head as he voiced Atlanta's other, unofficial motto.

"So that's the party line now," he told her. "This time, we gone keep it in the house and solve it on our own.

"*And* we make it plain that it don't signify whether the victims happen to be po' folks from out in the projects or rich dogs up in Buckhead," he said. "Or whether they black or white or jasmine with pink and purple polka dots on 'em."

"Just the way for a world-class twenty-first-century city to deal with a vampire," Kris agreed. "Thanks for letting me in the loop, Uncle Matt."

He waved her back in her chair as she made to get up.

"Set a spell," he said. "And I'll fill you in on Yuri. That's what you been wanting to ask me about, isn't it, Kris?"

Taking in his old sly look, she hauled up.

"Whoa," she said. "You really are a detective."

"Thank you kindly now."

He chuckled with her through his obvious fatigue.

"What give it away was that whiff of incense," he said. "I caught it when y'all come in together this morning."

At Yuri's invitation, she'd joined him for early Communion at St. Isaac's Russian Orthodox Church downtown. Accompanying them were Yuri's mother Ludmila and his uncle Vasily. Kris took it they were all pillars of the local émigré community from the former USSR.

"That boy's got to be my right-hand man," Matt said. "We're lucky to have 'im on the force. He was top of his class in criminology at Moscow State U., you know, and he got to be the youngest captain ever in the MVD over there.

"Sounds like he made it on his own, too, without relying on family ties," he added. "Guess you heard about Yuri's old man?"

"Gen. Andrei Chernenko?" Kris said. "Somebody at church said he made Hero of the Soviet Union early on, and then he had a really distinguished MVD career himself."

"Got to be commissioner of militia, and a damn good cop," Matt said. "Clean one, too, sounds like. Seems that wasn't the safest thing to be at the time.

"See, best I can tell," he went on, "Moscow in the 1980s and '90s was a lot like Dodge City in the 1880s, only with a sight more firepower to throw down with."

"And Yuri's dad got caught in the crossfire?"

"Man died with his boots on," Matt said. "That's when Yuri went and got his mom and his kid sister out to the States. That big-domed uncle of his was already over here at Georgia Tech, see, so that gave 'em connections here in town."

Matt looked away for a second and cleared his throat.

"And Yuri—well," he muttered. "Just say he left his hometown a little bit later than that."

Kris had already guessed what was to come.

"So with that kind of résumé," she coaxed him, "you'd think Yuri would be with Interpol now, or maybe the Feds."

"It's like I said about the time and place he was in," Matt said. "Look, Kris, I've come to think the world of that boy. But you got to understand, he might just be the last of the Wild West cowboys. It's like he's his own hired gun, now."

Kris nodded and tried to ignore the pulse that kicked up in her ears.

"It's not like there's warrants out for 'im anywhere," Matt went on. "But reports indicate that about the time young Capt. Chernenko resigned his commission, they was a major shakeup in what they called the Baumanskaya Mafia back there.

"That was the gang his daddy'd been cracking down on just before he got hisself shot down in the line of duty," he explained. "And right before Yuri chose to immigrate to the land of the free and the home of the Braves, well, the whole pack of 'em turned up splattered all over the walls of Moscow, down to the very last thug."

So that's how many notches he's got on his gun, Kris mused. Talk about a stone killer...oh, be still, my foolish heart.

"I see," she said aloud. "Thanks, Matt."

"One other thing I got to tell you, Kris."

He shook his head at her and seemed to think it over before he spoke again.

"You ever hear me talk about my granddad's old huntin' dog back in Jonesboro?" he asked after a little while. "'D I ever tell you about ol' Rocket?"

"No, sir," said Kris. "The stage is yours, Uncle Matt."

"Now ol' Rocket, he could flush a covey of quail like nobody's business and then go fetch 'em in the blink of an eye," Matt said. "He could tree a 'coon just about as fast as that, too. Fact is, he'd go track down just about anything you'd care to go looking for out in the woods.

"But it was a different story if you ever tried to call that dog off the scent and get 'im to come back from the trail to you and heel," he added. "Well, then, in that case it was just good luck, Charlie."

Kris started to say something. The look in Matt's eyes stopped her, though. He got up as she did and held out his hand to her at the door.

"That's what I mean about you and Yuri," he said. "You two might come from the ends of the earth, Kris, but there's this one way I can't tell y'all apart."

He gave her fingers a squeeze before she left, but in the end he didn't quite meet her eye.

"I'm not one to judge," he said. "But it's plain to see that both of y'all now, you live for the hunt."

CHAPTER THIRTEEN

The next day at twilight, Kris sat in the studio at Sun 99. Impatiently she fiddled with the earphones she'd settled over her head. She was poised at a microphone, waiting for the show to start.

Tilted back in a chair by her side, the host gave Kris a smile and munched a Snickers bar. A bulky young woman in a tracksuit, she had a spotty moon face under flyaway hair that was dyed the hue of chrome. Finally she sat up as the producer looked around from behind the glass panel in the wall.

He winked at large and flashed a high sign.

"Hel*lo* and welcome, everybody, to *Hot 'Lanta Nights*," said the host on the air. "Happy Monday.

"And if you're having a long weekend leading up to the big ol' Fourth of July celebration tomorrow," she trilled, "well, I'm just really and truly happy for you."

She brushed the wrapper aside and reached for another Snickers.

"I'm Kerry Jean," she went on. "And we have a very special guest tonight. She'll be chatting with us on a topic I think you can really sink your teeth into.

"Her name is Dr. Kristin Van Zant," she announced. "And she's a real live forensic psychiatrist. Hi, doc."

"Hi, Kerry Jean."

As the host prompted her, Kris sat forward and spoke square into the mike on its right-angled stand between them.

"And call me Kris," she said. "Everybody does."

"I believe we've had a colleague on some previous shows

who's also a relative of yours, Kris," said Kerry Jean. "I'm thinking of the renowned Dr. Henry Van Zant.

"Some of our listeners might remember him," she added. "He's the profiler who helped the police track down the East Point Slasher."

"Just lately, Uncle Hank's been a little under the weather," Kris said. "But now he's definitely on the mend."

Today Hank had wheedled the heart docs at the hospital into letting him go home in the care of a private-duty nurse. When Kris left him there, he was busy conspiring with Mrs. Hudson the housekeeper. Just as she'd feared, her uncle seemed all set to stage his backyard Independence Day blowout as if nothing had happened to him.

"Of course, my dear," he said to her. "I'll stick close to home for a week, just as I pledged to the eminent cardiologists of Emory.

"But as I'm sure even you will agree, Kristin," he went on before she could get a word in, "that doesn't mean the occasional revelry can't come to me. Now does it?"

"And so while my esteemed uncle's out of action," Kris said between her teeth, into the mike, "I'm going to try to fill in for him as best I can."

"Cool."

Sassy but languid, Kerry Jean's laugh peaked and faded.

"Now I take it, Kris," she said, "you're hunting vampires for Atlanta PD, huh?"

"Just one, Kerry Jean."

Kris reminded herself that her smile would be wasted here, so she concentrated on her tone.

"I'm hoping your audience can give me some help," she said. "Maybe one of your listeners in particular."

This time the host's laugh struck Kris as more than just a bit forced as she looked away and eyed the terminal screen in front of her.

"On that rather chilling note then, let's open up the phone lines," she said. "Well, hello there, Phyllis from Dunwoody. And what would you like to ask Kris, our intrepid little vampire stalker?"

The voice in Kris's headphones was staid and matronly.

"Dr. Van Zant," she said. "I beg your pardon. But that is your name, isn't it? Kristin Van Zant?"

"Yes, ma'am."

Kris glanced over the host's shoulder. Through the glass, she saw Yuri and Det. Kelly Sims listening in from the engineer's booth with the tech on loan from BellSouth between them. Kris shook her head at them.

"By any chance," she asked the caller, "have we met before?"

"No, Dr. Van Zant, we have not," said Phyllis. "But I believe I'm familiar with you all the same, from an incident some years ago. Weren't you that young girl who tried so hard to block the execution of that homicidal maniac in Alabama?"

"Well, I—"

"And wasn't that the very same vicious, bloodthirsty, murderous wretch," Phyllis cut her off, "who had slaughtered your entire family?"

"Yes, ma'am," said Kris. "That's me."

"Then in that case, doctor, you ought to be ashamed of yourself!" Phyllis said. "Why, for your family's sake alone."

"Yes, ma'am, exactly," Kris said. "That's why I wanted so badly to continue the dialogue with the killer. For their sake."

"*Uh*-oh," said Kerry Jean. "Sounds like we just lost Phyllis."

She winced between her earphones.

"Okay," she said. "Now let's hear from Tyrrell from Hapeville. How's it going, Tyrrell?"

The voice in Kris's ears was a baritone, bluff and resonant.

"I'm fine, Kerry Jean, and I hope you and your guest are, too," he said. "I've got just one question for Dr. Kris there."

Kerry Jean murmured encouragement.

"Doctor," said Tyrrell, "just why in the world are you so unalterably opposed to the death penalty in general?"

"I'm not," Kris said. "Nor to hanging, beheading, and

drawing and quartering. Or to public burning either, if you'd like to get specific."

"Say what?"

"Hey, whatever," said Kris. "I say, do what it takes to protect the tribe. But I also think certain offenders are best kept indefinitely under lock and key. For study."

"But c'mon now, doctor," Tyrrell said. "Beg pardon for getting personal here. But d'you really think that for somebody like the one that went and killed your folks, any kind of rehabilitation is possible?"

"No."

"But, but then why—?"

Kris waited until the caller's rumbling and sputtering had trailed off.

"I think it is possible to find out what makes somebody like Lyle McCandless tick," she went on. "And once we get a handle on the likes of him and Ted Bundy and Jeffrey Dahmer, we'll be all the better equipped to deal with another Adolf Hitler or Pol Pot or Saddam Hussein.

"That's what I think," she said again. "Fair enough, Tyrrell?"

"Dr. Kris, I still might not agree with you," he chuckled. "But I got to hand it to you, gal. You think big."

"I thank you," Kerry Jean came back on smoothly. "And I'm sure Kris thanks you, too, Tyrrell. Now let's hear from Madison in Alpharetta.

"Madison," she prompted the caller. "You're on the air with Kris."

Breathy and rushed, an adolescent voice piped up.

"Kris?" she said. "I'm logged into PsychokillerQuest.com right now. You know there's a whole bunch of sites on the Web about Lyle McCandless and your background, too, and how you—"

"Yeah, Maddy, sure I know," Kris broke in. "Question?"

"I just wondered how you can, like, *do* what you do anyway," she said. "I mean, spend your life talking to a bunch of dangerous, screwed-up creeps and psychos and pervs like that, you know?"

"I do it because I can," Kris replied. "And I'm very, very good at it."

"In other words, Madison," the host spoke up, "I think Kris is saying, why does Mark McGwire keep on stepping up to the plate?"

"Thanks so much for the sports analogy, Kerry Jean," said Kris. "*Love* it."

"That's what I'm here for, Kris," she said. "And now we've got time for one more call before the break."

Kerry Jean made a face at the screen and then looked up at the glass partition.

"No, really?" she said. "Well, okay, Bob. Why not? I guess it's that kind of a night.

"Folks," she said brightly, "my producer tells me we've got Vlad on the line from Transylvania. Okay, Vlad?"

The voice that came on sounded to Kris like stage Romanian. Still, she couldn't deny its timbre and conviction. Even Kerry Jean looked spooked.

"This is for Van Helsing!" snarled the caller. "You hear?"

"That's Van Zant," Kris said. "And it's doctor to you, pal."

"You listen to *me*, doctor," he growled. "I did it, you hear? I sucked all the blood from all of them. And I can prove it!"

"You don't have to, Vlad," said Kris. "I can tell."

She shot a glance at Yuri. He'd told her about the hundred or so confessions he'd already screened for the task force. Meeting Kris's eye now, he shook his head with her. Then he held up a finger and wagged it in front of the telecom tech who was knitting his brows under his headset.

"I'm curious," Kris went on to the caller. "Tell me something, Vlad. Okay?"

Vlad made a guttural noise of assent.

"Okay," she said. "Just what did you do with the victims' eyeballs after you ripped them out of their sockets?"

"Eyeb—? I mean, I boiled them in blood!" he thundered. "And then I ate them with, with—"

"'Fava beans and a good Chianti,'" she finished for him.

"Uh-huh. Now why don't you turn out the lights and go to bed before you wake your parents up? 'Night, sweetheart."

"Okaaay," said Kerry Jean. "And now let's have a word from our fantastic sponsors before we check back in with the children of the night."

She led into the break with one of her lingering, teasing chuckles.

But Kris saw the sweat sheen on her palms. She also noted the tremor in her fingers as she unwrapped another candy bar. Before Kerry Jean spoke again, she sucked in a lungful of air away from the mike.

"We'll be right back," she promised. "And then we'll talk some more with our truly fascinating little guest tonight."

It was getting close to midnight. With Kerry Jean handling traffic, Kris had fielded over fifty calls. More than a few of the people on the line had claimed to be the Buckhead Vampire. Most of the rest had offered theories as to his identity.

Now Kris judged the time had come to put up or shut up.

"If I may, Kerry Jean," she said. "I'd like to direct a few words to one of your listeners. Okay?"

Kerry Jean finished off a Hershey bar in one mouthful and gingerly returned to the mike.

"Well, sure, Kris," she said. "Friend of yours?"

"You might say," said Kris. "He's someone I've just recently come to share a bond with. A unique bond."

She took a beat and then made her words soft and clear and aimed them dead at the microphone she faced.

"I've looked at his work up close and fresh," she said. "And from reviewing his methods and drawing on my own experience and training, I can just about see his face. Right in front of me. Right now."

She looked down at the row of buttons on the touch screen. The host had told her that each marked a phone line to the station. Now for the first time since they'd gone on the air, not one of them was shining.

"Listen," she said fast. "Listen to me. I can tell you knew that with every bite you took and every drop you drank, you were cutting yourself off from the rest of your kind.

"You knew the stakes you were playing for," she went on. "You knew you were crossing the line. You knew how far you'd gone. I can see all that.

"And I know the need was too great to fight it," she added. "I know something else, too. I know the sheer hell that's facing you now. I know about the other need."

She paused long enough to let it sink in and go deep, and then she pushed on even faster than before.

"You've got to get it all out," she said. "You've got to tell. You've got to put a name on the drive that made you prey on your own kind and rend their flesh with your teeth and rip through their veins and drink their blood in the dead of night. You've *got* to tell it. Tell it all.

"The need demands it," she said like a warning. "You've got to let it out. If you don't, pretty soon it's going to burn through your guts and fry your brain and set your soul on fire.

"You know I'm right," she said. "You can feel it. You know it's true just as surely as you can hear me now."

Kris barely took a breath and didn't back off.

"You hear me, yes, yes," she went on. "And what's more, you know I'm the only one left who can get what you're about. You can tell that just by listening to me. So now, talk to me. Talk. Right now. Right here."

In Kris's voice, it was no more a plea than it was a command.

"*Talk*," she said. "Just talk. Talk to the only one in the whole world you *can* talk to anymore. Talk. To me."

Kerry Jean's mouth hung open. She'd drawn as far back from Kris as she could go without tipping her chair over. Now she stared at her as if she were something that had just flapped in through the window to perch at her side.

Inside the control booth, no one budged. Even Yuri stood frozen. Their eyes held fixed on Kris. Seconds went by with nothing moving.

Then onscreen, a light flashed on.

Kris grabbed for the console by the keyboard. She matched the number by the button and punched for the line. In one move, she pulled off her headset and pressed the receiver tight to her ear.

"Okay," she said. "Here I am."

True and clear, she spoke into the mouthpiece and kept it well away from the microphone.

"By now we know who we are," she said. "Don't we? So let's talk. Just you and me."

The line stayed quiet. For several moments, all she could hear was the hum of dead air. Finally came a sigh.

In it, Kris could make out recognition and something very close to resignation. That was enough. She broke into a big smile.

"*Oh*, my God!"

With a yell, Kerry Jean shoved back her chair and went down in a crash of springs and casters. Then she scrambled up and ducked into a crouch hard against the back wall. Fighting for air, she scrabbled with both hand at the panels and tiles.

"No, no, not—!" she got out between wheezes. "Omigod, omigod, omigod, oh..."

Kris didn't look up. She found an empty bag of potato chips on the desktop and held it out to Kerry Jean without turning around. In an undertone, she spoke out of the side of her mouth.

"Here, blow into this," she advised her. "You're hyperventilating pretty bad there. That's it. In and out. In and out. Good."

As calm and sure as she'd ever been, Kris got back on the phone.

"Hello, yes?" she said. "I'm all ears, here. Talk. Come on. Just talk to...?"

At length, the one on the other end of the line let out one more sigh. It was just loud enough for Kris to make out. Then the line clicked off in her ear.

"Kris?"

Very gentle about it, Yuri leaned down at her back and took hold of her shoulders.

"You did it," he said by her ear. "You made contact with Vampire."

"No doubt about it," said Kelly Sims. "Unh-*uh*."

The other detective came out to join them. Without breaking stride or looking around, she brushed past the host in the corner where she was still puffing for all she was worth into a plastic bag. Then Kelly hauled up in front of Kris and jerked a thumb back at the control booth.

"That geek from the phone company in there," she said, "he's giving us a hundred-percent match on the signal trace. Says whoever just called in was using some kind of high-end personal PCS cell phone that's got a distinctive ID with no way to hack it.

"Its number was registered to Macdonald Fisher," she added in a whisper. "See, that was part of our hold-back evidence from the last crime scene."

"Phone was only thing taken from Mr. Fisher's home, Kris," said Yuri. "Except for his blood, yes?"

"Sure," said Kris. "It's okay. I'm okay…"

All the phone lines stayed dark in front of her. For a little while longer, she watched and waited. Then she slowly got to her feet.

"See, now he knows me," she said. "He knows me for sure. And *I* know he'll call back."

CHAPTER FOURTEEN

The next day as the sun went down, Kris was still waiting to hear from the Vampire.

She'd stuck with the detectives and their liaison from the phone company as they briefed the staff at Sun 99. She stayed just as close while they did the same back at headquarters. All operators and receptionists went on alert for Macdonald Fisher's call ID. Like Kris, they got rigged for monitoring and digital recording.

Now she found it hard to focus as she helped out Uncle Hank with his Fourth of July party. Luckily, she'd pitched in for over twenty years at the locally famed event. So as she carried a tray through the crowd in the backyard at Baker Place, Kris could fall back on her reflexes.

"Canapés?" she said. "I made those little cheese puff deals in the middle myself."

Sampling the hors d'oeuvres, the dean of the med school and his wife offered their compliments as she passed by.

"Why, thank you," said Kris. "Oh, really, you're too kind."

With effort she put on a gracious smile. She'd charged her cell phone up to the max before she slipped it in her skirt pocket. Now as she kept an ear cocked for the ringtone, she tried hard not to make a face in anticipation.

"Kris!"

On her way back to the kitchen, she caught a voice she'd come to know well.

"Over here," Macdonald Fisher's daughter called. "Dude, thanks for like asking me to come tonight."

"Hi, Roan," Kris yelled back. "You look good."

She handed off the empty tray to one of the catering crew and cut across the lawn.

"Really good. Whoa," she added. "Knockout, really."

Tonight the heiress had on a long summer dress in black silk print. Over it, she wore a lacy gray shawl. Kris admired the way it suited the night breeze at the same time it served to hide Roan's arm tattoos.

"Thanks, Kris," she said. "You look..."

Meeting Kris's eye, she blinked and took a step back.

"Eager," she finished. "Way eager, man. Like you're ready to rock. I—heard you on the radio last night."

"So'd most of Metro," Kris said. "At least, that's what the station tells me."

As she clasped Roan's arm, she caught her uncle chatting up another guest she'd invited on inspiration.

"C'mon," she said. "I'll introduce you to the worst damn cardiac patient in the whole world. Our celebrated host, that is."

Courtly and towering, Hank had put on a tricolor bowtie with his white linen suit for the occasion. He greeted Roan with a bow from the waist. Then he turned to introduce a stately woman with graying auburn hair and a heart-shaped face.

"Ms. Roan Fisher," he said. "May I present to you the good Dr. Ludmila Chernenko.

"Or—I do beg your pardon, my dear Ludmila," he began to correct himself. "Would the proper Russian form of your name be Chernenka or Chernenya, or something quite beyond my modest linguistic ability?"

"Is no matter, Hank."

Yuri's mother, who'd turned out to be a doc on staff at Egleston Children's Hospital, had a laugh that reminded Kris of her son's.

"After all," she added, "as you say, we are in America, yes?"

"Yes indeed we are, Ludmila."

Hank gave her a pat on the hand and then spread his arms wide toward the refreshment table.

"Kristin," he said. "Now wherever are your manners, child? Have you not offered our Miss Roan a liberty mimosa?

"A humble concoction, I grant you," he called after the young women. "But tonight, my dear, it is the house specialty."

Kris conducted Roan to the punchbowl and passed her a flute of champagne and orange juice, topped by a maraschino cherry on a toothpick with a tiny Stars and Stripes attached.

"On me," Kris muttered. "Hey, go crazy."

"Oh, wow, thanks," said Roan. "I take it your family's got like a deep patriotic streak, huh?"

"I think it's got something to do our backing the losing side in the Civil War."

Kris helped herself to a glass of straight OJ and watched as Roan tossed her drink back in one go.

"Cheers," she said. "Packs kind of a sticky buzz, huh?"

"Trippy," Roan agreed. "Look, Kris, there's something I have to ask you."

She leaned closer and dropped her voice.

"There's this one issue I can't get my mind around," she said. "Especially after listening to you on the radio last night...?"

With her back to the gas-lit carriage lamps, Kris nodded.

"I've got to know," Roan said by her ear. "With you, is it like in the movies? I mean, can you really get inside some blood-crazed wack job's head like that and figure out what it is he's thinking and tell what he's going to do next?"

"No," said Kris. "I don't know anybody else who can do that either. Not in real life."

"But how'd you go and, like, make *con*tact like you did?"

"Call it empathy," Kris said. "It's not quite the right word, but it'll do."

She took a sip of her juice and shrugged.

"Say I've got a taste for human blood," she began to explain. "I really, really like the stuff. Got to have some. Yearning and burning for it. Okay?

"So I go out one night. First time ever, I sink my teeth in human flesh," she went on. "And whoa, sister, what a rush! What was I waiting for anyway?"

Kris went up on her toes in front of Roan and made some gestures of enthusiasm.

"So now it's my third time out," she said. "You can just bet I'm looking over my shoulder and trying to hide my tracks. And all the while, I'm listening hard for..."

A spray of fireworks burst overhead and lit up Kris's face. Then she realized her voice must have carried. Nearby, a group of Emory faculty folk cut off their talk. Looking unnerved, they spun around and stared at her. Kris in turn put on her brightest smile.

Then she raised her glass and dropped them a curtsy.

A few stray rockets and sparklers still shot up and made tracks in the sky from over by Lenox Square. Otherwise, the night's festivity was on the wane. Hank had loosened his tie, and to honor tradition he'd fetched his old Gibson guitar.

Now he led the remnants of the party in more choruses of "This Land is Your Land" than even Kris could remember. In back of the others, she sat and swung her feet on the edge of the weathered redwood picnic table. Looking on as the song finally came to an end, she shook her head fondly.

"Give my big uncle half a chance," she said, "and I swear he'll march you straight through the Woody Guthrie songbook."

At her side, Ludmila clapped and cheered.

"Is like—I must say," she chuckled. "I am very much reminded by this of my son and his singing."

Still gripping her cell phone with both hands, Kris looked up.

"Yuri?" she said. "He's not a folkie, too, is he?"

"Oh, no, Kris," said the pediatrician. "He has quite marked preference, I would say, for Allman Brothers Band?"

"No!" Kris burst out. "Gregg and the boys? *Really*?"

The others jumped and looked around startled, Roan most of all. Across the way, she'd been deep in conference with one of Hank's forensic fellows. He was a dashing young Brazilian psychiatrist whose name, Kris recalled, was Dario.

"Beg pardon there," she said at large. "I didn't mean to scare y'all. It's just that I've always had this guilty weakness for your basic dirty, down-home Southern rock."

"Oh, that's Yuri," groaned Matt. "Right, honey?"

The detective turned to his wife Irene, who was a professor at Spelman College. Together they'd shown up late for the party. Now Matt looked as at ease as Kris had seen him since she'd been back here.

"'Loord, I was boorn ramblin' man,'" he crooned. "'Tryin' to make livin' and doin' best I ca-a-an...'"

He broke it off at length, throwing his head back to let out a whoop.

"Talk about your country-rock 'n' roller from Moscow," Matt said. "Just you try listening to such as that over and over again. 'Specially when you out on stakeout with that ol' boy in the back of a van."

"Yuri sings like that, for real?" Kris marveled. "So he must be practically tone deaf. Like...like me. That's wonderful! I mean—"

All of a sudden she drew her heels back and sprang up. She'd just caught sight of a tall shadow. Squinting in the dark, she made out the figure that was headed for her at a steady lope.

"Yuri!" she called out. "C'mon over here. We were just talking about..."

Her voice trailed off when she saw his face. From a few feet apart, he matched her gaze. There was no way for Kris to mistake what she saw in his eyes.

Without a word, she held up four fingers between them. Yuri nodded. Then he put out his palm to her, and she took it. Hand in hand, they ran back to the street.

The yellow tape and sawhorses were just going up when they got to the scene. It was one of the new high-rise condo blocks at Centennial Park West. From all sides of the street, TV crews and press photogs were pushing in. Yuri dodged them as he pulled to the gate of the underground garage.

"Victim's name was Martine DuBarry," he said. "Apparently was her real name, too. That is, one she was born with."

"Son of a bitch," Matt said just over his breath. "Son of a bitch."

"'Mdub.,'" said Kris from the backseat. "That was how it showed up on Sister Night's list.

"'Mdub,'" she repeated. "Kind of like 'macd.f.' For Macdonald Fisher."

"Son of a..."

A patrolman with a clipboard leaned out by the parking attendant in her booth. He took down Yuri's and Matt's badge numbers and looked at Kris's med-center ID. Then he waved them down the ramp.

They cut across the first level between steel uprights and wheeled through ranks of cars. Kris made most of them out to be imports. All of them looked expensive to her. Yuri took a reserved slot at the head of the deck, and they got out together.

They cleared a second police checkpoint at the service elevator. Then they took it straight to the top. The doors opened on an airy hall between penthouse suites. Ahead of them, cutback lamps lit the way down a long stretch of dove-colored carpet.

"Building security is quite good," Yuri said. "According to log downstairs, no one came and went tonight except residents and known guests. But still..."

Matt put a hand on the door bumper and motioned for the others to stop right where they were.

"Okay," he said. "But what? Go on, partner."

"Turns out is possible to enter by side way. This is more private, you see," Yuri said softly. "If one has key.

"Or else," he added, "if someone on inside opens door for one, yes?"

"Sure," said Kris. "But then they'd have to keep surveillance cams trained on that door. Wouldn't they?"

"You damn skippy they do. They got to," Matt said. "So what's the story, Yuri? We got video?"

"Our people are reviewing tape as we speak, lieutenant."

They got back on the move at the same time, and Yuri led the way down the hall.

"Ms. DuBarry's is one over here," he said. "Eastern suite."

They rounded the corner, and a uniformed cop with smooth black gloves opened the door. Inside was another patrol officer, young and blanched. He saw them down a wide foyer with mirrors for walls. The room just past it was sparse and vast under track lights.

The far wall was solid glass, but gauzy sheers took the edge off the railing outside. Standing out white in the floods, the spikes raked back in a long thin line. Kris considered their pattern for a moment. To her they looked like the bones of a great ancient bird.

Then she looked down at the dead woman.

She lay face-up with her arms splayed out at her sides. Long and fine, her legs drew together. Her head was to the window with her hair trailing back. Thick and smooth like winter wheat, it lapped up over the marble ledge.

She wore a black silk negligee in no disarray at all. Her skin against it was paler than anything could be if it was still alive, and her dark eyes were open. Kris couldn't read her terminal expression. Still, she put it a long way past fear.

The victim's throat and the crooks of her arms gaped open, ripped white and gnawed down to the bone.

Kris heard a woman crying from another room. But it faded fast under the heartbeat in her ears. Too quick for the men to stop her, she broke away at the door. Skirting the body, she ran up to the wall at the side.

The hue of an eggshell, it was finished in bare plaster. Kris doubted that there had ever been a mark on it before tonight. But this time some blood had stayed behind.

"Kris, yo."

Matt caught up at her back and put a hand on her shoulder.

"We best stick to the drill now, doc," he said. "Look but don't touch, hear?"

She nodded. Straining hard not to reach out, Kris backed off a pace and folded her hands with her arms in front of her. She forced herself into the stance she'd take if she were now looking on in an operating room or a pathology suite.

"Kris?" said Yuri at her side. "Easy does it."

She started to speak to him, but her throat had gone dry and her tongue stuck to the roof of her mouth.

"Take some deep breaths," he advised her. "In and out, as you say. In and out, yes?"

"I—thanks," she said at last. "I'm okay. It's all right."

Still she kept staring dead at the four words on the wall. She noted how each stroke in them was sharp and clean, even the apostrophe. At least a foot above Kris's eye level, they stood out raw and red.

Then they ran down the plaster in long pink lines that only began to fade when they got close to the baseboard.

"Unh-uh," she murmured. "No way. *He* didn't write it."

"What?" Matt asked sharply. "What was that now, Kris?"

She shook her head. She hadn't meant to say it out loud. All at once Kris caught herself whispering.

"Nothing," she said. "But whoever wrote this had really, really steady hands."

YOU'LL NEVER CATCH ME, it read in blood.

CHAPTER FIFTEEN

Kris took some more deep breaths. At length her heart slowed down and she turned away from the wall. Ready to see what else she could read, she headed for the corpse.

She stopped on the way and took a look out the window. Ten stories down, people were still milling in the park. From this perspective, they might have been ants as they crossed the grassy squares and sidewalks by the rings of the Olympic fountain. Some stragglers looked up from inside the circle of obelisks and pointed Kris's way.

Then a last bright spray of fireworks bloomed from the skyline and burst apart against the stars. Kris shook her head and stepped back. Lightly she knelt on the carpet.

"He's getting hungrier all the time," she said. "Thirstier, needier, more driven. When he did this, I'll bet he could already feel the buildup to a great big boost. He knew it was about to come on strong. And boy, did he want the rush.

"Yeah, you can see how he's not holding back anymore," she added. "He's going straight for what he wants and ignoring everything else, even..."

Careful to keep her hands to herself, Kris nodded over the body.

"She's young," she said. "Isn't—wasn't she?"

"Thirty-two," said Yuri. "She used to be fashion model, I am told, at top of her profession."

He faced Kris across the ravening throat wound.

"More recently," he told her, "she was head of her own modeling agency here in town."

"No surprise."

Kris couldn't see any flaws in the dead face, which might have been marble. Set wide, the eyes were such a deep shade of blue that the irises nearly merged with the pupils. Scanning down, Kris considered the breasts that rode up high and full under wispy silk.

"Look like original equipment, too," she said aloud. "*Tres Vogue modele*, huh?Thanks."

She took the magnifying glass Yuri offered her. Methodically she ran it over all the skin she could see. All the while, Yuri shined his penlight on the body's wrists and ankles.

"And yet he didn't touch her except to bite her," Kris went on. "Our Vampire was obviously way more interested in blood tonight than in anything else this chick had to offer."

"And no more signs of resistance are apparent here than in others," Yuri said. "Merely same marks as we have seen before, yes?"

"Right," she said. "Same as the last time. Same as what the ME described in the posts of the first victims. All the same."

Kris sat back on her heels. Glancing up, she saw the evidence techs filing in from the hallway. Behind them came the medical examiner's crew, flanked by some more police personnel.

"I bet we're coming up dry searching the rest of the place, too, aren't we?" she asked the detectives. "Just like at the other scenes.

"No sign of bed restraints or rope or duct tape or bondage gear," she added. "And for that matter, no kind of medical kit. No IV needles or tubes or syringes or blood bags or phlebotomy equipment. Right?"

Yuri got to his feet with her.

"Nothing," he said. "So far."

"Hold on," Matt spoke up. "Is it just me, y'all, or is there a strong whiff of deja vu coming off the walls in here?"

Standing between Kris and Yuri, he spread his arms wide.

"I'm not talking about the wall with the writing on it now, " he said. "Or that glass one either. I mean these other two, here."

Kris took a step back with him, and then she let out a groan.

The words of Stephen Laszlo came back to her with a vengeance. The great profiler hardly deigned to visit crime scenes anymore. But over the past year of Kris's fellowship, he'd shared with her the bits of wisdom he'd picked up in the field.

Anytime anything catches your eye, said Laszlo, *ignore it. Wait until it lets go. Then back up and start to observe all over again.*

"That flocked wallpaper," Kris said between her teeth. "It's identical to what we saw in Macdonald Fisher's house. Even down to the garish, overbearing color scheme. Isn't it?"

"Just so," Yuri said. "Is very same shade of red, Kris, yes?"

Then he turned toward the sound of crying. Unabated since they'd come in, it picked up now. Loud and long, it carried from a nearby room.

Silently Yuri invited Kris to come with him, and she fell in step at his side.

From the patrolmen who'd been the first responders at the scene, Kris learned that there was only reason Martine DuBarry's murder had turned up tonight. And that was the arrival at the condo, unannounced and unexpected, of the victim's sister Gabrielle. She'd just blown into town from LA, she told Kris, off a video shoot.

"Gaby," she sobbed. "That's, like, always been my nickname, doctor."

"Call me Kris," she said. "Everybody does."

After introductions, Yuri dropped back and left them alone in the snug little breakfast alcove by the kitchen.

"I know there's nothing I can do or say that'd really help you now, Gaby," Kris said. "I can see how much she meant to you."

She took Gaby's hand and gave it a squeeze as she sat down facing her by the table.

"I can't tell you, Kris," she got out between sniffles. "It's like, like—"

Rocking back and forth in her chair, she took the handkerchief Kris held out to her and blew her nose in it with a loud honk.

"Thanks," she said. "It's—I don't know how to tell you what it's like. It's—d'you have, like, brothers and sisters yourself, Kris?"

"No."

"Well, it's like, Marti was always just, like, *there* for me."

She kicked off her hemp sandals and drew her taut, tan legs up in front of her. Tiny and curvy, Gaby was a sunstruck blonde with touched-up roots and chalky blue eyes. To Kris she looked like a cuter, sportier version of her late sister.

"Marti was always there," she said again. "You know, Kris?"

"Sure."

Carefully downcast with her, Kris let a beat go by.

"And I'll bet whenever Marti needed you, Gaby," she said, "you were right there for her, too."

"Yeah, uh-huh," she said. "Like, *sure*."

Clutching her knees and ducking her head, Gaby looked to be barely in her teens. Her faded cutoff jeans and floppy yellow tee added to the schoolgirl effect. But Kris had checked the plainclothesmen's notes and knew they were close to the same age.

"Right," Gaby snorted. "Like Marti'd ever really needed *me* since we were kids.

"See," she went on, "Sis was always this big ol' world-class success story, just about right from the start. And me, I was always this li'l snotnose punk fuckup she had to keep pulling out of, out of the..."

"It's okay, Gaby," Kris said. "'S okay."

As she gentled her, Kris got a fix on her accent. At first she'd taken it for outer-boroughs New York under a Valley Girl gloss, but then she caught a hint of a Gulf Coast drawl. It didn't take her long to pick out the strain of pure Vieux Carre in it.

"What about back when you and Marti were just kids growing up," she prompted her. "You know, back home in N'Orleans."

"It was just the two of us then, Kris," she said. "After Mom took off and *her* mom had to, like, take us in. As for where our dad was, huh, go figure.

"And, and I remember this one time," she went on. "I can't tell you how scared I got."

She brushed back her hair with both hands and then folded them under her chin as if she were at prayer.

"Marti was just fourteen, see," she said. "And I was twelve. And God, oh God, I thought I was going to lose her, like, forever. There she was, Kris, laid up in Charity."

"In—?"

Kris bit her tongue. Nowadays the official name for the facility was the Medical Center of Louisiana at New Orleans. But she knew that to folks down in NOLA, it was still just plain Charity.

"So Marti had to go in the hospital," she coaxed Gaby. "Because of all the blood she lost, in an accident? Some kind of serious injury?"

"Actually she—but how'd you...?"

Gaby blinked hard at Kris, but then she seemed to take her on faith and went on with her story.

"Swear to God, I just knew she was going to die then," she said. "'Cause nobody could figure it out at first. It was like all her blood was just breaking down on her. Then it turned out Sis had got, like, mono. You know?"

"Infectious mononucleosis?"

"Yeah, yeah," said Gaby. "But then the docs told us she'd come down with something else from it. They gave it some other kind of big-ass jawbreaker name."

"Postviral hemolytic anemia?"

"*Yeah*, like that," Gaby said. "Whatever, it damn near killed 'er."

While Gaby bobbed her head, Kris thought it over.

"Uh-huh," she said. "So I guess they had to give Marti a whole bunch of transfusions back then, huh?"

"It was like, God, she had to have every last drop of blood in her body flushed out and brand-new blood put in for her, all over again."

Looking in awe of her own memory, Gaby sat up and fixed Kris with eyes that had gone huge and wondering.

"And then it was like she'd come back from the dead, I'm telling you, Kris," she blurted out. "It was just like something in the Bible. Like—like Lazarus, right?"

Kris nodded.

"And, and ever since then..."

"Marti liked to take risks," Kris said for her. "Big-time, huh? Because that's the kind of survivor she was."

"She was like—I mean, c'mon, I'm telling you, Kris," she gasped. "Like f'r instance, that rock climbing she went in for. Last year Marti took off to Switzerland, to the Alps, for some righteous ice face action, like she said. And, and, like—*Jesus*."

Gaby hugged her sides tight, shivering.

"And sometimes, Kris, just riding in the car with her when she was doing the driving," she said, "I swear to Christ, it'd like to scare the livin' shit out of you, I'm here t'tell you."

Kris had heard enough. She murmured something else to console her. While Gaby buried her eyes in her hanky, she looked around and got set to go.

"Holy God...damn," Gaby moaned. "There were times, I got to tell you now, Kris, it made me like to think that Marti was in love with, with checking out like she nearly did before, back then."

Kris caught the eye of a policewoman who looked sympathetic, and then she gently handed Gaby off to her.

"I think Sis was all hot for—that she was all up for, for," Gaby sobbed. "For dyin', you know?"

Tonight, Kris mused, it looked as if Marti had finally met the suitor of her dreams.

Kris joined the bulk of the task force downstairs. They'd all crowded into the manager's office. Now they clustered around the TV mounted in the corner.

"Okay, y'all," said Matt. "Let's roll tape."

He went on just loud enough for Kris to hear right beside him.

"'Bout time we got us a break," he muttered. "Body turns up here while it's still fresh, just like at the Fisher place up in Buckhead. This time, though, the perp didn't get to the surveillance cams first and wipe 'em all clean.

"Okay now, let's go," he said louder. "Roll it."

Det. O'Riley, known as Bubba, punched buttons on the VCR remote and fiddled with the tracking control. At last he stood aside. On the video, jerky images showed up in black and white.

"Twenty-oh-three's when he hits the side door, looks like."

The redheaded detective pointed to the timestamp in the corner of the screen.

"That's three minutes past eight PM, doc," he added. "Or just 'bout four hours ago now."

Kris said thanks.

Then she caught her breath and stared. A tall, wide-shouldered figure had just appeared onscreen. As she watched, he elbowed the glass-and-steel door back from the portico. Not pausing, he stepped inside as if he knew the way.

He had on track shoes and jeans under a light-colored hoodie. Outsize glasses with dark lenses hid the rest of his face. Sticking a card in his pocket, he crossed the hallway in a couple of strides and used his free hand to haul open the door by the elevators.

For a second, he turned his back to the camera. Zipped shut, a backpack hung slack between his shoulder blades. Kris pointed at it and opened her mouth, but Kelly Sims spoke up first.

"Look at those gloves," said the detective. "Slick bastard's already snapped on latex, so you can forget about prints."

"From height of doorframe," Yuri said, "I would say he is six feet four or five."

"Mother's big," Matt agreed. "Fast, too."

Then he ushered in the resident manager. A carefully coiffed young blonde woman, she wore a Sea Island cotton pantsuit and a tense frown. Even with her arms folded tight in front of her, she was still trembling hard enough for Kris to see.

"You say there's no way in without a passkey, ma'am," Matt said to her. "Like the one it looks like he was using there?"

"In fact, officer, it's a plastic card with a magnetic strip," she quavered. "Each resident is issued one and one only. And I can assure you, they're designed to be quite impossible to copy."

"Thank you, ma'am."

Matt motioned for her to stay while he looked around. Holding up a hand, he called to a rotund detective at the back of the room. Kris saw him run a pen down a clipboard as he seemed to check off items on it.

"Say there, Dorf," Matt said. "Is Ms. DuBarry's pass card accounted for?"

"Sure is, lieutenant," said Det. Dorfman. "Turned up in 'er purse in the apartment. As to any extras...?"

He looked up from his list and raised his eyebrows, but the manager was already shaking her head.

"She never got one," he finished. "Didn't think so."

"Heads up, y'all," called Bubba. "Here he comes again."

Clutching the remote, he trained a finger on the TV screen like a six-shooter.

"See, house security's got this cam on the side rigged up to work off a motion-sensor trigger," he said. "So the next time we catch us a peek at this ol' boy, it's...

"Twenty-twenty-three hours on the day date," he read off. "That's what she's givin' us. So that'd make for a 8:23 exit from the premises."

Kris felt her front teeth start to gnash.

"The Vampire," she groaned, "has left the building."

"Son of a—?"

Matt ran his palms over his scalp, front to back, over and over again.

"Damn, y'all," he said. "Keep in mind we talking about barely twenty minutes door to door here. And yet he just drained that woman upstairs. Down to her very last drop, too."

"Bloodsucker moves like the wind," Kelly spat out. "Look at 'im."

She jerked her chin at the screen.

"Bang, he comes down the stairs," she said. "Doesn't even look like he's breathing hard. Then boom, he's out the door same way he came in. Doesn't look back either. He never misses a beat."

She turned to Kris.

"Does he, doctor?"

"Not even with a full load on, detective."

Kris felt everyone else's eyes on her. She stepped up by Bubba and took the remote from his hand. Then she hit reverse and froze the frame at the point of the intruder's departure.

"See that bulge in his backpack?" she said. "I'd say that's just about right for ten or twelve units of whole blood in phlebotomy pouches. But still..."

"What's the problem, doctor?" said Kelly. "Doesn't he fit your profile?"

"He fits it just fine, detective."

Kris got busy with the rewind.

"Now," she said aside, "I'm seeing him in a slightly different light. That's all. Just wait, wait...

"Okay, look," she demanded. "Look here!"

She waved an arm at the TV set as the first shot of their quarry came back onscreen.

"He's going in barehanded," she said. "That pack on his back's empty. Not a bulge to be seen at this point, okay? Trust me, even a bunch of IV bags that hadn't been used would take up more room than that.

"And for damn sure," she added, "he doesn't have the makings for the kinks going down in the penthouse. For crying out loud, you'd need more props to pull that off than a vintage Madonna video!"

"Kris, hold on there," said Matt. "Don't get too far ahead of what we'n already see with our own eyes. Awright, doc?"

"All right," she said. "But just take a look at how he's carrying himself."

She ran the opening sequence back one more time.

"C'mon, everybody," she went on. "Does this look like a mighty hunter to you? Like a steely-eyed, fiercely coiled stalker of the night? Like a vampire on the make, in short? Does it?

"Hell, no!" she burst out. "What we've got here's a strung-out junkie in a sweat to go line up with a connection. Nothing more, nothing less. Doper needs a fix, needs it bad. Real bad. Got to score. Right here. Right now. See?"

She caught her breath.

"Good point," Matt said fast. "Where's the gear anyway? We got nothing in the deceased's place. Nothing's showing up on the perp either, going in or coming out."

He switched to a command voice in a tight cadence.

"So we hit the bricks," he said. "We go through every trashcan and disposal chute and airshaft in the building and check under all the balconies and windows.

"Same time," he proceeded, "we get the techies back at HQ to blow us up some stills off this tape here and print 'em out for general circulation so's we can use 'em for canvassing witnesses and passersby.

"Then we gone ask every good citizen in the area if they saw anybody that looks like our boy coming or going," he wrapped up. "Y'all copy?"

"Yes, lieutenant," said Yuri. "But I believe doctor has even more critical point to make, yes?"

"*Yes*," Kris yelled. "I mean—"

She cupped her hands by her mouth and got even louder as a dozen voices threatened to drown her out.

"Hey, wasn't anybody at all listening to me just now?" she wailed. "Didn't you hear what I was trying to tell you?"

Still the babble in the room overrode her.

"The Vampire walked into a scene that was *already* in progress," she bellowed. "He was—he was *invited*. Now I'm sure of it. Can't you see...?"

"Yes," Yuri said by her side. "I must agree with Dr. Van Zant's conclusion."

Somehow, Kris marveled, he made the rest of the investigators shut up and look around at them without even raising his voice.

"No doubt," Yuri said. "In this way, you see, it was inside job."

CHAPTER SIXTEEN

Early the next morning, Kris joined Yuri for Martine DuBarry's autopsy.

"Guess it's not just for Buckhead anymore," said Rob Mackenzie during the post. "Even the *Constitution*'s switched to calling 'im the Atlanta Vampire now."

Otherwise, the ME had nothing new to tell them. After they'd shed their OR gowns and shoe covers by the locker room, they fell in step together. They'd decided to double-team Matt.

"In this instance, lieutenant," said Yuri, "I believe it would be most revealing if Kris and I were to talk to this person together."

"All we've got so far is circumstantial, sure," Kris conceded. "But c'mon, Uncle Matt. As a friend of mine who used to clerk for the Supreme Court always says, that is the hardest kind of evidence to fake."

"Okay, y'all," Matt said. "I—hold on."

He held up a finger as Kris and Yuri both started to thank him.

"I meant okay as in okay, I'm willing to listen to what you got so far," he said. "Play like I'm the judge here, see. Now y'all try to sell me on signing a search warrant you just went and put together on the spot."

"You remember what it said at the top of Sister's Night's list," Kris said from close by his side. "It was 'BAR/NN.' Right, Uncle Matt?"

"Uh-huh."

Slitting his eyes at her, the senior detective shrugged.

"I grant you, Kris, 'NN' might stand for Nurse Nell, that

outcall dom," he said. "Or whatever that woman was that had the mask on, the one you said Macdonald Fisher's girl walked in on with her daddy."

"Now as for 'BAR,'" Yuri said. "Look at this, lieutenant."

From Matt's other side, he held up a printout of the names of the residents of Martine DuBarry's condo.

"Name of occupant of unit one floor below Vampire's last victim is Blair Ann Rennie," he pointed out. "Is of interest that she has very same initials, yes?"

"Sure, partner," Matt sighed. "I find that interesting. Same way I do that some folks keep catching sight of Elvis from time to time. So?"

"So, lieutenant," Yuri went on, "I believe it is also noteworthy that Ms. Rennie is principal in interior design firm of Mancusi & Rennie."

"Mancusi & Rennie, as you might recall," said Kris, "were the decorators at the Fisher mansion."

With Yuri, she kept Matt hemmed in tight between them.

"And it turns out they did the DuBarry condo, too," she went on. "And it was you yourself, Uncle Matt, who picked up on that eerie similarity between the wall coverings and color scheme of the two places.

"Right down," she added, "to that really oppressive shade of—"

"Son of a—"

Matt shut his eyes and nodded slowly as he began to rub his scalp.

"Okay," he muttered. "I still doubt seriously that all this is going to add up to search warrant material. But for whatever it's worth, go for it. You two go pump 'er.

"Just—"

His voice faded at Kris's back as she banged back the door to the locker room on her way to change out of scrubs.

"Y'all be careful now," he called. "Hear?"

Mancusi & Rennie, LLC, took up the bottom two floors of

an old mid-rise on West Peachtree. Kris whistled in admiration at the Art Deco front. She was always pleased to see one of these little terra cotta gems holding its own downtown amid all the towers of smoked glass and steel.

"Hell of a thing," said Dante Mancusi. "Hell of a thing, really."

Kris judged the senior partner was in his mid-thirties. He'd greeted them in the foyer. Now with a flourish, he saw them across the bustling open-plan ground floor.

"Marti DuBarry was a fantastic human being," he went on. "Just fantastic, absolutely. Over and above her being a major client of ours, of course."

Yuri nodded and cut his eyes discreetly at Kris as she flanked the decorator opposite him.

"I couldn't help noticing," she said. "Ms. DuBarry's condo was really something to look at. That unique wallpaper, I mean, and everything.

"So I was just wondering," she added. "Did she pick out the decor herself?"

"Oh, no," said Dante. "Marti left all that up to Ms. Rennie."

Framed by a trim black beard, his smile struck Kris as forbearing.

"I must tell you," he said. "That rather vivid palette of colors is something of a trademark of hers."

Kris returned his smile. From behind it, she took his measure. While they headed for the stairs, she left the rest of the questions to Yuri.

Dwarfed by the detective who slouched beside him, Dante Mancusi was slim and of middle height. Kris noted his razor-cropped hair and the tiny silver ring in his left earlobe. She pegged his cotton blazer and open-necked silk shirt as Dolce & Gabbana, his jeans as Armani, and his loafers as Gucci. They all were black.

His accent tried for continental, too. But under the stylish gloss, Kris picked out more than a trace of New England. She put its origin south of Boston, likely toward the Cape and islands with some Providence on top.

"Looks like business is good," she said. "I've been away from town for a while myself."

At Dante's direction, they took a freestanding stairway with wrought-iron rails and gray marble treads. Kris gestured at the busy showrooms and cubicles below them. Near the top of the steps, she paused.

"So I confess," she added, "I'm not familiar with your name."

"Oh, M&R's only been on line for just about three years now, doctor."

Now Dante looked anxious, and his speech sounded practiced to Kris.

"I came to Atlanta straight out of an apprenticeship in New York," he said. "I started up here on my own. You might say this is still my first real job since graduating."

"From the Rhode Island School of Design?"

"Yes. And then after going solo for a while, I got together with Ms. Rennie," he went on as if by rote. "She already had a toehold here as a native, so to speak. And—"

At the head of the landing, he came to a stop in front of his partner's office and turned to stare at Kris.

"*Scusi*," he said. "But that's not on my—I mean, just how did you know where I went to college?"

"Wild hunch."

Kris smiled brightly at him. Then she took care to dim it as he started back from her. Still looking rattled, he knocked on the door and held it open.

Kris said thanks and ducked in under Yuri's arm.

"Oh," came a throaty contralto from inside. "Hi there."

A tall, busty woman in a white blouse and tartan skirt held up two fingers in greeting. Standing at the drafting table by the desk, she tossed back a mane of red-and-gold curls. Leonine was the word Kris would pick for her stance.

"Police, right?" she said. "I'm afraid I was rather short with one of your people when he knocked on my door last night and started asking me questions."

She put on a smile that was wide and white.

"But it was really late," she said. "Plus I'd been in bed with a migraine all day. And that was on top of having to find out about poor li'l ol' Marti like that.

"So just plain bitchy was the best I could be," she added before anyone else could speak. "And there, sir, 's an end on it."

"BA," said Dante. "This is Det. Chernenko from Homicide and Dr. Van Zant."

He seemed relieved to Kris as he excused himself and withdrew, closing the door behind him.

"Okay, no hard feelings toward the constabulary," BA said. "And no offense taken, I hope. So put 'er there, comrade."

As she offered Yuri her hand, the designer's drawl put Kris in mind of a jungle cat's purr at the zoo.

"And you'd be the little Werewolf girl from the radio show," BA said, turning. "Beg pardon, dearie. I meant to say the consulting psychiatrist."

"Call me Kris," she said with a grin. "Everybody does."

BA's hand was smooth against Kris's palm and felt as cool and hard as a freezer door.

"Everybody calls me BA," she said. "But not for what you'd think."

"No," Yuri chuckled. "Of course not."

As BA sat down and indicated the chairs in front of her desk, Kris admitted she found Yuri's laugh a bit annoying in this setting.

"Is very kind of you, Ms. Rennie, to assist us in this way in our investigations," he said. "Because as you would imagine, we find this murder of your neighbor quite baffling in many respects."

"It's BA," she said. "Remember?"

Levelly she met the gaze of both of them. Her eyes were smoky gray over high, full cheeks. Kris admired the way a cinnamon blush over a spray of freckles took the edge off her redhead's pallor.

"Okay, homicide detective and good doctor," BA said. "Now just how can I be of help to you?"

"You knew Ms. DuBarry rather well, I believe," said Yuri. "In professional sense at least, yes?"

"We were personal friends, too," BA said. "It always seemed as if Marti and I had a lot to talk about."

Looking down, she tilted her chair back and let her arms rest on the desktop.

"We were about the same age," she went on. "We'd compare notes on, oh, clothes, art, sports even, men we were seeing, former husbands. The usual."

BA's shoulders as well as her chest suggested heroic feminine statuary to Kris.

"D'you go in for rock climbing?" she asked her. "From talking to her sister last night, I gather that Ms. DuBarry was an avid climber herself."

"Not me, Kris."

As she looked up and met her eye again, she smiled thinly.

"Horseback riding's about as adventurous as I get," she added. "Marti was the daredevil."

"Oh, I don't know," Kris said. "I bet you're pretty daring in the saddle."

She nodded toward the photos on the wall behind the desk. BA wore riding pinks and jodhpurs in them. At various ages, she showed horses and took to the hunt.

"You come from hereabouts, don't you?" Kris asked. "I grew up around Emory myself, and your name sounds familiar to me."

"You're probably thinking of my father."

If still friendly, BA's manner had turned brisk as if to remind her visitors that time after all was money.

"He was Ewan Rennie, the surgeon," she said. "Daddy served on the clinical faculty of the med school. I went there for a couple of terms myself."

She seemed to follow Kris's eyes to the Princeton diploma on the wall at her side.

"Dropped out, though," she laughed. "I mean, stick my finger up where? Honestly now."

"To return to matter at hand," Yuri said. "We would like to ask you, Ms.—BA, if you and deceased had friends or acquaintances in common?"

"Of course we did."

She glanced at the portfolio sheets stacked up high on her drawing table.

"It'd be hard not to," she added. "As I'm sure you know, Det. Chernenko, this can be a very small town."

"Then we'll be more specific," Kris said. "D'you know Lu Ellen Reese?"

"Perhaps," said Yuri, "you are acquainted with her as Sister Night, yes?"

BA was good, Kris thought. Damn good, in fact. But still she couldn't keep from blinking like that.

"I can't say either of those names rings a bell," she said. "Was she...? Oh, I don't know. Some kind of gospel singer or palm reader, or what?"

"Not quite, Ms. Rennie," said Yuri. "But why do you use past tense like that?"

"I believe you did, detective," she said. "Didn't you?"

"I'm sure you're right," Kris said. "And we can see how busy you are, BA. Maybe we can set up a time to talk later, when it's more convenient for you."

She made to get up. Yuri was already on his feet as BA came around her desk to see them out. At the door, Kris paused and turned.

"Just one thing I have to ask you, BA, while I've got the chance," she said. "Wherever did you come up with those colors for Ms. DuBarry's condo?"

"Actually she did, Kris."

BA smiled down at her as if humoring a child.

"It was at a party we both went to, as I recall," she said. "Marti was taken with an interior I'd done for a mutual friend of ours. Mac Fisher."

"Mr. Macdonald Fisher," said Yuri. "He was also friend of yours, Ms. Rennie?"

"He was, yes," she said. "In fact, he picked out the wallpaper and paint for that job himself."

"Really?" Kris said. "But wasn't that an odd choice for the dominant color?"

"Well, we'd gone through about a thousand swatches and enamel samples," BA told her. "And Mac turned 'em all down. Then he noticed the nail polish I happened to have on at the time. It's a favorite of mine, and I suppose it's rather distinctive."

"Midnight red?" Kris asked. "Isn't that what you call that really tacky, lurid shade?"

As both women showed their teeth, Yuri stepped between them.

"Thank you for your time, Ms. Rennie," he said like a peacemaker. "But I cannot help but notice that, in fact, you do not wear nail polish."

In reply, BA kicked off a pump. Then she cocked her leg up and wiggled her toes at him. Under the light from the ceiling panels, the nails flashed crimson in the devil's own tint.

❧

"That Rennie woman," said Kris. "Clinically, I'd make her out to be a flagrant sociopath."

"This was my impression, too," said Yuri. "Legs were not bad, however."

Alone at the end of the day, they sat on the deep leather couch in Hank's office. Kris had sent for takeout from her favorite Cantonese place nearby. Now she sipped herb tea while at her side, Yuri used chopsticks to eat noodles from a carton.

"She had some other noteworthy appendages as well," Kris said. "But as to her personal history, here..."

She propped her feet up on a stack of journals at the edge of the coffee table. Stretching her legs, she sank back in the cushions. As she flipped through a legal pad, Kris took her time going over the notes she'd made.

"Take her late father," she said at length. "Eminent plastic surgeon. Widower. Single parent of an only child.

"Child molester," she added. "Right?"

"According to records," said Yuri. "Which were quite difficult to come by, I must tell you, Kris."

She reached across the table and topped off his coffee cup from the office pot.

"Ah, thank you," he said. "Upshot is that no criminal charges were ever brought against Dr. Rennie. But family of twelve-year-old female patient of his filed civil suit for assault. Then it looks like they settled out of court."

He shrugged but looked pained to Kris.

"Was not only such instance either," he went on. "At least that is what some people with long memories in Department's Sex Crimes unit were willing to tell me. All strictly hush-hush, you know."

"Sure."

Kris shuffled through some faxes of old records she'd wangled from the ME's office.

"According to the coroner's report," she said, "seventeen years ago, Dr. Ewan Rennie died at home. Alone. Of an acute coronary. Ruled accidental.

"Even though," she went on, "the nitrates he'd been taking to treat his heart condition should've been close at hand. The housekeeper found him dead in bed and hit 911."

Yuri referred to his own photocopies.

"According to police report of incident," he said, "Doctor's fifteen-year-old daughter Blair Ann said she could not imagine why her father did not make it to his meds that time. Claimed she had stayed out overnight with boyfriend. But refused to give his name."

He let out a heavy sigh.

"So you think Dr. Rennie was fooling around with his own little girl, Kris?"

"Sure do."

Still scanning papers, she nursed her tea.

"Just as sure as I am that he lived to regret it," she said. "If barely.

"Looks as if BA's uncle and ward mismanaged her trust fund," she went on. "Huh. Lucky he got out of that in one piece. Anyway, she barely had enough cash to cover her Ivy League tuition.

"That comes from some contacts of mine in the admissions office here," she added. "They also found out for me that BA had to take out a student loan for med school."

"Is your department," Yuri said. "They tell you anything else, Kris?"

"Just some gossip about a fling she had with the dean's son at the time."

Yuri raised an eyebrow.

"After one of their encounters back then," she said, "the young man apparently had to be rushed to the OR for some kind of emergency genitourinary surgery."

"Ouch!"

To Kris, Yuri looked impressed in spite of himself.

"So our BA is quite dangerous woman in many ways, yes?"

"Chick's got kinks," Kris affirmed. "Big-time."

She picked up a second ME's report.

"Then there's this older guy she married after she dropped out of med school," she said. "Also with a heart condition. Name of...Khachaturian?"

"Kocharian," said Yuri. "Barney Kocharian."

He looked rueful at the name.

"Old Barney was local high roller," he said. "Vegas gambler. Also speculator for high stakes in various enterprises, legitimate or otherwise. Some say he even did some gunrunning to Central America, before..."

"He died in the saddle, too," Kris said. "As it were?"

"Just so."

Yuri shook his head over his papers.

"Too bad for BA," he said. "Because it would appear also that Mr. Kocharian's debts outweighed his assets at time of his demise, some six years ago."

"Must've been a burden on the poor thing," said Kris, "having to fall back on interior decorating like that."

She took a sip of tea.

"No wonder she was ready and willing to link up with the likes of Lu Ellen Reese at that point," she mused. "Even if it meant working nights."

"No wonder, yes."

Yuri finished off his meal from the box and used his napkin.

"Is hardly necessary to say it, Kris," he added. "But we cannot prove even little bit of what is quite obvious to us here."

"Hell, no."

Sitting up, she knit her fingers tight behind her neck and softly groaned.

"No more than we can link 'Nurse Nell' to my—to the Vampire," she said. "But I know that's the way it is, Yuri. I just *know* it."

He was fastidious as he put a hand on her tensed shoulder.

"Me, too," he said. "May I?"

"Please," she murmured. "A little lower. Between the shoulder blades, if you would?"

"Is my pleasure," he said. "I believe that at this point, Kris, we both can put finger on BA's problem."

He paused as she moaned.

"Is good, yes?"

"Whoa," she said. "And by that I mean, don't stop."

"For sure," he said. "As I was saying, Kris, I believe we see eye-to-eye in BA's case, yes?"

Regretfully she checked her watch. She couldn't help thinking about all the plans she'd made for the next day. At last Kris sat up with a sigh.

"It's the same problem everybody has with murder," she agreed. "Once you get away with it, you'll always be tempted to try it again."

CHAPTER SEVENTEEN

Early the next morning, Kris sat at the desk in Hank's office and sorted through a growing stack of notes and files. Through her concentration, she heard footsteps padding closer. She looked up and gave her stand-in assistant a cheery greeting.

"G'morning to you, too, Kris."

Poised with a legal pad in one hand and a thick sheaf of callback slips in the other, Terri Frank took a deep breath.

"The movers called from Washington—DC?" she said. "They apologized about the delay and promised to come pick up the stuff at your apartment up there on Friday afternoon. If that's okay by you?"

Kris smiled and said sure.

"Okay. Also from our nation's capital," Terri pressed on, "Dr. Laszlo keeps calling for you. He says it's personal?"

"I'll take those, T."

Kris wadded the fistful of message slips into a ball and dunked them in the wastebasket by the desk.

"Next."

"Dr. Mackenzie's assistant just called from the Medical Examiner's office," said Teri. "She left word that they're pushing the DNA through on the individual bloodstains you queried 'em about and that they ought to be ready in another twenty-four hours."

Biting her lip, Terri looked over her pad at Kris.

"She said you'd know what she meant by that."

"I do," said Kris. "Did the program people at Sun 99 get back to us?"

"Sure did."

Teri was shaking her head as she held up the slip.

"That Ms. Cavanaugh's willing to have you back on her show tonight," she said. "*If* you'd call her in a prescription for some more Xanax."

"Do it, T.," said Kris. "And tell 'er I recommend doubling up on the dose right before air time."

"Will do, Kris. Oh," Teri said. "I almost forgot."

Backing gracefully out the door, she pointed to the phone tab flashing on the desk.

"That's that Mancusi & Rennie place you wanted me to get for you first thing," she said. "Ms. Rennie's secretary? She's holding."

"Way to go, T.!" Kris called after her. "Fine job, all around."

She waved her off and picked up the phone.

"Hi," she said on the line. "It's Dr. Van Zant, Kris Van Zant. I wondered if Ms. Rennie could spare me a moment."

Most of a minute went by, and then a husky voice spoke in her ear.

"Hi, Kris," said BA. "Think of some more questions for me, dearie?"

"BA, well, hel*lo*," Kris said. "Fact is, I need your professional help. I'm right in the middle of moving back here. So, I'm going to be needing some decorating done."

"I see," she said. "Well, while of course we're always happy to get the business here at M&R..."

Kris took BA's tone to imply that she'd never be able to afford her in a million years.

"Hey, I know how busy you are," Kris said as brightly as before. "But it turns out, too, we've got just a ton of mutual friends and acquaintances hereabouts.

"So," she added fast, "I thought maybe we could get together informally, just us two, and talk."

"You did?"

Kris read BA's cool little laugh to mean that while she didn't believe a word she was saying, she might just be willing to play along with her for a while.

"Lunch?"

"Oh, well," said BA. "By the strangest quirk of fate, it looks like I'm free today."

Kris said great. They set the time and place. Then she put on her perkiest Junior League of Greater Atlanta lilt to sign off.

"My treat now, hear?"

❧

BA had proposed that they meet at Ceres' Pantry. Kris found the restaurant on West Marietta Street near the King Plow Arts Center. From outside, it seemed to her to consist mainly of sloping planes of beveled green glass.

The dining room was close to the size of a warehouse. In every corner Kris passed was a ceramic tub sprouting multicolored gourds and fig trees. She found her quarry at last at a table for two in quiet, sunny alcove.

"*There* you are," she called. "Hi, BA."

"Hullo there, Kris."

Languidly she returned Kris's wave with two fingers and motioned for her to take the chair across from her. She had on a tailored cream suit over an open-collared green silk blouse and seemed prepared to be amused. The drink she was sipping looked like a Bloody Mary, but Kris was willing to bet it was tomato juice straight up.

"Where's that hunky Russky boyfriend of yours today?"

"Oh, Yuri's out chasing bad guys," Kris told her. "So I thought we could have us a nice, cozy li'l chat."

Kris sat down and shook out her napkin.

"Thanks again for finding time for me," she said. "Busy as you must be."

"As in, who's minding the shop?"

BA held on to her smile.

"As I'm sure you noticed, Kris, Dante's perfectly up to it."

"Must be good to have a talented partner like that, huh?"

"You mean it's lucky I hooked up with a trendy little Yankee hustler like that when I did," said BA. "Especially since the clientele I depend on consists with few exceptions of a bunch of blue-rinsed Buckhead ladies who've always dreamed of living in Tara."

She turned to the floppy-haired young man in black pants and a white shirt who had just stepped up to the table.

"Another one of these, Todd," she said. "How 'bout it?"

"Right away, Ms. Rennie."

Loose-limbed, the waiter turned to Kris.

"And what can I get for the young lady to drink?"

"I think I'll go ahead and order," Kris said. "How about a big ol' sirloin burger, medium rare, with ladled cheese on it and some onion rings and...?"

As Todd recoiled, gaping, she glanced at the menu and saw that the bill of fare was militantly vegetarian.

"No offense," she muttered. "I come from a long line of carnivores. How about the Portobello mushroom sandwich plate then, with some Worcestershire sauce?"

"I'll try to rustle you up some," the waiter said gamely. "Caesar salad as usual for you, Ms. Rennie? Very good."

"Oh, and hot tea for me," Kris called after him. "By any chance, d'you have Guangzhou Ginseng?"

"Doesn't everybody?" Todd said in motion. "Be right back with your drinks, ladies."

"So, BA, I hear your alma mater Princeton has a wonderful art history program," Kris led off on inspiration. "That must've been a great foundation for what you're doing now. I mean, what with all the restoration and design concepts and—"

"I was a psych major, Kris."

"And you finished summa, I hear."

Kris raised her water glass to her.

"Congrats," she said. "I know that doesn't come easy at Old Nassau."

"Thanks, dearie," said BA. "But then, I didn't whip through a master's program in abnormal psychology while I was still in my teens like some eager-beaver little prodigies I've heard about."

Beginning to enjoy herself, Kris said thanks in turn.

"We have med school in common, too," she added. "Right, Nurse Nell?"

"Nurse—?"

Not blinking this time, BA met Kris's eye and cupped a hand to her ear.

"I beg your pardon," she said. "Remember, I didn't come near to finishing medical school."

"But you went far enough in it to get a good handle on dog-lab physiology," Kris said. "And I bet you got to scrub in on some cases in the OR, too."

Kris kept her tone light and conversational.

"So naturally you learned your way around basic IV placement," she went on. "You probably got to do some cutdowns, too. And I'm sure you mastered fluid therapy, along with transfusion-reinfusion technique. Finally, you must've absorbed the principles of autologous blood and plasma replacement from what you'd seen in surgery and from dealing with shock patients in the ER."

Kris laughed softly, still cheerily eye-to-eye with BA.

"Just like riding a bike, isn't it?" she said. "Once you've picked it up it'll always come back to you, regardless of the setting.

"Even," she put in, "when it's for purely recreational purposes."

"Kris...?"

BA leaned across the table with a show of concern.

"I suspect I'm going to profoundly regret even thinking of asking you this," she said. "Here goes, anyway. Just what in God's name are you talking about, dearie? What *is* your point?"

"Just that we have a number of points in common," Kris replied. "And screw academics. Before either of us ever cracked a psych text, we knew we had a knack for spotting other people's weak points. And for turning 'em to our advantage.

"Works the same with all-but-suppressed obsessions and fetishes, no matter what their origin might be," she went on. "Even if they happen to be our own kinks as well, we both know how to punch the buttons and play 'em like a jukebox."

Kris shrugged.

"And that's just what Sister Night saw in you," she said. "Right?"

"Here we are, ladies."

Coming back in the middle of a display of alarm and confusion on BA's part, Todd set their drinks down from a tray.

"And I promise those entrees'll be right along now," he added. "All righty?"

"Uhm, yes," BA mumbled. "Thanks."

Kris envied the face of innocence she'd put on but didn't come close to trusting it.

"Dr. Van Zant...Kris," BA said. "I'm forced to ask this. Are you on some kind of medication? Strong medication, perhaps?"

"I'm fine, thanks."

Kris fought down the urge to reach across the table like a therapist and give her big smooth hand a pat.

"It's all right, BA," she said. "You don't have to react at all. That's not what I'm here for today. Just listen."

"Just—?"

BA took a sturdy pull on her drink. Then she shook her head hard. Beams from the skylight at her back made her hair shine like brass with a high buff on it.

"But—? Kris," she said. "Maybe I'm having a slow day. But I could've sworn you just implied that I'm a participant in some kind of...?"

"The most exotic, riskiest, high-rent edge of the local underground S&M scene."

Feeling the chill of the air-conditioning cut through her cotton blouse, Kris took a swig of steaming herb tea.

"Uh-huh," she added. "That's what I meant."

"S&...M?"

BA shook her head again and laughed.

"Oh, sure. I admit it, dearie," she said. "I always did have a thing for Scandinavian & Modern."

As BA's laughter got higher, Kris saw heads turning their way from tables nearby.

"Just listen," Kris said again. "I know what you've done.

I've got a fix on your specialty. Of course, I don't expect you to admit any of that to me.

"Nor do I claim I can prove anything," she added. "Yet."

"Oh?" said BA. "That's such a relief."

"Shut up."

Kris kept her voice down and held her gaze.

"This is what I've come to tell you, BA," she said. "If you think you can control the Vampire, you're wrong. Dead wrong. You hear me?"

BA narrowed her eyes and scowled at her, and then she spoke up louder.

"There's one thing I did pick up in med school," she said. "I saw how the ones who go into psychiatry are either seriously screwed-up themselves or else they're sheer, unmitigated control freaks."

"I don't mean to make your soufflé fall," Kris murmured. "But that's hardly a novel observation."

"Okay...okay."

BA shut her eyes and clenched her jaw, and then she let her next words carry.

"I know your folks got chopped up by a psycho when you were little," she said, just under a shout. "'S got to leave scars. I know.

"So *now*," she bellowed, "since you couldn't make the height requirement for the Gestapo, you've found your niche as the kind of shrink who thinks she's a cop and goes around rousting people for no good reason."

"Shut up," Kris repeated. "You're good. Even I can't say for sure what your game is now, okay?

"But trust me on this, BA," she said in an even lower tone. "With the Vampire, you're out of your league. He's not just playing. He's for real. So back off."

BA opened her eyes wide and sat back, and then she finished her drink in a gulp.

"Kris, Kris, Kris," she said. "Why, you li'l ol' silver-tongued devil, you. I declare, you've gone and twisted my arm.

"I'll make a clean breast of it," she said, still gaining volume.

"I freely confess it all, yes, ma'am. When the sun goes down, I pull on my boots and pick up my whip and turn into a great big ol' bloodthirsty dominatrix. Yes!"

She held up her hands and squared her thumbs to make a frame like a viewfinder, and then she went on in a voice Kris judged they could hear in the kitchen.

"What's more, I believe I have an opening for *you*, too," BA yelled across the table. "The way you get off on screwing with other people's heads, you'd surely be a resounding li'l success in 'the scene.'

"If only," she added at the same pitch, "you'd work a little more black leather into your wardrobe, say, and invest in some platform soles."

"Kind of you to say so, BA."

Kris smiled up at the white-faced server who'd just arrived with their plates. Taking the steak sauce from him, she sprinkled it on her grilled mushrooms. Then with an even brighter smile, she shook her head at BA.

"No, thanks, though," she told her. "I could never work with amateurs."

❧

Kerry Jean Cavanaugh rolled her eyes at Kris as she began to lead into the break.

"Well, well, well," she said on the air. "All right now, sports fans."

Together, they'd just dealt with the sixth caller of the night. He'd identified himself as a high priest and a practicing adept of the One True Church of Satan. The first five had merely claimed to be the Atlanta Vampire.

"Thank you for your thoughts, padre," said Kerry Jean. "Now what d'you say we take a li'l breather, here?"

"If I may, Kerry Jean," Kris spoke up into the mike in front of her, "I'd like to say a little something to your listeners."

Gripping a half-eaten Mars bar with both hands, the host looked unsteady.

"Well, Kris," she said, "I'm not sure it'd be a good idea to single out—"

"Beg pardon," Kris broke in. "I meant I'd like to say something to the audience in general. Okay?"

Kerry Jean swallowed tightly and said sure.

"Okay. Here goes," said Kris. "Listen up, people. Give me a break and quit trying to convince me you're the Vampire. By now it ought to plain to see that I know what I'm looking for. All right?"

She pushed ahead before Kerry Jean could get back in control of the broadcast.

"And now for the one I do want to talk to," she said, "I'm sure you can hear me. I know you want to talk. And believe me, I want to listen.

"So how about it?" she went on. "Here I am. Let's do it. Here. Now. Talk. I'm here for you."

At her side, Kerry Jean took a long breath and braced her shoulders. But the phone lines had all gone quiet. As the silence held, she opened her mouth to speak. Then all at once an urgent voice crackled in Kris's headset.

Kerry Jean let go a scream that rattled the wall tiles.

"I—beg your pardon," she said raggedly. "Sorry. That was Bob, my producer. He just jumped in to tell me we have a very special caller on the line now.

"So," she said, recovering, "I'd like to give a great big *Hot 'Lanta Nights* welcome to—"

"*No*!"

As everyone in the control room grabbed their ears, Yuri and Det. Sims included, Kris made an apologetic face.

"No," she said again, more softly. "Not on the air. Please, don't."

"K-K-Kristin?"

The voice in her earphones bore an accent of cradle Hungarian and adoptive Tidewater Virginia under an Ivy League finish, along with the stammer that Kris had a tendency to make worse.

"Doctor," the caller went on. "I am c-c-compelled to ask if you have you taken c-c-com-com—total leave of your senses?"

"Stephen," Kris said through her teeth. "This is not the time or the place."

"That's right, folks," Kerry Jean announced. "Joining us tonight from Washington, DC, is the world-renowned psychiatrist and analyst to serial killers, Dr. Stephen Laszlo!"

"Butt out, Stephen," Kris hissed on the line. "You're not wanted here."

"Oh, ho, ho," trilled Kerry Jean. "Quite the contrary."

Shaking her head at Kris, she reached aside and gave her a merry poke in the ribs.

"I can't tell you how long we've been trying to get Dr. Laszlo to grace us with his comments," Kerry Jean crowed. "And, doctor, since you've found it in your heart to call in to our humble show tonight, I can't begin to tell you how pleased and honored—"

"Yes, yes, yes," he broke in on her. "You're quite welcome, Ms. C-C-Cavanaugh, I'm sure. But if you please, I prefer to speak to Dr. Van Zant personally so that I c-c-can attempt to reason with her."

"Stephen," Kris said over the grinding of her teeth. "Go away."

"Very well, doctor," he said. "If you don't choose to be civil with me, then I would like to speak directly to the unsuspecting people of your city."

"Treat our airwaves like your own, doctor," Kerry Jean said. "Why don't you start by telling us what you meant by 'unsuspecting'?"

"Very well."

Stephen cleared his throat and dropped into the lecture tone Kris had often heard him use with federal agents, judges and others whose powers of comprehension he found dubious.

"To attempt to initiate a dialogue with a violently disturbed individual outside a c-c-controlled institutional setting is folly," he said. "Moreover, dealing with such 'free-range psychopaths' in this way poses a significant risk for all parties concerned. This is true in general for all practitioners.

"And I feel it is my duty to inform you people of Atlanta," he went on, steely to Kris's ear, "I believe this to be uniquely true in Dr. Van Zant's c-c-case."

"So I take it, doctor," Kerry Jean said, "you know our Kris here pretty well."

"I do," he said. "When we first met, I c-c-confess, I took her to be merely an exceptionally gifted and preternaturally energetic psychiatrist in the making."

Kris made a face at his chuckle, which was as rich and deep as it was dry.

"Unbounded personal ego and infinite professional ambition in a size-two dress, if you will," he added. "Then as our acquaintance grew, I came to realize just how gravely I had underestimated K-K-Kris—Dr. Van Zant."

Kerry Jean held out a warning finger as Kris balled her fists up and seethed.

"Please, Dr. Laszlo, just what're you saying?" she asked. "Is it the way she talks to psychos—?"

"What I'm saying, my dear Ms. C-C-Cavanaugh, is that any idiot who deigns to may talk to monsters!" he thundered. "But when *that* young woman c-c-calls them up, by God, they c-c-come running."

"You're missing the point, Stephen!" Kris yelled back on the air. "As usual. I'm not encouraging my—the Vampire. No, not all. I'm just here for him to talk to."

"You're missing your own point, K-K-Kristin, whatever your intentions," he said, much more softly. "For the love of C-C-Christ, my dear, there's no denying you have it in you to give aid and c-c-comfort to the devil himself."

"What the hell is *that* supposed to—?"

"Hey, hey, guys," said Kerry Jean. "I really and truly hate to step into a lovers' spat like this. But there's a personal call holding for you, Kris, and it sounds important."

Kris looked around at Yuri, who gave her a wink deadpan

from behind the glass partition, and then she picked up the phone by the terminal screen and said hello.

"Say, Kris," said another man's voice she found way too familiar. "How's it goin'?"

"Hi, Matt," she said with her hand around the mouthpiece. "Tuned in to the show, huh?"

"We all are, Kris," he said. "From the mayor on down."

"So am I fired?"

"Shut it down, Kris," he said. "Take the rest the night off."

"But—"

"Come see me in the office and I'll explain it all to you, first thing in the morning," he promised. "Way I see it, you've earned that much already."

"Okay," she said at last. "Thanks, Matt."

She hung up. After one more look at the faces around her, Kris started to get up to go. But then she grabbed the microphone back before anyone could cut her off.

"So goodnight, Atlanta," she said. "But as for *you*, just remember..."

She took a moment while frantic hand signals broke out over her head, and then she used her last bit of airtime.

"I'm still here for you," she said. "Whenever you want to talk, all you have to do is call me up."

CHAPTER EIGHTEEN

Back at Hank's desk early the next morning, Kris got her working papers ready to store for the time being.

"I just confirmed your flight to Washington with Delta, Kris," Terri Frank said at her side. "You're booked one-way on the 10:25 from Hartsfield, to arrive at National at 12:09."

"Perfect," Kris said. "Thanks, T."

She looked up at the young woman who had just appeared without a sound. Biting her lip, Terri seemed rueful as she met her eye. Then Kris caught the light blinking on her phone.

"Line one," she said. "'S that for me?"

"It's the Medical Examiner's office," said Terri. "Dr. Mackenzie just rang for you himself."

She seemed set for retreat, but Kris waved for her to stay as she punched the button and picked up the phone.

"Well, g'morning, Uncle Rob!"

"G'morning to you, Krissy," the ME grumbled back at her. "And don't you 'Uncle Rob' me now."

Kris held the phone away from her ear as his words carried like gunshots.

"Tell me what you knew about this DNA testing you were so all-fired interested in," he demanded. "And then I want to know just when you knew it."

"Yes, sir," said Kris. "That's easy."

She slipped a wink at Terri, who looked even more concerned on her behalf.

"I didn't know for sure what would turn up in the blood that message was written in, see, at the last crime scene," she said on the line. "Rather, the writing itself made me think somebody was trying to prove something.

"Very neat and precise it was, too," she said. "Better than you could do with a gloved finger, I'd say. No, someone must've used a brush to get those letters that sharp. I'm thinking, say, like an artist's brush or some kind of drafting instrument?"

"Some kind," the pathologist grunted. "Please proceed, child."

"But that didn't jibe with the Vampire's personality," Kris said. "I mean, after all, what's *he* got to prove? No, this looked to me like an extraneous touch. I figured it was meant not so much to throw us off the track as to point us a certain way.

"So naturally," she went on, "it occurred to me that it wouldn't necessarily be Martine DuBarry's blood on the wall. Or not just hers, anyway. How'm I doing so far?"

"Oh, the blood on the wall matched up serologically with the blood samples we got out of the victim's spleen and bone marrow, all right," Rob told her. "Which was just about all she had left."

The ME's voice had taken on a wondering tone, and now it began to trail off.

"Some of it made a match, anyway," he muttered. "Then, when you go on to the DNA we extracted..."

"But what about the rest of the message, Uncle Rob?" Kris prompted. "Now was it just me, or did those stains vary in shade from word to—?"

"Dammit, gal! We both know there's no way in hell you could tell the difference in 'em just by looking," Rob burst out. "So how'd you *do* that?"

"Wild hunch?"

Kris held the phone another inch or so from her ear as the ME set in to shout questions at her again.

"Okay," she said. "The 'me' in 'You'll never catch me' was Marti's blood, I'd say. But I'm betting the 'you'll' was in the blood of victim number one, Wade Hazlitt. And the 'never' came out of Halley Cantrell, number two. And the 'catch'—"

"Matched po' ol' Mac Fisher's DNA, God rest 'im," Rob broke in. "But now *how*...?"

"Four victims," said Kris. "Four words."

Rob let his breath out like a truck tire going down.

"I swear to God, Kris," he said. "If you'd been born three or four hundred years back, gal, they'd've burned your ass at the stake for sure."

"Well, hooray for progress."

Then while the senior physician was still making consternated noises in her ear, Kris decided to press him for one more piece of info.

"The blood from the first three victims was still in pretty good shape, too, wasn't it?" she asked. "Not lysed or clotted or anything like that?"

"Red cells looked good microscopically," said Rob. "Samples they came from must've been stored frozen, just like in a blood bank. So yep, Krissy, your Vampire knows what he's doing."

"Somebody does," Kris said just over her breath. "Well, thank you so much for confiding in me, Uncle Rob. Sorry I've got to run. G'bye now. You take care, hear?"

On her feet as soon as she hung up, Kris gathered in all her files and handed them off.

"Here go, T.," she said. "I'd be really grateful if you'd keep an eye on these for me."

"Sure, Kris, no problem."

Balancing the stack of papers under her chin, Terri followed her into the hall.

"I'll get your own filing cabinets all set up," she promised staunchly. "Your new office is just about ready for you to move into, you know, right down the hall from here."

"Sure," Kris muttered. "Soon as they clear all the brooms out of it."

Headed for the stairs with her flight bag over her shoulder and her purse in hand, she checked her watch.

"I meant in the short term, T.," she called back. "'Cause I expect to be back here on the job in a really, really short while."

Kris had the cab stop off at City Hall East on her way to the airport. She caught Matt in his office there. After greetings, he shut the door behind them in the half-windowed wall and offered her the chair in front of his desk. Facing her on the blotter was the early edition of the *Constitution*.

"Guess you've seen the paper already," he said. "Yeah, I thought so."

Kris mugged over the headline, *Police Take Dangerous Tack with "Vampire," Says Expert*. Side-by-side photos of her and Dr. Laszlo appeared above the fold. Not saying a word, she considered Stephen's likeness.

Parted high on the side, his hair was dark and bushy with flecks of silver in it. A full black beard took the edge off a face that was lean, aquiline, and saturnine. All in all, Kris reflected, he looked like the heir to the wisdom and expertise of a hundred years of Middle European shrinks. In her own picture, a recent one, she could pass for fifteen.

"Looks like right after you went off the air last night, one of our local reporters started working the phones," Matt said. "I don't expect it was too hard to get the good Dr. Laszlo to say a few more words about you on the record."

Matt put his reading glasses on and picked up the paper.

"The article quotes him as to how he always figured you were out to get hold of—let's see now, here it is—'your own Peter Kurten,'" Matt read. "I confess, Kris, I didn't get that reference right off."

"Before your time, Matt." she said with a smile. "It goes back a century or so, from Germany. Laszlo and I collaborated on a historical review of the case."

Matt lowered his paper and cocked an eyebrow at her.

"It's a landmark in forensic psychiatry," Kris said. "Peter Kurten, aka the Dusseldorf Vampire. He slashed and stabbed his way through a bunch of victims for nearly forty years before he got caught. He finally died by the guillotine in the 1930s.

"But before he got the chopper himself, he agreed to talk to the police shrink, a Dr. Karl Berg," she went on. "Of course, the documentation that followed made Prof. Berg famous."

Matt nodded and tossed the newspaper on the blotter, face down.

"Look here, Kris," he said. "It's not just a question of your ambition. Lord knows, a blind man could see that on you.

"But Dr. Laszlo," he added, "he sounds like he means it when he goes and calls what you been trying to do here a threat to public safety."

"He's right."

Kris realized she was still smiling.

"Attempting to make direct contact with the Vampire would be foolhardy as hell," she agreed. "That is, for anybody but me."

"Kris..."

With one hand, Matt pressed down steadily on the top of his scalp.

"Maybe there's such a thing as being too damn sure of yourself for your own good," he said. "And for everybody else's, too, for that matter.

"But still and all now," he began, "you know if it was up to me..."

"I know, Matt," she said. "But it's not just about me, is it?"

A snarl had edged through Kris's smile, and she didn't try to cover it.

"BA," she spat out. "She knows somebody, doesn't she?"

"Fact is, she knows a whole gang of somebodies," said Matt. "And one of 'em happens to be president of the city council at the moment."

He dropped his voice and glanced over Kris's head before he went on.

"Word I get from downtown is, Ms. Rennie went and told 'im how you took it upon yourself to go and roust her on your own initiative," he said. "Seems she didn't appreciate being accosted in public by, and I'm quoting here, Kris, 'some sadistic, sawed-off little Nazi-storm-trooper-wannabe bitch—'"

"*Hate* it when people allude to my height."

"'—who doesn't even have a badge to her name,'" Matt

finished. "Look, Kris, I'll be the first to say how much you've done for this investigation already."

He held up a finger before she could speak.

"But I'd be telling a lie," he added, "if I told you I can't see how you gettin' to be a liability to the case, too."

Leaving her bags by her chair, she stood up and leaned over the desk.

"It's okay, Uncle Matt," she told him. "As folks say back in Tuscaloosa, you don't have to go and spray-paint it up on the water tower for me to get the picture."

Looking relieved, Matt got to his feet with her as she turned up one of her business cards like a conjurer and palmed it to him.

"I just had 'em printed up," she said. "It's for my new office at University Hospital, see, with fax numbers and e-mail addresses and everything. And up at the top there in ink, that's the number for my cell phone. It's good for 24/7."

Matt said thanks. With obvious care, he put the card in his wallet. Meanwhile, Kris cupped her hands around the chipped old paving stone he used for a paperweight.

"This goes back to your very first homicide coup, way back when," she said. "Now doesn't it, Uncle Matt?"

He nodded as she gingerly hefted the chunk of pavement.

"When I was growing up," she said, "I remember how you told me it was an unsolved murder down in the Fairlie-Poplar district, on a side street.

"And you were the only one to notice how this one stone was out of place," she went on. "Then when you pried it up and flipped it over, it turned out to have the victim's blood on it where the murderer thought he'd hidden it. That's how you cracked the case, right?"

Matt nodded again, and Kris smiled at him for all she was worth.

"Good," she said. "'Cause that's just the association I want, here."

All at once she took an overhand grip on the stone and spun on her heel to face the door.

"Kris!" Matt yelled. "Don't—"

He dodged around the desk with an arm stretched out toward her, but she was too fast for him. With all her weight behind it, Kris heaved the paving stone into the glass wall. It starred wide on contact and cracked down the center.

Then the glass burst like a grenade with a thousand shards flying out, raining down on the floor outside.

"Kris," Matt sighed. "Aw, *hell*."

She waited for the crash to fade before she spoke again.

"That's what's going to happen to *this* case," she said at last. "Sooner or later, the phone's going to ring. And you know who's going to be on the other end."

Matt shook his head over the wreckage as she picked up her bags and stepped to the door.

"Kris..."

"It's not going to be just another lamer who wants to confess," she went on. "It won't be another tip that doesn't pan out. Uh-uhn."

A small army of homicide detectives stared in at them from the squadroom, but Kris ignored them as Matt opened the door by the smashed pane and held it for her.

"He's going to call," she said. "The one personality in ten million who could do what he did and still walk around on two legs in broad daylight, that's who it'll be.

"And I'm the only one who can talk to him," she added on the threshold. "At that point, I'll be the only one who put it all together."

"Kris," Matt groaned, still shaking his head. "For the love of God, girl."

Stepping nimbly over the broken glass outside, she smiled back at him over her shoulder.

"The city can bill me for this," she said. "Now y'all know how to reach me."

CHAPTER NINETEEN

Kris's flight set down right on time at Ronald Reagan Washington National Airport. Bags in hand, she marched up the street to the Metro station and took a Yellow Line train over the Potomac. At L'Enfant Plaza, she switched to Blue. That took her under Southwest DC and straight on to her stop on Capitol Hill.

Sticky heat boiled off the river flats and shimmered from the tide pools inland of Chesapeake Bay, but Kris ignored it. Unfazed by the noonday sun, she strode three blocks uphill to her apartment. She didn't stop at the front door, though.

Instead, she took the back steps down to the parking level. Her reserved space there tacked a hundred and fifty dollars onto her rent each month, but to Kris it was worth it. Bending down, she brushed a speck of dust off the grille of her white Saab 9-3 SE convertible. She'd named the car Flicka but would admit it to few.

Outside, she took a left onto South Capitol Street. Threading outbound traffic to the Anacostia bluffs, she crossed the river by the Frederick Douglass Bridge. Then she swung off the parkway onto Martin Luther King Jr. Avenue and kept going south.

Soon she came in sight of the rolling green campus of Saint Elizabeths Hospital, which took up three hundred acres of Southeast DC. A federal facility now, the place had played host over the past century and a half to such to such notable American head cases as Ezra Pound and John Hinckley, Jr. Kris flashed her ID at the front gate.

She pulled around the Gothic Revival main building to the redbrick forensic wing and parked in the staff deck out back. To placate Security, she fished her monogrammed white lab coat out of the backseat and shrugged it on. Then she took the stairs up to the fellow's office she'd used for the past year.

Predictably, the secretary was still out to lunch. Kris let herself in and went straight to her desk. She stacked reprints into cartons to take with her, signed off the last of her case notes, and dictated a summary memo for the service. Finally, she slipped her keys and laminates into an envelope on Saint E stationery to drop off at the unit desk downstairs.

Kris knew she was leaving one loose end. Still she hoped for a clean getaway. Then she recognized the footsteps bearing down on her from the corridor. With a long breath, she turned around.

"K-K-Kristin," said Stephen Laszlo from the door. "You realize why I said what I did last night, for everyone to hear."

He held out his hands to her, and Kris nodded as she took them.

"You were afraid for me," she said. "Because as usual, you thought I was biting off more than I could chew."

He winced primly at the phrase.

"Not just that, I must c-c-confess."

"I know, Stephen," she said. "You wanted me to come back here, to you."

She shook her head and let go of his hands.

"But in spite of appearances," she added, "it didn't work."

"K-K-Kristin..."

Scowling into his beard, he folded his arms tight against his chest.

"Oh, for God's sake," he muttered. "This is ridiculous, the two of us still going on like this."

Kris raised her chin and levelly met his eyes, which were as sharp as hers and nearly as dark on their way past blue.

"Glad to hear it," she said. "Because I think so, too."

Although his rep was larger than life, Laszlo stood just three or four inches taller than Kris. Much married and as often divorced, he always put her in mind of a lifelong bachelor. Fussy and solitary by nature, he was clearly in need of a kindred soul.

"I worry about you," he said. "K-K-Kristin, you know I've become c-c-convinced over the span of our, ah, our relationship that your gifts are truly unique.

"However," he added quickly, "I'm just as sure that in time these extraordinary talents of yours will present a very real danger to you if you don't seek out their sources."

"Stephen, I know you think I'm a prime candidate for analysis," Kris said. "But I still don't believe in it."

"K-K-K—"

He bit it off and grumbled under his breath before he got his voice back.

"I believe that such a measure is imperative for your continued functioning, let alone success, in both a personal and professional sphere," he got out in one breath. "In the vernacular, my love, you're a time bomb."

"Maybe," she said. "But I'll never go off. That's what *I* believe.

"Besides," she went on before he could, "I'm just no good at introspection. To me it's like trying to bite your own teeth."

"K-K-Kristin," he persisted, "I fail to see how in light of your background you still manage to be so single-minded, so zealous, so imaginatively accomplished, so wholly engaged, so—so damnably happy, even, in your pursuit of the most terrifyingly maddened and awesomely perverted reaches of human behavior.

"In the name of C-C-Christ, woman," he finished, "you remain a mystery to me."

Kris shrugged and went back to her boxes.

"I'd better be going, Stephen," she said. "It's been fun."

"I've never had any taste for 'fun' in my entire life, and we both know it."

Close at her back, he put a hand on her arm.

"K-K-Kristin, I—by now you must know this as well," he said. "I love you."

She patted his hand and sighed.

"Yes," she said. "But I don't love you, Stephen."

"Is this, my love, such an insurmountable obstacle to our being together?"

"Well, yes."

She thought in passing of Uncle Hank, who had been a couple of years ahead of Stephen at Harvard College.

"You know," she added, "I find it hard enough to put up with people I do love."

"There—there, you see, you're not without insight."

Facing her again in front of the desk, her suitor sounded desperate.

"Surely it must strike even you as peculiar, K-K-Kristin," he said, "that you reserve your deepest sympathies for those who have committed unimaginable acts of violence and c-c-crimes of an unspeakable nature."

"Goes with the territory, Stephen."

"K-K-Kristin," he said, "I admit that at the beginning of our association, I imagined that you were set on becoming the world's foremost forensic psychiatrist merely out of some entrenched sense of loss or even for revenge.

"The haunted hunting the hunters," he added, "if you will."

She smiled but kept on stacking the rest of her papers.

"But then," Stephen said, "I saw at last where your true ambitions lay. Even if you will not admit it to yourself, my love, nothing is plainer to me."

Putting his hands out to her again, he shut his eyes.

"At heart," he said, "I see you as a passionately c-c-caring woman who is driven to provide succor and nurture to all the tortured children and misfits and misbegotten heirs of a k-k-killing millennium."

"That's sweet," she said. "But..."

As fast and as sure of herself as ever, Kris gave him a hug and kissed his cheek just before she hefted her boxes and slipped out of the room.

"You're like Freud, Stephen," she called back. "You were always too much the poet."

Sounding wounded and proud, his bellow rang after her down the hallway.

"And you, K-K-Kristin Van Zant, were always too much the escape artist!"

❧

Back at her place on Capitol Hill, Kris dealt with the movers. Then she lingered at the end of the day with Jezreel Thornton, her roommate for the past year. They sipped iced tea her old friend had brewed Charleston-style, with spearmint and thyme.

"Well now, doctor," said Jez, "I assume you went and got shed of Laszlo the Great today."

"'S what I was aiming at, counselor."

"Uh-huh."

Padding around the flat in her stockings and pinstripes, Jez grinned at Kris like one canny down-home girl to another.

"So who else you seeing all of a sudden?" she asked. "C'mon now, Kris, you know you can trust ol' Jezreel to keep yo' secrets."

Kris rolled her eyes and drew on her tea.

"Whoa, girlfriend," she said. "Is it that obvious?"

"Is to me, sister."

"Okay," Kris relented. "Fact is, Jez, we've been working together lately. His name's Yuri Chernenko."

"Sounds about as Russian to me as you'n get."

"He is," Kris said. "I mean, of course, he grew up in the USSR. But to me, he, well..."

To her horror Kris felt a blush coming on.

"I swear, Jez," she confided, "if you met Yuri, you'd think he'd just stepped out of some kind of epic poem by Pushkin. I mean, I guess there's something about him that speaks to me of an earlier time.

"Of a way of being that's more straightforward and less screwed-up than we are today," she added. "And I really admire that. Uhm, 's that makes any sense to you?"

"Knowing you, it does, uh-huh."

Kris sensed some of Jez's courtroom manner coming back.

"And might one inquire, my dear Van Zant," she posed, "just what does this strapping Cossack lad of yours do? For a living, that is."

"He's a cop," Kris said. "A homicide investigator with Atlanta PD."

Jez blew her cheeks out and smiled at her.

"Oh, well now," she said. "That's a relief."

"What d'you mean, Jez?"

"Never mind," she said. "So have y'all done anything together, Kris?

"I mean," she went on hopefully, "besides exchanging smoldering glances and engaging in no doubt zesty banter over dead bodies and blood splatters and such as that at crime scenes?"

"We went to church," Kris said. "His church. It was so..."

Wondering, Kris shook her head at the memory.

"Funny thing," she added. "Yuri was telling me how on his father's side they'd all been good Party members. But his mom's folks tended to be, as he put it, 'old-fashioned God-believers.' And so I—*what*, Jez?"

"Kris, *you*—in church?"

Freckles ballooning on her bony cheeks, Jez doubled over laughing.

"You always struck me as such a li'l ol' dyed-in-the-wool skeptic of a lapsed Episcopalian," she chortled. "I mean, if there even *is* such a thing!"

Kris made a face back at her. Finishing her tea, she checked her watch. Then she caught herself using the same phrase she'd fallen back on when Yuri had spoken to her of his faith.

"I've always believed in God, myself," she said. "I've just never seen any reason to trust Him."

Deep in the night under a waxing sickle moon, Kris had just crossed the Georgia line on I-85. She'd left behind state troopers from three jurisdictions. After pulling her over, they'd let her off with admonitions to "try to keep this li'l ol' car down to sixty-five, little lady, hear?" Now she began to pray.

That was startling enough to her, but then the speed of the response made her catch her breath.

"*Hello*."

The ring barely registered with Kris before she snatched up her cell phone and flipped it open.

"Hello," she said again, in a rush. "This is Kris. Kristin Van Zant. Dr. Van Zant, here. Hello?"

"Kris, is Yuri."

Static crackled on the line and muted voices babbled from the distance as he spoke away from the phone.

"Okay," he said. "Here she is, lieutenant."

"Kris," said Matt. "He just called up."

Kris caught herself saying thanks under her breath.

"It was the Vampire for sure," Matt told her. "'Cause he knew all about the last of our hold-back evidence, right down to that buckle that got snapped off of Macdonald Fisher's belt.

"He hung up not more'n five minutes ago," he went on. "Said he's going to call right back. He wants to talk to you, Kris, just you and nobody else. Wise son of a bitch says he'll accept no substitutes. So let's us all keep the line open, awright?"

Kris had already slowed down, and now she homed on the welcome station just ahead.

"I'm holding," she said. "I'll be right here."

At the bottom of the off-ramp, white pillars stood out on the guesthouse. It looked closed for the night. Kris skirted the parking lot beside it. Doubling back, she passed a long row of tractor-trailer rigs and pulled into a slot right under an arc light.

She took her handgun out of her purse and checked the safety. Then she slipped it in the side pocket of her skirt. Getting out, she looked all around before she began to pace the sidewalk in the middle of the light. All the while, she pressed the phone to her ear.

Minutes passed. The night was warm and still all around

Kris. From the bush, crickets twanged like banjos. Nothing else made a sound.

Then the line clicked in her ear.

"Yes," she said. "Yes, I'm here."

"He is back on," said Yuri. "It appears he is moving around, most likely in car. So longer you can keep him talking, better chance we have to pinpoint his location, yes?"

"Got you."

"Very good," he said. "We are switching now. Next voice you hear will be...

"Wait. Yes," he whispered. "Now, Kris. Good luck and God's blessing on you. Now."

"Doctor?"

All the blood leapt to Kris's heart and her ears hummed at the soft, inhumanly calm voice.

"Call me Kris," she said. "Everybody does."

"Kris..."

The hiss he put on her name made her think irresistibly of a soul spitted and crackling in hell.

"I...don't really have a name of my own, Kris."

"That's okay," she said. "Say, may I call you Red?"

"I don't mind, Kris."

"Just seems to fit, doesn't it?" she coaxed him. "You know you don't have to explain anything to me, Red. I've been there, right behind you. I know."

"You know what it's like for me, Kris."

She couldn't hear a trace of a question in his voice.

"You know," he said. "I can tell you do. But how?"

"I've been there," she repeated, lulling. "Others have told me what it was like for them, too. I know."

"How?" he pleaded. "Kris, there's no way you can know if you haven't—if you haven't...done it, yourself? Have you?"

Kris could tell he wouldn't let her get by with a bluff, and at this point she knew better than to try to hold anything back.

"No, I haven't," she said. "I've watched, though. I've got close, too, really close. Hey, Red, you watch the news. You know how close I got to you."

"I—you're right," said the Vampire. "I'm sorry, Kris."

Kris smiled as she picked out the note of true contrition in his tone.

"Red, Red, hey," she chided him. "C'mon now, loosen up. You could just about be my brother, you know. In a sense, you are already.

"You're my blood brother, Red," she declared. "And nothing's ever going to change that. You know that, don't you, bro?"

"I—didn't think anybody else could...would understand, about..."

"The need, sure, sure," she filled in for him. "It's okay, Red. Don't even try to talk about it. Trust me, there really aren't any words for it."

She eased into a sisterly tack, bright and hearty.

"So why knock yourself out, huh?" she said. "The important thing for you now is, you know I'm here. And you know how to reach me.

"And I'm sorry I have to bring this up," she pushed on. "But in a little while you're really, really going to need me and maybe it won't be so easy for you to talk then.

"I want you to know now that nothing's going to change on this end," she told him. "I expect I'll have seen a little more of your handiwork by then, sure. But it'll be just the same between us. Okay, my brother?"

"Yes...thank you."

In her ear, his voice closed off like a tomb being sealed.

"Thank you," he said one more time. "Good night, Kris."

"'Night, Red."

A rapid sequence of beeps and clicks overtook the line, and at length she heard Matt's voice break out of the hum as if was talking to a whole crew at once.

"Hot damn," he said. "Tricky bastard must've got in the thick of it out on 285 before he punched in on that highflyin' PCS phone. Now he's switched off before we could angle in on 'im."

Then he dropped his voice and spoke directly on Kris's line.

"Damn fine job anyway, doc," he said. "I thought we'd gone and lost 'im for sure even before he got his second word out."

Climbing back in her car, Kris took some deep breaths to steady herself.

"Oh, he was ready to back out and hang up from the start," she said. "So I took advantage of his condition as best I could."

Matt groaned, and a small chorus answered in the background.

"Okay, Kris," he said. "What condition?"

"His high," she said. "You know, the way he was all blissed out like that?"

Kris buckled in with one hand and slid the key in the ignition.

"Oh, c'mon," she sighed. "Couldn't *any*body else tell?"

"Yes, Kris," said Yuri. "To me as well he sounded like junkie fresh from scoring and fixing, yes?"

"Bingo."

Gingerly she revved Flicka's engine before she backed up and swung the nose around toward the on-ramp to the highway.

"So you've got to know," she said, half to herself, "if that was victim number five that got him that way..."

"Kris," Yuri said in her ear. "You will drive safely, yes?"

"You bet."

She shifted up and fed in gas as she cut into the inside lane.

"I make it about an hour for me to get back to town," she said on the phone. "I'll be staying over at Hank's again, all right?"

"Easy does it now, Kris," Matt urged her. "We'll keep you posted."

"Y'all better."

She watched the RPM needle tach up in a smooth run. In seconds, the speed gauge hit ninety. Kris decided she could talk her way past any staties she might meet between here and Atlanta, so she kept her foot down.

"Because if there aren't any more names on that list for him," she said, "Red only thought he knew what it's like to get thirsty."

CHAPTER TWENTY

It was just past 3 AM when Kris rolled in at the house on Baker Place. Still she woke up fresh at sunrise. Before Hank was stirring, she hit the street for a run with her cell phone in her pack.

Feeling loose and strong after a shower, she put on a sky-blue polo and chinos with a clean pair of Nikes. Then she took a look out the window and saw an unmarked car from the city force parked at the head of the drive. Next to it was a civilian Volvo wagon she didn't recognize

Kris took the stairs down two at a time. Just then, the doorbell rang. At the same time, she smelled coffee brewing and caught a whiff of bacon broiling in the kitchen. All at once she knew what was going on.

"Yuri!"

On the front step, she greeted the two guests.

"And Ludmila, hi there," she added cheerily. "Welcome to Uncle Hank's famed brunch. So glad you could come."

The pediatrician smiled and glanced over her shoulder as the young investigator stood aside for her at the door.

"Is my pleasure, Kris," said Ludmila. "And for my son I speak also, I believe."

Yuri gave Kris a wink and a nod from the threshold.

The faint rings under his eyes were her only clue that he'd put in another night on the hunt. Otherwise, Yuri was spruce and looked sporty in a pressed khaki suit over a crisp white shirt with the collar open. He made Kris think of an officer in a war zone who was out to set an example for the troops.

"My dear Ludmila," boomed Hank. "Yuri my boy, welcome!"

He swept in with an apron over his weekend kit of an old knit pullover, cords and moccasins.

"And Kristin, good morning to you, too," he added. "I didn't hear you when you came in last night."

"But you were expecting me to be here all the same," she sighed. "I know, big uncle."

Leading the way back to the kitchen, she began to pitch in in that snug but cavernous space just as she'd done of a Saturday morning for the past twenty years.

"Don't think I'm going to let you eat any eggs Benedict even if you are fixing 'em," she warned Hank. "Not with what your serum cholesterol was on admission."

"Today I shall confine myself to fruit and fiber, my dear," he promised. "That should make you and the entire cardiology department happy."

Kris was already attending to all the pots and pans on the massive stainless-steel range.

"Yeah, sure," she muttered. "No butter on your grits either, hear?"

"Our Kristin was always such an imperious child," Hank said at her back. "I remember when she was a little girl cutting out paper dolls—"

"Hold on."

Spatula in hand, Kris turned to where Hank was presiding over the battered old butcher-block table in the middle of the floor.

"C'mon," she said. "I don't recall that I ever played with paper dolls."

Hank shook his head and regarded her over the top of the half-moon glasses perched at the tip of his nose.

"As I was about to say, my dear," he reproved her mildly. "I recall that in your case, you only fashioned paper dolls from the pages of Krafft-Ebing's *Psychopathia Sexualis*.

"Now then," he said graciously. "Who wants coffee?"

With Hank and Ludmila chatting at the head of the breakfast table, Kris pumped Yuri for details.

"Technical Services has already prepared voiceprints from recording of your conversation," he told her. "With digital spectral analysis, as you know, Kris, audio pattern such as this can be quite distinctive and specific for individual speaker."

While he munched wheat toast, she doused her home fries with ketchup and set in on her second helping of scrambled eggs.

"So you'll be comparing it to voice samples from known offenders," she said. "But that's still a long shot, isn't it?"

"Regrettably so."

Meeting her eyes, Yuri took a sip of coffee and used his napkin.

"Then lieutenant had us get linguistics expert out of bed to listen to tape," he said. "Perhaps you know this academician?"

"Prof. Breckburn? Sure," said Kris. "I sat in on a bunch of her seminars when I was in grad school here. There's not much about regional accents she can't pick up, especially in these parts.

"And you know, Yuri," she said, "Red sounded local to me, really local. What did the prof say?"

"She thinks that you are right."

Quick and boyish, his smile overran the tracks of fatigue in his face.

"From pattern of speech and accent," he said, "Vampire appears to her to be native and lifelong resident of Atlanta Metro area. Most likely, too, he is white and of lower-middle to middle-class social status with education in public schools.

"Professor thinks also he is high-school graduate with perhaps some college credits to his name," he added. "And..."

"Military," Kris put in when he paused. "He's got a military background of some kind, for sure."

As Yuri continued to encourage her, she caught Hank and Ludmila staring at her.

"What?" she said. "I mean, I beg your pardon?"

"The girl always had the most extraordinary ear," Hank

chuckled. “Her rather painful attempts to master the piano notwithstanding.”

He pulled a grimace as he inclined his head toward the music room.

“From her earliest years,” he went on, “our Kristin seemed to possess what amounts to perfect pitch for the human voice and all its shadings. She could be counted on to identify a stranger’s hometown with quite uncanny accuracy.”

“It comes from living in university towns full of people from all over the world,” Kris said. “Plus, growing up in a city with folks who’d moved around a lot before they wound up here.”

As usual when the topic of her oddly keen perceptions came up, Kris turned self-conscious.

“I’ve always kept my eyes and ears open,” she said with a shrug. “That’s all.”

“Go on, if you please, Kris,” said Yuri. “Military, you were saying?”

“Red—the Vampire, he had a touch of an Army drawl,” she said. “Even through that high he was on, you could tell he’d been a GI.

“Every major military reservation seems to have an accent of its own, you see, just like small towns,” she went on. “For instance, you could tell if a soldier’s spent time in training at Fort Benning, say, as opposed to Fort Gordon or Fort Stewart, which’re just across the state. And certainly you could distinguish his speech from a grunt who’d been stationed for a stretch at Fort Jackson in South Carolina or—”

“Please, Kris,” Yuri softly coaxed her. “Tell which base you think was home to Vampire?”

“Bragg, definitely,” she said. “What did Prof. Breckburn think?”

“Precisely same as you, Kris.”

Yuri matched her gaze as he leaned back in his chair and crossed his arms over his chest.

“So lieutenant had me on phone in wee hours, as you say, going over criminal records with office of commandant of military police at Fort Bragg, North Carolina," he said. "To no avail, however, I regret to inform you."

"Interesting, interesting," said Hank. "I invited Matthew to join us this morning, but it would seem he had more pressing matters to attend to. And so—"

Yuri's pager went off. As he checked the LED strip, Kris saw him begin to reach for his cell phone before he glanced up at her. She pointed the way to the phone in the hallway, and he excused himself from the table.

When he came back from using the landline, he was holding up five fingers.

"I see," Hank said, standing. "Then I must beg your indulgence, Ludmila, as a shamefully improvident host. For I fear I must take leave of you now."

Kris began to protest, but he squared his shoulders and stepped up to join the young people on their way out.

"No, no," Hank said. "I'm quite recovered now, I assure you. And I'd be more than remiss in my duty if I did not accompany you to the scene of the crime."

❧

Yuri drove them up to North Buckhead in the bright morning sun. At first Kris thought there was a riot up ahead. Then she realized it was just the media in a swarm. Shoulder cams and shotgun mikes jostled on all sides of them, and from overhead came the whir and chop of a helicopter's rotors.

"*11 AliveNews*, I presume," Hank murmured. "On the air, indeed."

They pulled up to a checkpoint by the gate in the Cyclone fence. On sight, the young APD officer gave Hank a salute. Then he took down Kris's name and Yuri's badge number before he waved them through.

Kris looked around as they followed a loop of gravel and blacktop up to the house. For a moment she thought they'd turned into Chastain Park. It took a beat for her to register that these grounds diverged from the golf course next door but were nearly as big.

"Hank," called Matt. "Thank God you're here."

Waving his arm at the rear window, he caught up with them at a trot.

"You, too, Kris," he added. "Damn, y'all."

Yuri pulled around a line of patrol cruisers. Together, they got out under a canvas awning. It ran from the pool house to an expanse of smoked glass, black timber and firebrick that Kris took to be the main building.

"Is correct, lieutenant?" said Yuri. "Victim was Gerald Zehner, himself?"

He kept his voice so low that Kris had to lean in close to hear. She stuck to the others as they hustled past a phalanx of blue uniforms, suits and lab coats. They cleared a second checkpoint and went in the back way.

"None other than," Matt whispered. "Uh-huh."

They took a sharp turn to the right and followed a narrow skylit hall to the corner room ahead. On the way, Kris noted how haggard and on edge Matt looked. Keeping his head down, he shook it as if he meant it.

"Maybe it's not like creeping y' way into the Oval Office and goin' and sucking all the blood out the President of the *U*nited States," he muttered. "But for hereabouts, I reckon it's close enough."

"Gerald Zehner," Kris said. "I bet his friends called him Jerry."

Sternly a crime-scene tech shook her head and held out a pair of paper shoe covers to Kris, who paused to fit them over her sneakers.

"So that would make him 'j.z.'," she went on. "The last name left on Sister Night's list. That'd make him the last recorded client of 'Nurse Nell.' And so, maybe the Vampire's final—"

"Kris, please," Matt hissed at her side. "Ssssh, now."

Nodding, she shut her mouth and folded her hands in front of her as she followed her uncle into the dead man's office.

The late Mr. Zehner might've been way up near the top of the Forbes 400, Kris mused, but you sure couldn't tell it from his workplace. Covering two walls were plain pine bookcases full of volumes with cracked spines. On the metal desk by the window, papers lay in neat stacks by a CRT monitor and a keyboard. That was just about all.

Even the body was dressed down. Laid out on its back beside the desk, the corpse had on a navy cotton polo, faded denims and old Top-Siders. Under graying brown hair trimmed as short as a Roman senator's, the face was thin and white. Its eyes were wider than any live man's could be.

The wounds in the neck and arms went deep. Ripped clean and gaping, they might have been the leavings of a raptor's feast. Still, Kris could tell from ten paces off that all the bites were human. Privately she admitted that anything else would have made her sad.

"Dear Lord." Hank said. "I had no idea from the photographs. In the name of God, this can't be..."

Faltering, he reached for Kris's hand as they knelt by the body.

"Easy does it," she said. "Deep breaths, in and out. That's good, Uncle Hank. Now just excuse me for a li'l bit, here."

She sprang up and whirled around. On the front wall, a map of the world in flat projection ran from floor to ceiling. True to Laszlo's dictum, Kris had done her best to ignore the big red letters that stood out there. But she couldn't help it anymore.

"Oh, that's cute," she said. "That is just *so* cute."

Straining to keep her hands down, she advanced on the message. Written high above her eye level, the crimson lettering squared off precisely with the margins of the map. It began over the western meridians of the Pacific Ocean and left a pink trail across the Americas into mid-Atlantic.

YOU'LL NEVER TAKE ME ALIVE, it read.

"Five frickin' words," Kris said through her teeth. "So the DNA'll count the victims off one by one from start to finish, back to front and inside out, no two ways about it.

"She's just not leaving any room for doubt!" she burst out. "She's keeping the spotlight on my—on the Vampire, I mean. Why can't anybody else see that?"

"Kris, hush!"

Matt grabbed her arm. Just as quickly, he let go. Patting her shoulder, he backed off.

"'Scuse me, doc, 'scuse me now," he said. "You just got to keep your voice down, hear? Please."

"Sure," Kris said. "Beg pardon, Uncle Matt. Sorry, there."

She took a breath and shifted to face him.

"Who found the body this time?" she asked. "I'm assuming the help got the night off, just like with all the others. So was it a family member?"

"There's no family," he said. "Not a one."

The senior detective ducked to meet her eye and shook his head again. Just now, Matt looked as wired and pressured as Kris had ever seen him. The way his rumpled seersucker jacket hung from his shoulders made her think of the tent being struck over the big top just before the circus left town.

"It was three of his buddies found him," he told her. "They come by here this morning for they regular golf game."

He tilted his head toward the door.

"They out there now," he said. "All of 'em major pillars of our fair city's business and financial community, and then some. And—Kris?"

All at once she broke away from him and made a sprint down the hall.

"Hey!" Matt yelled after her. "Whoa up, *Kris*—!"

Once again she was too fast for him, and this time Kris was bent on asking her own questions before anyone else tried to feed her an answer.

CHAPTER TWENTY-ONE

Under vaulted redwood beams that were nearly as high as a cathedral's roof, Kris sat down and squared off with three investment bankers.

"I'm Dr. Kristin Van Zant. Call me Kris," she said. "Everybody does."

"Oh, I think we know who you are, Dr. Van Zant," said Craig Billingsley. "And I believe I speak for us all when I say we'll do anything we can to help you find out who's responsible for this outrageous, despicable, downright sickening act."

Rangy with salt-and-pepper hair, he had a set of severe lines in his face. He struck Kris as the most imposing of the men, who were all dressed for the links. Facing her, they sat in a row on the right-angled couch at the center of the floor.

Meanwhile, Matt stood back with his head cocked to the side. Arms folded tight, he kept his gaze trained on Kris. His posture told her he was willing, if barely, to cut her some slack for now.

"Skydiving," she said fast. "As I recall, Mr. Zehner did some demonstration jumps at air shows hereabouts for worthy causes. That's not a pastime I'd associate with a venture capitalist of his standing."

"That's the kind of VC operator Jerry was, doctor," Craig told her. "You might say jumping out of airplanes was the least risky thing he did."

"Of course, he'd given that up in the past few years," Dave Rhinehart spoke up quietly. "Slipped disc, you know."

Silver-haired with precise features that were just shy of being pretty, he made a discreet gesture at his low back.

"Service to his country finally caught up with him," Tom Smitherman declared at his side. "You might not think so to look at him, doc, but ol' Jerry was one tough li'l piece of work."

Earnest and deliberate, he had a pink moon face under thinning yellow hair.

"Fact is," he added, "Jer joined the Army right out of Washington & Lee and volunteered for airborne infantry duty in Nam. Back before you were even born, doc, he won a Silver Star in a godforsaken place called Dak To for—"

"I think in fact, it was a Bronze Star," Dave put in. "I beg your pardon, Tom."

Kris gathered from his and Craig's faces that they'd heard the tale before.

"Okay, Dave, maybe it was bronze," Tom said. "But there's no disputing the color of the Purple Heart he got to go with it."

Bright-eyed, he went on with a soldierly relish that convinced Kris he'd never heard a shot fired in anger himself.

"Y'see, doc," he said, "Jer got into this big firefight in the Central Highlands back in '67 and got wounded bad defending his position. I hear he just about bled to death before his outfit could get him medevac'd out."

"No—? I mean, I see," said Kris. "And if I may, gentlemen, I'd like to ask about Mr. Zehner's more recent associations."

From the side of her vision she caught Matt biting down hard.

"In particular," she said faster, "did he have any connection you were aware of with a Ms. Blair Ann Rennie?"

"BA?"

Craig barked a short laugh as Matt gave Kris a determined headshake behind him.

"Funny you should mention her, doctor," he said. "My wife hired her on to do the inside of a place we keep in the Up Country. Way the job turned out, it'd just about give Scarlett O'Hara a migraine."

At his side, Tom bobbed his head and broke into a wide smile.

"BA, huh?" he said to Kris. "Talk about your high-risk behavior, now."

"What Tom's implying, I think," Dave sighed, "is that to use the vernacular, doctor, Miss BA Rennie is one fast filly."

"I see," Kris said again. "And could you tell me if Mr. Zehner and BA—Ms. Rennie had any dealings together, personal or otherwise?"

At that Matt uncrossed his arms and brought his hands together with a loud smack.

"Well now, y'all," he said. "I think that just about wraps it up here."

Craig raised a hand toward him but kept his eyes on Kris.

"Hold on, Mr. Judson," he said. "If you please, detective.

"Matter of fact, doctor," he went on, "I do seem to recollect that over the years, Jerry gave BA some investment advice. He'd done a fair amount of business with her husband, too."

Kris nodded as she called up a name from her shared research with Yuri.

"Barney Kocharian?" she said. "Is that so? I gather that the late Mr. Kocharian was quite a high flyer himself."

"Thank you for your cooperation with Dr. Van Zant, gentlemen," Matt broke in again. "Now we'd be very grateful if you'd wait here a little while longer to talk with some of our more, uhm, conventional investigators."

As he began to nudge her along, Kris dug in her heels.

"Just one more thing," she said, "if I may. To your knowledge, did Ms. Rennie ever—?"

"Kris!"

Calm but urgent, Yuri's voice rang and echoed in the hangar-sized room.

"If you please," he called to her, "we are in need of your assistance here."

She turned and caught sight of Hank shambling toward them. Slew-footed, he missed his step at the head of the hallway and two of the ME's people moved in to prop him up. As he slowly doubled over, his face went white and slack.

Putting the rest of her questions on hold, Kris broke away from the others and ran to his side.

❧

This time the docs in the emergency ward at University Hospital diagnosed Hank's condition as acute indigestion. Still, Kris was relentless. At her urging and with her uncle's resigned compliance, the attending cardiologist agreed to admit him overnight for observation and monitoring.

That left Kris with nothing to do but go back to Hank's office and sort through the Vampire files one more time. All the while, she couldn't shake the feeling that she'd been bumped out of the loop again. Now she judged she had only one chance left to get back on the case.

It was a good chance, though. As Kris thought back over her conversation with Red last night, she was sure he'd need to talk to her sooner or later. She'd put her money on sooner, too. So, she took care to keep her cell phone charged up.

She kept it close at hand even when she got ready to go to bed, toward midnight.

❧

Back at her uncle's place, Kris lay down in her old bedroom. It wasn't long before she felt a hypnic epiphany coming on. That was Stephen Laszlo's old tag for a brainstorm that blew up on the edge of sleep and served to crack a case like no amount of reasoning in daytime ever could. Now it blindsided Kris in a rush of pure logic.

"Of *course*."

Jackknifed, she up sat on the side of the bed and put both feet down flat on the floor.

"Why didn't I think of that to start with?" she went on out loud. "It fits. It all fits. Hoo *boy*, does it fit—with everything!

"That's it, exactly," she said just over her breath. "That's the way Red can be everything he seems to be and still keep from giving himself away. It's the *only* way. Really, he's got to be—"

She sucked her breath in tight as she caught a sound from

downstairs. Soft but unmistakable, it was the creak the tread at the bottom of the stairway made. All at once Kris thought of Rory, the hound that didn't bark on the night the Werewolf killed her family.

Without making any noise, she pulled on her sweat togs and laced up her running shoes in the dark. In one motion, she took hold of her handgun and her cell phone. In another, she lined up the pillows on the bed and drew the covers over them. Then she held her breath and kept still.

Seconds passed, and all was quiet. At length came a second creak from the stairway. This one was the sound of the loose riser three steps from the top. Kris dipped her head in recognition as she padded to the window.

Old reflexes cut in and took hold of her as she hoisted the sash, unhooked the screen, and swung it out from the frame. Lightly she stepped out onto the rooftop of the front porch. With one hand, she pulled the window back in place behind her and squared it off from the outside.

Rising, the quarter moon was bright at Kris's back as she went into a crouch on the shingles. She kept her face to the glass and drew her eyes down to slits while she watched and waited. A minute went by, and nothing moved.

Then as gradually as a shadow shifting on the wall, the door to her room opened. Kris couldn't see who was behind it. But she didn't wait to get a better look.

She pushed her phone and her gun deep in the side pockets of her sweatpants. With care Kris found her hold on the roof with her palms and the toes of her sneakers. Steadily she began to inch her way back.

She didn't stop until she reached the trellis at the edge. For a moment she tested her weight on the top of the lattice. Going hand over hand then, she climbed down.

As soon as she felt solid ground under her feet, Kris started to back up. Ducking low at the inside corner of the lawn, she flipped open her cell phone. She used her thumb to hit 911 on speed dial.

The operator picked up on the second ring. Before Kris

could respond, three sharp yellow flashes burst right overhead. In silence, they flared up and faded to black at her bedroom window.

"This is Dr. Kristin Van Zant," she whispered in the mouthpiece. "I'm at 332 Baker Place in Druid Hills, right off the university campus.

"There's just been a shooting," she said as clearly as she could. "I repeat, a shooting. Shots fired. Right here. The intruder's still inside the house. Got that?"

"Copy, miss, uh, doctor," drawled the woman's voice in her ear. "A squad has just been dispatched, and police officers are already en route to your location. Are there any injured parties?"

"Not yet."

Kris bit her tongue as she kept an eye on the window above and edged up on the front steps.

"I mean, no," she said on the line. "Nobody's been hurt. But I need backup. As in armed response. I need 'em here right *now*."

"Police officers are on the way," the operator repeated. "In the meantime, Dr. Van Zant, just you sit tight and stay on the line now, hear?"

"You bet," said Kris. "That is, yes, ma'am."

She slipped the open phone back in her pocket and used both hands to line her pistol up dead in front of her. With her feet spread and her arms locked in a marksman's stance, she got set to wait on the porch. Kris judged that whoever had tried to kill her must have just found out it was a miss.

Given her uncle's absentminded way of leaving a key under a rock by the box hedge, she was also counting on her wannabe assassin to come out the front door. Then she remembered how she'd always nagged Hank to put a deadbolt on the back way out. She doubted he'd got around to it yet. So, likely there was nothing else between the hall and the backyard but a rusty old hook on the porch screen.

"Uh-oh," Kris said through her teeth. "Oh, *damn*."

From the side she caught a flicker of twirling blue lights and heard sirens headed her way. Just now, though, Kris's heartbeat overrode everything else. She wheeled where she stood and took the front steps down. Digging in, she charged around the back with her gun held high.

As soon as she got around the corner, Kris saw the door standing open inside the screen. By the glow of the carriage lamps at the foot of the lawn, she made out a lone figure going full tilt in front of her. Now it was closing on the border hedge off the side street.

The runner had on a dark jumpsuit and some kind of bulky headset over a hood. Still, Kris couldn't mistake that long springy stride and the thrust of the chest. She bent her knees with her arms braced in a vee. Looking steely down the sights, she led the legs with the muzzle.

"Hey, bitch!" she sang out. "Not so fast now, you hear me?"

She aimed low and swung straight through her target as she squeezed off a round. Bucking back in her hand, the 9mm cracked on the air like a big dry twig. Dirt and grass kicked up in a spurt, and the figure in flight stumbled to one side and dropped something.

Then it pitched back up and kept pounding away from her in a sprint. In the same move, Kris rode the recoil down and raised her sights by a hair as she pulled her lead in tight. She trued in the next shot to drill her quarry clean through the knees. Catching her breath, she eased a pound of pressure on the trigger.

Suddenly the world turned stark white, glaring all around fit to blind her.

"Freeze!"

From close at her back, the man's voice burst and rolled on her like a clap of thunder.

"You drop that gun right now," he yelled. "Get y' hands up there, boy!"

"Okay," Kris called back over her shoulder. "Okay."

Carefully she let the little SIG semiauto fall to the grass at her feet. With her hands over her head, she squinted in the high beams. All the while, she watched the leaves rustle apart in the hedge at the side of the lawn. Then they went flat and closed off on her for good.

Blowing out her breath, Kris tried not to grit her teeth as she turned her head to deal with the suburban police.

"First things first, officers," she said. "I am *not* a boy."

CHAPTER TWENTY-TWO

Kris dealt with Druid Hills' finest in back of the house. Meanwhile, neighbors from up and down the street came over to check on her. In various states of dress, they milled around the yard and mingled with the police.

"I was so alarmed, Kristin, for your sake," said Prof. Teitelbaum from down on the corner. "I sleep less and less these days, you know. And as I chanced to look out from my study tonight, I thought I saw shadows moving in your backyard. And then..."

Wearing a pullover and wool slacks with his bedroom slippers, the gray-bearded physicist shook his head and shuddered.

"Then," he said, "I saw a stealthy, agile figure like—like a ninja, yes. It might have been a little ninja climbing out of an upstairs window. Well, then, what could I do but alert the police straight away?"

Paternally he took Kris's hand, and she squeezed back.

"Thanks, prof," she said dryly. "And you say you saw somebody come up through the backyard?"

"Of that I cannot be sure, Kristin," he said with a shrug. "What with these old eyes of mine, and tricks of light, ach. I just couldn't say, my dear."

Hulking and grizzled, a plainclothesman in shirtsleeves loomed over Kris with a notebook in hand.

"But you say you think you recognized the intruder, Dr. Van Zant?" he prompted her. "That is, this person you just took a shot at."

"The one who took a shot at me," she said. "Three shots, in fact."

Balling her fists, Kris raised her voice over the buzz of the crowd that was still building out front.

"And if you'd care to take a look in my bedroom, detective," she said, "I predict that's the number of bullet holes you'll find in the pillow."

"All in good time, miss, uh, doc," he said. "Now, I take it you got a good look at the intruder's face?"

"No, of course not."

With effort Kris kept her jaws from clenching at the recurring question.

"As I told you before, detective, she had on a headset of some kind," she said. "I'm pretty sure it was a night-vision rig."

"But, Dr. Van Zant, if you didn't see her face," said the investigator, "then how can you be so sure who it was?"

Kris fought down the urge to use her hands.

"Her silhouette, her shape," she said. "She has a really distinctive figure."

"Could you be more specific there, doctor?"

"Well, I bet nobody's ever taken *her* for a boy."

"Sarge?"

Trudging up the lawn, one of the patrolmen held up a big Ziploc evidence pouch.

"Got us a weapon here, sarge," he called again. "Looks like."

"That's it!"

Crying out, Kris went up on tiptoe to get a look at the bagged pistol as it changed hands.

"See, it's got a silencer built right onto the barrel," she pointed out. "That's why it didn't make a peep when she went gunning for me upstairs. C'mon, y'all, there's got to be some way to trace this thing. How about—?"

She broke it off as she made out the big shadow loping toward them and holding out a badge.

"Chernenko, Metro Homicide," said Yuri. "I would be

most grateful merely to check serial numbers here if you please, detective, officers?"

He passed Kris his penlight, and she held it up for him as he took out a printout sheet and checked the handgun against it.

"Yes," he narrated. "Ruger Mark II semiautomatic, long-barrel model in .22 caliber with post-manufacture addition of integral suppressor on muzzle..."

Pushing in close at his shoulder, Kris craned to read the numbers on the metal.

"Is no question," Yuri said at last, looking up. "Federal registration of both handgun and silencer here match those issued to Mr. Wade Hazlitt of Buckhead."

"And as you recall," Kris added to the others, "he was the number one victim of the Vampire."

"Okay, boys," called the senior investigator to the patrolmen. "I guess that's it."

Then he dropped his voice and turned to Yuri.

"So like we discussed on the phone, Det. Chernenko," he said just loud enough for Kris to catch, "we're more than willing to cede jurisdiction to APD on the spot."

Kris felt Yuri's hand close on hers. At the same time, she saw a line of city uniforms fan out across the head of the lawn. Right behind them came a deluge of light bars, lenses, mikes, and shoulder cams. Half a dozen voices of broadcast quality yelled as one.

"Dr. Van Zant! Over here!" they carried over a rattle of film-advancers. "Is it true you're the first victim ever to escape from the Atlanta Vampire?"

"Sorry, Kris, sorry," Yuri muttered, shielding her. "Would appear they picked it up on scanners."

Ducking in front of him, Kris led the way up the steps of the back porch and through the screen door.

"The amazing thing," she whispered, "is how they never get anything quite right.

"And why do I feel like I've just slipped even farther away

from the case than I was before?" she demanded. "And without even getting any sleep to show for it."

"We have name now, Kris."

Stepping inside with her, Yuri made room for the APD evidence personnel to get past them.

"We got tip this afternoon," he went on. "Anonymous, you understand."

"And...?"

"Tip panned out," he told her. "In suspect's apartment we found blood stored which matches serotypes of victims. Already we are going over his dental records. Now is merely matter of time."

As another barrage of shouts and questions broke through from outside, Kris shook her head and tried to clear it.

"Whoa, whoa, whoa, big fellow," she said. "Hold on, there. You're saying you've already put a face on Red—that is, on the Vampire?"

"I will tell you everything, Kris." Yuri pledged. "But first I think it would be best that we get you to secure site for rest of night, yes?"

"Uh-huh," she said. "Got any place in particular in mind?"

Inclining his head to her, Yuri held his grip on her hand.

"My apartment is in area that is very well patrolled," he said. "Also, building security is excellent. I will stay there with you as well while we wait for word from search that is ongoing for suspect's vehicle, yes?"

"Best offer I've had tonight, thanks," Kris sighed. "I'll go pack a bag."

❧

At Kris's insistence, she followed Yuri in her car. His digs turned out to be in a snug modern building just north of Midtown. A block off Peachtree, it looked like any number of more or less anonymous residential complexes nearby.

"Treat place as your own, Kris," he said as he held the door for her. "Would be good to get some sleep tonight while is still possible, yes?"

She agreed.

Then she said thanks but turned down his offer of a snack or tea or something else to drink. Out of habit, Kris looked around for personal touches. She saw as little of them as she'd expected from a man who seemed to have lived for much of his life in dorms or barracks or bachelor officer's quarters.

Yuri's bookcases looked homemade to her. They overflowed with criminology texts and law books in Russian and English and a few other Euro tongues. The fiction she saw there ran to Mark Twain, Zane Grey, Bret Harte, and Jack London.

Thinking of his mother's remarks, Kris confirmed that Yuri's CD collection featured the Allman Brothers, the Marshall Tucker Band, the Atlanta Rhythm Section, and Lynyrd Skynyrd. On the mantelpiece were a couple of framed photos of mother, father and teenage son and daughter. Street posters of Moscow and St. Petersburg and a few wildlife shots filled in most of the bare spots in the front room.

But a large photograph in a plain silver frame drew Kris's eye to a wall that was otherwise empty.

Its subject was a man with fair hair and a hulking chest and shoulders. He had on a gray uniform with gold braid, and his pale blue eyes were as keen and direct as a boy's. Except for deeper lines by his mouth and a straighter nose, his face was a match for Yuri's.

Kris turned around when she felt Yuri watching her.

"You said you'd been in the suspect's apartment already," she said. "I'd like to see it."

"I believe this can be arranged," he said. "But later, Kris, if you please."

He took an armful of sheets and a pillow from the hall closet and dropped them on the end of the couch, and then he opened the door to the bedroom and bowed over the threshold.

"You take bed," he said. "I insist. Now is better to get some rest."

"Later," she said, dropping her voice to mimic his. "If you please."

Kris plopped down on the middle of the couch and patted the cushion beside her.

"C'mon, pard, bring me up to speed," she urged him. "Hey, I know Matt and the brass downtown are antsy about keeping me in the loop just now. 'Cause you can bet our pal BA's still pulling strings with 'em, even as she came over to pot me tonight."

"Ms. Rennie is spending night in Braselton, Kris."

Yuri crossed the room to face her but stayed on his feet.

"She is supervising big restoration project there at old planter's house," he added. "So her firm assured me when I made inquiry earlier today."

"Good alibi."

Kris bobbed her head as she thought it over.

"Great one, in fact," she added. "It's an easy commute but just far enough away from here to make it hard to keep tabs on her."

Yuri took a seat by her side.

"Tip on suspect," he said, "it came from public phone downtown. Clearly caller had put on voice-changer."

"You know it was BA, don't you, Yuri?"

"Was my first thought."

He blew his breath out in a long stream and rested his hands on his knees.

"Not that either of us could prove it," he added. "Or for that matter provide motive for her."

His jacket hung open on a Glock in a shoulder rig. Kris made the big handgun out to be a .45 or maybe 10mm. In passing, she wondered what caliber he'd used back in Moscow when he tracked down the men he'd fingered for his father's killing.

"The suspect's apartment didn't give much away, did it?" she said aloud. "You probably had to look hard before you turned up that blood in the freezer.

"As for pictures in plain sight," she went on, narrowing her eyes. "I'd say there was maybe an old family snapshot or two. Right?"

"There was one formal, posed photograph on wall," he

said. "Was of suspect and his parents. Foster parents, that is. Occasion was—"

"Graduation," she cut in. "No, no, wait. An award, say. He did a military stint, didn't he, probably a long hitch? So I bet it was a decoration of some sort."

"It was on occasion of his receiving Distinguished Service Cross," Yuri told her. "After Gulf War."

Kris let out a whistle.

"That's just a notch down from the Medal of Honor," she said. "So he was Army, huh? Then it must've been for a really high-profile mission, maybe some kind of rescue operation?"

Showing no surprise, Yuri kept his eyes fast on hers.

"All but single-handedly, I am told, he saved his recon unit after most of them were wounded in ambush when they were well ahead of their lines," he recited. "He was noncommissioned officer, Kris, in US Army Special Forces."

"That explains Fort Bragg."

Kris got up to pace in front of the couch.

"I hear Green Berets specialize in their duties," she went on. "So our man must've been, oh, a medic?"

Yuri nodded and let her have a grin of admiration.

"Perfect, perfect," Kris said in motion. "And his name, I bet it rang some bells in the squadroom. But not for priors. Right? No, not for something he'd done.

"Unh-uh," she fretted, picking up speed. "It had to've been the other way around."

"Lieutenant remembered case, " Yuri said at her back. "As soon as he heard name 'Lawrence Fitzhugh,' he recalled all details."

"Uncle Matt's got a memory like elephants wish they had."

"He says same thing about you, Kris."

Holding her gaze as she turned, Yuri was impassive.

"Goes back twenty-five years or so," he said. "Boy was orphan only five, perhaps six years old. Very big scandal for Human Resources Department, so story goes."

"Before my time," Kris muttered. "Still, I'd predict little

Lawrence went through some kind of hell at home. Physical abuse, sexual abuse, out-and-out torture even, it had to've been sheer fire and brimstone for a little kid. Maybe of a ritual nature, too."

"First family to take in him and his siblings, they were something of cult locally," Yuri said. "Fancied themselves to be devil worshipers, according to reports."

Kris saw he was sitting up straighter than usual, but he kept his voice low.

"There was good deal of bloodletting," he went on. "For ritual purposes, yes, you are quite correct, Kris. Lawrence was only one of children to survive."

She arched her eyebrows at him.

"Fitzhughs were good people, older couple, schoolteachers," Yuri added. "They are dead now, but it would appear they were willing to adopt little boy then in spite of all publicity at time. They gave him good home, Kris."

"God bless the Fitzhughs," she said with feeling. "And to hell with those white-trash Satanists from the '70s who drank Lawrence's blood."

Thinking out loud now, Kris cut sharp turns up and down the carpet.

"Jesus, Yuri!" she burst out. "Why the hell didn't he stay in the Army? He'd survived, for God's sake. He was functional there. He'd got to be a hero even, for real. Why'd he have to come back here?"

"He was medically discharged year and half ago, Kris," Yuri said. "While serving with UN peacekeeping mission in Kosovo, he received direct laser-sighting injury to eyes."

Kris thought of the big dark glasses she'd seen in the surveillance tapes from Martine DuBarry's building.

"A permanent retinal burn, sure," she said just over her breath. "That'd allow for correction of his vision by refraction. But he'd still be sensitive as hell to sunlight...

"Okay," she pushed ahead. "Lawrence Fitzhugh gets MD'd out of the Army after serving with great distinction. So he comes back to his hometown. He gets a job in a medical setting where he can work nights. At a hospital, say, or on an ambulance crew?"

"For past thirteen months he has been paramedic with Fulton County Emergency Medical Services," Yuri told her. "His coworkers describe him as very good man at accident scene but not much for small talk and—"

"Damn near impossible to get to know," she finished for him. "At his apartment, Yuri, did he have a computer by any chance? A modem? Net access?"

"He had good desktop PC and AOL account, Kris."

He got up to join her and held out his hands.

"Also Mindspring and maybe some other ISPs as well," he added. "Before you ask, we have techies in Department working over hard drive now. They are attempting to find out which Web sites and IRC chat rooms he frequented."

"Great."

She took both his hands and bore down on them.

"But you've got to put the pressure on him and keep him on the run," she said. "Because at this point he's got just one way out."

"Kris..."

"And that's through me," she insisted. "He's got to see that, Yuri. For him there's no other exit. You've got to do everything you can to make that clear to him."

"We are, Kris," he said. "Trust me, we are doing just that."

He took a deep breath and slouched some more so they were nearly eye-to-eye.

"But I must tell you this," he said. "It scares me very badly to think that you would place yourself in such position."

"What can I tell you?" she said. "It's not easy being right. Not this right, anyway."

Tilting his head to the side, he looked wry but deeply in earnest as he kept hold of her hands.

"Would you like to hear little theory of mine, Kris?" he asked. "You see, I believe there are two kinds of people in world."

"You mean those who believe there are two kinds of people

and those who don't?" she countered. "Didn't Oscar Wilde say that?"

"Is quite possible he did, Kris."

To her, he looked all the more determined to speak his mind and plead his case.

"Me on other hand," he said, "I believe there are professionals and then there are amateurs.

"Most people are professionals in one way or other," he went on without looking away from her. "With them is merely matter of doing job, of taking care of business and balancing books, keeping score, and so on."

"Pros do it for money," Kris summed up. "And amateurs?"

"For love."

As if shy to state the obvious, Yuri looked more than a bit sheepish to her now.

"That is why they are so unpredictable and heedless of danger," he pressed on. "Is why their lives are so risky. Is also why I—others, I mean, why others become so afraid when we come to care for them, very much."

He cleared his throat.

"When we come to love them, you see."

"So what am I?" Kris asked. "Pro or am?"

"You are easy case," he said. "From first time we met, Kris, I have had no doubt in this matter."

He let go of her hands and seemed regretful as he took a step back.

"You are so far past being professional in all you do," he stated, "you have never lost amateur standing."

At that Kris blinked and stared back at him.

All at once she recognized what she'd seen from the start in his eyes. Now she knew why he'd never been able to share it with her. Not just a bright mirror image, it was pure knowledge of her. It was plain to Kris that he had her down, dark side and all, well past what words or looks could tell.

Neither of them spoke as seconds went by. At length Yuri began to say goodnight, but Kris shook her head. She threw her arms around him and twined her hands behind his neck as he covered her mouth with his.

Then he picked her up like a rose from a vase, and together they made for the bedroom.

CHAPTER TWENTY-THREE

Dawn was still to come when Kris hopped out of the shower. Toweling off and getting into a beige knit pullover and chinos with her running shoes, she came close to breaking into handstands.

Yuri Andreyevich Chernenko, she hummed to herself, you are indeed a talented man.

He'd seemed just as appreciative of her. Kris thought in passing of an erstwhile flame who had taught physics at MIT. Thermonuclear between the sheets had been his phrase for her. Hairbrush in hand, she hit her wash-and-go cut a few strokes and stepped back from the mirror. Then she headed for the way out.

Once she stepped into the hallway, though, Kris caught a whiff of steam from the bath by the bedroom. Then she smelled coffee and a familiar herbal blend on the boil. At that point, she judged her chances for a clean getaway had gone from good to zero.

"To you very good morning, Kris."

Well shaved and looking as spruce as ever, Yuri loomed dead ahead in crisp white shirtsleeves and held out a steaming mug to her.

"Tea perhaps?"

"Thanks."

Hauling up, she followed him to the kitchen and took a sip on the way.

"Guangzhou Ginseng," she said. "That's not easy to come by. Thanks, really."

"You are quite welcome."

He pulled back a chair for her at the plastic-topped table with a big straw basket of fruit in the center.

"I am making oatmeal," he said. "If you please?"

"Great," said Kris. "No borscht?"

"Was not breakfast food at my house."

As he shifted pots and pans at her back, she heard him let out a heavy sigh.

"Kris," he said, "was not merely to sleep with you that I wished, you see, but to wake up with you as well."

"You're an early riser."

"One of great many things we share, I am sure."

He turned to face her with his hands hanging down at his sides.

"Kris, please," he said. "I cannot pretend that I live merely for moment. And I find it impossible to believe that this is case with you either."

"Yuri. I..."

Shaking her head at herself, Kris got up and went to him.

"We're alike in many ways, I'll grant you," she said. "But please, don't push it. Just don't."

"I will say it just this one time, Kris, okay?"

He opened his arms to her. Otherwise, he kept still except to tilt his head toward the front room. Kris followed where he looked and saw the photo of his late father.

"Both of us, when we were young," he began. "Well, I was not so young as you. But still, quite early in life I found myself in dangerous situation in which I had to make hard choice. Like you, I had not so much time in which to consider my actions."

He shrugged and met her eyes.

"In my case, I merely shot my way out," he said. "Bang bang bang, boom boom, and that was end of it.

"You, on other hand..."

He reached out to her and very gently settled his palm by the side of her head.

"To make your escape you used much more deadly weapon than I did," he seemed to conclude. "One that is not so easy to put away, yes?"

Kris razzed her breath out loud between her lips.

"Yuri," she said, "you sure you're not just a shrink trying to pass for a cop?"

Before he could respond, she grabbed him around the middle. Planting her feet apart, Kris shook him hard enough to throw them both off balance. Yuri dropped his head and laughed as his arms closed around her shoulders.

"Hey!" she piped up at him. "Want to go back to bed?"

"This, my love, you must ask?"

Then her cell phone shrilled from her belt. At the same time, his pager went off. A second later, every phone in the apartment began to ring.

In the small hours of Sunday morning, the Northwest Expressway was as empty as it ever got.

Yuri drove them down the six-lane outbound in an unmarked APD car with the radio crackling. Mute and tense, Matt rode beside him up front. Kris sat forward in the backseat with a hand on her cell phone and her eyes wide and watchful.

A BellSouth Mobility van dogged them in the outside lane. Mounted on its roof, a microwave dish was spinning slowly. Kris knew the techs inside were set to nail the relay signal of Macdonald Fisher's cell phone and ride it down to its source.

"Bloodsucking bastard's being cute, is what it is," Matt spoke up at length. "He calls the *po*lice number from way out this way and says he wants the doc. Then he buttons up and slides right back off the radar."

Turning in his seat, he looked from Kris's face to Yuri's and back again.

"I reckon the 'sucker decided to run silent, run deep for a spell," he added. "Hell's the man's game is what I want to know."

Yuri clicked on the wipers against the misting rain.

"Perhaps he is merely taking his time, lieutenant," he said. "Has only been half hour since he called, yes?"

Matt scowled at his watch.

"Thirty-four minutes," he said. "And countin', man."

"He wants me," Kris said. "Don't worry, Uncle Matt. He just wants to be sure I'm close when he breaks cover again.

"He feels the hunt closing in on him," she explained. "And he can see his supply's been cut off. Now his need's bigger than ever and he knows he can't keep running.

"He knows," she said again. "Trust me, he knows. It won't be long now."

Matt appeared to smile in spite of himself.

"Doggone it, Kris," he said. "How can you be so rock-solid sure?"

"If I could tell you that," she said with a shrug, "I might be even better at this than I am now."

"Heads up, lieutenant."

Keeping his eyes on the road, Yuri picked up the microphone from under the dash and passed it to him.

"Is Det. Sims," he said. "She says they have made visual contact up ahead."

"Yeah, Kelly, it's Judson," Matt said in the mike. "*What?*"

After some more chatter from the speakers, he put his head back and punched the air with his fist.

"Patrol car ID'd his plate!" he crowed. "Our boy's pulled over at a truck stop. I make it not more'n a mile away from here up I-75."

Yuri ran his window down and put the blue flasher on the roof. Then he hit the siren and floored the gas. As they took off due north, Kris sat back with her phone between her hands.

"He let 'em see him," she said. "He knew I was right behind him and he knows just as well how much I want him. He's weighed his options. He knows the score."

She spoke louder against the wind rush.

"What we're dealing with here is smart," she went on. "Pure evil, granted. And it's only a useful approximation of human, sure, right. Still, it's smart. Very, very smart. Please, y'all, let's not lose sight of that."

Matt braced an arm on the seatback and leaned toward her.

"Kris, hey," he said. "He's got a name now, you know."

"Not what I'm dealing with."

Kris knew better than to let the depth of her desire show. Even to herself, she'd barely admit how close she wanted to get to this unique entity. At last she knew what it was, and now everything depended on taking it alive.

"Unh-uh," she said aloud. "Don't confuse the jagged bit of psyche I'm going to be talking to with anything close to a human being. That'd be a big mistake. So don't, Matt, just don't. And please, pass it along."

"You don't mind my saying so, doc," he muttered, "that sounds kind of cold. I mean, he trusts you. You and nobody else, right?"

"It can't trust anybody," she said. "Not even if it wanted to."

She was loosening up, getting primed for the dialogue to come.

"Right now," she said, "it's like a junkie in a corner with the kick shakes coming on bad. It needs a fix in the worst way. All it wants is survival, by any means."

Matt raised an eyebrow and gave her a narrow frown.

"It wants me," she said one more time. "As to why, it's just a matter of options like I said. I guess you could call it the principle of the devil you know."

Her phone rang.

She answered right away. A tech whispered that the circuit was open and the Vampire was on the line. He gave her a tone, and Kris settled the speaker by her ear with her lips close to the mouthpiece.

"Hello, Red," she said. "See? It's just the way I promised it'd be. Nothing has changed between us. I'm still here for you, like nobody else."

She might have been soothing a baby in its blanket.

"I'm here, Red," she crooned. "Right here. For you."

Against the arc lamps, the rain came down like quicksilver

and made bright puddles on the blacktop apron. A dingy white Dodge Ram van had pulled up in the middle of the lot, thirty yards from the gas pumps. Its headlights were out, and the engine wasn't running.

A ring of police cruisers had it hemmed in tight with ranks of uniformed officers fanned out at the sides. Behind them, a SWAT team was deploying from a tactical wagon. Kris stayed close to the detectives as they crouched in the open in back of the cars. Now she was worried.

"I lost him," she said, mainly to herself. "At the end he just disappeared, right in the middle of talking to me. And then..."

For a moment she'd thought she heard a child crying on the line, but she couldn't be sure. Now as she looked around, Matt caught her eye. He motioned urgently for her.

"Over here, Kris," he called. "C'mon."

She joined him by the telecom truck. At his side stood a wiry young man in plainclothes with earphones on. Hollow-cheeked and freckled, he had a sensitive look.

"This is Det. Jones," Matt said to her. "He's the best crisis negotiator we got on the squad."

Kris said hi. Then before Matt could finish his introductions, she turned to a young woman with short dark hair. Waiting by the men, she wore scrubs under a hooded raincoat and was close to Kris's size.

"You're a doc," Kris said without thinking about it. "I mean, aren't you?"

"This is Dr. Angelina Sanchez," Matt said. "She's—well, she knows Lawrence Fitzhugh pretty well."

"We grew up together," she said in a rush. "We go back to grade school. We'd just got to know each other all over again, too. See, I bumped into him when he was bringing a patient into NICU at Grady."

Kris picked up an edge of NYC on top of her Metro accent, maybe from the South Bronx but more likely uptown Manhattan.

"I'm a neonatologist, you see," she went on with a quick

breath. "Up to a year ago, I was still in training. I'd just moved back to town to join the med school faculty."

"Me, too," said Kris. "Even more recently. In psych."

She clasped a hand that was as small and slim as hers and felt just as strong.

"Call me Kris, doctor," she said. "Everybody does."

"I'm Angie, Kris."

Tiny white teeth flashed in a tan, fine-boned face.

"Glad to meet you," she added, "doctor."

Angie turned her head a bit to the right, out of the shadows. Then Kris saw the big purple stain that ran from her hairline down past her cheek on the left. She recognized it as a vascular nevus, one of the congenitally disfiguring lesions that not even a skin laser could take off.

"You say you knew him from childhood," Kris pressed her. "D'you mean right after he got placed with his foster parents, the Fitzhughs?"

"That's right, Kris."

Leaning closer, Angie set her jaw and dropped her voice.

"We all knew what he'd been through, or at least we'd heard the rumors," she said. "But Lawrence would never talk about it. Not a word, as far as I know. Not to anybody."

Trying not to fix on too many people who were moving too fast around them, Kris thought even faster.

"I need to know something, Angie," she said. "Did he ever have any nicknames?"

"Nicknames—Lawrence?"

Angie made a face, but her eyes stayed serious and never wavered from Kris's.

"That'd be way out of character, believe me," she said. "It was always just plain 'Lawrence' or 'Fitzhugh.' Only way he'd have it."

"Not 'Larry'?"

Wrinkling her nose, Angie shook her head.

"He *hated* that name, Kris," she said. "I think it had to do with—well, maybe what they called him before..."

Kris nodded. At their side, Det. Jones looked bewildered

as he clutched at his headset and shifted from foot to foot. At last Kris stepped back.

"Thanks," she said. "Now, I need to—*Je*sus!"

Like a line of thunder, four rifle shots cracked on the air.

"Is okay, Kris," Yuri called over to her. "They just blew tires."

"That's *not* okay," she yelled back. "They're going to spook the mortal crap out of him. Jesus."

Brushing rain out of her hair, Kris spun around and tried to push closer to see.

"Kris?" said Matt. "What's this sudden concern for the perp's nerves, and all? Didn't you just tell me what we dealing with's not even human?"

"I was talking about Red, not..."

She ground her teeth. Squinting ahead, she caught something moving at the side window of the van. Cropped hair like pale straw showed just over the rim.

"For Christ's sake, Matt," she pleaded. "Do we really need all this firepower out here? C'mon, can't you do something to call off this Rambo mission?"

"Command authority goes to the cap'n over there, Kris."

Matt gestured toward a tall, craggy figure in black fatigues.

"Not to mention the chief," he added. "Word is, she'll be on the scene herself any minute now."

"But—but—"

Kris groaned out loud and caught her breath.

"All these tight-jawed, flinty-eyed SWAT jocks running around with the Fritz helmets and the MP5s," she said between her teeth. "They're just waiting for a clean shot so they can blow him out of his socks. Aren't they, Matt?"

"They're pros," he said. "Yes, they heard what was on the wall at the last two victims' places, if that's what you're asking, Kris. Plus, they know about that stash of guns that went missing after victim number one got all his blood drained out of 'im."

Looking steeled to act and set to go, Matt shook his head at her.

"They've got the word about Lawrence Fitzhugh's service record," he added. "For that matter, too, we let 'em know his dental records've already matched up with all the victims' wounds."

"*Jesus*."

Desperate now, Kris pressed her phone tight to her ear and spoke into it.

"Larry, Larry, listen to me," she begged. "It's Kris, Dr. Kris. I'm your friend, Larry, and I want to help you out. Larry, please talk to me, please. Larry?"

She strained to hear on the open line. For way too long, there was nothing but dead air. Then once again, she heard a child's voice.

This time it sounded like a little boy to her. His words were faint, and Kris couldn't make out what he was saying. But still she sensed he was scared clear through.

"Here!" she yelled as loud as she could. "Listen!"

Waving over her head, Kris shook the phone at the SWAT leader.

"See, see, captain?" she called. "There's a kid in there!"

"Dr. Van Zant's right," Det. Jones sang out. "It is a child."

Pushing his headphones into his ears with both hands, the negotiator straightened up by the phone truck.

"And he's talking from inside the vehicle," he added. "No doubt about it."

"Hostage onboard!" the SWAT leader bellowed to his men. "Repeat, subject is holding a hostage. There's a kid in the van!"

"Here go, doc."

One of the tactical officers had lumbered up beside Kris, and now he helped her belt into a flak jacket.

"If you gone be this close to the fire zone," he said, "you best get you a vest on."

"Don't you have one in a floral pattern?" she muttered. "Never mind. Thanks.

"Larry, please," she said back on the phone. "Listen to me. It's Kris, and I want you to just sit tight. Stay right where you are and let me come and get you. Okay now?

"I know you're afraid, honey," she went on softly. "Yeah, I know. It looks bad out here, sure. But you've got to—no, don't. Please! Don't—oh my God."

While she watched, the panel of the van slid back. The gap widened to a couple of feet. Then, slick with rain, a blond head stuck out.

Gun barrels came up and leveled off on all sides. Kris heard safeties snapping and bolts hauled back. She didn't give herself time to think.

Ducking low, she spun away from the men. She broke through the police line with her knees up and her elbows pumping high. Shouts and static roared at her back, but she paid them no heed now. Kris ran headlong for the van.

She got to it just as a big gaunt man in dark glasses stood up from inside. Jumping in front of him, she grabbed hold of his arms just above the elbows. Then she pulled down with all she had. Caught off center, he tumbled out the door and took a dive straight into her.

Kris bucked a neat sidestep. Then she kicked back with both legs and spun up in midair. She came down on top as the two of them hit the ground and splashed on asphalt. With the impact, orders and warning shouts burst in her ears.

Suddenly another body leapt over Kris from behind. As big as the one underneath her, it shoved her down flat and covered her full length in the middle of the pile with the weight off her. Then the world went black. Minutes seemed to go by before she saw light again.

"*Mmmff*—?" she sputtered. "Yuri?"

"Is okay, Kris."

Finally he rolled off to the side on his hands and knees and helped her up.

"Everything is under control now," he said. "See?"

The tactical crew snapped cuffs on the suspect. Then they heaved him to his feet. Flanking him close, they led him to an APD wagon waiting on the apron off to the side.

His glasses had come off in the scuffle, and for a moment

Kris met his eyes. They were a light, soft blue. Like a terrified child's, they blinked and darted from side to side.

Then they went dark and sharp like killing a klieg light. Kris smiled at that. She knew that at last she'd come face to face with Red.

He inclined his head to her as if they were old friends. With grace Kris returned the gesture. Not looking away, she called out to the others.

"He won't put up any fight for now," she said. "But listen to me. For God's sake, don't turn your back on him! Don't let your guard down. Not for a second, hear?"

One of the SWAT detail let out a yell from inside the Dodge van, which now stood derelict in the middle of the lights.

"All clear," he shouted. "There's no sign of a kid in here. No hostages. Repeat, no hostages."

Looking concerned and exasperated at the same time, Matt jogged up and took Kris's hand.

"Doc," he rasped. "Kris, please now. Tell me, just what in the hell was that all about?"

Before she could open her mouth, a rattle of metal broke out all around them and a whir and flap churned down from on top.

They ducked together and went into a crouch. Then Kris saw that the press had formed a ring of its own around the police. She realized she'd just heard shutters, not guns. Looking up, she made out a helicopter breaking to the side and closing in on where they stood.

"You wouldn't've believed me if I'd tried to tell you before," she began. "But it's the truth. In fact, it's the only way he could be..."

Startled, she felt something warm and wet tracking down her face. She ran her palms over her cheeks and took a look. Relieved, Kris found it was only muddy water. There wasn't a scratch on her after all.

She tossed her head back and raised her voice against the wash of the chopper blades that beat down on them.

"See, Uncle Matt," she said in his ear. "All along, he's been multiple."

CHAPTER TWENTY-FOUR

The way the media covered the capture of the Atlanta Vampire didn't surprise Kris. She'd expected them to get it wrong. But this time even the editorial cartoon in the *Journal-Constitution* struck her as unfair. Conferring with her uncle in his office, she held up last Sunday's paper and folded it back to the op-ed page.

"Just look at this," she said. "Oh, c'*mon* now."

The drawing's central character was a girlish form in a lab coat. Confronting her was a towering, shadowy figure in a black cape. As blood dripped from her adversary's fangs, the pint-sized heroine stood her ground and held out a reflex hammer like a crucifix.

"I mean, my nose isn't really as pointy as that," Kris insisted. "Is it?"

Hank took the cold Meerschaum pipe from between his teeth and shook his head.

"I assure you, my dear Kristin," he said, "exaggeration is the very soul of caricature."

"You think?"

Tossing the newspaper aside, she began to pace up and down the carpet while Hank settled back in his chair behind the desk.

"I need your help, big uncle," she said. "Please, tell me if you think I'm charging in where shrinks ought to fear to tread."

Resting a hand on his belly, Hank looked judicious. To determine Lawrence Fitzhugh's competence to stand trial, the court had appointed them experts. Together, they'd visited the prisoner in his medical isolation cell at county lockup over the past several days. The senior psychiatrist had given Kris her head all the while.

"As to the diagnosis, Kristin, I think we're in substantial agreement," Hank said. "Clearly the man has become dissociative as a consequence of a chronic post-traumatic stress syndrome of the highest order."

He looked down and fussed some more with his empty pipe.

"And in his present persona of implicitly believing himself to be an immortal, nameless vampire, legally he's as insane as the day is long," Hank went on. "But then comes the question of whether it's possible for him to recover even a vestige of his dominant premorbid personality."

He took a reflective pull on the Meerschaum.

"Well, with conventional therapy and mainstream analytic approaches, I'd put his prognosis for significant improvement, let alone cure, as guarded, to say the least," he said around the stem. "But with you on the case, my dear..."

Kris held her breath but didn't slow her pacing.

"I think it's worth a try," he said at last. "I'm willing to state as much to the court, too, Kristin. As to what the outcome will be, though, I can certainly make no promises."

"It's okay, Uncle Hank," she said. "That's all I could ever ask of you. Thanks."

She gave him a buss on the temple.

"I already talked to Judge Merrihew," she told him. "And she'll take formal notice of my status as a putative defense expert, without prejudice to our findings so far."

Hank patted Kris's head. Then as she got set to go, he spread his arms wide after her. Equal parts benediction and wonder, it was an old sign between them.

"Excuse me, Dr. Hank," Terri Frank called at the doorway. "I wanted to let Kris know that Sgt. Mackey from Fort Bragg—that is, the US Armed Forces Joint Special Operations Command?—he just got here. So did Dr. Sanchez from Grady Memorial. I put 'em in your office, Kris."

"Thanks, TF," Kris said, back in motion. "And did you get

hold of all that old material I asked for from the Department of Human Resources?"

"I had to go digging in the state archives," Terri said. "I used your name and Dr. Hank's along with Judge Merrihew's order just like you told me to. That got 'em to unseal the records so I could make copies. Now the whole file's on your desk."

"Attawoman, T.," Kris told her. "Outstanding job. Way to go."

As she hit her stride in the hallway, the young assistant skipped to keep up.

"Oh, and Kris," she said at her back, "one of the paralegals at Clarke & Associates just called to confirm your meeting over there, in an hour?"

"Check, T."

"They're all set," Terri said. "And you know, in the background, I could hear Hapgood Clarke himself talking. He sounded like—I don't know."

Terri folded her hands and made a face of awe as they hauled up together by the door to Kris's office.

"I don't know," she said again. "Like, Moses meets Matlock?"

"That's why he's the best criminal defense attorney south of the Mason-Dixon line, T.," Kris said. "And did my suit ever get back from the cleaner's?"

"I hung it in your closet, Kris," said Terri. "Hard to picture you in designer chalk stripes like that. I'll bet you look like, well, like a lawyer."

"That's the concept, T.," Kris said. "If you can't lick 'em..."

Sergeant Major Ross Mackey blinked hard and cleared his throat as he came near the end of his war story. Then he looked down. Facing him across the high-buffed top of the conference table, Kris averted her eyes.

For a few moments she gazed through the panel of smoked glass at his back. Twenty stories down from them was the

Fulton County Courthouse. Gleaming white in the sun, its front loomed right across Martin Luther King Jr. Drive.

"To tell you the truth," the Green Beret went on, "Fitzhugh surprised me. I confess, before that day I just didn't think the boy had it in him."

Kris watched his face and posture. The hue and texture of weathered teak, Ross's features were planed down square and gave little away to her. As he sat up ramrod, she took in a chest full of combat ribbons and the arrowhead-shaped Special Forces patch on the left shoulder of his Class A greens.

"But you said he'd always been a good soldier," Hapgood Clarke coaxed him from the head of the table. "Isn't that so, top sergeant?"

"Yes, sir," Ross said. "As to discipline and motivation and general competence, there never was any problem with Fitzhugh. He was a damn fine medic, too."

Glancing around at the women who flanked him, he looked apologetic.

"Begging your pardon, ladies," he said. "Er uh, doctors, counselor, I mean."

"Sure," Hapgood said. "But...?"

As the senior lawyer smiled, long seams and creases drew out in a face framed by a brush of hair like steel wool and a squared-off Brillo pad of a goatee. But his eyes didn't change. Icy blue and keen, they put Kris in mind of a buccaneer who'd spent a lifetime on the high seas but was still up for a raid.

"Maybe Fitzhugh just didn't seem to you like the stuff that heroes are made of," he said as if prompting a witness on the stand. "'S that it, top?"

"I'm not sure I know a whole lot about heroes, sir," Ross said. "But up to that point, I've got to tell you that personally Fitzhugh struck me as a pain in the—in the neck, that is."

He coughed behind his fist.

"Man just wouldn't ever unbend," he said. "Never would. That's all."

"Lawrence was always a dry stick, a cold fish," Angie

Sanchez said beside him. “I mean, he’d always come across that way, until you got to—well, okay.”

The neonatologist set her chin and tugged on the lapels of a tailored pinstripe suit much like Kris’s.

“Even after you got to know him,” she admitted, “Lawrence could still be a prig.”

“It was like having some kind of Baptist preacher in the outfit,” the sergeant major said, nodding at her. “Without even knowing any good hymns, I mean to say, or having the rhythm to do the sermonizing right.

“Man was stiff as a poker on top of that,” he added. “He’d just keep his peace all the time, you know what I’m saying. Always seemed like he had something on his mind but he just wouldn’t let it out.”

Silent now, Hapgood inclined his head and opened his palms to him.

“Okay,” Ross said. “But then came that day back in ’91, in Kuwait. Our unit got cut off way ahead of our lines. An Iraqi Republican Guard advance battalion got the jump on us. Liked to chewed us up, too, for good and all.”

Kris saw his eyes go bright with the memory.

“Well, just say that’s when I saw something come out in Fitzhugh that must’ve been there all the time,” Ross went on. “And it wasn’t just that he risked his life for his outfit to start with either, after we got pinned down trying to pull out under fire.

“No, sir,” he said. “It’s how he kept coming back for the wounded, one after the other, picking us up and carrying us out on his back. One by one, all by himself. Lord knows, it had to be a temptation for him to turn tail and run.

“Maybe it’d even been best in a tactical sense,” he added, “to pull stakes and take off while the getting was good.”

The commando met each of the other’s eyes in turn and then shook his head.

“But no, sir,” he said. “No, ma’am. He didn’t run, and he didn’t look back. And he made sure he got every last mother’s son of us out of harm's way before he ever even stopped to catch his breath or pull his socks up.

"Maybe if it'd been a different kind of war without so much politics involved," he went on, "and maybe if he'd made some more friends along the way, Fitzhugh would've got the Medal of Honor. Way I see it, he surely deserved it."

He shifted to face the head of the conference table.

"And I'll testify to that, sir," he said. "Whenever and wherever you please."

At the foot of the table sat a senior associate whom Hapgood had introduced as Jenny Miller. She struck Kris as a paler, heavier version of her friend Jezreel Thornton. Now Jenny looked up from her legal pad and stopped writing for the first time since they'd all sat down here.

"The military seemed to bring out the best in Lawrence," Angie broke the quiet. "I could tell he hated having to leave the Army."

Kris saw her tracing the long purple discoloration on the side of her face without seeming to notice what she was doing.

"I was with him in Yugoslavia when he got picked off by that Serb bugger with the Russian laser gear," Ross said. "And—beg pardon again, ladies."

He made as if to bite his tongue.

"I went up and visited Fitzhugh in the hospital after he got lased," he went on. "He'd just got word about the medical discharge. But you know, even after he'd saved my life in the Gulf like that, he still wouldn't say a word about it."

"He did to me," Angie said. "We were talking after he'd come back here. As usual, I had to pry every word out of him. But finally he said maybe it would've been best if he'd died in combat."

"And?" Kris spoke up at last. "What'd you say to that, Angie?"

"To shut up, dammit!" she snapped. "That that was just morbid, self-pitying, romantic bullshit."

Suddenly her eyes overflowed, and she put her head down and dug a handkerchief out of her purse.

"I—I'm sorry," Angie muttered. "I beg your pardon."

"Of course, of course," said Hapgood. "That's all right, doctor, quite all right."

He gave his associate a nod, and then he met Kris's eye across the table.

"I thank y'all for sharing this with me," he said. "And now if you'd care to kick back and maybe take another question or two from Jen here, I believe Dr. Van Zant and I need to have us a li'l talk back in m' office."

Unlike the conference room with its view from on high of the courthouse square and its wall of photos of famous clients, the lawyer's workspace was close and cluttered and smelled of cigar smoke.

Hapgood dropped Kris a bow and indicated a wooden chair in front of his desk. Kris said thanks. But before she sat down to face him, she put the file she'd brought with her on top of a stack of folders on the blotter.

"Word I get, doctor," he said, "is you've already got you a working theory about this case."

"I sure do, Mr. Clarke, and call me Kris," she said. "Everybody does."

"Make it Hap."

He gave her a crinkly smile, but still she could just about feel the coolness of his eyes on her skin.

"Maybe I can save us a little time here, Kris," he said. "I've already got wind of all the stories that's going around the DA's office."

Not surprised, Kris smiled back at him.

"I heard about 'Sister Night's' book," he told her. "From what the late Ms. Lu Ellen Reese wrote down before she got herself shot by a party or parties unknown in a nearby jurisdiction, I gather that some recently deceased pillars of our community may've been engaged in, well..."

"Barely imaginable S&M practices," Kris filled in for him, "involving the repeated tapping of their veins followed by reinfusion of the bulk of their blood volume. All consensual, of course."

"C'mon, Kris," he said with a frown. "It's hard to think some folks'd really take pleasure in that kind of thing."

"Guess that's why there's strawberry *and* vanilla, huh, Hap?"

"No disputin' taste, I reckon," he sighed. "But why in the hell'd they keep going in for that particular kind of recreation when there was bloodless corpses turning up in the neighborhood?"

"Because their form of blood play didn't involve biting," Kris said. "And because at the heart of S&M is trust, pure and simple. In the accepted course of things, betrayal of one player by another would be unthinkable."

"You're the expert there," Hap grunted. "But getting back to the case at hand, I take it from certain sources that the individual who was hiring out to satisfy these peculiar cravings went by the moniker of Nurse Nell."

Impressed this time, Kris nodded.

"Not that the media's even got close to that angle," she began. "Her real name is—"

"If you don't mind, Kris," Hap cut in, "unless you've got some solid proof to back you up on that, I'd just as soon keep it at no names."

"No names," she agreed. "But I'm convinced she's the one who got to Lawrence Fitzhugh's vampire personality. Then she made it come join in her games."

"Okay," Hap said. "But how'd she link up with him to start with?"

"I don't know yet," Kris said. "But that's exactly how she's covered her tracks so nobody's inclined to dig any deeper."

"Can't rightly say I blame the prosecutor on that call, Kris."

Tilting his chair back, Hap stretched his legs and put his feet up on the edge of the desk.

"More than likely it'd be one thankless can of worms to open up," he said. "What with all the juice the victims' families've got to keep their names out of the tabs.

"Then there's the matter of motive here," he added. "Or its lack."

"I admit I don't know why Nurse Nell killed her clients."

Finally Kris gave in to the urge to get up and pace in front of the desk.

"I just know that to get away with it, she used the Vampire as a pawn," she went on. "And as for Lawrence Fitzhugh, he's an innocent man."

"ME's forensic people matched up his teeth with every last bite mark in the victims," Hap said, ticking off the points on his fingers. "Samples of the victims' blood turned up in the freezer at his place of residence. And I hear there's even some manner of computer evidence that he made contact with the victims via the Internet, in chat rooms and such."

Shaking her head, Kris tracked up and down a carpet that was already well worn.

"Nurse Nell set it up," she said. "All of it. I know it."

"Maybe so," Hap chuckled. "But you got to admit, Kris, it sure doesn't make Mr. Fitzhugh sound 'innocent.'"

Then he looked thoughtful as if to console her.

"But we both know how the defendant's background'll play out in the media," he said. "Abused child grows up to be a war hero, and so on. And what with his present state of mind, you'n bet not even Tricky Nick's gone want to see that ol' boy fry."

Kris caught the reference to Nicholas Atkinson. She knew he was the longtime Fulton County District Attorney. She'd also heard rumors that his political ambitions were even more flagrant than was traditional with that post.

"I hear the DA'd be happy with a plea of not guilty by reason of insanity," she said out loud. "And if I thought that'd be best for my—for Lawrence, I wouldn't mind if the greenest rookie in the public defender's office entered it for him either."

Holding her hands up, Kris went on before Hap could respond.

"But we both know what that'd mean," she said fast.

"Commitment. Automatic institutional commitment, unreviewable de facto. And in this great state, you could be sure Lawrence Fitzhugh'd never see natural light again for the rest of his days."

"Oh, I've had some dealings with our state psychiatric hospitals, Kris," Hap said. "In general, sure, they're understaffed, overworked, and underfunded. Still, they got some good people workin' in 'em."

Locked on her gaze, he propped his chair back against the wall and looked sly.

"Hardworkin', ordinary folks like that, though," he went on, "I guess it'd be natural that they wouldn't take kindly to some young Ivy League hotshot poking around, looking over their shoulder at one of their prize patients."

"Okay, I admit it, Hap," Kris said. "I know what this case could do for my career And I know how rare it is to take one like him alive."

Pausing by his desk, she pointed to the thick sheaf of Human Resource documents she'd put down between them.

"So sure, I'd hate like hell to lose him," she went on. "But I also know what I can do for him."

She took a beat for her conviction to build, and then she let it all out at once.

"And I'll be *damned* if I'll stand by and let a dissociative identity disorder with highly evolved vampire tendencies wind up warehoused in the back ward of a state mental hospital like some dime-a-dozen schiz off the street!"

"Okay, okay," Hap gentled her. "Who'm *I* to make any bones about ambition anyway? Still and all, one other consideration touching on you does come to mind here."

Still overlooking the file in front of him, he gestured at the newspaper clippings heaped up beside it.

"Not to get unduly personal about it, Kris," he said, "but you can see how the newsies've been having 'em a field day about what befell you and your family at the hands of another serial killer, way back when."

"Screw my background," Kris said. "Look, Hap, we've all

got our demons to deal with. In my case I just chose to give 'em a big ol' hug and put 'em on the payroll. Okay?"

Hap watched her for a little longer. Then he threw his head back and gave a laugh that sounded to Kris like a proud papa's. Finally he put on a pair of bifocals and began riffling through the photocopied pages of Lawrence's old file.

A few minutes later, he looked up. Kris could swear she saw a mist taking hold in his eyes then. He coughed behind his hand and leveled a finger at her.

"Say I stood up on Mr. Fitzhugh's behalf," he began, not blinking. "I'd have to turn down every deal the DA could come up with and buck the court on it, too.

"That is," he added, "if I was to enter a plea of not guilty by reason of altered capacity on account of this post-traumatic multiple personality syndrome or dissociative identity disorder, or whatever the hell else you want to call it here."

"That's why I came to you," she said. "You're the only one who could make it stick, Hap. Just as I'm the only one who can bring Lawrence Fitzhugh back."

"But they—"

His voice broke as he reached for the file again, and he cleared his throat with a growl.

"Those sorry-assed bastards who had 'im when he was just a li'l kid, Kris," he choked out. "For God's sake, they kept 'im penned up like a veal calf. They cut 'im and drank his blood. They...

"I mean, Jesus," he groaned, "why didn't he just wind up a basket case?"

"That happens with certain types of personalities, Hap," she said. "The more heat and pressure you put on 'em at an early stage, the harder they get and the more sides they form. That's how they survive."

Facing him square, Kris shrugged.

"But even diamonds'll crack," she added. "If you hit 'em right."

"And you think you can put 'im back together again, Kris," Hap demanded. "Just like that?"

"With your help."

She dropped her voice but spoke even more in earnest than before.

"Keep him out of the faceless, dehumanizing system and put him in my hands, Hap," she pleaded. "Do that for me for just a little while, and I'll make him whole again. I can do it. And I will. I swear it by God."

He looked away from her and seemed to peer through the wall. Kris hoped he was thinking of what his prospective client meant to the likes of Sgt. Maj. Ross Mackey and Dr. Angie Sanchez out there. That's why she'd brought them with her.

"Okay, Kris," Hap said at last. "I'll take the case. Pro bono, natch.

"But first," he added, "I want you to answer me just one thing."

He got to his feet with her and held out his hand.

"A pitiful tortured child, a bloodsucking nightcrawler of a killer, a tight-assed geek GI who turns out under fire to be a red-blooded American hero and no mistake about it, all rolled up in the same package," he said in one breath. "Can you put a name on that condition for me, doctor?"

Kris smiled and then solemnly joined hands with him.

"I sure can, counselor," she said. "Human."

CHAPTER TWENTY-FIVE

"All rise for Judge Merrihew!" the bailiff sang out. "The Superior Court of Fulton County is now in session. God save this honorable court!"

Kris caught herself watching the jury box out of habit. Since this was just a pretrial hearing, it now stood empty. By all the signs, though, this should be a crucial day in court for her.

She felt dwarfed standing up. Looming blank-faced in front of her, Lawrence Fitzhugh had on a pair of blaze-orange coveralls fresh from the county lockup. To the defendant's left, Hapgood Clarke towered like a weather-beaten monument to all the downtrodden. As Kris glanced to her right, she noted how Nicholas Atkinson struck much the same pose.

For a moment she considered the DA's dashing mahogany face with his trademark straight-edged mustache. Then she nodded to her uncle right behind him. Acting as state's expert, Hank got to his feet with the dignity of a bull elephant on old ground. The chair at his side was vacant.

That was ominous. The prosecution had been coy so far about naming its other psych consultant. But Kris had no doubt as to whom they'd called in.

"Please," said Judge Evelyn Merrihew from the bench. "Be seated."

Spare and looking strict, the judge had salt-and-pepper bangs and a bun drawn up at the back of her head. A pince-nez sat on the bridge of her long, straight nose. She made Kris think of a prairie schoolmarm with winter term ahead of her.

"All right," the judge said. "I believe I've been adequately briefed by the defense as to its findings to date. I have before me its petition for a continuance for additional psychological evaluation prior to lodging a plea of not guilty.

"Not guilty," she added, "by reason of altered state of mind or diminished mental capacity of a temporary nature. Not, that is, by reason of insanity."

"Your honor!"

The chief prosecutor was on his feet with a squad of assistant DAs bobbing up at his side.

"Once again," Nick intoned, "I'd like to register my strongest objection to this obvious delaying tactic on the part of the defense."

"You have," the judge said. "Duly noted, Mr. Atkinson."

Then she narrowed her eyes as Hap stood up, too.

"Yes, Mr. Clarke?"

"I'd just like to make it clear, judge," he said gravely. "The very farthest thing from my mind right now is putting off by so much as a minute the proper care and treatment that my client here needs and deserves."

"Okay, Mr. Clarke," Judge Merrihew sighed. "It's on the record."

She glanced down at the papers on the lectern in front of her.

"First," she announced, "the court has some queries of its own to put directly to, ah, Dr. Kershaw. I believe he has performed an independent medical evaluation of the defendant.

"And then, if the district attorney will be kind enough to present him to us," she went on with asperity, "I would also like to ask...oh. There you are."

Kris heard brisk footsteps from the back of the room, but she didn't have to turn to look to know who it was.

"Good morning, doctor," said Judge Merrihew. "So kind of you to work our proceedings into your busy schedule."

She gave a brittle smile and raised a hand in greeting to the newcomer, who paused and bowed to her.

"Your honor," the DA said, standing very straight by his chair. "At this point, I'd like to state for the record that acting as expert witness in this matter on behalf of the citizens of the State of Georgia is the greatly esteemed and renowned Dr.—"

"Yes, thank you very much, Mr. Atkinson," the judge broke in. "Certainly the witness requires no introduction in this court. Mr. Clarke, any comments or perhaps objections you'd like to make now?"

Kris kept her eyes fixed on Lawrence's back and away from the prosecution table. Hap turned in his chair and cocked an eyebrow at her. She shook her head. Standing, he made a gracious gesture across the aisle as he addressed the court.

"No, ma'am, your honor," he rumbled. "In fact, the defense would like to extend a warm welcome to the learned Dr. Stephen Laszlo."

"Very well," said Judge Merrihew. "Let's get on with it then."

❧

Kris knew Horton Kershaw from the med school as a neurology prof of high regard and long tenure. A personable and good-living Louisianan, he had a shrewd beaky face under dark curls. Once he took the stand, he made short work of the results of his exam of the defendant

"Bottom line is this man's brain works just fine," he said in his bayou brogue. "The neuro workup checked out okay. EEG, head CT, PET scan, and fMRI studies all indicated normal structure and function of the central nervous system."

He shrugged under his pincord jacket and then let his shoulders drop.

"Guy thinks he's a vampire, sure," he concluded. "But trust me, your honor, it's not due to an organic lesion."

"Thank you, doctor," said the judge. "That clears up my questions as to Mr. Fitzhugh's state of physical health. Now if there are no further queries from either Mr. Clarke or Mr. Atkinson and their associates...?"

Raising her eyebrows over rimless lenses, she seemed to scan the courtroom from front to back.

"No? Very well," she went on. "I'd very much like to hear from Dr. Laszlo now."

Still avoiding his eyes, Kris recognized Stephen's battle dress. He had on the charcoal Brioni suit with a white shirt and silver tie by Charvet that she knew he favored for court appearances. With understated grace he went up to the bench, took the stand, and got sworn.

"Dr. Laszlo," Judge Merrihew said at his side, "I gather from the clinical report you filed with the court that you are in general agreement with the Drs. Van Zant in their assessment of Mr. Fitzhugh's mental state."

"That is so, your honor," said Stephen. "In sum, I believe this man is suffering from dissociative identity disorder. Multiple personality, if you will."

With not a trace of doubt showing, he sat up straight in the box and inclined his head slightly toward the microphone.

"And now holding sway over the remainder of his psyche," he went on, "is the entity whose primary reason for being is to seek to drink human blood."

"I see."

The judge impressed Kris with her manner, which implied that she'd heard a story like this more than once before and now was expecting with little pleasure to hear it again.

"Based on your training and experience as a psychiatrist and psychoanalyst then," she asked the witness, "what chance would you give this patient for recovery?

"And by that," she added, "I mean for his getting back to a state of mind where he doesn't want to go out and drink people's blood all the time."

"In general, your honor," Stephen said, "multiples are very difficult to treat, let alone to c-c-cure. The process is very demanding for all involved, to say the least. But in this instance..."

From the stand he finally caught Kris's eye, and she sucked in her breath and held it as she waited for him to go on.

"You see," he began, "I believe that the potential here exists to break through the wall of the persona that is dominant at present and in this way to revive and reinstate Mr. Fitzhugh's normal, previously maintained identity.

"And this is solely due to a link, a unique path of empathy if you will, that is already well established," he proceeded. "Now I must admit that I myself most strongly recommended against the attempt to forge such a link at the time."

"Yes, doctor," the judge said. "I'm sure we're all aware of your opinion in regard to young Dr. Van Zant's communication with the defendant prior to his arrest. It was, after all, quite widely broadcast in this vicinity."

Leaning closer to him, she used both hands in a gesture of dwindling patience.

"My question is," she said, "how much of a chance remains to get through to him *now*?"

"I think at present there is only one such chance, your honor," said Stephen. "And that chance lies in K-K—in Dr. Van Zant herself."

Kris saw how he braced himself even harder as he frowned and drew a breath. At the same time, she caught a rustle and hum from the table across the aisle from her. If there had been a script up to this point, she could tell that now her onetime mentor and thwarted suitor was getting set to depart from it.

"It's a matter of her damned—I beg you pardon, your honor—of her methods," the analyst blurted. "She works from the inside out, as it were. Her therapeutic approach poses the very greatest emotional and functional risk, I must tell you, to patient and therapist alike.

"But still," he said after a beat. "Still, her results, as I myself have witnessed over and over again in c-c-cases that by every objective standard were quite hopeless, have been nothing short of astonishing. She—"

"Your honor!"

The DA's voice rang over Stephen's in spite of the amplification.

"Your honor," he called again. "If you please, I wish to enter an objection even if this is the state's expert. I object to—"

"You're out of order, Mr. Atkinson," Judge Merrihew cut him off. "Sit down."

Never turning her head, she kept her eyes on the witness stand.

"Now tell me, Dr. Laszlo," she charged him. "Is it your opinion that the defendant can regain a mental state in which he'd be competent to stand trial for the crimes he's accused of?"

Kris watched as Stephen closed his eyes and seemed to fight down a shudder.

"Only under the management and c-c-care of Dr. K-K-Kristin Van Zant, your honor," he finally said. "God help him."

While the DA's team made some more noises to be recognized, a buzz broke out in earnest from the press and spectator's gallery. Judge Merrihew banged her gavel once and sat back. For several moments she set her gaze fast on Kris.

At last, still intent, she held up a long bony forefinger and crooked it at her.

❧

Overshadowed by Nick Atkinson and Hap Clarke, Kris stood at attention between the men in front of the bench. She stole a glance over her shoulder and saw Lawrence raise his head. Even though she couldn't make out his eyes behind his dark glasses, she still felt his attention come to rest on her.

She sensed the same from Yuri and Matt. Both of the detectives craned forward in their seats in back of the DA's table. Closer to the front of the courtroom on the defense side sat Angie Sanchez. Her eyes never left Kris either.

"Dr. Van Zant," Judge Merrihew said. "I believe, if I may borrow a phrase, that extraordinary situations call for extraordinary measures."

"Me, too," said Kris. "I mean yes, your honor. So do I."

"Therefore," the judge said, "I hereby order that Mr. Fitzhugh be transferred with maximum-security precautions in place from County Jail to the special neuropsychiatric evaluation facility within Grady Memorial Hospital.

"He is to be confined there for the next thirty days," she went on. "Further, Dr. Van Zant, I order that the defendant be placed exclusively under your care throughout that period."

She cast stringent looks from side to side at the lawyers who flanked Kris before she focused on her one more time.

"That is," she wound up, "if you're agreeable to such an arrangement, doctor."

Kris realized she'd been holding her breath again and let it out all at once.

"Yes, thank you, your honor," she said. "That's all I need."

CHAPTER TWENTY-SIX

Kris took a meeting with the ward staff of the lockdown psych unit at Grady Memorial. They got together in the conference room by heavy metal doors with triple-pane Plexiglas panels. As they sat down around the long tabletop with its ancient pattern of cuts and scuffs and burns, Kris briefed them on her patient.

"Keep this in mind at all times," she said. "What we've got here's the real deal. Don't for a second mistake it for just another flaky, grossly delusional patient who thinks he's a vampire.

"Uh-unh," she said deliberately. "We've got to take it seriously. Dead seriously."

She paused and looked from face to face at the nurses, counselors, psych techs, and security personnel. Meeting her eye, they all made it plain to her that they were veterans. Kris knew that to pull duty down here, you had to have seen everything at least twice.

"I know what it's capable of because I've observed what it's done," she went on. "I've been there even before the bodies could get cold. I was right behind it.

"So trust me," she said at large. "No matter how diffident and cooperative it might seem to you, you'd be a lot safer trying to get up close and personal with a hungry king cobra than you'd be letting your guard down and giving it any advantage over you."

Just as she'd hoped for, Kris caught a few frowns of disapproval at the phrase she'd used.

"And by 'it,'" she added, "I'm referring to a complex and highly organized independent psychopathological entity that'll answer to the name 'Red.'"

She got a nod from Naomi Webley, RN, at that.

Kris had heard she'd been unit supervisor here for close to twenty years. About six feet tall and a solid two hundred pounds, the boss nurse had a serene round face with anthracite skin and pewter hair. Behind shell-rimmed glasses, her eyes were clear hazel and made Kris doubt she'd ever missed anything that went down on her watch.

"At the same time," Kris went on, "I don't want any of you to confuse the personality we're going to be dealing with here with a man named Lawrence Fitzhugh. No, not at all.

"Mr. Fitzhugh," she added, "is a highly trained and dedicated professional, much like yourselves. He's a decent and honorable man."

If not, she said to herself, the easiest guy in the world to cozy up to.

"He's shown himself to be extraordinarily compassionate and immeasurably brave, even under fire," she said out loud. "Of course, he also has a history of abuse in his earliest years of a type and to a degree that'd be hard for most people to imagine. I'm sure we've all heard the stories.

"Well, they're true," she added softly. "I'm here to tell you that the truth's even worse than the rumors made it out to be."

Kris saw a number of the staff taking notes. She wondered if they'd made any more out of the case so far than she had. As she saw it, great evil done to a child that then spawned kindred evil in the man he grew up to be was hardly an explanation. To her it was barely a clue.

"So let's get down to basics," she said louder. "Red wants blood, pure and simple. So I want everyone on this unit to make every effort to cover up any sign of blood or any stimulus that might be related to bloodletting or the shedding of blood.

"For instance," she told them, "I've talked to Dietary. I want to keep Red healthy and well nourished, of course, but not on meat. I don't want anything on its plate that so much as hints at a living, animal original.

"Hell," she muttered, "not even ketchup for that matter."

She smiled in return for the few laughs she got.

"Keep any cuts or abrasions of your own under a dressing," she proceeded. "And not to sound like a park ranger at Yellowstone warning you about the bears, but if any of the female staff is menstrual I want you to keep clear of this patient until your period's over. Seriously, now. Okay?

"Okay," Kris said. "No TV for it either. Keep all violent imagery of any kind away from it, especially on the news. So, no magazines or newspapers either.

"Avoid even having conversations of a possibly exciting nature that it might overhear," she added. "No conflict, in short, for it to feed on."

"Dr. Van Zant," said a gravelly voice from the side of the room. "Question, here?"

She nodded to a sandy-haired nurse with sad eyes and lines etched deep in his face.

"Aren't you outlining a plain old-fashioned no-frills D-tox protocol?" he asked her. "Isn't it like goin' pure ol' cold turkey off a bad habit?"

"Exactly!" said Kris. "I want to keep it on edge and off balance to start with. In the end, I want a burnout vampire that's way too far past being strung out to put up a fight.

"At that point," she added, "I predict Lawrence Fitzhugh'll show up and we can welcome him back to life. From then on, it'll be like dealing with any multiple once you've got all the personalities in the same room together. Yes?"

A young psych assistant held her hand up, her eyes bright and troubled behind round lenses.

"I was just wondering, doctor," she said. "What if, uhm, Red offers resistance or creates some kind of conflict himself?"

"It won't," she said. "It's smart, remember, way smart. Just letting itself get locked up like this means it's hedging its bets to get what it needs."

"But you just said he wants blood, doctor, 'pure and simple,'" a seasoned-looking RN spoke up from the foot of the table. "D'you mean he might try to use something else to score—uh, to get at some blood? And if so, what?"

"Two great questions," said Kris. "The answers are yes and me."

She got up and started to pace by the side of the table.

"Me," she said again. "It knows how bad I want to get a closer look at what's inside its head. That's why it's willing to play along with me. That's why it'll risk losing its strength in the short term.

"See," she went on in motion, "I'm sure that's how Red broke out of the deepest and best defended recesses of Lawrence Fitzhugh's personality in the first place. That's how it took hold and started to grow like a malignancy in him.

"It made a deal with someone," she confided in them. "Someone who thought she could control it and who was willing to meet its needs, for a while."

"Doctor," said the supervisor. "Please. We need to know something from you. Now."

As she turned to her and came to a stop, Kris felt like a mortal waiting to hear from an Olympian goddess.

"You say somebody went and cut a deal with this dangerous, complicated entity before," the nurse said. "Well, are *you*?"

"Thank you so much for asking me that, Nurse Webley," Kris said with a serious face. "The answer is maybe."

It was a lie. Kris didn't plan to give Red anything except a bad time. But she couldn't risk his finding that out now. And to get what she wanted from him she was set to use any leverage she could lay hands on, even hope.

❧

Colleagues had told Kris that within the hospital, the Neuropsychiatric Evaluation Unit was nicknamed "deep shrink." On admission here, each patient got assigned to individual quarters. The accommodations struck her as being equal parts private hospital room and max-security prison cell.

For her sessions with her patient, though, Kris favored a setting that would give them both a bit more room to breathe. She found an open empty space off the end of the corridor that ran between individual rooms. That's where she set up a table for two.

The only light that wasn't fluorescent came from a pair of heavily barred ground-floor windows set high in the wall behind the nurses' station. From there, the nearest door out of the unit was past two lock-ins. Adding to the sense of sunken confinement was a color scheme that ran to muted blues and greens and shades of dun.

So every time she took a chair facing Red, Kris couldn't help but imagine they were in a cave together at the bottom of the sea.

"You're always on the lookout for yourself, thinking two moves ahead," she said to him. "Take the way you swiped that fancy personal-communications cell phone from Mac Fisher's place without letting Nurse Nell catch you."

Kris gave him a long, admiring whistle.

"Talk about getting ready to grab hold of another vine while you still had a strong one to swing on," she said. "As a new friend of mine would say, dude, whoa. I mean, you didn't even know I was out there."

Her patient sat tall but at ease with his long, sloping shoulders squared under a scrub shirt. Behind dark lenses like the bottoms of Coke bottles, his eyes were of a piece with his face. Stark and pale, they gave little sign of life.

He could be good-looking if he weren't so damn stolid, Kris mused, kind of like Jimmy Stewart in old movies.

"You just won't rat 'er out, though, will you?" she probed. "Even after she left you high and dry like this, you won't turn on her. If I didn't know you so well, Red, I might take that for loyalty.

"But in fact, you're just keeping your options open," she went on. "Just like from the start, huh?"

His smile might have been molded on a mannequin. Dead as it was, Kris picked up the thanks behind it. So far, she'd found that gratitude was the closest thing to emotion she could get out of him.

"I hoped you were 'out there,' Kris," he said. "I always

believed there'd be somebody I could talk to, somebody who could understand."

He kept his voice deep and low but focused his words on her as if they were exchanging secrets in a churchyard.

"I believed," he said again. "And I was right."

"You mean somebody else to talk to," she said with a nod. "I knew it, too. To get what you needed, you had to tell. You still do."

The greater the transgression, as Laszlo put it, the greater the drive to confess. Kris had heard that lecture from him more than once. She wondered in passing what Stephen would make of this chat. For her part, she was sure that Red's willingness to talk to her came straight from his will to endure.

"Tell you what," she said at length. "I'll skip the BS if you will, okay?"

"You're not really interested in how I did what I did, Kris," he said in the same tone as before. "I know what you want."

She reached across the table and rested her palm on top of his folded hands.

"You know I want you to let go, Red," she said. "Just for a little bit. C'mon now, blood brother. What d'you say?"

"I did, Kris, once before," he said. "You met the child."

Chilly and fixed, his smile came back.

"You're not interested in him either."

"Pull your horns in," she said. "Give me a crack at good ol' Lawrence Fitzhugh himself."

He shook his head, and just for a second Kris thought she saw regret in his face.

"Lawrence," he sighed. "No, Kris. The soldier's moved on."

Maybe, she marveled, just maybe there was a glimmer of remorse there as well.

"Lawrence has taken his last order," Red whispered. "There are no more battles for him to fight, you see, no more bids to be a hero. He ran out of time...

"So now he's folded his tent," he said, his voice fading. "He's gone away."

Kris caught her breath.

It was the first time Red had acknowledged Lawrence's primary personality to her. She felt the strain building in her to keep her triumph out of sight. It was just a crack of the door, but now Kris could see where it would lead her.

It was all she'd ever desired.

She admitted to herself that a dialogue with a devil behind steel doors wasn't nearly enough for her needs. It was good for publication and tenure, sure, and maybe even movie rights. But what she'd come to covet was primordial evil, true as a cancer and too pure for words. Now she wanted to cut it out of the man it had grown in and keep it like a prize.

All at once Kris was seven years old again, back in the shadows at the foot of the stairs. No matter what anyone had told her, she'd always known what was waiting in the dark. Finally she had the monster she wanted in her sights.

"Kris?"

Red was smiling thinly at her, his lips like snow heaped on snow in the dead of winter.

"Kris," he whispered again. "Are you all right?"

"I'm fine," she said. "Thanks, Red."

She gave his hand a pat and got lightly to her feet.

"Hey," she said, smiling. "Looks like it's suppertime."

Behind them stood an orderly built like a defensive lineman. He'd just wheeled in a plastic rack of steam trays. With a flourish, Kris swept the cover off her patient's plate. Then she smiled even wider over the spread of tofu, mashed potatoes, boiled collard greens, and pintos with cornbread.

"Okay, Red," she chuckled. "Later."

She gave him a cheery wave and then motioned for a nurse behind the unit desk to hit the buzzer that would trip the electronic bolt on the door.

"Till then," she called back on her way out. "*Bon appetit, mon frere*."

Kris cleared the last checkpoint in deep shrink, but she still wasn't ready to leave the hospital.

Instead, she took the steps up and crossed over to the OB wing. Then she threaded the winding halls and climbed another flight to the Neonatal Intensive Care Unit next to the high-risk nursery. Finally she slipped into the docs' lounge to wait out late rounds in NICU.

"Kris?"

Breaking off her pacing between the half-sprung couch and a row of dictation cubicles, she turned and saw Angie Sanchez come in. The neonatologist had on hospital scrubs and an OR cap, and she was shedding a long gown and a gauze mask. Her eyes went wide at the sight of Kris.

"Is he—?" she began. "Did Lawrence...?"

"Nothing to report yet," Kris told her. "I just wondered if you wanted to go get a bite to eat."

"Eat?"

As she pulled up a chair and picked up a phone, Angie seemed ready to fire off one last clinical note and get out of here.

"Sounds good," she said. "Got anywhere in particular in mind, Kris?"

"Oh, I don't know," Kris said deadpan. "Know any good Mexican restaurants nearby?"

"Well, there's this place my folks still run," Angie said. "It's back in the old neighborhood where Lawrence and I grew up, right around..."

Pausing, she looked up and mugged at Kris.

"Jeez, you shrinks really don't believe in accidents, do you?" she muttered. "You knew exactly what I'd say and where we'd go in advance."

Kris smiled brightly at her and jingled her car keys in her hand.

"My treat," she insisted. "I'll drive us if you like, in Flicka."

"Sure, sure," Angie said. "Just give me a...Flicka?"

As she looked up again, Kris noted how she tended to tilt

her head to the left to cover the long port-wine stain on the side of her face.

"Hold on," Angie said. "You mean you *named* your car, Kris?"

"It's from a book my folks used to read to me when I was a kid, called *My Friend Flicka*," Kris explained. "About this headstrong but lovable li'l horse, you know. And after all, she—I mean, it's a Saab."

"Yeah, yeah, I know the story," she said by the phone in her hand. "But still, Kris, giving your car a name like that. Isn't that kind of a, well, girly-girl thing to do?"

"Your point being…?"

"Never mind," the other doc sighed. "Gimme a minute here. Then we'll go catch a meal at Sanchez's Café Grande de Monterrey and I'll give you a guided tour around the 'hood where Lawrence and I grew up, okay?"

"Thanks," Kris said with a smile that was even bigger and brighter than before. "That's totally what I was hoping for."

CHAPTER TWENTY-SEVEN

The restaurant gave Kris the impression of a small Latin American nation made up for the most part of Angie's relatives. Various Sanchezes fixed their meal, served it, and then hung around to entertain them as they ate. For their part, the family seemed impressed as Kris put away three big helpings of poblanos in walnut sauce.

After dinner, she dropped the top on the Saab and drove through the streets of East Atlanta.

"The old neighborhood's changing," Angie said from the passenger seat. "Back when I was growing up here in the '70s and '80s, you really got a feel for…I dunno."

They passed low-slung blocks of modest old storefronts and houses that had a lived-in look. On all sides of them, Kris picked up the signs of spillover from Downtown development. She sensed that gentrification was set to take hold here like kudzu.

"Call it community," Angie said. "For lack of a better word."

Watching and listening, Kris nodded in encouragement.

"Not to get all rosy about it," Angie went on. "But we were pretty tolerant for the times, given how mixed we were around here. I mean black and white, sure, like you'd expect.

"But there was a bunch of us Mex and some Guatemalans and Hondurans, too," she added. "Some Namese and Lao even, no big deal. And it wasn't just putting up with each other either. We'd pitch in to help all around. We got along."

"'Community' sounds about right," Kris said. "Lawrence was a Boy Scout, wasn't he, in the local troop?"

"Yeah, he made Eagle Scout in record time, too," Angie said. "He had merit badges up the wazoo."

Angie laughed, but to Kris she sounded as if they were talking about a friend at his funeral.

"Lawrence was one hell of a scout," Angie told her. "I remember this one time, he set up a dog patrol..."

Her voice trailed off as the holdout residential squares and local businesses began to thin out on their way. Taking the place of the old fixtures were vacant lots, derelict mid-rises and some raw construction sites. In the near distance, Grant Park and Oakland Cemetery were vast shadowy plains of green and white.

"You say Lawrence took the lead," Kris prompted her softly. "In some kind of neighborhood watch?"

"His dog patrol," Angie said again. "He might be standoffish with people, see, but he always loved dogs. And vice versa."

Nodding, Kris watched sidewise as her smile broke through and shone bright and fine around the edge of her birthmark.

"And, see, somebody started going out in the middle of the night around here," Angie went on, shaking her head. "It was some sicko. He was slashing dogs, spilling a lot of blood on the sidewalk. Lawrence got mad.

"Really mad," she added. "I'd never seen him get that worked up about anything before. He went out on his own and organized this citizens' patrol. And every day around sundown we'd go on alert with him and be on the lookout for strays. He was bent on catching the vicious, cowardly son of a bitch who was responsible. But, but..."

Angie slumped back in her seat and rubbed her eyes with both hands.

"But we never caught him," she muttered. "Jesus, Kris, it was really Lawrence, wasn't it? I mean, he didn't even know it. But he had to be the one, right?"

"Maybe," said Kris. "Red's been around for a long time, I'd say."

"He's always had this thing inside him, hasn't he?" Angie pressed her. "And it's got to be bigger and badder than those sadistic bloodsucking assholes who got their hands on him when he was just a little kid. That's how it works, isn't it, Kris?"

Kris shrugged and kept on driving.

"Oh, lord," Angie muttered. "Lawrence..."

Her voice tightened and began to fade again, but then she sat up and pointed ahead.

"Hey, look," she said. "Up there. It's our old school, Woodrow Wilson High."

With only a tinge of irony to Kris's eye, she mimed waving pom-poms.

"Goooooo, Wildcats," she chanted. "Yeah!"

Peering between streetlights, Kris made out a weathered two-story building with cinderblock walls. Its whitewash was spotless. The compact stadium and playing field in back had a sandblasted brick front and a shiny marquee beside it. Meant to last was how Kris saw the place.

"So was Lawrence valedictorian of your class?" she asked. "Or were you, Angie?"

"I was."

She gave a dry, knowing laugh.

"I honestly think he shaved some points on a chemistry final we took together, just so I'd come out on top and he'd settle for salutatorian," she said. "That's the kind of thing Lawrence'd do."

"He did a year at the University of Georgia." Kris said. "Top marks in premed, as I recall from his transcript, before he dropped out. Say, Ange, did you two go off to college together?"

"We were both freshmen at UGA," Angie said. "I could tell from the start he didn't fit in there. Not that Athens, Georgia, was some glittering cosmopolitan city or a Bohemian paradise, or anything like that.

"But still," she added, "Lawrence just didn't seem to know what to do with himself when he wasn't in class or out drilling in ROTC. I guess he, uhm, needed structure."

Kris thought of her patient's Army service jacket. Early on, he'd got accepted for Rangers and Special Forces training and had made sergeant in short order. Then came a long stretch of puzzled notations from his commanders as he kept turning down offers of admission to Officer Candidate School.

"Maybe he needed some kind of rigid, predictable framework to function in," Angie went on. "But he *did* prove himself. It sounded like he was going out on these hardcore military operations all the time, swooping down on the Gulf and the Balkans..."

"And all the while," Kris coaxed her again, "you got to be a doc in New York."

Angie blinked and looked around at her.

"You mentioned your training before," Kris said. "I can still hear a little Noo Yawk in your voice, too. Was it NYU or Mt. Sinai or—no, unh-uh. Farther uptown than that, I think."

"You're not kidding," Angie said, narrowing her eyes at Kris. "You can do that, just by listening?"

"It's a knack," said Kris. "It was Columbia, right?"

"I got a scholarship to Columbia P&S for med school," Angie said. "I stayed up there for my residency and fellowship, too, at Presbyterian and Harlem Hospital. Then I took a job back here in the old hometown when Emory came courting me. Like you did, too, huh?"

"Yep."

Kris turned into a broad, empty street. Signs with the Fisher & Wales logo declared that the The Shoppes of Plaza East were coming soon to this site. To make way for progress, most of the buildings were razed flat.

Still standing were a pair of seven-story redbrick apartment houses with their windows boarded up. They loomed ahead on the corner, at the end of a row of dusty old oaks and sycamores. Kris took her bearings and decided that now they were only a dozen or so blocks from the hospital where they'd started out.

"This is it," Angie said. "This is where Lawrence grew up, Kris. The Fitzhughs always lived in that building to the right.

"Third floor in the far corner, see?" she directed, pointing up. "Lawrence's room was away from the street, right there."

Kris pulled to the curb and parked. In the light from the

dash, she saw the color rising in Angie's face. As she cut the engine, she nodded to herself and let her eyelids sag. All of a sudden she pictured Lawrence and Angie on the dance floor together, swaying to the music cheek to cheek.

"I need more," Kris said aloud. "C'mon, Angie, keep talking. Tell me something else about the man."

"Kris, I—"

Her words came out strangled. Without opening her eyes, Kris passed her a handkerchief. Angie sniffled and blew her nose, and then she went on in a steady voice.

"Thanks," she said. "After we met up again here, I could see it on him. It'd always been there, I guess, his being a survivor. But now it was worse, a lot worse.

"People who've gone through hell like that before they'd even got a chance to grow up," she went on just over her breath. "I don't think you can ever get a hold on them, not really, no matter how hard you try...Does that make any sense to you, Kris?"

"Uh-huh."

Angie sobbed again, but then she bit it off.

"And he said maybe he'd used up all his time," she said. "He told me he was just going through the motions now and nothing seemed real to him anymore. Maybe there wasn't anything left for him, he said. Maybe it was time to..."

"And you told him to shut up with the morbid bullshit," Kris reminded her with her eyes still closed. "Go on, Angie. Please."

"He—oh, I couldn't help it, Kris," she said. "I tried to pull him out of himself, just like old times."

Angie laughed suddenly, and to Kris it sounded like the real thing before her tone turned wondering.

"I even dragged him over to that big Monet exhibit with me," she said. "Back in the spring, you know, when it came to the High Museum. And then it was really like old times with him."

Kris judged that at last she was getting close to something she could use, so she kept quiet and waited.

"He always reacted that way to—I don't know, to anything new that wasn't so much a threat as just the opposite," Angie went on fast. "It'd take him off guard and overwhelm him, but in a good way, really good. Oh, man, you should've seen him, Kris."

In the other's excitement, Kris made out the opening she'd been searching for.

"I mean, Lawrence was standing there in the middle of all those unbelievable old Impressionist paintings," Angie explained. "It was like every single brushstroke was special to him, you know? Like they all hit home at once.

"Real beauty and then some," she added. "And he was all wide-eyed, breathing fast and trying so hard not to let it show how it really went deep and touched his heart and...Kris?

"Hey, Kris!" she said. "You okay there?"

Kris said sure and opened her eyes.

Then she realized she'd brought her arms up high in front of her. Clenched tight, both her fists were lined up over her head with the wrists cocked back to strike. She might have been clutching a stake.

Back in deep shrink, Kris hung her white coat on the back of a chair and sat down on the mat by the table. She had on her working outfit of chinos, a bright pink polo and white Nikes. Gazing over her patient's shoulder, she held up a box of Crayolas for him.

"Way to go, Larry," she said. "Yeah, you know I kind of thought your favorite color'd be blue like that."

It was another late session for them. Over the past few days, Red had begun to wane. Kris had found that if she kept pushing him hard enough and long enough, he'd falter and then start to fade right in front of her eyes. That's when Larry came out to play.

She leaned closer now and bobbed her head over the sheet of poster paper she'd spread out between them.

He'd filled in a sunny day with birds flying high, and the

ground below was full of flowers and trees. Larry liked to draw. But when he added people to his pictures, Kris had noted how his mood went as dark as the colors he chose.

"I saw what he did, Kris," he said, still busy with the crayons. "I was with him, right there."

His voice was a small boy's, hurt and troubled.

"I got to look at what he did," Larry told her. "But he didn't know I was there. He didn't even see me. But I saw him, Kris. I saw. I saw it all."

Kris patted his arm.

Next he drew a night scene for her. Carefully he sketched a stick figure in crimson. Face-up, it was spread out between two bigger figures. The man had big dark glasses on, and the woman wore a white mask. Her cap was white, too, but the hair that peeked out from under it was like brass.

"He did bad stuff, Kris," said Larry. "She let him do it."

As he kept his eyes on the paper, he looked scared to Kris but still sure of himself. She sensed all the outrage he was holding in. In each of his movements she recognized the wariness and dignity of the violated.

"She was the one who let him in the house, too," he said. "Every time, uh-huh. And she kept those people from fighting back or getting away from him when he went and bit them all up like that.

"And after he did it," he went on, "she made him pick up the dead people. She made him wash them off and dress them up again. And then he took them and he put them down, right where she said."

Most of it Kris had heard before. Larry had dropped bits of his memory like breadcrumbs down the whole maze of their talks together. But this was the first time he'd got it all out for her at once.

Kris couldn't help grinding her teeth as she considered how far from admissible this would be in court, just as she knew she had zero chance of ever getting a judge or jury to listen to her tell about it.

"It's okay, Larry," she said. "Hey, take it easy, pal."

He was biting his bottom lip to keep from crying, and Kris reached up to cradle his shoulders.

"Everything's fine, partner, just fine," she crooned. "Your ol' buddy Dr. Kris's right here for you. See? Whoa, you're brave. So brave. Yes, yes, you are. Attaboy."

Blinking, he set his chin at last and bucked up.

Kris sat back and waited. This time, it took a couple of minutes for Red to come back. As baleful and watchful as a starving wolf, he fixed his eyes hard on her from behind his glasses.

"Say there, sport," Kris cheerily greeted him. "Another busy day huh?"

She got to her feet with him.

"Tell you what," she said. "Let's make it an early one tonight. What d'you say?"

He gave her his most wintry smile. Still, she could see the life force trickling away from him along with his will. Kris couldn't come close to imagining what his hunger and thirst were like at this point. For that, she gave thanks.

"Okay, so now it's time to call it quits," she kept chiding him. "Let's pack it in and go beddy-bye, hm?"

She motioned to a burly orderly behind his back and caught the eye of Vergil, the seasoned psych RN with the melancholy eyes.

"Back to your room, Red, that's the way," she said. "And sweet dreams now, hear?"

Flanked by the big attendant, he stepped into his cell with his head held low. The steel door clicked shut at his back. Through the mesh-backed Plexiglas port, Kris kept watch on him.

Then all at once his head jerked up and he recoiled and spun around.

Pounding on the door and staring through the glass, he flushed deep red. But then he met Kris's eyes, and his face went white as he took a step back. Fear and betrayal were what she read in him. Those were the strongest emotions he'd shown her so far.

"No!" he bellowed. "What is this? Doctor, you can't—*nooo*!"

Kris had persuaded the ward staff to slip into his room during their last session and line all the walls with museum prints of Monet. Now she bent down by the door and picked up a big manila envelope. It held one more reproduction, plus a couple photos she'd had blown up to poster size.

"Great job, Vergil, just great," she said. "Now once he's done tearing those pictures to shreds in there, I want you to tape these other ones up at the window here where he can't get at 'em."

Ignoring Red's yells and pleas, she pointed to the door and fanned out the reproductions between her hands.

"And then, if you please," she said, "just rotate 'em from time to time through the night."

The last print was of *The Water Lilies*, which according to Angie was Lawrence's favorite Monet of all.

The first of the photographs was of young Sgt. Fitzhugh. He stood tall by his white-haired foster parents while his commanding officer pinned the Distinguished Service Cross on his uniform. The second pic was from the senior prom of the Woodrow Wilson High School Class of '86.

Before she handed them off, Kris took a moment to admire the figures caught on film. Gangling and awkward in his tux, Lawrence gazed down in awe at his date by his side. Angie wore an evening gown with an orchid corsage and kept her face in right profile to the camera. Kris had to admit she looked just like a princess from a fairy tale.

"Dr. Van Zant," called Naomi Webley. "A word with you, doctor, if I may."

Kris had just hung up her lab coat in a locker in the staff lounge. As she took out her purse, she turned and tilted her head up politely. Bearing down on her, the formidable supervisor looked around the otherwise empty room before she went on.

"I've got to tell you, Dr. Van Zant," she said in an undertone.

"In my day, I've seen a lot of shrinks come and go around here. But watching what you've been doing with Mr. Fitzhugh all this while, I have to say..."

She stopped and shook her head before she went on.

"Without a doubt, doctor," she said, "you are the most single-minded, cold-blooded, downright relentless therapist I've ever seen in action."

Kris nodded. She glanced over her shoulder as she paused on the threshold. Just past them, a member of the hospital security detail was minding a bank of closed-circuit TV monitors.

"And what's more, Dr. Van Zant..."

Kris blinked as the nurse cracked the first smile she'd got from her since she'd been on the unit.

"I just hope if ol' Sister Naomi here ever comes unglued," she chortled, "you're around to put the pieces back together again. I surely do, Dr. Van Zant."

"Thank you," she said, touched. "Thanks. And call me Kris. Everybody does."

"Yo, doc!"

Following a loud buzz and a clank from the bolt, Vergil pushed through the unit doors.

"Look here, doc," he said. "That ol' boy's already getting pretty agitated back there. So you want to go on and leave a sedation order for 'im overnight?"

"No," said Kris. "Hell, no. I don't want Red to miss a thing."

"But, doc," Vergil persisted, "he says he wants to talk to you again. He, he—

"Well," he said after a big breath, "I think it's pretty clear now, he wants to go and make some kind of a deal with you."

"Tell him I want to talk to Lawrence Fitzhugh," she said. "And if Larry wants me, I'll be right there for him, too."

Kris checked her watch and turned to go.

"But as to Red, just tell 'im I don't time for any damn vampire," she said. "I've got a date."

CHAPTER TWENTY-EIGHT

On Yuri's recommendation, Kris went to meet him at Ivan & Alyosha's. The restaurant was in Midtown, in the basement of an office block just off North Highland Avenue. Its sandstone front looked to Kris as if it went back to the turn of the last century or before.

She liked the inside, too. The lighting was dim and confidential, and tonight the place was packed. Not far from the table where she joined Yuri, a Gypsy trio strummed guitars and balalaikas and belted out one ballad after another. More than a few patrons joined in, in Russian and with feeling.

"Owners are old friends of mine from Moscow," Yuri had said when they made the date. "Also they are militant neo-Czarists and quite diehard traditionalists.

"So I must warn you advance, Kris," he added. "There is constant threat of dancing breaking out between courses."

Facing him now, Kris spoke up between her last forkful of beef Stroganoff and a sampling of lamb from his shashlik Caucasian.

"There's no doubt anymore, Yuri," she said. "Larry told me everything."

Finishing off the barley mint pilaf, he nodded thoughtfully.

"And who knows?" she sighed. "If there weren't so many debacles from 'false memory' testimony on the record, I might even get it into evidence."

"Pity, yes."

Across the candlelit table, Yuri opened his hands to her and turned up his palms.

"But as psychiatrist yourself, Kris, it would seem that already you have earned reputation for being—ah, how is best way to put this?" he said. "Somewhat manipulative, yes?"

"Hell, *yes*, I'm manipulative!"

Even through all the festivity in here, Kris startled the young couple in Soviet Army shades and black Diesel tees at the next table.

"I beg your pardon," she called aside and then leaned forward again. "But in all humility, Yuri, I have to tell you I'm one of the most facile li'l manipulators ever to put on a white coat.

"That's how I've found out enough to put it all together," she said more directly to him. "The real killer, see, she needed a fall guy. And so naturally, BA went trolling for one on the Net."

Sipping from his glass of lemon water, Yuri cocked an eyebrow at her and held up a cautionary finger.

"Okay, no names," said Kris. "So let's just say a part-time leech dominatrix we both know, she of the IV-transfusion-nurse-from-hell shtick.

"The nighttime working girl, that is, who'd hire out to a certain carriage-trade clientele whose lives apparently lacked a certain zing if they didn't have the occasional brush with death from exsanguination and hypovolemic shock," Kris went on, warming to the sketch. "Or, not to be so clinical about it, they really got off on bleeding to the brink. You know?"

"Yes, Kris," said Yuri. "So is much better, I think, without names."

"Well, she needed a fall guy," she said again. "Even if she did pop Sister Night and purge her business records, she still had to cover her tracks. Okay?"

As he nodded, Yuri looked a lot like a cop to her.

"So what better diversion could there be than a big ol' bloodsucking publicity hog of a serial killing spree?" Kris proposed. "And throw in a potential scandal for the well-connected for good measure.

"Oh, my, yes, dearie," she said huskily. "Now *that's* the ticket."

Yuri laughed as she matched BA's theatrical drawl right down to the slur.

"So, she starts logging on and lurking in chat rooms for vamp wannabes and aspiring blood fetishists," Kris proceeded. "Of which there's not a few, by the way, even locally. Likely she was just looking to hook up with some half-bright teenage stoner of a neck-chomper she could use to take the rap for her. But no.

"Oh, no, no, no," Kris trilled. "Such a lucky, lucky girl! Instead, she found Red."

Yuri looked up and waved off the waiter, who held out a bottle of Stolichnaya embedded in a block of ice. After Kris passed on the vodka, too, he put his napkin aside and leaned across the table. Somehow he projected his words to her without raising his voice.

"I recall how you predicted what turned up in suspect's apartment," he said. "Including PC with modem. At time, Kris, this seemed to me like witchcraft."

Kris said thanks and raised her glass of steaming herb tea to him.

"I'd just figured out he was dissociative then," she explained. "As a rule, you know, multiples love to surf the Web.

"And so," she went on, "it was in the trackless wastes of cyberspace that Red met up with B—"

"No names, Kris," he warned her again. "If you please, yes?"

"Right," she said. "With our acquaintance with the bonnie auburn hair and the D-cups, then. Talk about a union made in hell. Now we've only got the less dangerous of those two monsters locked up."

"Perhaps, Kris."

"I know it," she said. "Because I know Red. I've just about got that personality dissected now. At heart, it's nothing but raw blood need and a compulsion to strike.

"Trust me, Yuri," she added. "It's not equipped to act on its own. All it boils down to is a creature of opportunity.

"And Lord knows," she said between her teeth, "*she's* all

about opportunity. To her, Red's strictly disposable. He's just a cat's paw for her. That's why she tipped you off to Lawrence Fitzhugh's place right after the last murder. She knew with his background, they'd sic a SWAT team on him.

"And then if I hadn't been there when Red gave itself up," Kris challenged him, "all those hard-eyed boys in Kevlar would've mowed Lawrence down and aired him out for good, wouldn't they?"

Yuri nodded one more time.

"So to keep Red from talking to somebody who might just know how to listen to it," Kris summed up, "she even took the risk of going out to whack *me*, for crying out loud."

Yuri slouched in his chair. With his head tilted to one side, he watched her deadpan. Kris couldn't help thinking of a great big Siberian husky that wouldn't bark.

"C'mon, partner," she coaxed him. "You're the homicide pro. You're the real-life murder cop. Aren't you supposed to tell me what I'm leaving out, here?"

He smiled and reached for her hand but still said nothing.

"Okay, I'm the shrink," she said, squeezing his fingers. "So I can tell a sociopath from a psycho on sight. But we both know she ain't crazy, right?"

"She is sociopath," Yuri said. "Sure, Kris. Even though she has no conscience, still she needs motive for killing."

"Thanks for using the M word, finally," she said with a smile. "Your turn, then."

He lowered his head and spoke even more privately against the singing, shouts and clapping around them.

"I asked for this time with you tonight, Kris, because I believe we have in common something which few others share," he said quickly. "Unusual desire, compulsion, call it what you like. Perhaps it is not such healthy thing to have, after all. Fetish, if you will."

Eye to eye with her, he paused with his brows heaped up like snow banks.

"Fetish for justice," he said. "Yes?"

"It's good for me."

"Very well," he said. "This is why I have continued to work on these cases even though they are officially closed now.

"Even lieutenant," he told her, "he said to me, is best not to bother with what Kris is up to now. One should not come between girl and her vampire, yes?"

"Sounds like Uncle Matt."

"But still," he said lower, "I cannot ignore certain facts which turned up in course of investigation and have never come to light."

Kris pricked up her ears at that and held her breath as he glanced around the room.

"On night of murder of victim number five," Yuri went on, "Gerald Zehner made sizable on-line transfer of funds from one of his Swiss bank accounts to what turns out to be merely shell corporation offshore.

"Such transaction required use not only of his personal password," he added, "but also of fail-safe protocol. This had to do with echo feature that could be carried out only on his personal PC terminal. You see how I mean this, Kris?"

She nodded eagerly.

"And even if someone were to persuade him to reveal password and at same time had access to his computer itself," Yuri went on, "Mr. Zehner had standing arrangement with his bankers in Zurich for built-in delay. This, you see, would give him option to cancel transaction and block final transfer within twenty-four hours of its initiation."

"He should live so long," Kris muttered. "Yuri, you've got to tell me. Please. Where'd the money go?"

"Is impossible to say for sure now," he said. "Because exactly twenty-four hours after entry of transaction, you see, corporation that received funds dissolved and had its assets wired elsewhere under strictest of security measures."

"C'mon, Yuri," she wheedled. "You were a big-time MVD investigator in Russia in the wild, wild '90s. For pity's sake, there can't be a whole lot you don't know about following a money trail."

"Yes, I have some knowledge of such things," he said. "Also

friends and colleagues with considerably more expertise in these matters than I myself possess."

Kris bit down hard. Al the proprietor had chosen that moment to mount the bandstand beside them. Picking up a guitar, he broke into a chorus of *Ochi Chorniya* that rattled her teeth.

"I found out that our redheaded acquaintance, decorator, you know," Yuri said behind his hand, "she likes to go to Caribbean. Even now she is on holiday—vacation, yes?"

"*Hate* to think of that," Kris said. "She's probably tossing back rum drinks on the beach right now, laughing her head off at us."

"She is hard woman to keep tabs on, as you yourself have observed," Yuri said. "But in past she has favored Cayman Islands to visit. Grand Cayman in particular."

"Grand Cayman," said Kris, shutting her eyes. "I hear the banks are lovely there."

"Through channels that are quite illegal for me to use, Kris, and in such manner as would allow our acquaintance to file suit against whole Department if she found out," Yuri said in one breath, "I have determined that at very same time shell that absorbed Mr. Zehner's fund transfer dissolved, her private account in Caymans received credit by wire of identical sum."

Kris opened her eyes and caught a tang like copper and ashes as her mouth went dry to the back of her throat.

"Yuri," she began to plead, "I've got to know the stakes she's playing for here. For my—for my patient's sake. I just left him alone, see, where people can come and go and...and if he's all that's standing between her and a clean getaway with...

"For God's sake, Yuri!" she blurted. "How much money? Tell me."

"Relatively small sum," he said. "For late Mr. Zehner, anyway. Less than one half of one percent of total estate, you see."

For the first time since they'd sat down together, he looked away from her.

"How much, Yuri?"

"Kris, please," he said. "Perhaps now is better for us merely to try to live with our suspicions and go on with our—"

"How *much*?"

"In US dollars," he said, "thirty million."

The soles of Kris's shoes smacked on the floor tiles as she ran down the corridor and skidded around the corner on the way to deep shrink. Still ringing in her ears, her scream had cut through the night like an air-raid siren. With it, she could hear Yuri's parting words as she bolted from the table.

"Is no mean feat," he'd said at her back, "to cause scene in Russian restaurant, yes?"

Bearing down on the nurses' station by the first lockdown point, Kris saw that the monitor screens at the security desk had all gone blank. She clipped her ID on her belt and reached for the metal doors with one hand. With the other, she dug in her purse.

"Hey!" she yelled. "What happened to the closed-circuit TVs out here? And why isn't anybody watching 'em?"

A nurse she didn't recognize looked up wide-eyed from behind the counter.

"Hospital engineer just called, doctor," she told her. "He said they'd had a bunch of electrical wiring to short out tonight."

"Okay," Kris said. "So where's Security?"

"They just got a call to go over to see to this emergency out in the main parking deck, and—"

Kris let go a loud groan as both doors to the locked unit swung in under her hand.

"Dr. Van Zant?" said another nurse. "What's the matter, doctor?"

"You tell me," Kris snapped. "The electric bolts're all shorted out, too, right?"

"Doctor!"

The first RN squealed and pointed as Kris pulled out her handgun and held it up in front of her.

"Doctor, you can't take a firearm into the unit like that!" she yelled behind her. "Besides, there's a special security man just went back there."

"'Special'?"

Kris took a grip on her pistol with both hands and put her elbow to the door.

"That's *not* how things work around here, and you ought to know it," she called back before she went in. "Get hold of the head of Security! Stat!"

"Doctor!"

"Tell 'im we need some armed guards down here right now," she said over her shoulder. "*Real* guards, hear?"

❧

Kris knew there was a mechanical lock for backup as well as the electronic one on the deepest ward in the unit. That's where her patient was. But now as she came up to the door, she saw a thin wooden wedge plugged into the bottom of the jamb.

She eased through it on her toes and looked around. Up ahead of her down the hall stood a lean, leggy man in a hospital security uniform. He had his back to Kris and was holding his hands out in front of him. As she watched, he used a key to open the door of her patient's room.

"Hey, you!" Kris shouted, raising echoes off the ceiling panels. "You, get away from there right *now*. Get your hands up! You hear me?"

"Doctor?"

Mild but deep, his voice carried easily. Kris padded up on him from behind. But all the while she got closer, he kept his hands where she couldn't see them.

"I beg your pardon, doctor," he said without turning. "But there's been an emergency in the hospital. And you see, doctor, I have orders to move this man to—"

"Hands up!"

Kris had heard enough from him. Now she could tell what was going on. She took her stance and covered him from ten feet back. Then she drew a long breath and held it.

"Don't move," she said one more time. "Please..."

He bent his knees and pivoted on her. She caught a glimpse of a narrow brown face under bushy dark hair. But the gun in his hands held her eye. At the end of its barrel was a long, flattened cylinder.

Before he could get his arms up, Kris had her sights trued in on the thick of his chest. Smooth and even, she squeezed off the first round. Then she kept on firing till the mag ran dry.

The man in front of her crumpled up. Then he pitched down flat on his back with his legs splayed wide and his arms thrown out slack at his sides. All Kris could see of his face was his chin. His limbs twitched for a second or two before his head fell back and he went limp.

It took a little longer for all the thunder to fade in the corridor. Over the last roll of echoes and the pulse that beat at the base of her skull, Kris barely heard the door as it let out a squeak. Gradually it swung out down the hall. Gritting her teeth, she looked up to see who it was.

"Larry...?"

Kris's own voice sounded distant in her ears.

"No, no, Larry," she begged over her gun. "It's okay, see? Please."

She couldn't mistake the little boy she saw in the eyes of the man who sidled out the door and let it swing shut at his heels. Towering in his scrubs, he hugged the wall and edged along the floor. Then as fast and as light on his feet as a child with the wind up his back, he dodged right past her.

"Larry!" she called after him. "No, please, come back. Don't—!"

Kris swallowed hard and tried to catch her breath. Her heart was knocking at her ribs fit to break on through, and the blood was still rolling like kettledrums in her ears. Reluctantly she hung back from trying to chase him down.

Instead, she turned and kicked the gun away from the man she'd shot. Dropping to her knees beside him, she felt under the angle of his jaw. She could barely pick out the carotid pulse as it went thready under her fingers.

Raising her head, she saw a squad of nurses and orderlies running up to her.

"Call the ER stat!" she ordered them. "Tell 'em to scramble CV Surgery right now! We've got to get the pump team ready to go for this guy up in the OR."

She put her head back down and blew some air in his lungs before she started to work his chest like a bellows.

"I think there's still a chance," she said. "Just a chance, here."

While she braced her arms and put her spine into trying to save a life, Kris heard screams and shouts break out from the front of the unit. Close after them came the clash of steel doors as they banged back on their hinges. Then she knew that Larry had broken loose for good. Now he was on the run.

Once again, Kris sighed, she had a patient at large.

CHAPTER TWENTY-NINE

"Kris...damn."

Matt Judson strode back and forth in the conference room by the ER. He had a crackling two-way clamped tight in one hand with a cell phone beside it. He was using the other hand to give his scalp a hard rub.

"Damn," the ranking detective said again. "I mean, c'mon now, Kris. I can't hardly believe you just went and let the prisoner run right on out past you like that."

"He's my patient, Matt."

She made a face in the steam that rose from the Styrofoam cup in her hand. Kris hated coffee, but it was all they had to drink here. Hospital coffee was her least favorite blend of all.

"What was I supposed to do?" she said. "Shoot him down in cold blood?"

"Yeah, well, you did have a gun," said Matt. "And it's plain to see, Kris, you sure's hell knew how to use it."

He turned around and looked pained. Another one of his men had just ducked in the door. He shook his head at Matt and then whistled at Kris.

"Dang, doc," Det. O'Riley said from the threshold. "That ol' boy that went and drawed down on you, you know you put nine full rounds right square in the 10-ring on 'im?"

He still looked awed by the sight. Kris had helped wheel the man she'd shot over from deep shrink. The patient never made it up to the OR, though. What was left of his heart gave way before he could get on the pump.

"I swear, doc, I doubt Annie Oakley could've done any

better," the young investigator went on. "Where in the world'd you learn how to shoot like that anyway?"

"Girl Scouts," Kris said distantly. "Sometime I'll have to let you see my merit badges, detective."

While the policemen conferred, she thought of her patient's escape. Bright scraps of the museum reproductions Red had ripped up had swirled at his heels and trailed him down the hallway. He'd fled from her at last in a swarm of beauty made real on paper.

"Aw, c'mon, Bubba," Matt said from across the room. "You're telling me nobody around here even saw a hair on him? We got us a six-foot-four Green Beret vet vampire on the loose and can't any of the local citizenry tell us so much as which way he went?

"What'd he do then?" he demanded. "Turn hisself into a bat and *fly* away?"

"He didn't have to, Matt," Kris spoke up. "He just had to keep his head down and mind his own business. Remember, this is Grady Memorial territory.

"With an eight-hundred-bed teaching hospital in your backyard," she added, "who's going to notice one more pale, clean-cut, thirtyish white guy passing by in glasses and scrubs?"

Matt opened his mouth, but just then Yuri loomed in the doorway with a notebook in his hand.

"We have ID on deceased, lieutenant," he said. "His documents were all forged. Very nice fakes, I might add. Walther 9mm he had on him had all serial numbers ground off with emery wheel, and so did suppressor on it.

"But I had hunch his prints might be on file with Federal Firearms License database," he went on. "Indeed, they just AFIS-matched with name of naturalized US citizen. He is originally from..."

He raised his brows and cut his eyes at Kris.

"Brazil—Rio?" she hazarded. "I thought I caught a trace of a Carioca lilt under that South Florida accent of his before—well, before our conversation got cut short."

"Is amazing."

Looking as indulgent as ever to Kris, Yuri shook his head and winked at her before he went back to his notes.

"Name of deceased is Jorge Dos Santos, born in Rio de Janeiro in 1969 and more recently resident of Miami," he read off. "There he was nominally on payroll of import-export concern that would seem to require him to do good deal of traveling both in US and out of country."

"High-class contract trigger, sounds like," Matt grunted. "Right, partner?"

"For sure, lieutenant."

Yuri slipped his notebook in his jacket pocket and folded his arms.

"Question is," he said, "who was paying way for late Mr. Dos Santos on this job?"

"Oh, come *on* now."

Kris snorted and tossed her coffee cup in the trashcan.

"For crying out loud," she said. "We all know BA Rennie used to be married to a gunrunner who did business in the tropics. Who else in these parts would have a clue how to get in touch with the likes of Jorge the hit man?"

"Oh, don't sell this community short, Kris," Matt said. "I expect a fair number of our more sophisticated residents might have the wherewithal for it. Not to mention some hard feelings toward that hot-footed patient of yours."

With a stern frown, he met Kris's eyes head-on.

"For instance, take Macdonald Fisher's li'l ol' bereaved daughter, Roan," he said. "That girlfriend of yours, Kris, she strikes me as the kind of citizen that might just lose patience with our criminal justice system and decide to take up where her tax dollars left off. You know what I mean?"

"Uncle Matt, you—!"

Kris tried to bite it off. For now, she meant to hold her peace. But as she faced off toe-to-toe with Matt, she felt her back teeth start to grind in earnest.

"You, sir," she said through her jaws, "are a true credit to the force."

"Kris, lieutenant," said Yuri. "If you please."

He stepped between them and held up his arms like a fight ref in the ring.

"Perhaps would be best if I saw doctor home now," he said. "Is quite some ordeal she has been through tonight, yes?"

Matt dipped a curt nod and waved both of them out. But before Kris turned away from him, he held up a finger and leveled it dead at her. The glare he gave her was fierce and paternal. Unmistakably, it was also a warning.

In the hall outside, Kris pointed to the back way out. She was hoping they could slip past the press who'd come out in force up front. Then suddenly Angie Sanchez ran up in scrubs and a lab coat. Her eyes were red, and she was blinking hard.

"Kris!"

Angie grabbed her by the shoulders and put her face up close to Kris's.

"What the hell happened to Lawrence?" she demanded. "I've been dealing with a crisis up in NICU all night, and I just heard. *What*?"

"It's okay, Angie, okay," Kris said. "Don't worry."

She patted the other doc's arm and gently broke away from her as she motioned Yuri ahead.

"I can't explain just yet," Kris said. "But I promise you, I'm going to bring him home now."

❧

With Kris beside him in an unmarked car, Yuri pulled out of the visitor's parking deck. Waiting to merge with traffic on Butler Street, he inclined his head to her. His voice was low and calm when he finally broke the silence between them.

"Okay, Kris," he said. "Where to now?"

She took her handgun out of her bag. After she'd checked the action, she slid a fresh mag in. Then she jacked a shell up the spout and chambered it.

"I believe you know exactly where he is now," Yuri said. "No one else could get so far inside his head or even follow in your tracks, yes?"

He pulled into the street, and Kris noted how he kept checking the mirror as they began to circle the block.

"I guess it'd be out of the question," she said, "to ask you to drop me off here?"

"No," he said. "I will not let you go chase vampire all by yourself."

"There's no vampire," she said. "Not anymore."

"You think you killed it, yes?"

"I hauled Red out in the sunlight and burned its ass good," she said. "If it isn't dead by now, it's so close it doesn't matter."

She couldn't quite keep the note of regret out of her voice.

"But the child's still in there," she went on. "And where Larry goes, you can bet Lawrence is bound to follow."

"Yes, Kris, but please," he said. "To where?"

He stopped to idle at a red light. Kris could tell from his eyes just how much it was costing him to put on this show of cool forbearance for her. After a beat, Yuri spoke up again.

"Directions, Kris," he said. "If you please, where to from here?"

She thought it over one more time, and then she told him.

"Thank you," he said. "Just one other thing."

He took off from the light and speeded up down the block, and then they headed east on side streets.

"Before tonight," he said, "you had never killed anyone, yes?"

For just a moment Kris thought of Lyle McCandless the Tuscaloosa Werewolf, but she shook her head.

"Only in a professional capacity," she muttered. "And never on purpose, before."

"Is important," Yuri said softly. "In this matter, Kris, please remember I am not without experience. So now is best for you to let it out before you have too much time to think about it on your own."

"All right," she said. "I'll tell you how it felt."

She slipped her gun in the side pocket of her chinos and sat back in her seat, rubbing her temples with both fists.

"Killing that man back there made me sick," she said. "Sick

to death. But I had to do it. I had to protect my patient, not to mention saving my own tail. And—and so, I…"

"Please, Kris, say it."

"Okay, okay."

As she folded her hands in her lap, Kris felt her forefinger go tense as if once more she were drawing back on a trigger.

"Satisfaction," she said at last. "That's exactly what I felt when he went down in front of me. Pure satisfaction.

"I'm glad I killed that snake!" she spat out. "Cold-blooded, mercenary, murderous son of a bitch had it coming to him, and then some. Just like that…okay, Yuri?"

"Is better."

He reached over and squeezed her hand.

"Is best to get it out in open like this all at once, yes?" he said. "Now, Kris, there is more? You can tell me, please."

"Yeah, I couldn't help thinking of something else back there," she fretted. "About that 9mm of mine, you know?"

Without words, he kept encouraging her.

"Well, it just doesn't seem to have the stopping power I always thought it did," she said. "Maybe I ought to go with a .40 S&W. Maybe even a .45 ACP?"

"Would not be so difficult for you to master such caliber at that," he told her. "Soon we will go to practice range together, and I will help you.

"Now, Kris," he said one more time. "Which way?"

"Take another right up here," she said. "It's in the middle of this big retail development."

Kris sat up straight and pointed ahead.

"Just follow all the F&W signs, Yuri," she said. "You can't miss it."

They parked at the curb on the empty street. Trees lined the sidewalk under spotty lights, and at the end stood two buildings with boarded-up windows. Looming against the sky, they faced each other from opposite corners.

"*Gavno,*" said Yuri. "I beg your pardon."

Kris turned to look at him as they got out.

"Bad word, you know," he said. "In Russian."

"I figured that out from the context," she said. "What's the matter, Yuri? 'D you see something?"

She caught herself whispering on the warm, rising breeze.

"Someone following us perhaps," he said. "I thought I lost them on way over. But just now—ah, well, I was mistaken maybe."

He shrugged as they crossed the sidewalk, but Kris saw how taut and wary his face had gone.

"Or else," he said just loud enough for her to hear, "perhaps they are very good at it, yes?"

She took his arm at the elbow and felt the muscles drawn out like high-tension cable next to the bone.

"Yuri," she said. "I'm going to have to get into this old hulk up here and take a look inside."

She led the way around to the stoop at the front of the redbrick mid-rise.

"And please," she added before he could speak, "I have to be by myself when I do it. Otherwise Larry'll get spooked and we'll lose him for good. Okay?"

He shook his head as they took the steps up to the entrance.

"Ten minutes," she said. "That's all I'll need to go in and get him."

"No, Kris," he said. "I must go with you."

"I know what I'm doing, Yuri," she pressed him. "See, he's in his safe place. This is where those good folks the Fitzhughs took him in. They made a real home for him here.

"And he trusts me now just the way he trusted them back then," she went on, fast and steady. "Just me. He knows I mean him no harm. So there'll be no danger at all, for him *or* for me."

"Kris..."

Cutting around him in the shadows, she tried the caved-in door. It creaked loud and shuddered. She gave it one more shove with the flat of her hand, and it swung back wide. Abruptly a vast dark space gaped in front of them.

"You've got a mobile phone on you, right?" Kris said even faster than before. "It's one of those Nokias that APD issued to all the members of the task force, isn't it?"

Still eyeing her narrowly, he nodded and held out the cell phone to her.

"Great," she said. "And the number is..."

She flipped open her own phone and punched keys so he could see his number on the LED screen.

"Give me just ten minutes on my own in there," she pleaded. "And I promise I'll keep my gun in my hand and a thumb right on the send button. Deal?"

He shook his head again. But after meeting her eye for a few moments more, he seemed about to relent. Reaching in the side pocket of his jacket, he pulled out a sturdy-looking flashlight sheathed in plastic.

"All right, we will make bargain," he said as if he'd rather not. "Ten minutes. And take this, please, Kris. You will need torch in there."

"Unh-uh," she said. "It's too big, and it puts out way too much glare."

She took out her penlight and snapped it on. Then she fitted the handle in the hollow of her palm and pressed it against the bottom of her phone. As she raised her hand, the lens lay snug between her fingers.

"See?" she said. "This'll be perfect, just perfect. Ten minutes, Yuri, and I'll come right back to join you out here."

"Yes, Kris," he sighed. "Still, I must tell you that for you I am very much a—"

"Then," she broke in, "I'll have the honor of introducing you to Sgt. Lawrence Fitzhugh, US Army, retired. Something tells me you guys'll hit it off like old comrades, too. Agreed, Yuri?"

He mugged at her and began to shake his head.

Then all at once he took Kris in his arms and kissed her full on the mouth. They held on to each other without moving. Seconds went by. At last Kris gave him one more hug and stepped back.

She didn't give Yuri a chance to stop her again. Quick and sure, she darted through the door and began to thread her way in. Past the edge of the light beam, the gutted space spread out as black and sheer as a coal pit all around her. But Kris wasn't afraid.

She crossed the old timber on the balls of her feet. Now she was headed for the rear wall. From the street she'd spotted an open window. On the ground floor in back, it was the only one she could see that had all the boards pried off.

She didn't take long to find it in here. As best Kris could tell, it was a short drop from the sill to the ground outside. Drawing her legs up with her back to the opening, she eased out over the casement until she was clear of the sash. Then she turned and hopped down.

Back in the open, Kris found her footing in the dirt and rubble by the wall. She craned her neck and put her head back. With care she checked in all directions.

Nothing she could see out here was moving. So she ducked and hit the pavement. Keeping to the dark spots where she could, she crossed the street at a sprint.

On the other side, she stopped and checked her back. Now she was right behind the old apartment house Angie had pointed out to her. Looking overhead, she picked out the window of Lawrence's old room. It was at the far corner on the third floor.

Kris took some deep breaths. For a few paces, she ran in place and swung her arms at her sides. She was getting set to go in.

She felt bad in passing about the trick she'd just played on Yuri, leaving him to stand guard in front of the wrong building. But she knew it was the only way to keep him close enough to back her up but far enough away to keep him from charging right in on her. She'd come to trust him in most things.

Still, Kris doubted that Yuri could ever stop trying to save her from herself.

CHAPTER THIRTY

Kris came up on the derelict old building from the back.

A rusty gate in the area fence hung open in front of her. Just past it was a service door with some fresh pry marks by the latch and a long gash on the jamb. Raw wood showed through old whitewash. Kris looked closer and saw splinters by the latch.

Bending down, she ran her light over the ground by the concrete steps. Beside them, she found a padlock with its hasp snapped off. She reasoned that Larry would know how to get in here. And even though his personality might still be at bay, Lawrence could lend him some muscle.

Kris smiled in the dark.

Straightening up, she took a last look up and down the street. All she could see there were the tree shadows that spread out long and gray between the lights. She put her head down and slipped through the door without a sound.

Inside, she saw that all the non-weight-bearing walls on the ground floor were knocked out. In front where the lobby must have been, there was nothing left but some exposed brickwork between two-by-four studs and uprights. Plaster lay like snowdrifts along the sides.

Kris hung back at the threshold and listened. She was barely breathing in the warm, musty space. Methodically she swept the walls with her penlight. The wind outside buffeted loose boards in the windows. From closer in the background came a soft rustle and scratching that sounded like rats in the walls to her.

High overhead, a floorboard creaked. If she hadn't been

listening so hard, Kris would never have caught it. Clearly a man's step but as light as a child's, the lone footfall just carried from the near corner. She had no doubt whose it was.

"*Larry?*"

She let the echoes die before she raised her voice again.

"Hello, Larry?" she called out. "It's me, Kris. It's Dr. Kris. Please, Larry, don't be afraid.

"I'm here for you," she said more quietly. "You see, I've come to help..."

As she let her words trail off, Kris heard more footsteps from above. Headed away from her, they fell soft and fast. They were going higher, too.

Kris held her light up to one side and took a grip on her handgun with the barrel pointing down. She scanned the wall in front of her until she found the stairwell in the corner. The door to it was half open, and she pushed it all the way back with the toe of her sneaker. Then she gingerly took the first flight up.

The treads were all warped, and the wooden risers were close to rotting through. Kris stayed to the outer edge of the steps until she got to the landing. She paused there and listened some more. Nothing was stirring, so she turned and kept climbing.

On the second floor, she leaned through the doorway and swept her light across the open flat. It was much like the one she'd left below. With a nod to herself, Kris went back to the stairs.

She stepped out on the third floor and padded across it. As she took her bearings, she edged up on the corner away from the street. That was where she put the Fitzhughs' old apartment. Kris took her time tracing the molding along the wall.

Before long, she found the outline of a snug room at the back. She mused that the window here must have given a sunny western exposure in its day. Now there was a stack of canvas tarps heaped up under the sill.

On top of the pile was a gritty old blanket. Slowly Kris ran her hand over the flannel. She felt a long, wide indentation in the middle. It was still warm.

"It's okay, Larry," she called again. "Don't you worry, my friend."

Backtracking to the stairs, she checked the action on her pistol and thumbed off the safety.

"Dr. Kris is right here for you," she crooned as she climbed steps. "And it's all going to be fine, just fine now. You'll see. Nobody else is going to chase you or hurt you, ever again..."

Something was wrong. Kris was sure she hadn't let anything get past her in the dark, and she'd already checked all the floors except the top one. Still, she heard footsteps at her back.

Shaking her head, she stopped in the middle of the stairs and listened. Each step was gradual and furtive, but there was no mistaking them. They were getting closer and closer behind her.

She knew Larry's step, and it wasn't his. It didn't sound like Yuri's to her either. Even if he'd lost patience and come looking for her on this side of the street, Kris was sure he'd be calling her name by now.

She judged it was even too stealthy for Red.

Silently she made her way to the landing on the sixth floor and turned around. Holding her light up high to the side, Kris aimed the beam straight down the staircase. She was just about to yell out a challenge when a noise made her jump.

Heavy and slow, metal clashed on metal over her head. Kris jerked her neck back and heard the groan and squeal of old hinges. Someone had just shoved open a door on the roof.

"Larry?"

Kris wheeled around and hit the stairs to follow him.

"Larry," she called out again. "Hey, Larry, wait for—*yaaaaaah*!"

She'd got midway up the flight when a tread gave way under her feet. Cracking like a rifle, the rest of the boards caved in beside it. All at once Kris dropped in deadfall between the rails.

She threw her arms out and grabbed for the next step up. As

she fought for a hold, her pulse battered her eardrums. Finally she got some leverage at the top of the tread and bore straight down on it flat-handed. With a grunt, Kris heaved herself up out of the hole.

Between her feet, she saw her penlight flickering far below. Twirling end over end, it seemed to take seconds to hit the ground under the staircase. Then it went out with a faint crunch of glass. Her gun and her cell phone rattled down right behind it.

Kris took some deep breaths, in and out over and over. She let her heartbeat ease off before she made her next move. In reflex she ducked her head.

Then something hummed by her ear. In the same second came a thud like a hammer blow on the wallboard right beside her. A spray of dust and splinters blew out and stung the side of her face.

Kris blinked and hopped back. She didn't wait for the next shot. With her neck tucked in, she dropped flat and then pushed off with her hands. Leaping up, she made a dive for the head of the landing.

She came down light on the hardwood and cleared it on the balls of her feet. Then she kept on pumping up the steps by the wall, crowding the edge on the outside. At the last turn, she swung around tight and took the last of the stairs two at a time.

The steel door stood partway open at the top of the flight. Bright as a new dime, moonlight glowed and streamed through the gap. Kris charged for it flat out.

The footsteps behind her got louder and faster. Over them, she heard a bolt snap back. The tinny thump that came with it could only be a shell case bouncing on wood. Now Kris was six feet from the way out and closing on it fast.

She held her arms out stiff in front of her to catch the panic bar. Suddenly a sharp breeze cut over her shoulder. The edge of the door pinged just before she touched it, and the metal rang down the side and shivered like a gong under her hand.

Jackknifed headlong, Kris slammed the door at her back and plunged for her life straight into the night.

As she scrambled for cover, Kris was grateful for the light out here. She wound up crouching low with the moon at her shoulder. Waxing silver and close to full, it hung high to the west in the southern sky.

The rooftop was windswept gravel-and-tar with a sheer drop on all four sides. If it weren't for the rusted-out compressor hoods and the hulking ductwork between them, there'd be nothing up here to hide behind. Except, Kris corrected herself, for the vinyl-sided box at the head of the stairwell. And that had to be where Larry had gone.

"Oh, Kri—*iss*?"

Trilling from the top of the stairs, the voice was one she knew too well.

"Ollie ollie oxen free, dearie."

With a crash the door pitched back open, and a dark figure burst out through it.

Kris took in the tight Lycra cat suit. It was matte black with a hood to match. On the visor headband, a set of night-vision goggles tilted up at jaunty angle. She really didn't need to see those broad shoulders and long supple limbs.

No, Kris sighed, the warhead tits were quite enough to clench the ID for her.

"Damn good shootin', sister, with ol' Jorge back at the hospital," BA said just over the wind. "And God knows, good help is *so* hard to come by these days."

As Kris watched, she brought up a long-barreled semiauto with a silencer on it. Then she leveled it out double-handed in front of her as if she knew what she was doing. Moving crabwise down the length of the roof, she swept the muzzle from side to side.

"Silly me, I should never have sent a boy to do a woman's job," she called softly. "And I must say, my little friend, it wasn't very smart of *you* to drop your gun back there. Now was it?"

Kris squinted past her in the moonlight, and then she started and stared.

A cropped blond head with big dark glasses was peering around the corner of the stairwell housing. But now she could tell it wasn't Larry. And for damn sure, Kris knew it wasn't the vampire's face.

Instead she saw a rigid line of jaw and a finely steeled, vigilant set of the head that had never come through in all of their talks.

"Oh, be a sport, Kris," BA went on. "C'mon out."

Scouting around, she'd come up almost level with Kris on the other side of the ventilation ducts.

"Endgame, after all," she said. "Now isn't it, dearie? And I promise I'll make it quick.

"Trust me, Kris, it'll be so much better for *both* of us this way," she drawled. "*You* won't have to keep chasing after monsters in the dark. And *I'll* get to keep my hair appointment on St. Barths in the morning."

Her voice had gone husky, and the slight slur in it put Kris in mind of a viper trying to spook a mongoose.

"Yes, so now," BA hissed, "what d'you say, Kris?"

Kris took one more look at her patient as she cast the odds and plotted the angles. Then she scooped up a clump of loose tar and pressed it tight between her hands until she'd put a stiff, sharp point on it. Satisfied, she cocked back her arm and let out a shriek with all her breath behind.

"Bi—*itch*!"

BA jumped back and whirled on her at the same time Kris took aim and chucked the lump through the piping at chest level.

"Okay, sister," Kris shrilled. "Suck on *that*."

BA fell back yelping and swearing but still got a shot off. The round clanged on a fan blade and skipped along the roof. Gravel kicked up at Kris's heels.

"Medic!" Kris bellowed from the bottom of her lungs. "*Yo*, mediiiiiiic!"

Doubling back, she cut for the door at the head of the stairs and kept on yelling as loud and deep as she could.

"*Medic*," she thundered. "For Christ's sake, help me, Fitzhugh. I'm hit! *Help* me, Fitzhugh."

At a trot she rounded the corner at the end of the ductwork. Then Kris held back for a beat. BA lurched to the fore and got between her and the stairwell. All at once they faced off head-on in the open.

Now BA had her back to Lawrence with no sign that she knew it. He took a step up out of the shadows and bent down right behind her. His hand was inches from taking hold of her arm.

Kris tried her best not to look, but something in her patient's eyes caught her up then and she couldn't help it.

BA thrashed her head around to see over her shoulder. Before Kris could reach her, she'd whipped her gun out to the side. Feinting and turning on her heels, she lined up and squeezed the trigger. She shot Lawrence three times point-blank in the chest.

Kris made a grab for her, but she'd already wheeled back to round on her. The pistol came up in her face like a tollgate. Suddenly Kris looked straight down a deep black bore.

She knew she was as good as dead. Still she made a lunge for the muzzle. But it swung up out of her reach. Then it kept on rising, lifting higher and higher over Kris's head.

She blinked and looked down, and Lawrence met her eye through his thick dark lenses. With a death grip on both of BA's arms from the back, he was hauling her up like so much rope right off the ground. She snarled and kicked back at him. But even with his spine wrenched concave, he didn't let go.

For a long moment he held Kris's gaze. His face never budged, but he dipped his chin to her. It was a small move but sure and crisp like a salute. Then he fell back full-length and went down hard.

Kris jumped for him, but he was too far off for her to catch. She could see that now he was locked with BA to the end. When they hit the edge of the roof, their bodies bounced but didn't come apart. Cleaved together, they kept on falling.

To Kris they seemed to stay in the air for a hell of a long time. Lawrence didn't make any noise she could hear, but BA screamed all the way to the ground. Then came a hard wet smack like the breakers that rolled when a big wave hit a reef. Silence followed.

As deep as the grave's, the quiet held on in Kris's ears while she looked down after them. She couldn't say how long she stood like that at the lip of the roof with the wind in her hair. In the distance, lights and sirens were rising. But even as they picked up their pitch and bore down on her, she barely saw them or heard them.

She could just make out her patient's face from here. Turned up at her from a wrack of flesh and bone, it was white and sharp against all the blood on the sidewalk. As Kris shaded her eyes and peered between streetlamps, the gore spread out wide. At last it seeped in the gutter and glistened there as if to jeer at all she'd ever done and to mock her for what she'd tried to do.

Bright and vile in her eyes, the spilled lifeblood was a threat to leave a stain on the dark around her and to turn this midnight red.

"*Kris*!"

The door banged open at her back, and Yuri pushed out with his head down low. He darted his eyes to look all around them. Then with his handgun braced up in front of him and his arms locked in a big vee, he crossed the roof to join her.

"Kris," he called by her side. "Kris, are you—? You are all right, yes?"

She raised a hand to him to signal all clear. But when she opened her mouth, she gasped and choked. It hurt her to get the words out. She was shaking bad now, and she couldn't stop. Doubled over, Kris began to cry.

"I lost him, Yuri!" she wailed. "I *lost* him."

Carefully he took her in his arms and led her away from the edge, and then he held her to his chest.

"It was in his eyes," she sobbed. "I could see it! Right in

front of me, plain as anything. It was redemption, Yuri! Pure redemption, like I've never seen in my life."

"Is okay, Kris," he said in her ear. "Okay. Everything is okay now."

"He was a soldier again, a hero," she insisted. "You should've seen 'im, Yuri. He just totted up his options like he was balancing his checkbook, and then—and then he..."

Yuri made some more gentling noises and cradled her shoulders.

"He gave his *life* for me," Kris bawled out. "Just like that. He didn't even blink. Not once!"

The sirens were louder now. They were keening right at their feet. With them came red and blue lights, spinning up and flashing.

Suddenly the street below filled up with cars. Voices called back and forth and crackled out of radios and loudspeakers. Kris raised her head as a flurry of chopper blades cut high and beat down on the air, coming closer.

A helicopter sailed in overhead and broke right over the scene. It swept the block and then homed straight on the roof. Swinging to center, a searchlight picked them out. Kris cupped her hands by her eyes and gritted her teeth.

"All *right*!" hailed a man's voice from seven floors down. "It's all right, y'all."

He might have been leading a cheer, Kris thought.

"It's him," cried another voice by the first. "We got the Vampire!"

"*No*!"

Yelling back, Kris twisted away from Yuri and marched out to the edge of the rooftop.

"No, no, you *don't*," she kept shouting. "You don't know! He wasn't—no!"

Yuri looked concerned and on his guard at her back, but she warned him off when he tried to stop her.

"Hey, you people," she called out even louder. "You *listen* to me."

Faces looked up at her with their mouths hanging open.

Kris knew they'd get it wrong again if she let them. They always did. But now she was bound to bear witness. Furiously she brushed off the last of her tears and stood up straight with her arms held out wide at her sides.

"Lawrence Fitzhugh came back!" she yelled full-throated. "Right here, you hear me? He came back! I'm telling you..."

Her words rang down in the street, and at last the night wind took her cry up and made it soar like a praise song.

"Home!" Kris pleaded. "He came home..."